AN
OCEAN
APART

Sarah Lee has been a journalist and editor for the past twenty-five years, working across news and features, and writing for regional and national newspapers, as well as commissioning for women's true-life magazines. More recently she has focused her attention on the world of travel, creating luxury blog *LiveShareTravel*, and working with destinations and brands worldwide on storytelling marketing campaigns and conferences through her company, Captivate. *An Ocean Apart* is her debut novel.

SARAH LEE

AN OCEAN APART

PAN BOOKS

First published 2022 by Macmillan

This paperback edition first published 2022 by Pan Books
an imprint of Pan Macmillan
The Smithson, 6 Briset Street, London EC1M 5NR
EU representative: Macmillan Publishers Ireland Ltd, 1st Floor,
The Liffey Trust Centre, 117–126 Sheriff Street Upper,
Dublin 1, D01 YC43
Associated companies throughout the world
www.panmacmillan.com

ISBN 978-1-5290-8681-2

3 5 7 9 8 6 4 2

A CIP catalogue record for this book is available from the British Library.

Typeset by Palimpsest Book Production Limited, Falkirk, Stirlingshire
Printed and bound by CPI Group (UK) Ltd, Croydon, CR0 4YY

Visit **www.panmacmillan.com** to read more about all our books
and to buy them. You will also find features, author interviews and
news of any author events, and you can sign up for e-newsletters
so that you're always first to hear about our new releases.

*To my adventurous, courageous mother, Margery,
and other Windrush Generation women who
dedicated their working lives to caring for others*

Chapter One

Connie

19 February 1954
Somewhere in the mid-Atlantic

There was a ping and clatter of metal against wood as Connie Haynes snatched her tweed coat from its hanger. Throwing it on briskly, she grabbed at the cold brass door handle to escape the claustrophobic confines of the cabin she shared with her sister, Ruby.

'I need some fresh air,' she said, desperation dulling her tone.

Ruby glanced up from the *House and Home* magazine she had picked up in the ship's library. It was well thumbed after being pored over by countless passengers, each searching for a first taste of their end destination. But its smudges, creases and torn pages hadn't dampened images of British life for Ruby.

'You know, we going to have to learn to knit, and make jumpers to keep warm in England. It says you can buy wool for this pattern in Woolworths,' Ruby's cheery chatter chased Connie from the room.

'They don't sell much wool in shops back home . . .' Ruby chortled. But her frivolous last words stuck in the door jamb as her twenty-two-year-old sister made for the deck of the ship.

Will she ever stop licking her mouth about how wonderful everything will be?

1

Connie was looking forward to the ship reaching England just as much as her nineteen-year-old sister. But today was the last day of their three-week sailing and the sun-filled skies Connie was familiar with at home in Barbados had long turned grey. It was as though someone had turned out the light, leaving them in a constant semi-darkness. And these gloomy seas were now a reflection of Connie's mood.

She staggered and bounced off the walls of the corridor. The Atlantic was building up to yet another stormy day, turning Connie into a drunken sailor. Fighting against the force of the wind, she used all her strength to slowly prise open the door to the outside deck. It greeted her with a powerful blast to the face that stung her skin, instantly making her eyes water and blowing her neat curls up and back into a scarecrow-like mop.

Pulling up her collar to shield her neck, she persevered, despite other passengers taking advantage of the door she had left open to race for the warmth of the ship's interior. But Connie was impervious to the numbing gale, oblivious to the other passengers who converged into a river of dark winter coats, trilby hats and the odd bright headscarf, who flooded into the ship.

The SS *Sorrento* swayed and reared as waves crashed upon the bow. Water was thrown high up onto the deck, forming salty streams that raced to the back of the ship. Connie felt equally unsettled, emotion churning deep inside her like the swells in the Atlantic below. There was definite excitement – they would soon be in England – but it was being smothered by something else.

Apprehension was natural, their father had told them both before they had left home, and Connie remembered Ruby beaming confidence back at him. *She doesn't know what apprehension is.*

Connie considered her younger sister for a moment – the almost childlike enthusiasm with which she greeted every decision, every action. She could be so flighty. And yet Connie smiled, wishing in that moment she could be more like Ruby. After all, if it weren't for her sister, Connie wouldn't even be on the ship, a new chapter of her life being written as the *Sorrento* charted its course across the waves.

It was Ruby who had picked up the leaflet explaining that Britain was looking for its Caribbean citizens to train as nurses.

'The National Health Service needs us. They're looking for people to go and help. We should do this.' She'd had a seize-the-day urgency in her voice.

They weren't exactly pioneers – Connie wasn't sure she would have wanted to be one of the first to go to England. In recent years, a lot of people she knew had packed up and left Barbados to make their way to the Motherland. First there were the ex-servicemen, like Devon Grant, and Connie remembered her awe when she heard he was leaving for England. The Grants and Haynes families had been close ever since the Grants had arrived sixteen years earlier, building their blue chattel house on a vacant plot around the corner from Connie and Ruby's home. When Devon left for England, that wasn't his first time sailing across the waves to Europe, but this time it was different. He wasn't going to just fight alongside his English brothers like he had in the Second World War, he was going to live with them.

For Connie, it was different too – actually knowing someone who was going to England made it so much more real; it was no longer just hearsay, or something other people did.

So, although Ruby's suggestion had caught her off guard, it didn't take long for Connie to come around to the idea, and they applied for the government-backed programme. For once England wouldn't just be somewhere that she had learned about in text-books at school. A slight smile now brightened her face as she thought about all the places she had read about back then and how she would soon be able to see them with her own eyes.

Shifting her coat sleeve to cover the fingertips of her right hand, she formed a barrier between them and the frigid steel rail running the length of the ship, as she grabbed it to stabilize herself. *Am I doing the right thing? It's . . . it's just so far away . . .*

Connie's left hand, jammed deep into her coat pocket, found the edges of a photo and as she pulled it out, tears ran down her face, this time no longer provoked by the blistering wind. An infant with white ribbons in her hair beamed a toothless smile from the photo.

'Martha, I hope one day . . . one day, you'll understand . . .' Connie whispered, her words whipped away by the wind in an instant.

It was the same gust that nearly picked Ruby up, bowling her out onto the deck, and she grabbed her sister's right arm to steady herself.

'Man, Connie, you really getting yourself ready for the weather in England. What you doing out here in this wind?' she shouted. Connie hurriedly thrust the black and white image back into her pocket, then surreptitiously wiped her face and brushed stray strands of hair back in one movement, fixing a smile onto her face. Ruby didn't see what her sister had put in her pocket, she didn't catch her tears, but she saw through Connie's bravado in an instant.

'Come here,' she said, hugging her sister close, Connie's cheeks instantly freezing Ruby's face. 'I going to have to warm you up,' she said, rubbing her hands briskly along the length of Connie's arms. 'I know you'll miss her,' she comforted.

'No, don't, Ruby,' Connie said. 'We agreed we wouldn't talk about this.'

'Yes, but it's just you, me and this vast ocean here – who would know?' Ruby chuckled a little now. 'Everything will be OK.' She paused for a moment as they both looked out once more at the grey skies.

'I think I can see the sun coming through over there, you know,' Ruby said, pointing in the direction in which the ship was sailing.

Connie looked up and laughed; it was still steely grey to her, but, as ever, her sister was looking for the silver lining in each of the clouds before them.

'Just think of all the stories we can tell her one day! And, who knows, maybe she'll sail to England just like us and be real fancy and drink tea like the Queen,' Ruby said, sensing her sister's tension easing.

'Only you would come out with such nonsense at a time like this,' Connie said with a slight smile.

'Serious! I read in that magazine there are tea houses and they got all kinds of cakes you can have with it.'

'Oh, Ruby!' Connie laughed, mildly exasperated. 'You and your magazines.'

'It's true, though,' Ruby replied. 'And you just wait – when we get there and get settled in at the hospital in Harpfordshire, we can do all of those things.'

'Ruby, it's not Harpfordshire,' Connie laughed. 'We're going to *Hertfordshire*.'

'Ah yes,' Ruby said, giggling too. 'St Mary's Hospital in the town of Four Oaks and that's in East *Hert*-fordshire,' she said grandly, taking her sister by the hand and spinning around the deck in a gleeful waltz.

The SS *Sorrento* juddered over a wave and the girls stumbled, Ruby spinning out of control and into the arms of a tall, willowy man who had just left the warm confines of the ship.

'Oh, oh, sorry, mister,' Ruby exclaimed, flustered. 'I didn't mean to dance into you – I was just trying to cheer up my sister.'

A kind face looked down at her from under a trilby hat and he smiled. 'No problem; we could dance all the way to England if you wish. But we best hurry – it's right over there!'

Ruby spun around, spotted the outline of a green land mass emerging from the grey and squealed. 'Look, Connie! Look, it's England!'

'Lord, Ruby, we're nearly there!' Connie said, wide-eyed, Ruby's excitement infecting her now too as they hugged and jumped together on the spot.

The man, too, was smiling, all of them oblivious to the bitter wintery day, because in that moment every passenger of the SS *Sorrento* was being kept warm by their hopes and dreams.

'Errol Alleyne,' the man said, holding out his hand. The sisters paused their celebrations for a moment to hurriedly shake his hand and introduce themselves.

'We're going to Harp . . . Hertfordshire,' gushed Ruby. 'We're going to be nurses.'

'Oh, that's wonderful! You already have jobs, and that's some important work,' Errol said, in a strong Barbadian accent. 'I read all about England's National Health Service in the newspaper. They said it has been doing big things in the past six years – saving so many people's lives. But I read they need more nurses. It's good that us from the Caribbean can come up here to help them.

'My brother lives in Birmingham, so I'll be going to live with him up there while I try and find some kind of work. He tells me there's work on the railways and that sort of thing.'

Connie nodded. 'Yes, our friend Devon works on the railways in London – he found work pretty easily, I think, what with the labour shortage since the war and everything.

'He's coming to meet us when we dock in Tilbury. Our dad insisted on it – "Get dat boy to collect you, I don' want my girls landing in England and not knowing anyting or anybody",' she said, her voice deepening and her accent thickening with her impression. 'So I wrote to Devon and he's going to escort us to the hospital's meeting point in London.'

Errol smiled. 'Ah that's good, that's good, you all will have somebody to show you the ropes right away.'

'Yes, it's very good of him. But he knows what it's like to come here and have to start completely from scratch,' Connie explained.

'I'm so glad we won't have to do that,' Ruby said. 'At our interview, the liaison officer back home said we'd be very fortunate as we have a job and a home at the hospital straight away. She said as we had passed our General Certificate of Education at school we had all the qualifications we needed to be trainee nurses. Then we only had to get our passage money.'

The sisters had borrowed money from the government, on the understanding that they'd pay it back each month from their wages. 'And of course, we also have our *show money* . . .' The girls had ten pounds to tide them over until their first pay day.

Errol nodded enthusiastically. 'Yes, you always need your show money. I hear they won't let us off the ship without being able to prove we can stand on our own two feet financially,' he chuckled. 'Lord, it took me so long to save the money to come up here. Well, I wish you luck in England, ladies, and I hope that you transform the health service.'

The next five hours of the journey seemed longer than the previous three weeks, as the passengers prepared themselves to dock in England. As the ship sailed through the Thames Estuary and towards Tilbury, the driving wind and choppy seas of the Atlantic faded and on either side of the ship they were surrounded by the green countryside of Essex and Kent. But that seemed to be the only bright colour in this overcast scene, as the fields soon gave way to gloomy warehouses and sooty factories with slate grey rooftops. It wasn't quite what the sisters, or the other passengers, had expected of England. But nothing could dull this adventure.

The ship's whistle blew, heralding their arrival, and the girls looked at each other, grins spreading across their faces. They were finally in England.

'Connie, Connie!' Searching the crowd on the dockside, Connie's eyes met with Devon's.

'Come, Ruby, he's over there,' she said. They showed their

landing documents to border staff and rushed towards Devon through a melee of disorientated passengers, luggage lining walkways, and greeters whose experience of all things England was clear, even from a distance.

It was the same look that Devon had – the experience and confidence of a man who had long since settled in.

'Welcome, welcome,' he said to the girls, hugging Connie warmly first and then Ruby.

'You must tell me about your trip and fill me in on all the news from home on the way to London. But we need to hurry for the next train,' he said, grabbing Connie's suitcase in one hand and Ruby's in the other. The girls looked at each other as they followed him through the crowded docks, impressed by both his physical strength and his poise.

Entering Tilbury Riverside station, Connie and Ruby's eyes widened at the sight of a steam train on the platform. Hurriedly buying tickets from the counter, Devon ferried them onto the train and in minutes puffs of sooty smoke rose from its engine as it chugged its way to London Fenchurch Street.

The sisters settled beside each other, Ruby already peering out of the window next to her as Devon adjusted their luggage and slid the door to their compartment closed. They were soon chatting, Connie and Ruby sharing details of their twenty-two-day voyage and messages from friends at home.

'Oh yes, and your brother Joseph asked me to give you these,' Connie said, passing Devon a letter and a bottle of Barbados rum she'd retrieved from her case.

'Ah man, I can't wait to open this up, and it's great to get news from home.' Devon smiled. 'I miss the family. Well, I miss a lot of things. But it's so good to have you here, it's like you've brought a piece of home to England.' His gaze lingered on Connie's face.

Devon was seven years older than Connie and, when he had left Barbados, he remembered her being little more than a child.

But now there was a woman before him, a woman who, like him, had taken the opportunity to sail to another country for a new life. He only hoped she would find everything she was looking for.

As they chatted, he began to tell her about his life over the years since they'd last seen each other, his updates coming in edited snippets before the conversation moved on, almost as swiftly as the train rushed through the countryside.

Connie recalled how women in their neighbourhood would always refer to the Grant smile as a thing of devilish charm. She hadn't remembered him being quite so handsome before, but as he spoke about his life, she was taken by his broad smile and deep brown eyes. England was clearly good for him.

'You said the hospital management have people to welcome you at Liverpool Street station, is that right? I don't want to put you girls on the train to Four Oaks on your own,' Devon said with care in his eyes.

'Yes, they're meeting us there because they say there are other girls coming from all over England to start work at the hospital and it is a good central point,' Connie replied, a part of her hoping there would be no one from the hospital at Liverpool Street at all, and that Devon would escort them further on their journey. And maybe he was thinking the same, she mused. Connie had caught his long gaze more than once, but unsure of what to make of it, she turned her attention to Ruby.

Chapter Two

Ruby

Scenes of her new homeland rushed before Ruby's eyes. It felt familiar, yet strange and wondrous all at once. She felt she could almost be back in Barbados, at the Empire Cinema in Bay Street, watching one of her favourite dramas made in London. To everyone else, the rush of green countryside fading into towns huddled with houses were at best unremarkable, on this increasingly gloomy, dank winter's day. But nothing could stifle Ruby's first impressions.

'Devon, they must like a lotta bread in England. I seeing chimneys everywhere – it's as though every next building is a bakery,' Ruby said, perplexed.

Chuckling at her innocence, Devon replied gently, 'No, Ruby, those chimneys are on houses – everybody has a coal fire inside the house. There ain't no sunshine like back home to keep people warm, you know. At least, not until the summer.'

'Ohh,' she said, then returned to her window, transfixed for the duration of the journey.

'Look, Connie! This must be London now, look at the buildings!' Ruby gushed minutes later, her eyes almost as wide as her mouth in awe. 'But wait . . . is that the Tower of London?'

'Yes, that's it,' Devon replied.

'Lord h'mercy! It's just like in the pictures. Beautiful!' she finally exhaled.

Devon smiled, again catching Connie's eye.

'Connie, how you can make this whole journey without once looking out the window?' Ruby said, all but oblivious to the chemistry bubbling between Devon and her sister.

From Fenchurch Street the trio hopped on a bus the short distance to Liverpool Street station. 'Come along, we haven't got all day to be waiting on your sort,' bristled the conductor. Devon stiffened a little as they boarded and found seats. 'All aboard!' the conductor bellowed. There was a ding-ding of the bell and the crank of a ticket machine as the bus juddered into action, spewing exhaust fumes into the evening air. The fumes mingled with the stench of the city: smoke whirling from chimneys, a stale earthy odour emitting from underground stations, and the reek of beer from a rabble of pubs. Every sound, every sight, every smell seeped into Ruby's consciousness.

This is what England is all about, she thought, excitement building inside. But questions swirled in her mind – what would the hospital be like, what would their rooms be like, what would the other nurses be like? So many questions that Ruby couldn't wait to get answers to.

Arriving at Liverpool Street station, Devon escorted the girls to their meeting point, then, giving them both a hug, he wished them well for the next stage of their adventure.

'I hope you enjoy Hertfordshire,' he said to Ruby, then paused as he spoke to Connie. 'I think you'll like it here, but keep in touch and let me know how you're getting on. I'd love to hear from you when you are settled.'

Waving him off, Ruby met the woman at the small desk with a broad smile. 'I'm Ruby Haynes and this is my sister, Constance Haynes.'

'Ah, yes, you are the last two we're waiting for,' the prim woman replied, putting a tick next to their names on her list.

'Come, Connie,' Ruby said, linking her arm with her sister's. 'We need to get on that train over there.' She gave her sister a sideways glance. 'Did you even see all the sights on the journey? Or were you too busy with just one of them? I saw the way Devon looked at you as he left us just now,' she teased.

'Stop it, Ruby, man!' Connie protested, a little sheepishly. 'I'm sure Devon isn't interested in me. He's been up here all this time with those girls in London. He is nice though, and such a gentleman for meeting us . . .' She trailed off as they boarded the train.

By the time the train pulled into Four Oaks station it was dark, and every shop in the small market town was shuttered for the day. A biting wind blew along the platform, and the girls were pleased to find some warmth as they boarded an Austin K8 minibus to the hospital.

'Welcome, welcome, ladies!' At the nurses' home, a tall, slim woman in her mid-fifties greeted them from beneath a portrait of Queen Elizabeth II. 'I'm Matron Valerie Wilson and we are delighted to have you here with us at St Mary's Hospital.'

The matron struck an elegant figure and spoke eloquently. Ruby was immediately impressed with the smart silhouette of her uniform, which seemed to make her ivory skin glow, even in the pale light of the nurses' home lobby.

'As many of you are aware, Great Britain has undertaken a remarkable project these past six years. This has always been an incredible country, and our strength of spirit and character revealed itself as we held strong against the tyranny of fascism in the war. But if we had one failing, it was in the nurturing and care of our citizens. We, however, are a pioneering nation, and you girls will be playing a vital role in the development of our National Health Service. According to its architect, Mr Bevan, it will become the jewel in the crown of British life and it is already proving to be a model of exemplary healthcare for the rest of the world. You all here will be contributing to its future.'

Ruby grinned at Connie, who smiled back, pride filling the air as each of the young women felt the weight of their place in history.

'Some of you are joining us from other parts of the country, while others have come from many miles away,' Matron Wilson concluded. 'This hospital is at the heart of the community here in Four Oaks and I'm sure the locals will make you feel very welcome. As for you girls from our Caribbean colonies, I hope you quickly feel at home here, because England is an extension of each of your homes.'

'You see, Connie,' Ruby whispered. 'It's just like we were told in Barbados – they need us here. We're going to make England better for everyone.'

Connie nodded enthusiastically as Matron Wilson escorted the girls into a room with tables piled high with items of nurses' uniform and a desk where the girls would be issued with room keys.

Ruby made straight for the uniform table while Connie gave their names for the keys to their accommodation.

'Ruby, come, you need to sign the form to agree to the room lease and deductions for meals and board from our wages,' Connie beckoned to her.

'But, man, did you see the uniforms? We got to wear the white coats for our preliminary training, but then, when we've qualified we'll be getting one of the dresses. But I like the cloaks best of all. And didn't Matron look smart? She seems real nice,' Ruby babbled. Going to sign the sheet before her, she turned to Connie. 'Do you see how much we get paid? Eighteen pounds a month!'

Connie nodded. 'Yes, sis, but don't forget we'll lose some of that for our board and more.'

'Of course, but I would've done this for less money than that,' Ruby whispered. 'Nursing is very noble work and this is a chance for us to contribute, just like Matron said. And think of the money we can send home to Mum and Dad! It will help pay for Harold's schooling. Ahh, I miss that little brother of ours.'

'Me too,' said Connie, signing her form and picking up her key. 'But we'll get back to the family one day soon. I'd like to see Harold before he goes to secondary school, so I have just over three years to learn everything here and save the money to get home.'

'I might come with you . . . for a holiday. But I ain't going home for a long time yet,' Ruby said grandly. 'I got too much to see and do here.'

She caught Connie slightly rolling her eyes, but Ruby didn't mind. She knew England afforded her an opportunity for adventure – it had already given her the chance to travel to the other side of the Atlantic. But it was so much more than the job and the salary. Ruby loved family, and for her, that extended way beyond her parents and siblings. This was a chance to help her brothers and sisters in England. Meanwhile, the job also gave her a shot at building her life, and she was ready to seize it with both hands.

Even Ruby was aware that she could be a dreamer, and that perhaps that was her failing. She thought back to when she'd started dating Sylvester Adams the previous spring, and how she had thought they would be together for ever. Ruby had all but started planning their wedding, despite Connie warning caution. Looking back, Ruby knew she had been headstrong, but she had really wanted to be married and soon after that, to start a family with Sylvester.

Sylvester hadn't viewed the world in the same way, though, and two weeks after ending their relationship, word reached her that he was dating Sandra Blake, a girl who couldn't have been more different to Ruby.

'Miss Haynes?' A voice pulled her out of her thoughts. 'Here's your uniform – you can pick up your cloak next,' the administrator said.

'Thank you,' Ruby beamed.

Heading upstairs, each of the soon-to-be nurses found their rooms – Ruby's was next to Connie's at the end of the corridor. It was a box room with a washbasin in the corner and a huge pipe running underneath a sash window. The pipe, which ran through each of the nurses' rooms, was the only source of warmth on this frigid February night, so Ruby kept her coat on and wrapped the cloak over her shoulders while she unpacked and made herself at home.

Home.

This small, chilly room in a corner of the English countryside was a long way from her real home, and the family Ruby adored in Barbados. She already missed her mum, dad and Harold too. But if home is where the heart is, Ruby's heart was quickly warming to life in England.

Chapter Three

Billie

'Wait, Billie, are you still not ready? You can't miss your train,' came a concerned voice, as twenty-three-year-old Billie Benjamin tried to force the lid closed on her suitcase. Taking a moment to adjust its contents – stilettos, fitted jumpers, pencil skirts, lacy bras, and a make-up bag bursting at the seams with bright lipsticks, eyeshadow compacts, mascara and fake eyelashes – she sat on the lid and was finally able to force the two clasps closed.

'Ugh, Esme. I can't move any faster, man, my head hurts real bad,' Billie replied, looking fragile in the dim light of the tiny room her friend Esme rented in a house near Caledonian Road.

'You got to get yourself to Four Oaks and arrive at the hospital looking all business and thing,' Esme replied. 'You need to make a good impression, girl, you don't want them thinking they getting some little pickney from Jamaica that ain't up to the job. You're going to be a nurse, people's lives will be in your hands,' she said dramatically.

Billie looked at her friend wearily. 'That's fine, just as long as they don't put their lives in my hands when I got a hangover. I need someone looking after *me* just now.'

'Girl, I told you from early o'clock last night that it was time for we to head home. But you wanted to follow those boys to the dance. Where did you end up anyway?'

'But Esme,' Billie said, a pleading forgiveness to her voice as she recalled flashes of the previous night, 'they were soooo nice, and that Philip had such lovely brown eyes. I like these English boys, you know. I mean, I like the boys back home too, but the boys here are just, you know . . . different,' she gabbled.

'We had so much fun! I think . . .' She paused thoughtfully, then continued: 'I mean, we did – we went dancing. Yes, that was it – we went to the Tottenham Royal or something so.'

'What?!' Esme interjected. 'You went all up into Tottenham with those boys? We'd only met them last night, Billie!'

'Oh, but they were proper gentlemanly, Esme, you didn't have to worry about a thing with me and them. That Philip, he hugged me up and made sure I didn't get too cold while we waited for a taxi home.'

'Hmm . . . I bet he did, the wretch!' Esme said, flicking Billie a knowing look.

'Yes, but he wanted to protect me.' Billie smiled wistfully. 'There were some Teddy boys at the dance all dress up in their long jackets and tight, tight trousers and thing. He said they could be a bit funny sometimes.'

'Billie, man, you does get into some situations. Anything could of happen. You gonna have to be sensible when you get to the hospital. I want you to show them your smarts. That there's more to you than just having fun.' Esme's tone was maternal now.

'But Esme! I like having fun, man. I didn't come all up here to England to sit in the house. And there will be plenty, plenty time for me to get the book smarts I need to become a nurse. But I came up here for adventure too.

'We're in England!' she said now, stretching her arms out to her sides. 'This ain't little Jamaica where everybody's up in your business. Besides, Kingston is so downmarket. I been in England a week and already it feel like here, anything is possible,' Billie added, sliding her stockinged feet into black heels, then buttoning a coat over a plum dress with leopard-print trim that hugged her every voluptuous curve.

'I understand. I just want you to be ready, because the countryside ain't like London, you know,' Esme soothed, gently pulling at her friend's coat collar.

'Well, yes, but they going to have to get ready for me, Esme, and if there ain't much action there, I will just have to create some.' Billie laughed mischievously and Esme couldn't help but laugh too at her friend's confidence.

'Right, get going. Don't forget – it's the number fourteen bus from the stop round the corner. I've got to get ready for work,' Esme said. 'Take care of you, and write and let me know how you're settling in and when you will get a chance to visit again.'

'I will, and thank you for letting me come up to London early and stay with you a few days – I knew I'd love it. It's so good to see you all settled here, girl. I only wish I'd have come from the small island to the big one sooner,' Billie said, hugging her friend, then going to walk out of the door.

'Don't forget this,' Esme said, handing Billie a striped brown and grey woollen scarf.

'That's not mine,' Billie said, then a second later as a memory flashed through her mind: 'Oh, wait. Philip gave it to me last night – to keep me warm. Well, I don't suppose I'll be able to get it back to him, and I'm sure it's still cold out there,' she concluded, wrapping the scarf loosely around her neck. As she waved to her friend, Esme listened to the clip-clip-thud of Billie's heels on the stairs as she dragged her case behind her.

'Lord Jesus, now she's going to wake the whole house,' she muttered, rolling her eyes.

Closing the front door to the house behind her, Billie made her way out into the bitter winter's day. It was bright and sunny, but a hard frost made the trees look to Billie like the snow she'd heard so much about, and the air was tinged with the grubby smell of coal fires as soot billowed from chimneys the length of the street.

As she stepped onto the back of the bus, a man lightened the load of her suitcase as he took it to help her. 'Thank you,' she smiled.

'You're welcome, darlin' – can't have a pretty girl like you building up too much muscle now, can we?' he replied, eyeing her from head to toe, his lecherousness quickly overshadowing his gentlemanly act. But this was an everyday occurrence for Billie. She had garnered male attention since she'd hit puberty and her tomboyish physique transformed, first when breasts budded and bloomed to fill out her blouses, and then as her body rounded out to an hourglass figure.

Sitting as far from the open platform and the man's gaze as she could, she'd hoped to find a little warm comfort on the bus. But, despite the bright sunshine that sparkled off London's pale grey, icy pavements, it was no match for the hot sun back in Jamaica.

Pulling Philip's scarf up higher to shield her neck against the bitter cold, she could smell the Old Spice aftershave and Brylcreem that impregnated the wool. It gave her a fleeting flashback to the previous night and she felt a tingle of excitement deep within. She remembered using the scarf to pull him closer to her for a kiss and then again to drag him into a doorway, passion over-whelming them. But then there was a void.

As London's streets passed by, Billie, who had till now enjoyed spotting the city's sights on each journey, could only think of the previous night. But huge parts of her memory had been erased by the cherry brandies she'd been drinking.

Did I . . . did we . . . ?

No, we can't have.

I would've remembered. There's no way that could have escaped me . . . could it?

But in that moment, Billie, who usually saw a boundary and looked at just how she could extend it, really couldn't be sure how far she'd gone with Philip. The only thing she did know was that there was an opportunity for a new life before her that could crumble to dust if she had been stupid.

She had enjoyed the evening, though, despite the fact that Esme had gone home early. But Esme had known Billie wouldn't follow until she'd well and truly made her mark on the night. Esme knew Billie all too well. They had become firm friends five years earlier while working at Pints and Pounds, a grocery shop in their home town of Kingston, in Jamaica.

It was Esme who had given Billie her nickname back then, and she'd embraced it even though her friend had likened her to a horny old billy goat. The nickname, though, was as much a tribute to eighteen-year-old William Clarke, who'd also worked at the shop, and whom Billie had fixed with her big eyes often enough for him to get a sense of her infatuation with him. Despite her having subsequently had little more than a brief fling with William, Billie ended up keeping the nickname, and, five years on, she was only ever called her real name, Dionne, by her family in Jamaica.

Getting off the bus, Billie was caught off guard in the rush of people flooding into King's Cross underground station. London was so much busier, noisier and faster than she had expected, even though she had thought she was ready for somewhere much busier, noisier and faster than Kingston.

Checking the directions Esme had written for her, she headed to the Tube, placing her suitcase on the step of a wooden escalator as it gently juddered deep underground. Waiting on the platform of the Metropolitan Line, she became aware of the gaze of two separate men.

If there was one thing Billie knew, it was the power she had over men. They were quickly and easily intoxicated by her – consumed not just by her buxom body, but hypnotized by her deep brown eyes and overwhelmed by the broad smile on her ruby red lips.

The one thing they were never taken with, however, was her mind. They didn't seem to care what went on behind that electrifying smile, or to ask her opinion on anything. They wanted to have her on their arm, and to devour her body. The fact that Billie was sharper than most of her beaus and idle flirtations was overlooked by them.

This proved a source of frustration to her, but she was never one to see an obstacle and be defeated by it. Billie concluded that sex was power, and she had been known to wield it to get what she wanted. This was never anything nefarious, and she hadn't slept with every man that showed her attention, but she had occasionally used her head-turning assets to her advantage; and, if she was honest, to soothe the pain of her teenage years, when she felt she had lost more than she could bear. Having someone to hold close made Billie feel complete.

As the train arrived, its doors slid open to a fog of stale smoke and glum faces, and one of the men took a seat beside her.

'I – erm – I hope you don't mind me sitting next to you,' said a voice with a familiar accent. 'Good afternoon, my name is Clive.' The man held out his hand.

'Billie.' She smiled slightly awkwardly, shaking his hand. 'You here from Jamaica too?'

'Yes, I come up here, ooh, must be seven months ago. I mostly like it so far,' he said, removing his hat to reveal closely cropped hair topping warm features that shone like a beacon amid the gloomy faces of Londoners. 'Well, the weather ain't much to write home about, so I didn't send a letter to the family about that as yet,' he chortled; then, sighing, he added: 'And some of the people . . . you know, they don't like to mix with we too much. But mostly it's been going good.'

'Which part of Jamaica you from?' Billie enquired.

'I from a little village not too far from the town of Wiltshire. And you know, when I get up here, I laughed when I find out there's a place name Wiltshire too.' He smiled now, recalling this revelation. 'You can find a little piece of home up here in England. And what are you doing here? I see you have luggage but you look too experienced for someone who just get off the boat.'

Billie smiled. Her beauty and confidence often seemed to dazzle people like the full-beam headlights of an approaching car, bewildering and blinding them to her vulnerabilities. But she was as exposed as every arrival in this strange new land.

'I got here last week, but I have been staying with my friend. She's been teaching me the ropes, but now I'm leaving London for Hertfordshire. I'm going to train to be a nurse – I'd like to help people, and an old schoolteacher of mine told me: "Billie, you best get yourself off this island because you got too many smarts to be wasting them in a shop." I used to work in a grocer's back home,' she explained, 'so I applied to the National Health Service. But I don't even know how to take a temperature.'

Clive laughed, charmed by Billie's innocence as much as her good looks. 'Ah, it's a real shame to see a pretty girl like you heading to the country. I'd love to take you out sometime, maybe for dinner, or to the pictures. Here, take the telephone number for my lodgings and we could see each other when you get free.

'I haven't yet been to Hertfordshire, but I hear the country is nice, and you know, it would be good to have *someone* beautiful to see there too,' he went on, taking a pen from his pocket and scribbling down his phone number on a piece of paper.

As the underground train rattled into Liverpool Street station, Billie decided she liked Clive. He had a good strong jaw, deep brown eyes and his chiselled cheeks squished into dimples when he smiled. Add to that, she mused, having another friend from home could only be a blessing. 'OK, Mr Clive, when I get settled and find my bearings, we can make a date.'

'Wonderful! Now, wrap yourself up – make sure that scarf is protecting your neck – it's going to be even colder up in the country than down here,' he said, looking at Philip's striped scarf around Billie's neck.

'I will,' she said.

He took her hand and slowly, purposefully, kissed the back of it, looking up so his eyes locked with Billie's. 'I'm looking forward to seeing you again very soon.'

Making her way to the mainline station, she did as Clive suggested and pulled Philip's scarf tighter around her to block out the bracing wind that whipped across the platforms.

The train journey to Four Oaks flashed by and as the city faded into a landscape of green fields, Billie buried her fears about the previous night with thoughts of when she would next see Clive. She never liked to linger long on past liaisons, and it felt easier to brush away her fractured memories than to face the possible realities. With her period due any day, if anything untoward had happened, she knew she would find out soon.

It was just before four o'clock when her taxi from the station pulled up at the guard house at St Mary's Hospital. 'Hello, I'm Dionne Benjamin. I'm a trainee nurse. Or, I will be.' The guard telephoned the nurses' home and some minutes later the taxi was waved through. Pulling up outside the grey Victorian building, the driver carried Billie's suitcase into the reception area. 'Hope you enjoy it here, gorgeous,' he said, winking at her as she paid him.

Stepping into the reception, Billie looked at the portrait of Queen Elizabeth that hung on the wall and felt awed by the grandeur of the moment, even though the room itself was fairly unremarkable, with parquet flooring and green-painted walls above dark brown tiling. She could hear a persistent click, click, click, ding of someone typing in a back office.

'Miss Benjamin?' the clipped voice of the hospital administrator, Miss Bleakly, enquired. 'I'm sure we expected you with the other new arrivals, yesterday.'

'Ah, well you see, I was staying with a friend in London and I knew we wouldn't be starting training till Monday so I could make my way here myself today,' Billie replied, unbuttoning her coat and unwrapping Philip's scarf to reveal an impressive bust bursting from the top of her dress.

Miss Bleakly glared at Billie from behind round glasses, as though inspecting her and mentally judging her choice of outfit. Miss Bleakly's silver hair was braided on both sides of her head, pulling her features back and making her pale white face stark in the room's glum shadows. Her stare made Billie feel as though her blood could freeze in her body.

Pursing her lips, she shuffled through some papers, then shoved a clipboard with a form and a pen across the desk towards Billie. 'I'm not sure Matron will be impressed by your tardiness but here you are, fill this in and sign the contract, which details your pay and deductions.

'Fred, please show Miss Benjamin here to her room in the nurses' home. She has arrived late and missed the tour of the premises that the other girls have had, so she'll just have to figure things out for herself.' The gruff disgust in Miss Bleakly's tone was unmistakable, and Billie feared she may have got off on the wrong foot before even starting her training.

'I'm sorry, I didn't know I'd miss anything important,' she stammered, as hospital porter Fred Jones picked up her suitcase and led her to the second floor of the building.

'Here ya go, Miss,' Fred said, opening the door to Billie's room. Then he whispered: 'I wouldn't go getting upset about Bleakly Bloomers down there. She's a bit of an old dragon.'

Raising his voice again, he added: 'You'll find the bathroom and kitchen down the hall there, and I think you might find more of your lot are in the common room right now. But you may want to unpack as it'll soon be time for supper.'

Thanking Fred for his assistance, Billie closed the door, and immediately slumped on the bed of the box room, the highs and lows of the past twenty-four hours weighing on her. Over the next two hours she slowly unpacked, finding a home for her hot comb and hair curlers, and setting aside one of the smaller drawers in the room for her make-up. She left two items in her suitcase, though. While she'd given one bottle of Appleton Estate rum to Esme – who'd enthused that she'd brought the 'good stuff' from home – Billie had kept two bottles for herself. She was hoping she would soon make friends, as she had big plans to celebrate her twenty-fourth birthday the following weekend.

Just as she'd secreted the bottles away in her case, there was a knock on the door. As she opened it she was greeted by a face of wide-eyed enthusiasm. 'Hello, I hear you just got in. My name's Ruby. Are you from Barbados too?'

'Hello, I'm Billie. I'm from Kingston. In Jamaica,' she added hastily. But it wasn't necessary – Ruby picked up instantly on Billie's strong accent.

'Well, it's good to meet you,' Ruby said, immediately dazzled by Billie's beauty and the way her dress hugged her figure in all the right places. 'I'm here with my sister Connie,' she added, as Connie wandered down the corridor.

'Hello, you just got here?' Connie said, holding out her hand. 'I'm Connie. We were about to go down for dinner, you want to come?'

The three girls were soon joined by other young trainees, still in their casual clothes, then uniformed nurses, sisters and the hospital's management flocked to the dining room.

'I'm hoping it's better than yesterday's dinner,' said Ruby ruefully.

'Yes, that was disgusting,' Connie replied.

But the girls were equally unimpressed as they reached the front of the queue and found a large pan of greying potato and onion, labelled bubble and squeak, alongside bread and dripping.

'What . . . what is this?' Billie squawked. 'It look like somebody ate it before.'

'It's onion and potatoes, lovey, it's beautiful,' said a server behind the counter. The girls exchanged cautious looks, but with nothing else available, the server loaded up their plates and they took their seats in the capacious dining room. They pushed the food around, but with empty tummies, each girl was driven to eat just enough of this peculiar new dish to appease their hunger.

'Lord, what I would do for some chicken and peas and rice now. You know like how Mum would do it, with some proper seasoning and thing,' Connie said.

'The only seasoning I've seen here so far is the salt and pepper on the table,' Ruby said, nodding dolefully.

'I don't know that I can stomach this,' Billie grimaced. 'I ain't been feeling too well today and I was hungry, hungry, but this isn't helping me feel any better.'

'Oh, are you sick?' Ruby enquired. 'You should speak to someone – it's a hospital after all, somebody should be able to help you.'

'Well, not exactly sick,' Billie replied. 'It's my own fault. I was in London last night and I let some young men keep me out late at a pub and then a dance. But they were so nice, and handsome too,' she grinned, a glimmer of excitement in her eyes.

'Were they friends from back home?' asked Ruby.

'No, I just met them last night, dear. These nice English boys took me drinking and dancing, and then, well, one of them saw me home afterwards.' Billie's smile was enough to suggest that things hadn't ended there.

'Wait! You mean to say . . .' Ruby's shock played on her face. 'What was it like kissing an English boy?'

'Ruby! You shouldn't ask such things,' Connie scolded. 'A lady never tells.'

'But a lady doesn't do things like that either,' Ruby said, putting her foot in it long before she realized she may have already insulted their new friend, and Connie shot her a look.

'Ladies, it's 1954, not 1904 – relax your corsets a little,' Billie said, unperturbed. 'We can enjoy life just as much as the boys, you know. We just have to be a little more sensible is all.' She suddenly looked thoughtful as the dark voids in her memories of the previous night continued to play on her mind.

'Anyway,' she said, steering the conversation on. 'What brought the two of you to England? You real lucky you're up here together, you got yourselves instant friends.'

'Well, you have instant friends in us too,' Ruby smiled, thrilled to already have a chance to claim a friend in England. 'We came because we heard they needed our help, but it's also such an exciting adventure, isn't it?'

'You're right there,' Billie replied. 'Once my mind was made up, I could hardly wait to leave Kingston. I felt so trapped there. Don't get me wrong – I had some good times, and there were plenty of nice young men back home who would take me out and thing. But I knew I could achieve more here. I worked at a grocer's, but I had my General Certificate of Education from school, and that should've been more than enough to get me into a job at a bank or something. But I soon found out those jobs were only available to the white Jamaicans, or those from certain connected families.' She sighed now as Connie nodded in agreement, some of Billie's experience mirroring her own.

'And, well, my family could barely connect to itself, let alone Kingston's society.'

'I understand that,' said Connie, then sensing Ruby's glare, 'I mean, our family is wonderful, we have Mum, Dad and Harold, our little brother, at home . . . But we didn't have any of the

27

connections that might get us places either. So you know, this is an opportunity to make our way in life.'

'Yes and my mother died when I was sixteen, leaving me and my older brother, Samuel, and Candace, my little sister, to fend for ourselves,' Billie continued. 'It's not that we never knew where to find our father, but I would only see him if I passed by the rum shop and caught him playing dominoes with his friends under the tamarind tree there. When Samuel joined the merchant navy, I would have done anything to follow him. But you know, there aren't any jobs at sea for us girls.

'So when I saw the advertisement to get into nursing up here in *The Gleaner*, I thought here was my chance to escape.'

Ruby studied Billie now. Even though she was considerably younger than her, she couldn't help but feel a maternal instinct towards the Jamaican girl; as though Billie were a baby bird that had fallen from its nest. 'I'm sorry, what a sad story,' Ruby said.

'Oh, it's OK. Besides, it's not all bad. Not at all,' Billie replied with a wicked smile. 'I already had a great time in London this past few days.'

Later that night, though, as she lay awake in bed, Billie's mind was racing with the possible outcomes of the previous night's dalliance, and it was nearly four o'clock in the morning before she was able to get to sleep. So when Ruby knocked on her door the next day to see if she'd like to join the sisters at church, Billie sleepily told her she needed more rest. In reality, Billie hadn't been to church since her mother's funeral, and she had no intention of starting again now she was in England.

Chapter Four

Connie

There was no need for Connie to set her alarm clock for Monday morning; she woke at six o'clock – a whole hour before it was set to go off. She lay in her white metal-frame bed for a while, excitement bubbling inside for the first day of preliminary training school.

Tiptoeing down the hall so as not to wake the other girls on her floor, she took a lukewarm bath in one of the communal bathrooms, shivered her way back along the hallway and, getting dressed, she put on the white coat each of the girls had been given to wear over their own clothes during training, then fastened it at the waist with a white elasticated belt. Only when they were on the wards would they be able to wear the coveted nurses' uniform. Looking at her reflection in the mirror, she smiled – she was ready. It was still only ten minutes to seven.

As alarm clocks rang up and down the corridor and the other girls started to stir, Connie realized she had about forty minutes spare, so she sat at the desk in her room. Pulling out her Bible from a drawer, she took a moment to study the photo of the little girl she had hidden away between its pages. Next she found a pen and notepad and started to write a letter home. But the letter wasn't to her mum and dad; instead Connie chose to write to her mother's sister, her Aunt Agatha. She told her about their voyage to England, how Devon had met them at Tilbury Docks, and how they were safely ensconced in Hertfordshire, ready to start their course. Staring at the photo again, she finally asked the question that had been burning in her heart: 'We've so much to look forward to, but I can't help but think about my little Martha. How is she? Maybe one day, you can tell her for me that I've done this for her. I want to make her proud of me, and give her a life I could only dream of.' Promising to send her aunt some money for the little girl when she got paid, Connie sealed the letter in an envelope just as there was a knock at her bedroom door.

'Connie, are you ready?' Ruby's voice was hushed but urgent.

'Yes, just give me a second.' Connie opened the door, then put the envelope into her bag. 'I wrote to Aunt Agatha – I must post it later. Oh, Ruby,' she smiled proudly. 'You look so smart in your white coat – like a real medic already.'

'I know it's not the proper nurses' uniform yet, but I'm ready!' Ruby beamed back.

Then as Connie went to close the door, she rushed back into her room, mild panic on her face. 'I nearly forgot to put this away. I don't want anyone seeing it,' she whispered as she secreted Martha's photo back between the pages of the Bible and placed it into the drawer.

'Good, you put it up safe,' Ruby said. 'Let's go, sis – a quick breakfast and then we gonna get started at this nursing thing!'

Entering the dining room, the girls were happy to see bacon and scrambled eggs on the menu – finally something they recognized. 'Come, Ruby, those girls over there have white coats too, they must be trainees like us.'

'Hello, do you mind if we sit with you?' she enquired of a table of fresh-faced recruits. The only thing Connie and Ruby had in common with them, though, was the white coats. With skin far paler even than the white people they knew in Barbados, the sisters figured the girls were all English. That is, until Kathleen O'Hare piped up.

'Of course – take the weight off yer,' she said in a warm Irish accent, pointing to the two spare seats at the table. 'There you are. Now, what yer after calling yourselves?'

'I'm Connie.'

'And I'm Ruby, I'm happy to meet you. We're sisters and we've come from Barbados. But where are you from? You don't sound English.'

'Ruby, don't be so forward,' Connie interjected.

'Ach, no, yer fine,' Kathleen smiled. 'I'm from Cabra,' then, sensing the sisters' mild confusion, she elaborated: 'It's in Ireland, a corner of Dublin.'

'Ohh, yes, Ireland, there are plenty people in Barbados with Irish roots,' Connie said knowingly.

'Well, given the choice, I would much rather be in the sunshine of Barbados than freezing my bones here in England,' Kathleen grinned, rubbing her arms with her hands as if to warm herself up.

'I would go with you,' a girl with long, mousey hair and glasses said. 'It's so interesting that there are all these girls coming from the Caribbean here. I'm Grace, by the way.' She smiled at Connie and Ruby, who were by now tucking in to their breakfasts.

'I wouldn't go there,' spat another girl from across the table, her mouth tightening. 'And I don't know why they're all coming here either.'

'Margaret, that's awful mean!' Kathleen said, chastising the brunette. 'Take no notice of her, girls, she seems to have got out of the wrong side of the bed this morning.'

'I'm a Hampshire girl, and in my family we were always encouraged to speak our minds,' Margaret replied, scooping up the last of her eggs, then she gulped down her tea and slammed the cup on the table.

'Well, there's a few of us coming from the Caribbean these days. They said there aren't enough nurses up here so they needed us,' Ruby replied.

'Yes, I already miss home, but I'm excited to be in England,' Connie said, then turned to Margaret and added, slightly wistfully, 'If you were ever to get to the Caribbean, you might be surprised. It's so bright and warm there and people are real friendly.'

Margaret's chair legs screeched on the parquet floor, providing a noisy punctuation to the conversation as she got up and left the room.

'Ach, Jesus, Mary and Joseph and all the saints, she's a funny one,' Kathleen sighed.

Grace nodded in agreement. 'Yes, she can be. Anyway, are we all looking forward to today?'

Connie looked a little perturbed, but then said to Grace: 'Oh yes, I love learning. And I'm excited about when we will actually get onto the wards and start taking care of patients.'

'My God, I damn near overslept,' Billie said as she put her tray at the place Margaret had vacated, and joined the girls. Connie paused, taken for a moment by Billie's big, beautiful cat-like eyes, red lips and perfectly coiffed hair that fell about her shoulders. Then she introduced her to the others at the table, telling them Billie was from Jamaica.

'But you said you're from Barbados, isn't that in Jamaica too?' Grace enquired. 'You have very different accents.'

Finishing breakfast, the three Caribbean girls gave their new friends a brief geography lesson, explaining that the two islands were separated by more than 1,200 miles of aquamarine Caribbean Sea.

Within the next hour, all the trainees were lined up in the classroom.

There they were met by a portly woman with greying brown

hair pulled back into a taut bun, revealing stern features on a plain face. Sister Shaw, one of the hospital's trainers, was renowned among previous charges for her sharp edges, and from the outset Connie could tell she would take no nonsense from the latest batch of trainees.

Her tone was as starchy as her pointed linen cap as she demanded the ten new recruits stand in a line before her. Connie had never been in such a multiracial group before; not only was there her, Ruby and Billie from the Caribbean, but there was Irish Kathleen, Grace Roberts and Margaret Allen, who they'd met at breakfast – one more joyfully than the other – and two other English girls, Phyllis Richmond, who lived with her family on the other side of town, and Jean Lewis from Shropshire. Completing the group were Lin Chang from Hong Kong, and Mei Chen, who originated from Singapore.

'St Mary's Hospital is more than a place where we heal the sick. Over the years, it has become a place of learning too. But I want you girls to be aware that we have very high standards, and that starts with the way you're dressed and how you carry yourselves,' Sister Shaw said.

'You are expected to dress appropriately. There should be limited make-up, and certainly no red lips.' She turned to glare at Billie. 'Your hair should be neatly cropped, or if it is long, it should be pulled back into either a high ponytail or a bun so it is out of the way. And nails should be kept short, natural and neatly filed. You will, of course, have your uniforms, all ready for when you finally start working on the wards, but in the meantime, you will be expected to wear respectable clothing beneath your white coats. That means high necklines and long hemlines.'

Connie started to look at Billie now too, sensing her tension as Sister Shaw quite clearly highlighted her as a picture of inappropriateness, and she couldn't help but feel sorry for her.

'So, Nurse,' the sister said pointedly, staring Billie in the face,

'I expect you to come here more respectably dressed tomorrow.' As she turned away, Connie caught Billie's eye, but instead of seeing shame spread across it as she would have expected, she saw a flash of defiance. Behind Sister Shaw's back Billie even shared a slight smile with her.

'You are expected to represent this fine establishment well, and that begins with how you carry yourselves. Posture is very important in building a good first impression and creating confidence in patients, so you must stand tall and straight at all times, with your shoulders back,' Sister Shaw continued.

'You are expected to know your place. This hospital has many learned people, who are your seniors, so you must show them respect; for example, you should stand back at doorways for people walking behind you to proceed first. You should refer to Matron as "Matron", me and others like me as "Sister", and doctors as "Doctor" – you must never use their first names. You should spend most of your time here listening, and if you do, you will no doubt be well equipped to pass this twelve-week preliminary training. Only then can you continue your training to become state registered nurses, as you learn on the job over the next three years.'

After this less-than-welcome speech by Sister Shaw, the trainees spent their first day learning what constituted a nurse's working day.

'Your preliminary training will begin with the basics of nursing, then you will learn more about looking after patients with individual needs such as bed care. You will also have to understand the structures of the body, or anatomy, as well as developing a deep understanding of how the body functions, physiology. We will look at the nervous system, cardiovascular system, the respiratory system, the renal tract, and study digestion, during which you will learn all about the alimentary tract. We will also examine the basics of pharmacology and dietetics,' explained Sister Shaw.

Later that afternoon, as Connie and Ruby started to walk back to the nurses' home, Billie caught up with them. 'So what did you think to the first day?' Billie asked.

'I enjoyed it. Well, mostly,' Connie replied. 'Sister was a bit stern, but it sounds like the course will be interesting and I really like the other girls.' Then, pausing, she recalled Margaret's frosty reception at breakfast. 'Well, except for Margaret, I guess.'

'Lawd, God yes, I saw how she was carrying on like she was the Queen. But she's going to be doing the same work as all of us here.' Billie gestured to the sisters and herself.

'It's all right for both of you – Sister paired me and that Margaret for practical work later this week. She said I couldn't work with Connie,' Ruby grumbled.

'Ah, don't worry, sis. You just do your best work and ignore Margaret,' encouraged Connie.

Back at the nurses' home Connie headed to the reception desk. 'I'd like to send a letter home to Barbados please, I was told you had stamps.'

'Yes, that'll be two shillings please,' said the administrative assistant and handed her a stamp and an airmail label, which Connie stuck to her envelope, then wrote her name and address on the back. 'Oh, are you Miss Constance Haynes? There's a message for you.' The assistant sorted through some notes. 'Ah yes, here it is: a Devon Grant telephoned for you. He'd come through on the main hospital number but they put him through to the nurses' home. He left this telephone number and asked that you call him.'

Taking the note from the assistant, Connie couldn't help but feel a spark of excitement. Ruby looked at her with big eyes. 'Well,' she said dramatically. 'You can't say the man ain't got any initiative.' She was grinning now.

'Man, don't be making that face at me,' Connie giggled bashfully. 'He is probably just checking that we're safe and well.'

'Well, he didn't leave no message for me.' Ruby gave her sister a knowing look. 'It's OK, I'll let you go and call him, but be sure to remember ev-er-y-thing about the conversation because I need a full run-down. I mean to say, if I'm going to be getting a brother-in-law, I'm gonna have to check out this boy – we ain't got Mum and Dad here to look out for us,' she teased.

'Ruby, man, hush now. We've barely even talked yet!' Connie looked coyly at her sister, following her upstairs.

'Wait, you ain't going to call him?' Ruby enquired.

'Yes, I was just going to get changed first.'

'All right, but don't waste time, a good man waits for no one!' Ruby called as she tramped up the stairs.

Half an hour later, Connie emerged from her room to find Ruby's door ajar. 'OK, I'm going down to call him now, but you have me all nervous. What if he wants to see me?'

'Say yes!' Ruby exclaimed. 'Maybe he'll invite you to London and you can go see all the sights.'

'Oh, but if he said that then I'd have to be sure you could come too. We should do that together.' Connie put her arm around her little sister's shoulders.

'OK, I'm glad you said that actually,' Ruby beamed. 'But anything other than that, you tell him yes, you will go out with him. Who knows, maybe he'll even come up here . . .' She was thoughtful for a moment. Then she looked up at her sister's gentle face. 'Then I'll be able to keep an eye on the two of you.' Ruby roared with laughter. 'Now go phone that boy, and whatever he says to you, say yes.' With this she removed her arm from her sister's waist and chased her from the room with shoo-ing arms.

Sitting in the wooden telephone booth in the reception area, Connie dialled the number.

'Hello, Kentish Town 6874, Rachel Silver speaking,' a woman answered.

Connie hesitated then said: 'Hello, erm, I was looking for Devon Grant . . . I was given this number for him.'

'Hold for a minute please,' the woman said. There was a moment of silence, then Devon's deep tone came down the phone line, instantly warming Connie's heart – a sensation that took her quite by surprise.

'Connie, it's so good to hear from you. That was my landlady.' Devon explained how he'd called the hospital to check that all was going well for the sisters in their first days in the country, and enquired if there was anything he could do to help them. Connie, unsure of herself and of Devon's intentions, had started to convince herself that he was just being a good friend.

'And Connie, I don't know if you're going to be too busy with your training and everything, but I wanted to ask if you'd like to go out sometime? You could come to London for a day, or I could get the train up to Four Oaks. It's just – I really enjoyed talking with you on the train, and I realized how nice it was to have someone from home here as well.'

Connie's palms started sweating and her cheeks burned with shyness. 'Um . . . yes, um, OK,' she said, then immediately realized that didn't sound like the most enthusiastic acceptance, so she put a shine on it. 'Yes, that will be lovely,' she replied with much more assuredness. 'Would you like to come here?'

'That will be wonderful,' Devon said and Connie could hear a smile in his voice. 'I have a day off work on Sunday, is that OK with you?'

Agreeing to the date, Connie raced back upstairs and into her sister's room.

'Ruby, you were right!' she gushed, excitement dancing on her face. 'He's coming here to take me out on Sunday.'

'You see,' Ruby enthused. 'I told you!' She pointed at Connie, then, grabbing her hands, she jumped up and down. 'I told you he had it bad for you. And he's so handsome!' She now looked wistfully at her older sister.

'I know,' Connie replied. 'I was thinking that from the time I saw him pick up our suitcases at the docks, but I didn't think for a minute he would be interested in me.'

For the rest of the night Connie had an indelible smile on her face. So much so that it drew the attention of a few of the other nurses as they relaxed in the sitting room after dinner.

'Penny for your thoughts?' enquired Jean, pausing from her knitting.

'Where I come from, they say a girl who smiles like that has a good story to tell,' Mei grinned.

'Well, where I come from women only have that sort of cat-who-got-the-cream expression when they get their claws into a fine man,' Billie said, knowingly.

But Connie just smiled, keeping close counsel, as if sharing her news might jinx this relationship before it even began.

Later, though, when the other girls had left the sitting room, Connie shared her big news with Billie.

'I knew it had something to do with a fella,' Billie grinned. 'But imagine you come all the way up here to England only to fix up with a boy from home.'

'I know. Though I bet you have all the boys here and at home chasing after you, Billie,' Connie said, eyeing her beautiful new friend.

'Oh my dear, I do. But that can be a problem. I have a whole lot of fun with them, and I love the feel of a man's arms when they hold me close, and I like when they open doors for me. Real gentlemanly like, you know. But there aren't too many of them around, and even the ones who are gentlemen at the outset. Well . . . let's just say you can find out that they aren't what you thought they were. Maybe they just wanted something pretty on their arm. I never felt like any of the men I dated before really took the time to get to know me.'

'Ah, Billie, that's so sad. Maybe the boys you meet here will be different – you already said you met a nice fella in London at the weekend. What about him? Maybe he's the marrying kind,' Connie suggested.

Billie took a deep breath and Connie saw her expression change, but perhaps didn't know her well enough to recognize it as the same sort of anxiety she herself had once felt.

'Well, maybe,' she sighed, then, smiling at Connie, she said: 'I hope that Devon is, for you.'

Chapter Five

Ruby

The rest of the week passed in a blur of new experiences and new learnings for Ruby as she and her fellow trainees were taught the basics of nursing.

'Now, Nurse, you need to unravel that and bandage that wrist again,' instructed Sister Shaw. 'It looks like that of a two-thousand-year-old mummy. It will never do that loose.'

'But Sister, I did it as tight as I could,' she protested momentarily, then quickly realized her error of judgement in questioning the experienced trainer. 'Yes, Sister,' she replied, unpinning the bandage to restart the process.

The next day the trainees were taught how to give bed baths and how to carry and empty bed pans; the following day was all about bed-making.

'You need to be sure that you hold the sheet perfectly perpendicular to the ground before you tuck in the first section, which *must* be eighteen inches long. Then you fold, Nurse, F-O-L-D the top part of the sheet over and tuck it in. *That* is how you make hospital corners,' explained Sister Shaw, as she began to take the girls through the make-up of many different bed set-ups.

Unfortunately for Ruby, co-ordination wasn't one of her strengths, and Sister's instructions only left her more confused. Margaret, her partner for the exercise, seized on this in a moment, as they worked on a bed in the far corner of the room, away from the main group.

'Ugh, you can't even make a bed,' she hissed. 'Don't they have them where you come from?' She paused for dramatic effect, then said: 'Well, I heard you all live in trees, so I guess not.'

'What?' Ruby huffed, feeling the sting of tears in her eyes. It wasn't the first time that week that Margaret had been rude to her. They'd worked together on a number of practical exercises and Margaret had been awkward the entire time, demanding that she practise it first, then being uncooperative when it was Ruby's turn to take her pulse or blood pressure. Margaret had even deliberately broken a needle they were using to practise injections on an orange and told Sister Shaw it was Ruby's fault.

'How could you say such nonsense? I don't know why you are so nasty to me – I didn't do anything to you,' Ruby said, fighting back tears. She didn't want to cause a fuss and for Sister Shaw to see this disagreement – she had already made it clear that disputes were to be kept out of the training school and the wards. But more importantly, Ruby didn't want Margaret to see how hurt she was and to feel that she had the better of her.

Margaret, the other English girls had discovered, was from quite a privileged background. Her parents had a small country estate in the New Forest. This information had left Ruby and Connie confused. Why would she be taking a job as a nurse if her family had so much money? But, Ruby had said to her sister, maybe Margaret had just heeded the call to service like they had.

'Now mind you fold that corner properly, else Sister will have our guts for garters,' Margaret said, a snarl curling her lips as she waved her right hand in the air dismissively.

Soon Sister Shaw made her way to their bed, inspecting the perfect corners on Margaret's side, then the aborted effort that Ruby had made of hers. 'Nurse Haynes, what in heavens is this?' she demanded, shoving Ruby aside and yanking the sheet out from under the mattress. 'I told you, you have to fold it like this. Then like that,' she blustered. Margaret looked on, flashing Ruby a sly snigger as Sister Shaw berated her for her efforts. Connie now caught what was happening from across the room and her brow furrowed as she watched her sister looking on in frustration.

'Don't worry about it, Ruby,' Connie implored as the day's classes finished and the girls made their way back to the nurses' home. 'I'll teach you how to do the bed corners, we can practise on your bed tonight.'

'Thanks,' Ruby grimaced. 'I tried my best with them, Connie, but I just didn't understand. I'm more upset about Margaret though, she was really nasty to me.'

'Ruby, you've got to try not to be too sensitive to things. We're in a whole new world here in England, you know; people might have different ways, but I'm sure she wasn't deliberately being rude to you.'

Billie nodded in agreement with Connie. 'Yes, you shouldn't let anyone else play on your mind. Just try to focus on you, Ruby.'

'I guess you're right. Maybe I'm seeing trouble where there isn't any,' Ruby said.

That evening as the three girls headed to dinner, Ruby's stomach was rumbling, as though the day's trials had only fuelled her hunger.

Reaching the counter, though, her heart sank along with her appetite she saw a stew of carrots, swede, potatoes, celery and onions, with just a few spots of shredded beef in a gloopy gravy.

'What is that?' Ruby enquired.

'It's beef stew, dear,' said a dinner lady.

'Wait – the same beef we had for dinner last night?'

'Look, miss, there's still rationing going on, you know, and we all have to make do with what we have,' the dinner lady bristled. 'My kids would've loved a bit of this stew back during the war.'

'Fine, I'll take it,' Ruby said unenthusiastically, as the woman behind the counter ladled her up a plate of another uninviting dish of the day.

'Don't worry, Ruby, we'll go into town on Saturday and see if we can't pick up a few snacks to keep in our rooms,' Connie said, sitting down beside her in the cavernous dining room.

'Ooh yes, I remember we said we would check out the town.' Ruby perked up. 'I want to see what materials they have for a new dress or two, and I need some Posner's Ebonaire for my hair. Is that what you said you use, Billie?'

'Yes, but I use the Creme Press with my hot comb – you should get some of their Creme Curl as it will give more condition and body to your hair, I read about it in *Jet* magazine,' Billie replied.

'*Jet* magazine! Did you get that here?' Ruby was excited now at the prospect of finding the black American magazine in England.

'No, I got it before I left Jamaica,' Billie explained. 'But everybody is pressing their hair now. I can always press yours for you on Saturday if you come out with me into town. It's my birthday and I need to celebrate, so who else should I go with than my favourite Bajan girls?'

'It is? Gosh, how old will you be?' Ruby enquired.

'Ruby!' Connie shot her a look.

'I don't mind. I'll be twenty-four, but just don't tell everyone. I might start telling people I'm twenty-one, I don't want any good-looking young men to think I'm past it, you know,' Billie said thoughtfully, and Connie and Ruby couldn't help but laugh at her unabashed fancifulness.

'But it's true! Which man wants to date a broken-down old maid?' Billie demanded.

'You're a long way from that,' Connie said. 'And have you seen the way men behave when you walk into a room?'

Ruby nodded. 'Yes, everybody notices you,' she chortled. 'It's as though the rest of us are invisible.'

'Oh, wait till Saturday and I'll help you get real fancied up, then no one will be able to keep their eyes off you,' Billie promised to a beaming Ruby.

'Hmm, I'm not sure I'm keen on where this gonna end up – I see trouble on the horizon,' Connie warned and the three girls giggled. 'OK, just let us know what you're wanting to do for your special day,' she conceded. 'Phyllis says there's a milk bar in the town but I don't know of much else yet.'

Saturday morning came around and Ruby woke to the sound of lively chatter seeping in from the hallway. The other girls were up early and having fun, from the sounds of things, but Ruby wanted to sleep a little longer. While she was good with her hands, and quite creative – it was Ruby who had taught her older sister to crochet – she had never been academically gifted. So this first week of study – not to mention the stinging comments from Margaret, which lingered at the back of her mind – had proved heavy going for her.

Ruby embraced everyone she met warmly, as family, so she struggled to understand Margaret's hostility. She'd been so excited to come to England and begin her training, yet in this moment she felt that joy slipping away, and tears now rolled down her cheeks and onto her pillow.

She knew she could talk to Connie, of course, but her older sister was always so together and so much more competent that Ruby sometimes didn't think she truly understood her worries. But this sense of not being good enough was nothing new for Ruby – it was what had driven her to journey to England in the first place, to finally achieve something herself, and maybe to find a husband along the way. Yet here she was struggling in the first week and fearing she might soon see that dream turn to dust.

'Ruby, are you up?' Connie's knocking pulled her out of bed and somehow seemed to lift her spirits right away. But as she opened the door, Connie could tell instantly that something was wrong with her younger sister. 'Oh no, what happened?' she said, shutting the door behind her.

Ruby crumpled into a heap on her bed. 'I don't know – I just don't know that I'm good enough to be a nurse, Connie. I can't even make the beds how they want them.'

'Now stop that nonsense, Ruby Haynes. This is only week one, we have a big, long road to travel. It sounds to me as though you're letting Margaret bother you, and you mustn't. You got so much more to offer than she has. Just you wait and see if you don't pass the course with flying colours. So much here is new, Ruby – we just got to take our time and we'll get used to everything.

'Speaking of new things, we said we would go into town today to take a look around. We might even be able to find some fabric you like for the dresses you're thinking of.'

Ruby felt comforted by her older sister's supportive words, and the thought of a little shopping while they explored their new home town soon put a smile back on her face.

An hour later the sisters walked the thirty minutes into Four Oaks, starting out along a country lane from the hospital that transformed into a main road surrounded by large houses, and, eventually, into a busy high street.

Beneath the spindly spire of a fifteenth-century church, the market was in full swing. 'Sprouts, two pence a pound,' bellowed one barrow boy. Then: 'Get yerselves some lovely spuds, ladies. I'm sure your husband will love 'em in a stew for his supper,' another shouted, enticing a woman in a grey woollen coat and red headscarf to stop at his stall.

A deep, warm, earthy smell came next as billows of smoke filled the air. 'Hello there, have a look at these lovely chestnuts,' a man said as Ruby and Connie rounded a corner and discovered the source of the aroma. It was not something they'd ever come across before, but for Ruby, the day was all about adventure.

'How much are they?' she asked, inspecting the shiny blackened husks with interest.

'Penny a bag,' the man said, thrusting a steaming paper bag into her hand before she'd even confirmed her purchase. But this wasn't something Ruby was going to miss out on. The chestnuts were just one of many strange new fruits and experiences in Four Oaks town centre, and Ruby was ready to sample them all.

'These are nice, nice, nice,' she said, shoving a chestnut to one side of her mouth to let the steam out, momentarily looking like a chimney as her breath billowed in the cold air.

'Let me try one,' Connie said, plunging her fingers into the paper bag to gather a sooty, roasted nut. Then something caught her eye. 'Ruby, look at that,' she said, tugging on her sister's coat sleeve to show her a dress in the window of Faulkner and Sons, a department store they'd heard the other trainees talking about.

'Man, that would look so good on you, Ruby.' Connie's eyes widened as she took in a red, wispy chiffon dress with a figure-hugging bodice that floated from the waist into a full skirt. 'That colour would really suit you. Let's go in and see if you can buy the fabric and if they can recommend a seamstress.'

'Ohh yes, that's beautiful!' Ruby said, her eyes wide.

The girls wandered around the store until they found a haber-dashery counter, behind which reels of brightly coloured ribbons and lace hung from bobbins, and rolls of fabric lined the back wall. Finding the exact same red chiffon as the mannequin in the window was dressed in, the assistant calculated the cost of five yards.

'That'll come to two pounds, six shillings,' she said, then, seeing the look of horror on the sisters' faces: 'It's actually one of our more affordable chiffons.'

'Lord h'mercy!' Ruby exclaimed as Connie took her by the

arm, as much to steady her as to lead her gently out of a potentially embarrassing encounter. 'Connie, that material is almost half a month's wages for us after deductions.'

'I know,' her sister muttered from the side of her mouth.

'I had no idea things would be so expensive here,' Ruby replied, now a little sullen. 'And there I was thinking we would be able to get a little gift for Billie's birthday in here, but this shop's prices are running us out.'

An hour later, after perusing the market, picking up crackers and a slab of cheese tightly wrapped in parchment to enjoy in their rooms on days they couldn't stomach the hospital dining room, Ruby and Connie headed into Woolworths. A spectacled man behind the counter, wearing a black apron, helped them decide on a gift for Billie – a small bottle of Yardley English Lavender bath oil, which he wrapped in a brown paper bag.

'It's not a lot, but it's what we can afford,' Connie commented, and Ruby nodded her approval.

'Though I remember reading on the ship that this is one of the most popular fragrances in England, so now she can smell just like she belongs here and get all the English fellas chasing her,' Ruby said, winking.

'Ruby, man.' Connie rolled her eyes, but also couldn't help but smile.

Then Ruby remembered: 'And could I have a jar of Posner's Ebonaire, please?' The shopkeeper looked at her, perplexed. 'It's for your hair.'

'Nope, I've not heard of that before,' he replied as he looked at women's hair products in a cabinet. 'What is it? We've got Black & White Pomade and, um, there's Revlon Satin-Set, or some shampoo?'

'I don't think those will be any good for what you need, Ruby. It's a good thing I brought some extra things from home for our hair,' Connie said.

'Yes, you might find that sort of thing in London, but not out here,' the man explained.

As the girls left Woolworths, shop shutters started rattling down and streetlights flickered into life. Heading back to the hospital they were struck by a long queue of people and the smell of deep-fried goodness that travelled its length.

'Ooh Connie, I heard the English girls talking about this – it's a fish and chip shop. We should get some for our dinner, then we won't have to eat whatever disgusting thing they got for us at the hospital tonight.'

When the girls reached the front of the queue, they found that they could only afford a bag of chips and a piece of cod between them if they were going to have money to go out with Billie that evening. But having to share didn't bother them one bit.

'Maaaan, that was delicious!' Ruby said, licking the last greasy morsels off her fingers. 'This is the best thing we eat since getting up here to England – the best!'

Connie eyed Ruby, pleased to see her mood had transformed since that morning and that she was bubbling with enthusiasm once more. Her effervescent sister was back to herself.

Back at the nurses' home, Ruby rushed into their new friend's room and nearly bowled her over with a hug. 'Hey, Billie, happy birthday! We got you a little something from town.'

Ruby looked at Billie expectantly as she opened the brown bag, pulled out the bottle and immediately went to smell the bath oil. 'Oh, Ruby, Connie, this is lovely. They say this is a real popular scent here, thank you!' she said, hugging them both.

'Yes, you can pretend you're a proper English girl now,' Ruby laughed.

'Ha, I guess so. But I think I'll always be a Jamaican girl in England,' Billie replied.

'So tonight – I'm thinking we might as well get the party started now,' she added with a knowing smile. Then she popped open the lid of her suitcase and pulled out one of the bottles of Appleton Estate rum.

Ruby's eyes grew larger. 'But wait! You brought liquor here? You ain't frightened that they would inspect your room and find it?'

Billie laughed at Ruby's innocence. 'They can come look all they like,' she sighed. 'But they ain't taking my rum. Besides,' she added, 'I ain't planning on it being here long enough for anybody to find it,' and she lined up three glasses on her desk and poured a generous measure into each.

'You ain't got nothing to mix it with?' enquired Connie.

'No, unless you want to get a drop of water,' Billie replied with a mild look of horror. 'I prefer to have it as it is, or with a few ice cubes, but they don't have ice like they make at home.'

'But I ain't drunk rum like this before.' Ruby was staring into the glass, a picture of puzzlement and trepidation. 'I only had it when it was warmed with honey, ginger and some lemon – you know, when I had a fever and Mum would say I needed something to help me sweat it out.'

'Lord, you girls are out here in this big old world, all up here in England, and you ain't even experienced things from home yet. How can you be under your mother's skirt when you're on different continents? And Connie, you're supposed to be going out with the delicious Devon tomorrow – I'm sure he would like a woman that's lived a little. Someone who knows herself,' Billie cajoled, as the sisters each took a sip from their glasses, Ruby's significantly larger than Connie's.

'Ugh!' she exclaimed, scrunching her face and shuddering as the rum burned a course down her windpipe. 'I'm not so sure this is meant for anything other than medicinal purposes – only medicine tastes this bad!'

'Ah, you'll get used to it. Alcohol is an acquired taste,' Billie informed her.

'I ain't sure it's a thing I want to acquire,' Ruby replied, her face still contorted. She looked over at Connie, who seemed much more at ease with the tipple in her glass, and wished she was more sophisticated and able to handle this new experience.

'OK, no problem, we'll have to find something lighter for you as we build you up to the strong stuff. Maybe a little port and lemon,' said Billie as she turned her attention to her wardrobe. 'Now, what are you girls planning to wear? And Ruby, don't forget I said I'd do your hair, and I have a lipstick that will really suit you and rouge to bring out those lovely cheekbones of yours.'

An hour and a half later the three girls walked into town, and Ruby was especially excited. Not only was it going to be their first night out in England, but Billie had given her a hair and beauty makeover that made her feel a foot taller, five years older and infinitely more stylish.

Chapter Six

Billie

Billie didn't tell the Haynes sisters but it wasn't only her birthday celebration that made her want to get acquainted with one of the bottles of rum in her suitcase. She wouldn't admit it, but her week had not been without its challenges, and she was happy to see the back of it.

She wasn't the type of person to allow people's opinions to undermine her confidence, but she had quickly recognized she would have to bend to fit in at the hospital, or at least to appease Sister Shaw – something that didn't make her very happy.

But after being on the sharp end of a few of the sister's acerbic remarks, Billie felt she needed to change her outward appearance before the sister started judging her character and abilities as well. Although frustrated, she dug out the highest necklines she could find in her wardrobe – three V-necked sweaters that Esme had given to her when she got to England – and wore them under her white coat for the rest of the week's training. She had also done away with her trademark red lipstick, and even went to training what she considered to be bare-faced – with just a little eyeliner, mascara and a smear of Vaseline to moisturize and add gloss to her lips. This did nothing to conceal her beauty, however. The trainees that noticed this change in how Billie presented herself, Connie included, thought she was even more arresting, and it didn't stop male heads turning wherever they went with her around the hospital grounds, be it those of patients, visitors or doctors alike.

Following this transformation, Billie's first week's training had gone quite well – Sister Shaw even commended her knowledge of the different bed set-ups.

But something was still niggling at the back of her mind and seeping into her consciousness even as she tried to focus on all the new things she was learning. Billie had been due a period earlier that week, and with Aunt Flo not putting in an appearance so far, the big question about the previous weekend still plagued her. Billie tried not to let it worry her; she had always told herself that she was a big girl, and whatever happened in her life, she would have to face the consequences of her actions. Besides, having a baby couldn't possibly be the worst thing in the world – Billie loved children and, added to that, it was the 1950s now, and the Second World War had changed so much. She knew that women in England had been working, for more than ten years, in jobs that had traditionally been reserved for men.

She considered Jamaica to be fairly enlightened. More than one girl Billie had gone to school with had had a child before she was out of her teens, and none of the relationships with the fathers had outlasted the pregnancies. Gossips would gossip, of course. They concluded these girls had let their families down, but the mothers weren't spurned or subjected to the same level of shame she understood existed for unmarried mothers in England.

'They have special homes where they hide these girls away until they birth the baby, and then they post the children for adoption. They treat them worse than a criminal,' Esme had told her. Added to that, Billie knew she couldn't be a nurse and a mother; women were expected to leave their jobs when they got pregnant, not be starting a new career.

By Saturday evening however, she was ready to quash any fears for her future and celebrate her present. When her mother, Clara, had died at just thirty-nine years old, Billie had realized that a long life was not promised to anyone. Despite being a teenager, she was convinced she had no time to waste. Life was for living, she told herself, so she did so with a seize-the-day urgency, embracing every experience – and every man – along the way. Walking into Four Oaks, she was ready to paint her new home town the same shade of red that she'd glossed onto her lips.

As the three young women found themselves in the shadow of Four Oaks' old church, they scanned the town for life and were struck by how quiet the high street was.

'This place is a bust,' Billie stated flatly.

'I can barely believe it's as quiet as all this,' Ruby said as they walked past the marketplace that had bustled with life earlier that day.

'Right. It's like a ghost town compared to this afternoon,' Connie added. 'Let's carry on down the road though and see if we can find the milk bar Phyllis mentioned.'

At the far end of the street, beneath a sign that said 'Minstrels' in a fancy script, the girls were glad to step into the cosy warmth of the milk bar. Being Saturday night, it was full of groups of teens and twenty-something couples on dates. Conversations died down and the girls became aware of heads whipping around as they headed to the counter. 'Table for three?' a waitress in a red pinafore dress behind a chrome-topped counter enquired, then led them across a black and white checked floor to a booth with pale blue and white leather seats.

'I guess they're not used to seeing people like us here,' Connie said meekly.

'It ain't that, it's that they're dazzled by our beauty,' Billie replied with a self-assured wink. 'Besides, they better get used to us, as there's more like us coming to England to help out. And if any of them get sick we'll be the ones caring for them.'

Billie picked up a menu from the pink Formica table and scanned past cold dishes of egg sandwiches and tinned crab with tomatoes, then hot meals of ham, egg and chips to get to the drinks. 'You got to be kidding me! They only look to have milk-shakes and a whole heap of soft drinks. What kind of a place is this?' Her disappointment was palpable – this was far from Billie's idea of a good time.

But Connie tried her best to look on the bright side. 'Well, they got ice cream sodas. There's no booze in them, but they can be nice.' Her voice weakened as she sensed Billie's discontented stare burning into her. Despite Billie's irritation, the girls ordered three lemonade ice cream sodas, which were delivered in tall footed glasses with red and white striped paper straws.

'Oh, that's delicious,' Ruby said, sucking noisily on her straw as a man in a brown leather jacket with indigo jeans rolled up at the ankles walked past their table and to a spearmint jukebox trimmed with chrome.

'It's OK,' Billie shrugged, taking in the man at the jukebox's backside. 'But I wish I had brought a little of my rum to liven it up.'

'Yes, that would've given it some zing,' Connie replied. But Billie didn't hear her; she had locked eyes with the jukebox man as he headed back to his table.

It was just after eight o'clock when they finished their sodas and Connie suggested they go for a walk just in case Four Oaks offered anything more lively. Wandering outside, Billie came face to face with the jukebox man.

'Hello, darlin', had a good night?' he said, from astride a motor-bike.

'Well, this place isn't exactly exciting,' Billie moped. 'Tell me, what do boys like you do for fun? It can't be hanging out here.'

'Nah, you need to come down the Woodman's,' the man said. Then curiosity got the better of him: 'You up at the hospital, are ya? I hear they've got a lot of people coming to work up there.'

'Yes – we're from Barbados and Billie's from Jamaica,' Ruby told him, pointing at Connie and then at Billie.

'Jamaica, eh? I saw the Queen went there a couple of months ago.'

'Yes, my little sister was one of the school children who sang to Queen Elizabeth at Sabina Park in Kingston,' Billie said. 'She couldn't stop talking about how pretty she was.'

'Yeah, she is a bit of all right, much like yerself.' The man winked at Billie. 'So what brought you to Minstrels of all places?'

'Good question. There didn't look to be much other than this place, though it's not how I planned to spend my birthday.'

'Oh, it's your birthday, is it? Well, then we'd better show you a good time, darlin'. Hop on and I'll whizz you over to the Woodman's, it's a nice little pub,' he said, motioning towards the space in between him and the motorbike's chrome handlebars.

Billie looked at Connie and Ruby.

'But you can't go off with him! You don't even know his name,' Connie said.

'John Whicker,' the man interjected. 'Pleased to make your acquaintance. And that's my mate Ted over there, who's driving round in his car – he could take you two ladies over.'

Connie had considered arguing against the plan, but then she saw a look of devilment on Billie's face and knew right away her protestations would fall on deaf ears. Minutes later, Connie and Ruby followed in Ted's car, as Billie rode at the front of John's motorbike, her figure-hugging pencil skirt forcing her to sit sideways on.

'Wheeeeee!' she squealed as the bike raced round the corner and they came to a stop outside the Woodman's Arms. John's hand slipped from the bike's handlebars to Billie's slim waist to help her down, then he wrapped an arm around her shoulders as Connie, Ruby and Ted followed them into the pub.

Two hours later the group's table was straining under the weight of their glasses, Connie and Ruby settling on a sweet wine each, while Billie started with cherry brandies and ended up joining John and Ted for a couple of whiskies.

As Billie went to the toilet, John escorted her to show her the way, leading her to a dimly lit entryway where the toilet block was located. As she turned to thank him, his blue eyes locked for the second time that evening on her big brown ones, and he pulled her towards him, kissing her intently. His hands moved swiftly from her waist to caress her pert, round bottom.

'Wait a minute, I really do need to go,' she giggled, pulling away from him.

Minutes later as she walked back into the pub John was waiting by the door, and they joined Connie, Ruby and Ted with a rabble of people huddled around a man playing the piano. John wrapped his arms around Billie as she stood in front of him, his warm breath caressing her neck. She enjoyed the sensation of his muscular arms around her, making her feel safe, and the seductiveness of his breath as the group around her sang 'Roll Me Over in the Clover' along with the pianist.

'What kind of lyrics are these?' Billie laughed.

'I dunno – they're a bit dodgy, ain't they, but I guess they get right to the point!' John chuckled as he looked purposefully into Billie's eyes. Meanwhile, the rabble continued to sing with bawdy delight:

> *Roll me over*
> *In the clover,*
> *Roll me over, lay me down*
> *And do it again.*

Oh, this is number nine,
And the baby's doing fine.
Roll me over, lay me down
And do it again . . .

Suddenly the niggling worry of the previous weekend that had
spent the last few days at the back of Billie's mind pushed its way
to the front, riding a wave of alcohol in her system to dull her
mood in an instant, and she froze in John's embrace.

'You all right?' he enquired, sensing her body tense in his arms.

'Yes, yes, it's nothing,' she said, painting a weak smile on her
face.

'I know what you need . . . Barman, another round!' John
bellowed.

Another hour and yet more drinks passed before the pub rang
the closing bell. As Connie and Ruby retrieved their coats, they
spotted Billie slip outside with John, and when they followed they
were shocked to find them sharing a passionate kiss by his motor-
bike.

'Boy, Billie, you don't waste any time,' Connie said, as the girls
started walking home.

'Time waits for no man . . . or woman, for that matter,' Billie
replied with a smile. 'And by the time John had fix me with them
piercing blue eyes . . . I couldn't help myself.'

All three girls laughed raucously now. 'Really, though, I just
couldn't say no,' she said emphatically. 'He was some hot stuff!'

'Do you think you might see more of him?' Ruby enthused.

'Ohh yes, I'd be very interested to see *more* of him,' Billie
replied suggestively. 'But I don't know, I have another friend I
need to see in London yet – I met a nice fella called Clive, from
back home, on the underground last week.'

'Billie, you behave just a like a man!' Connie observed.

'If you mean I have fun, then yes, I do behave like a man. But if you're suggesting that sex is only for men to enjoy, then I would have to disagree with you.'

The two sisters looked shocked now. Connie was in awe of Billie's liberated outlook, while Ruby hadn't even considered sex as part of the equation. Within herself though, Billie didn't know if she would make an effort to see Clive or John again. Although she enjoyed being in a man's embrace and having his eyes fall on her adoringly, she was starting to feel that men were much more trouble than they were worth.

'Calm yourselves, girls,' Billie laughed gently. 'I got my head screwed on. It's men whose brains are always in their pants.'

'Are you sure it's only the men?' Connie teased as they arrived at the hospital grounds.

There, the girls were surprised to find the nurses' home all in darkness and as Connie tried to open the main door it stuck in its lock. 'Oh no, they must lock the doors come a certain time!' she said.

'Let me have a go – they don't lock it till after midnight,' Billie said, rattling the door handle as if to try to jimmy the lock. But it was to no avail. Peering through the window, she caught sight of a white clock face in the shadows of the reception area that said quarter past twelve.

'Oh no, we've missed lock-up,' she said.

'My God, what we gonna do? We can't stay out here the whole night, it's freezing,' Ruby fretted. But just then a window opened in a room above the doorway.

'Jesus, what in the world are you girls doing out there at this time? I thought you were all tucked up in bed like the rest of us,' hissed Kathleen. 'Wait there, I'll come and let you in, but you'd better be quiet, you don't want to wake Sister Shaw.'

The next two minutes felt like an hour as the girls' alcohol-fuelled joviality gave way to anxiety. 'What if she can't get it unlocked and we're out here the whole night in this cold?' Ruby asked. 'And then we'll be in trouble for not representing the hospital well, like Sister Shaw said we had to.'

'Shh, Ruby, we just got to wait for Kathleen, and then we can sneak up the stairs quietly,' Connie whispered, her teeth now starting to chatter in the numbing night air.

Soon Kathleen appeared at the door in a quilted dressing gown, her hair in rollers under a pink headscarf. 'Come on, you'd better be creeping up those stairs dead quietly now,' she said, locking the door carefully and silently behind them.

Billie took off her stilettos; Ruby and Connie followed suit with their kitten-heeled shoes, and they started to silently tiptoe up the stairs. Reaching the second set, Ruby's hand slipped on the handrail and one of her shoes clipped the banisters as it went crashing to the floor below.

'Oh no!' she hissed as she raced back down to retrieve it. Picking it up, she turned to begin her ascent again, but came face to face with Sister Shaw.

'What time do you call this, Nurse?' Sister Shaw said, her face stern. Then she caught two things – the first being the other three girls as they hovered on the stairway. The second was the smell of alcohol and the pub – stale beer and cigarette smoke – that hung around Ruby.

'This is *not* ladylike, and it is most definitely *not* the way nurses at this hospital are expected to behave,' she blustered. 'You've woken me, and you've clearly woken Miss O'Hare here who really ought to know better than to get involved with your shenanigans. I will not have you disturbing any more of the residents, so get yourselves to bed. But I want you three girls to report to the matron's office in the morning. That means bright and early at 8 a.m.!'

The girls shuffled upstairs, Ruby and Connie looking deflated, as Kathleen said goodnight and went back to her room. Billie paused at her door. 'Goodnight, my Bajan girls, and thanks for coming out with me – I had such a good time and we managed to paint Four Oaks r— well . . . at least a good shade of pink.' She smiled. 'Everything will be all right with Matron – you just wait and see.'

'Goodnight,' Connie and Ruby chorused, their enthusiasm deadened by the threat of what punishment might befall them later.

But as Billie closed the door and got ready for bed, her spirits were pretty high – she felt it had been a great first birthday in England. And she was never one to let small hiccups bother her.

At eight o'clock that same morning, the sisters had been waiting outside the matron's office for five minutes when Billie raced along the corridor.

'Lord Jesus my head hurts real bad,' she panted. 'And now we got to see what's going to happen here. This is not how I wanted to mark my birthday.'

A minute later, Miss Bleakly gave the girls a steely stare from behind her round glasses as she ushered them in to see Matron Wilson, whose heavy wooden desk seemed to signify her importance. 'Now, ladies, I understand that you caused a bit of a to-do late last night. We simply cannot have our charges arriving back at the nurses' home at an ungodly time. It's just not acceptable behaviour. What in heaven's name were you up to out at that hour?' Her voice was calm and measured.

Ruby looked at the floor like a naughty schoolgirl, Connie attempted to frame her answer, but Billie jumped in. 'It was my fault. I asked Connie and Ruby to join me to celebrate my birthday. They didn't want to stay out late, but I made them come to the pub with me,' she said.

'I do hope you didn't embarrass yourselves and the good name of this establishment – the people of Four Oaks look upon St Mary's as a place of knowledge and healing. They can't be seeing nurses behaving irresponsibly and falling about the town drunk. This is the kind of insubordination that could lead to you having your wages docked. You have to realize that things are different here in England and we hold all of our charges to a high standard.

'However, I was once young just like you are, and so I am prepared to overlook this incident on this occasion. But girls, do not let me down again; you must be back at the nurses' home far in advance of midnight in future.'

'Yes, Matron,' the three girls said quietly, as they made for the door.

'And girls, I expect to hear good things from Sister Shaw about your progress – I hope you invest more time in your studies than you do in exploring the pubs of Four Oaks.'

'Oh God, I feel sick. I was real frightened of what she would say. She could've had us on the boat back to the West Indies,' Ruby said, relief brightening her face.

'No, they need us, Ruby,' Billie replied. 'You ain't seen the news reports of how many more girls like us are coming to England? They got to cover these labour shortages somehow. Anyway, I would've taken all the blame for it. I wouldn't see you two getting in trouble for me, you're too sweet for that.'

Chapter Seven

Connie

Devon arrived on the midday train from London and Connie was waiting at the station to meet him, her relief from seeing Matron that morning now mixing with anticipation, causing her to feel a little unsettled.

As Devon strode off the train, Connie held out her hand, a little unsure of how he would greet her, then felt awkward as he used it to pull her towards him and placed a gentle kiss on her cheek.

'I hope I've not been too forward,' he said, his brown eyes looking down at her tenderly.

'No, er, not at all,' Connie replied, surprise and excitement dancing inside. 'I don't know where you'd like to go. I tried to ask around and see what sort of things we could do today but no one had any ideas. The local girls said as it was a Sunday it would be very quiet,' she stammered, while Devon just smiled, taking in her fine features.

She was right – as they walked through the centre of Four Oaks, it resembled the graveyard at All Saints, the church with the steeple. Even Minstrels was closed. But Devon was happy merely to be in Connie's company.

'Let's just walk and talk,' he said. 'This looks to be quite a nice place. I've not been this far out of London yet – well, not into the countryside, I've been to Birmingham and Nottingham. But, as you know, I started working on the railways a few months ago, so I guess I'll get to see a lot more of England soon enough,' Devon said. As they walked, his hand swung in time with Connie's, and suddenly they were as one. 'You don't mind if I hold your hand, do you?'

'No. I don't mind at all.' Her voice quivered as a hot flush of embarrassment caught her. Connie wasn't used to men asking to hold her hand. It wasn't that she was wholly inexperienced in matters of the heart, far from it. But she hadn't met anyone as gentlemanly as Devon before.

Despite there being a chill northerly wind, the pair wandered the town's streets for hours, as though warmed by the glow of this burgeoning relationship. Devon told Connie about his time in England, how he had been working in a factory in London for most of the previous four years, but he was now thrilled about his new job, which offered better pay and prospects. 'It's not easy living here sometimes, you know, Connie. The English . . . well, they haven't exactly welcomed us with open arms, and things are very expensive, especially in London. So it's been a struggle to get settled and feel like you making a little progress. But I'm hoping I can move out of the place I'm living in now and into a flat in time.'

'You don't like it there?' Connie enquired.

'Oh yes, you spoke to my landlady the other day. Rachel is a good woman. She lived and worked in the East End of London for a long time, in the fabric mills there, before her and her husband were able to buy the house in Kentish Town. He died some years back so she rents out rooms to a few of us to pay the bills. She's Jewish, so she knows what it's like to feel you don't fit in. It's been good living there, but I can't go on living in one room for ever.'

'I understand,' Connie said, even though she knew she couldn't truly understand his perspective. Everything was fresh for her and she was enjoying her time in England – making friends, having adventures, and learning so many new things. Turning a corner, the pair came across Memorial Park and wandered along its oak-lined pathways. Then, in a field dotted with plane trees, with the town's cenotaph at the centre, they took a seat on a green bench as a chill wind blew towards them.

Placing his left arm around her shoulders, Devon pulled Connie closer to him. 'I hope you're OK with us cosying up. The English winter has a way of getting people closer,' he joked.

'I'm fine, yes,' Connie smiled, enjoying the closeness and the warmth of Devon's body as their breath made steamy trails through the cold air of the afternoon. Connie found herself unusually quiet. She was feeling a little shy, but she enjoyed listening to Devon as he shared his experience of life in England with her – though she did notice that his enthusiasm for Britain appeared to be dulling.

Devon started to tell her about his early years in England. 'The war was tough on everybody. No one had it good, you know. Whether you were living here where bombs were falling on your house, or you were like me, in the army and heading into occupied Europe. I used to wake up in the morning and wonder what could have possessed me to leave home and say I'm going fighting in this war, thousands of miles away. But my grandmother had told me, Hitler is the devil. She said, if we don't go and fight him for Britain, we don't know what could happen back home. That we may even find ourselves back in slavery.'

'Yes,' Connie nodded. 'I remember hearing the old folks saying that sort of thing. It was like they were frightened the war would soon spread to us.'

'Well, it was never very far from our shores in Barbados. Do you remember when the SS *Cornwallis* was torpedoed while it was moored in Carlisle Bay?'

'Oh yes, I was just a little girl, but the noise it made!' Connie's eyes were wide now as she recalled the incident. 'Then everyone sat around the Rediffusion, waiting for the news to come on before they would venture out the house.'

'It rocked the whole of our small island, eh?' Devon said, shaking his head slightly. 'So when the forces were recruiting I joined up to fight the evil of the Nazis. But really, I don't think any of us from back home knew what we were getting into. We were kids.' Connie looked up at Devon now, as the soft features of his face seemed to tense momentarily.

'But eventually the war was over, and it felt as though the whole world took a sigh of relief. It was just a matter of a couple of weeks before we got our discharge papers and I came to England for a few days before heading home to Barbados. Back here there was bunting all over the place and people were welcoming us back like heroes.'

'And you *were* heroes,' Connie enthused. 'You all played your part, fighting beside our English brothers.'

'Yes, we did. But later I realized – people didn't have time for prejudice when there were bombs dropping on their heads and we were the ones there helping them. But it was different when I came back a few years ago. It seemed as though Britain had changed and people were scared – but not like how they were during the war. This time they were scared about the future and the economy.

'A man from Guyana I met when I first got back to London, he said to me, "Don't worry about a job – there's plenty work out there – you should worry about finding somewhere to live." The first couple of places I went to look at to rent, I was turned away by the landlords who said they didn't rent to blacks.'

'But why would they say something like that? What on earth did they think we would do?' Connie asked him, shocked.

'I wish I could tell you, Connie,' Devon replied. 'It's a complete mystery to me, but I learned quickly that not everyone was going to welcome us here.'

'I guess I'm lucky I already had a place to live here at the hospital,' Connie considered as the wind whipped up and Devon pulled her closer, then shielded her from the gust by wrapping his other arm around her in a warm embrace.

'Doesn't all this cold weather make you miss home, though?' Devon said wistfully.

Thoughts of home were certainly not far from Connie's mind. She was starting to miss her family, and the warm Barbados sunshine that kissed her skin. But she also felt her great English adventure had only just begun. She couldn't plan a future back home just yet, but the idea of a future with Devon was certainly an exciting prospect.

'That said, I miss a lot of things beyond the sunshine,' Devon continued. 'I long to get back to see my mum and dad and my brother. And I miss the friendliness – people in Barbados . . . you just know where you are with them and everyone you meet has a friendly disposition. Here, people can be very cool with you.

'I do think the weather makes a difference, though. Just wait till the summer comes. Boy, when the sun is shining the English people can be full of merriment, you know.' His eyes lit up at the thought. 'But it's not like that here all the time, so I'm saving, and I hope to go back home some day soon. Perhaps with you on my arm, Miss Haynes,' he said warmly.

Connie felt a rush of blood to her cheeks as her apprehension took hold until she could keep the thought in her head no longer. 'I thought you'd be looking for an English girl to take home after all this time. I expect all those girls in London are real glamorous.'

'Really? No, Connie, they're not my style at all. I've dated a couple English girls, but they're from a different world. They seem to want to do everything fast – you go to the pictures and next thing they're inviting you back to their place and want to get your trousers off you. It's not how I was brought up.

'You hear about girls here who say they're going away to visit a friend or an auntie, but really they're pregnant. I mean,' he said, shaking his head, 'who goes on holiday for weeks on end? Next thing, they come back, the baby's gone, and they carry on with their lives as if nothing happened.'

Connie shifted uneasily. 'So . . . wh-what happens to the babies?'

'They get adopted by some nice family in the countryside who brings the child up. I don't know for sure, but I don't think the mothers see them again. They have these homes here, you see, where they send unmarried mothers and once the babies are born, they're put up for adoption and that's that.'

'Oh dear, that's terrible,' Connie said. 'Imagine them never seeing their babies again.'

'Well, I think they're encouraged to worry about their future and not the past, and they know that no man would marry a girl who has that kind of background. It's tough on the girls, but I can understand the reasoning.'

'Yes. I-I suppose so.' Connie sounded meek now as she buried her face in the folds of Devon's coat.

As the afternoon's light began to dim, the mood between the couple lifted as Devon escorted Connie back to the nurses' home and they reminisced, sharing stories from their neighbourhood in Barbados. 'And do you remember Fat Pig and the time he stole a breadfruit from Mr Beckles' tree? He came out his yard and chased and chased him for miles, till Fat Pig couldn't run no more. He was bent over in the road panting and saying: "But Mr Beckles," pant, pant, "why you couldn't just let me have one little breadfruit for ma' dinner?"' Devon roared with laughter and Connie did too.

'Fat Pig, though? What kind of a name is that to call somebody?'

'Oh, you know how it is at home, Connie, they've got all kinds of creative nicknames for people. They used to call me Skin Teeth, because of the way I was always smiling.'

'Ha ha, yes they did! I remember it now,' Connie giggled. 'Everyone used to talk about your smile. They'd say it could get a girl into some trouble.'

'Really?' Devon beamed with flirtatious purpose, as the pair arrived back at the nurses' home. 'I don't think it has such power. At least, I hope not!' And Connie loved seeing his smile.

'Are you coming into the lobby for a while? We're not allowed visitors upstairs, but Ruby will be excited to see you. Oh, and she keeps saying how she needs to check you out seeing as Mum and Dad aren't around.' She gave Devon a sideways glance and a knowing smile.

'Ah, really? That sister of yours is such a card! Sure, I'll come and say hello. And I'll be sure to be on my very best behaviour,' he said, removing his hat and bowing slightly. Then he opened the door and ushered Connie in. 'Miss Haynes, allow me,' he said, replacing his Barbadian accent with a very formal English one.

'Well, thank you, kind sir,' Connie laughed.

'Devon Grant! I see you escorting my sister up the path, all very fancy. And look at you in that hat and coat, you look like a real English gentleman,' Ruby said as she made her way down the stairs.

'Well, a man has to look sharp when he's out with a beautiful girl.' He smiled at Connie. 'I hope you've been enjoying yourself, Ruby. Now, tell me, have you been eating up all that English bread?' he teased.

Ruby pulled a face. 'The food hasn't been my favourite thing so far,' she started to reply, then, realizing Devon was referring to her observation about all the chimneys she'd spotted in London, she launched herself at him in a mock tantrum, playfully hitting him on the arm. 'Don't you pick on me, Devon Grant. How was

I to know they were for the fires? It seemed real strange.' And the three of them laughed with glee.

Minutes later, Ruby feigned busyness by looking at the previous day's copy of the *Financial Times* she found on a coffee table in the reception area, while Connie saw Devon out.

'It's been such a nice afternoon. I really enjoyed our walk.' Connie smiled.

'It was lovely seeing you again,' Devon said as his hands brushed Connie's face, then he pulled her towards him and planted a kiss firmly on her lips.

'Oooohhhh!' they heard Ruby cry from reception, and the pair looked at each other and smiled for a moment.

'I'll call you this week and perhaps you could come and visit me in London sometime soon.' Devon was looking right into Connie's eyes and she felt her heart racing.

'I'd like that very much,' she replied, as Devon set off for the train station and Connie closed the door behind him.

'Wait a minute – was that who I think it was?' said Billie as she wandered down the stairs. The look of joy on Connie's face was all she needed to answer her question.

'Yes, it was him – Devon,' Ruby enthused. 'He was even more handsome than I remembered.'

'So how was your date, Connie? Do you think you'll be seeing *more* of him?' Billie enquired pointedly.

'Billie, you're too much,' Connie chuckled. 'But yes, he said he wanted me to visit him in London sometime. We had such a nice walk and we talked for hours. I really like him.'

'I'm happy for you, dear,' Billie replied, taking in Connie's glow. 'He's really brought a smile to your face, and any man that does that is worth keeping hold of.'

'I agree,' said Ruby. 'Now, who's ready for dinner? I'm hungry.'

Later that night, Connie struggled to get to sleep. She was unsure if it was the thrill of this new romance, or if she was a little uneasy. She could see herself falling for Devon. Any girl would fall in love with his good looks, confidence and considerate nature. And yet, some of the things he had said bothered her. She felt sure she could trust him with her heart, she just didn't know if she could trust him with her secrets. Or what he would think of her if he was to find out that the young girl he knew years ago in Barbados was not the woman he had met in Four Oaks that day. But just before sleep overtook her, Connie pictured Devon's smooth skin and handsome features, then his soft lips as they caressed hers, and she fell asleep with a slight smile on her face.

The following morning as the girls arrived for that week's training, Sister Shaw took a moment for a rather grandiose introduction.

'So far, you have been learning the very basics of nursing care. But today, we are starting on anatomy and physiology,' she announced.

Connie was excited at the very prospect; it was as though their training was really getting started.

Biology wasn't a subject that had been studied in any depth when she was at school. Or rather, it wasn't a subject girls had been encouraged to study, so there had been little opportunity for her to learn until now. And if there was one thing Connie loved, it was learning.

As Sister Shaw handed out textbooks, Ruby caught her sister immediately starting to flick through its pages as though already soaking up the information within. 'This is the bit I was looking forward to,' she beamed.

'I can imagine,' Ruby replied, looking less enthusiastic.

'Now, of course, we do not have a lot of time – you only have a few more weeks of your preliminary training for us to cover a huge amount of information,' Sister Shaw told them. 'You will, of course, learn much more on the job, and during your further studies in the next two to three years before becoming fully fledged state enrolled or state registered nurses. But for this part of your training, we need to move swiftly, in order to get you on the wards working and receiving first-hand experience.

'We will start today by looking at the skeletal structure,' she continued as she pulled forward a skeleton that had, up till then, been gathering dust in the corner of the room.

'The skeleton is the framework that provides structure to the rest of the body and facilitates our movement. At birth, the human body is made up of 270 bones, but these fuse over time so that by adulthood, the body has 206 individual bones. You will need to become familiar with each and every one of them, and how they work with bands of connective tissue such as ligaments and tendons. We will be covering this first and it is, of course, vital that you learn it all to the letter!'

Most of the trainees felt daunted at the prospect of the challenge ahead of them. But Connie had a self-assuredness that she only felt with academic study, and soaked up all of the information Sister Shaw shared with them that day.

'What are you girls doing this evening?' Billie enquired as the day's classes drew to a close. 'I was wondering if you fancied having a little drink after dinner – I still have that Appleton's, you know.'

'Oh, no can do for me. I plan to study this evening – we have a whole lot of things to learn, and I'm fascinated by how all our bodies work. I'm keen to get into my textbook.'

'I knew it!' Ruby said. 'Connie, you always had your head in your books when we were kids.'

'Yes, and maybe you should too, instead of your head being in the clouds all the time,' Connie retorted.

Ruby feigned shock, then looked thoughtful for a moment. 'Well, maybe you're right. I'll give some time over to study tonight too. I don't want my big-brained big sis getting all the praise from Sister Shaw.'

After dinner, Connie sat at the wooden desk in her room, poring over the pages of her textbook for hours, until the moon was high in the sky outside.

Seeing light coming from under Connie's bedroom door, Billie knocked on it, almost imperceptibly.

'Billie, what are you doing up? I thought I was alone, studying this late. Even Ruby has long gone to bed.'

'I thought I'd see if you were finished for the night. Maybe you fancy that rum after all your hard work,' Billie said.

Connie looked at her, sensing there had to be a reason why she was drinking at quarter to twelve on a Monday night. 'Erm, OK, I'll come to your room. But just a very small one for me.'

In her room, Billie took a clean glass off a shelf and put it alongside her own, which still had a little brown liquid in the bottom. Topping it up, she passed the other glass to Connie. 'I don't have any mixer, but I know you can handle it,' she said.

'I don't even know how you can be back on the booze so fast after Saturday,' Connie said, slightly mining for information.

'Huh, I guess I needed it to settle me down. I'm not a drinker really, you know, Connie. Don't get the impression that I drink every day – I usually only get rum out for special occasions. And I'll have a little cherry brandy now and then.' Then Billie sighed. 'The truth is, I think it's cherry brandy that has me in this mess in the first place.'

'What mess? I don't understand, Billie,' Connie said, concerned, and as she looked at the Jamaican girl she could now sense her inner turmoil.

Billie shifted in her chair, looking down into her glass and seeming far removed from the confident girl Connie had got to know. 'It was the night before I came here. If I'm honest I don't even know what happened. Maybe nothing happened at all. But I'm scared, Connie,' she rambled, her face contorting as she recalled the fractured memories of her last night in London.

'What could have you so upset?' Connie asked.

'I might have got into some trouble,' Billie said, then paused, Connie hanging on her every word.

'It was that English boy I was telling you and Ruby about when I got here. We had such a good time at the dance, then when it finished he took me to my friend Esme's house in a taxi. I know we had a kiss . . . and there was more too. But . . .' and now the words caught in her throat, as though to let them out would realize her fears, 'I can't remember *how much more*. And I'm scared, Connie. I'm scared that I might be pregnant.' Her voice quivered as a tear now started to run slowly down her right cheek. 'I just don't know what I would do. I can't go back to Jamaica. Not with a baby. But really, not at all. I left there for a reason – I had to get out.'

Connie reached for Billie's hand and clamped hers on top, as though trying to physically transfer her strength to the other girl. 'It's all right. Billie, do you know when you're due to have your monthly?'

'It should've been the middle of last week. But there's been no sign, and I'm usually regular as anything,' Billie replied solemnly.

'Oh, but you're really not late yet. If it don't come in maybe another week or so then you might have reason to worry. And maybe then you should think about going to the doctor.'

'Ah, no, I ca—' There was panic in Billie's voice now.

'Shh, shh,' Connie soothed. 'Billie, it's OK, it probably won't even come to that. And, let me tell you this, a baby is not the worst thing to ever happen to a woman.'

'Connie, come on – you know it would mean a one-way ticket back to the West Indies.' The anxiety in Billie's voice was plain. 'And besides, how would you know?' she pressed, more out of fear than exasperation.

'I do know, Billie. I do,' Connie said. 'You're not the first to go through this worry, and you certainly won't be the last.'

Connie looked at Billie, and for the first time since meeting her she saw her fragility. It was as though she were a pretty porcelain doll that now had a crack across its delicate face. She placed her arm around Billie's shoulders for comfort, as her friend, by now, could do nothing to contain her sobs.

'You're confiding in me, and so I will confide in you, because I want you to understand that you can overcome any situation, you hear?' Connie's voice was low now as Billie nodded.

'A few years ago I was in the same place as you. I didn't have a new job, and I wasn't thousands of miles from home. Although sometimes I wished I was,' Connie said, a little sullen.

'What do you mean?' Billie mumbled, staring at Connie in the amber glow of her bedside light, as though her story might start to play out on her face.

'I knew when I met Cedric Worrell that my life would never be the same. I just didn't realize it would be in a bad way,' Connie began. 'He was ten years older than me, and frankly he had ten years more experience in matters of the heart. Though if I think about it, I don't suppose he was ever really driven by his heart.

'But he was my first love, he was my first . . . well, my first everything. I'm not sure I was his love, though – he didn't want to be tied down to *only* one woman and when I got pregnant, he told me he did not want to be a father again.'

'What, Connie, you've been pregnant?' The revelation stopped Billie in her tracks, and she momentarily held her breath, waiting for the other girl to continue. 'But you're the most sensible girl I know.'

'Well, I wasn't very sensible back then. Truth be known, I didn't have much experience of love or of men at all. We're Catholic, Billie. Our mum and dad . . .' She sighed. 'They loved us, but I don't think they did Ruby and me much justice. They didn't teach us much about love, least of all . . . you know.' She pulled a face in a bid to conceal her unease.

'So when I had missed my monthlies, and then a few weeks later when my belly began to bulge, I went to Cedric. I don't know why now, but I expected to get love and support from him.' Connie's voice started to tremble. 'But you know what he said? He told me he already had a wife and two children. I had no idea till then.'

Billie could see Connie was fighting back tears herself now, the pain still cutting deep into her heart, more than three years on. 'Then he told me, "I ain't got no interest in you or your damn pickney.'"

Connie continued telling Billie her story. How she had been scared of her God-fearing parents' reactions, and that her mother's temper had flared at the news. 'What kind of disgustingness you bringing on dis house?! This is a godly house, an' you telling us you made a mistake. You inn't made no mistake. The devil musta get into you, girl – simple as dat.'

But Connie said it was her father's quieter response, his seething disappointment, that tore at her heart so much more than her mother's acid tongue.

'Then I was banished to the countryside,' Connie continued. 'My mum's sister, my Aunt Agatha, looked after me. She lives way up north in a parish called St Lucy, far away from where we lived in town.'

So struck was Billie by Connie's story that she forgot her own worries for a few minutes, perhaps for the first time since she'd left Esme's house. Instead, she was transfixed by Connie – a girl she'd had down as far too sensible to get into the kind of mess that she had. But now she was seeing her in a new light, and observing a strength in Connie that Billie only wished she had herself.

'I grew real close to Aunt Agatha in those months. She helped me a lot. I don't know, I felt kind of abandoned by the rest of my family. Ruby and I were always close, but I even felt distance from her because she wasn't allowed to come and see me. I missed her and my little brother, Harold. I missed my parents too.'

Billie now took hold of Connie's hand, their roles reversed as she tried to be a pillar of strength. 'This is terrible, Connie, and it happens so much. It's like we girls get punished. Even though it takes two people to make a baby. But . . . what happened to your child?'

Connie was silent for a moment. Before Billie had shared her worries, Connie had been terrified at the prospect of someone discovering her secret. She feared it was the kind of information that could have hospital managers looking down on her or, worse still, put her on a boat back home. But she felt sharing her story was helping, and if there was one thing Connie wanted to do for any young woman like her, it was to help them realize they were not alone. That what they'd done wasn't sinful, or wicked.

'She's beautiful,' Connie said, after a longer pause than she realized. 'Her name's Martha. She's two now and she has the prettiest smile. Ruby came with me to see her the week before we set sail. We snuck into town and got the bus up to Aunt Agatha's to see them.

'If I'm honest, though, it didn't matter too much. Martha thinks I'm her cousin. She doesn't really know who I am,' she said bleakly as Billie felt Connie's sadness fill the room.

'Aunt Agatha is the only mother she's ever known. And I can't be the mother to her I would like to be – not while I'm here and unmarried, anyway. So I have to accept it.'

'Oh, Connie, I'm so sorry. It must be so hard for you being here away from her.'

'Well, not really. I miss her something terrible, Billie. But I missed her when I was at home, too; there's no way I could be a mother to her there or here,' Connie explained. 'But I was here to listen to you and now I'm telling you my sad story.'

'No, I was happy you were able to tell me, and I hope you get to be the mother to her that you would like to be one day,' Billie replied.

Connie looked thoughtful. 'Yes, maybe one day. Maybe after I've become a nurse and can go home and show everyone what I've achieved, give Martha someone to be proud of.'

As the night turned into morning, the two girls finished their conversation and Connie headed back to her room. 'Promise me you won't worry yourself any more,' she said, hugging Billie tightly. 'We've all been through some big changes – it could easily be that upheaval mixing things up for you. And as we Bajans say, there's never a bad happening, you just trust in the Lord and everything will be all right.'

Billie smiled at her God-fearing friend. 'I will do. And I hope you know your secret is safe with me too. Goodnight, dear.'

Chapter Eight

Ruby

'Good morning,' Ruby piped up as she spotted Billie in the hallway at just after half past seven the next day. 'You ready for breakfast?'

'Ugh, I'm feeling a little tired. Think I'm going to give it a miss today, maybe just get some tea in my room, but I'll see you at lessons,' Billie replied. 'Where's Connie?'

'I'm here – how are you doing this morning, dear?' Connie chirruped as she caught up with her sister, then exchanged a brief knowing glance with Billie.

'I'm OK, just feeling a little fragile. I'm going to get tea and rest a little more.'

'OK, well don't be late – I'm sure there's a sleeping dragon within Sister Shaw, and I for one wouldn't want to wake that,' Ruby joked.

As they walked down to breakfast, Ruby was thoughtful, then she turned to her sister. 'Do you think Billie is OK? I wonder if she's feeling lonely. It must be real difficult if you come up here *all* on your own. I'm so glad we have each other, Connie.'

'Me too, sis. Actually, I had a talk with Billie yesterday. I got the impression that she has a few things on her mind and yes, she is missing home a little too.' Connie wasn't comfortable not

78

being completely open with her sister, but felt Billie's concerns weren't hers to share. She knew Ruby wouldn't think badly of Billie. Ruby had done all she could to support Connie when she became pregnant, and it had taken courage to stand up for her older sibling when their parents found out, even though she had been little more than a child herself at the time.

'Well, I hope she feels brighter soon. Maybe we need to organize something fun to do at the weekend to take her mind off things. Perhaps we could make a cake, and see if they'd let us bake it in the kitchens, or we could do each other's hair or something like that.' Ruby sounded enthusiastic now.

'Hmm . . . maybe the hairstyling. I'm not sure Billie's the cake-baking type, Ruby.'

'Well, she might be if we make a black fruit cake like we have at home, you know, with all the rum soaked into it. She seems to like her rum,' Ruby said in a weak jibe at the Jamaican girl.

'Ruby, you behave yourself,' Connie cautioned. 'Before you know it, people hearing you talk will be making all kinds of judgements about Billie.'

'Yes, but you know what I mean, Connie. She is a bit . . . I don't know. People back home would probably say she's a wild cat.'

'Well, I like her,' Connie replied, now getting a little frustrated with her sister. 'She's just lived more than you is all.'

'Oh, but I like her too,' Ruby rushed now to ensure Connie knew her thinking was in step with hers. 'She's fun and friendly and very beautiful. She's just, well, different is all. She says and does things we wouldn't dream of. Like how she was carrying on last Saturday,' Ruby continued as the sisters took their seats in the dining room.

'Good morning! How are you doing?' Kathleen was perky as she took a seat across from Ruby. 'Hope I'm not interrupting your conversation.'

'No, we were just talking about Billie and—' Ruby started, then felt a sharp prod in her leg under the table from her sister.

'Oh, what, about the other night? I meant to ask you, how did you get on with Matron – I take it she didn't rip you all a new hole?' Kathleen enquired.

'What?' said Ruby, confused by the Irish girl's vernacular.

'I mean she didn't tell you off too much, or threaten you with the boot?' asked Kathleen.

'Ohh, no. Oh my goodness, we were all real frightened, but she told us she was young once too, and gave us a telling-off. But there will be trouble if we do it again – no more staying out until all hours,' Connie explained.

'Ah, thank the heavens! It must've been such a relief to you all. That Sister Shaw – she's a true fire-breathing dragon, but Matron Wilson seems a more reasonable woman. She reminds me some-what of me old mammy,' Kathleen said. 'She's firm, but you could talk to her about anything on your mind. I'm impressed that you found somewhere to go out in Four Oaks till that hour, though. Back home we have plenty of places to go for a bit of the craic, but I've found it pretty staid here so far.'

'Well, we had to work pretty hard at it, but we're learning that Billie is irrepressible. If there's a good time out there, she'll find it!' Connie chuckled, Ruby and Kathleen laughing too.

'We'll have to go out sometime too, even if it's just into town for a browse around the shops. It's not that we can buy much with the wages we'll be left with,' Kathleen enthused.

'Gosh, I know,' Ruby replied. 'I thought what with our room and board covered and us having a few pounds still each month, that we'd have enough to send money back home and enjoy ourselves a little. But things here are much more expensive than I thought they would be. It's a good job we still had some of the money we brought with us so we could go out for Billie's birthday.

That said, the gentlemen who took us to the pub bought our drinks, which was very nice of them.'

'Yes, and I'd dare say they were expecting you to repay them somehow too,' Kathleen said with a knowing look.

'Oh, I don't think so. Well, we didn't anyway, but I'm not sure what he might have said to Billie . . .' Ruby giggled.

'Ruby, hush now. You know Billie would say "it's a woman's prerogative" how she interacts with a young man,' Connie said, putting on a grandiose imitation of Billie. 'She's a real modern woman,' she smiled, unable to hide her awe at her friend's temerity.

'Ach, ain't that the truth, I can tell already. That Billie is awful bold,' Kathleen agreed.

'And Kathleen,' Ruby said in a conspiratorial tone, 'what about you, do you have someone at home? What are Irish boys like?'

'Ach no. Not that there aren't some lookers in Dublin, but my mammy would tear strips off me if she thought I was messing about with boys. It's part of the reason she was happy for me to come here and get my training. I think she wanted me to be a nun deep down, but the Sisters of the Trinity at my school said I was too unruly for a life serving the Lord. So my mammy decided I should train as a nurse, because then I could still give my life in service to others – it was the next best thing to the convent for her,' Kathleen laughed. 'But I think you would like the boys back home, Ruby. Like James Murphy,' she said wistfully. 'He has dark brown curls and eyes like big blue pools that you could swim in for days.'

'He sounds like a catch!' Ruby said with a cheeky grin.

'Ah yes, he's a definite catch of the day. Every day!' Kathleen replied and the girls fell about laughing.

After breakfast, as they took their seats in class, they were unsurprised to see Billie rushing through the door just as Sister Shaw was about to shut it.

'Good morning, Nurse Benjamin,' said the stern-faced sister. 'Do take your seat, we were just about to begin.'

The sister told the trainees that they would be grouped together for the day's tasks, and later would be put in pairs to test each other's knowledge.

First the girls were split into two sets of three and one of four to discuss the various functions of the respiratory system. 'The body's cells need a constant supply of oxygen for them to carry out the metabolic processes that are required to maintain life,' Sister Shaw explained. 'The respiratory system works along with the circulatory system to provide this oxygen. It also removes the waste products of metabolism and helps to regulate the pH – in other words, the acidity or alkalinity – of the blood.

'Now I want you all to take these models of the thorax in your groups and break them down into their constituent parts, and then rebuild the respiratory system.'

Ruby and Connie were grouped with Lin and Phyllis for the class, and each girl sat looking at the clay model before them for a few moments before Connie picked it up and started removing each piece.

'This should be fun,' she said as the other girls looked on.

'What's that big thing there?' Ruby enquired.

'That's the diaphragm,' Connie explained. 'I was reading about it last night. It's a muscle and when it contracts, the volume of the thoracic cavity increases, creating a negative pressure. This then draws air into the lungs.'

Lin nodded approval. 'Yes, it runs right under the lungs. But doesn't it go lower on the left-hand side because of the presence of the heart there?'

'Yes, that's right,' Connie enthused, taking off the last part of the model as the girls then discussed each piece and their function, then furiously scribbled notes in their exercise books, knowing that they would need to remember all of this for their exams.

'Oh my goodness, there's so much to this,' Phyllis said, sitting back in her chair exasperated. 'How they expect us to learn all this in a few weeks is beyond me.'

'Me too.' Ruby looked a little dispirited. 'And this is just the one organ. There are so many more to learn yet.'

'Well, it's actually a few organs,' Lin interjected. 'The pharynx, larynx, trachea, lungs . . .'

'Yes,' Ruby rushed to cover herself, 'I mean it's a system of organs. But there are just so many things we have to learn.' A grimace now tarnished her usually cheery face and as her brow fell into deep furrows she said, 'I don't know that I'll ever get the hang of all this. I never thought nursing would be this complicated.'

'What did you expect to find?' Lin enquired. 'My father is a doctor back home in Hong Kong, so I had some idea of the competencies we would need for the job. He actually was able to teach me some things already too.'

'I don't know,' Ruby replied, perplexed. 'I guess I just didn't think it would be so *hard*. I thought we'd be making beds and looking after people – bringing them food and making sure they were comfortable. Keeping an eye on their temperature and blood pressure – that kind of thing.'

'Oh, but this is modern nursing, Ruby,' Lin said. 'The NHS needs us to be much more than bed-makers.'

'Yes, Ruby, it's not enough to just take temperatures and so on, we need to know *why* we're doing it and *how* we can help to make people better. Part of that is about understanding how the body works,' Connie explained.

'Hmm, I suppose so,' Ruby replied, but she was more exasperated with the extent of things they were expected to absorb than with her sister.

'Don't worry, Ruby, I understand what you mean. This is all very complicated, but we will get to grips with it – you know what they say in the magazines these days: us girls can achieve anything we put our minds to,' Phyllis encouraged.

'Right, nurses, I hope you have all got your models back together correctly. Please hand them to me as I come round, and then it will be time for lunch,' Sister Shaw instructed.

An hour later, as the girls returned from their lunch break, Sister Shaw divided them into pairs for that afternoon's task – they would test each other's knowledge on what they had learned so far on the skeletal system. Connie was put with Grace, Billie with Mei, and Ruby was paired with Margaret for the test.

'Ugh,' Ruby muttered under her breath to her sister. 'Her again.'

'Come on, Ruby, if you don't try you'll stand no chance of making friends with her or anyone else,' Connie encouraged.

Each girl was given a list of questions and tasked with testing the other's knowledge. But as Ruby took a seat at the table with Margaret, she was already feeling uneasy. Despite having studied the previous night, she feared she didn't quite understand the make-up of the skeletal system.

'I'll start because I know this stuff already,' Margaret said with a self-assuredness Ruby could only dream of.

'OK, the first question is, how many thoracic vertebrae are there?' Ruby began.

'Twelve. The vertebrae relate to the nerves in them, T-1 to T-5 affect the upper chest, mid-back and abdominal muscles that control the ribcage, lungs and diaphragm; T-6 to T-10 relate to the abdominal and back muscles,' Margaret shot back confidently.

'Erm . . . yes,' Ruby said slowly, while scanning the answer sheet for all the details. 'That's correct. The next question is, what is the thoracic cage made up of?'

'Well, there is the sternum and that connects to twenty-four ribs, which protect the respiratory system, and a host of organs.' With every question Ruby posed, Margaret's confidence shone and Ruby immediately felt under pressure, even though she had learned all of this too.

'Right, it's my turn to test you now,' Margaret said in a clipped tone, picking up the list of questions she was set to pose and going through them one by one. Ruby didn't answer as confidently as her partner, but she was surprised and delighted at just what she did remember, even though there were many questions she had to pass on.

'The vertebrae of the thoracic spine connect to the lumbar spine, then the sacrum and coccyx. What is the purpose of the coccyx?' Margaret asked finally.

Ruby's jaw fell; she couldn't help but look at Margaret as if she had just said something in a foreign language, and she slumped back in her chair. 'I haven't heard of the sacrum and coccyx before. We haven't gone beyond the thorax and thoracic vertebrae so far, have we?' She searched Margaret's face for an answer, but all she could see was a saccharine veneer that barely disguised her insincerity.

'Does it support the diaphragm?' Ruby said, a wariness to her tone.

'No, no it does not,' Margaret announced, her eyes filled with spite as they bore into Ruby, who sat puzzled for a few more seconds that seemed to her like minutes.

'Well, I don't know,' she said finally. 'You'll have to tell me.'

'It's the tailbone. It supports you when you're seated. And I would have thought you'd know all about *tail* bones,' Margaret said pointedly, her off-script question now providing a stage for her ignorant agenda. 'You lot most of all.'

'What are you talking about?' Ruby was perplexed.

Margaret's pursed lips broke into a cynical snigger. 'Well, you've all got tails, haven't you? I guess you lot just haven't evolved as much as the rest of us, so maybe that's why you've never heard of a coccyx – yours probably doesn't work in the same way.'

Ruby was so flabbergasted by Margaret's comments that she found herself sitting open-mouthed for a moment. Then a low, uncontrollable and slightly nervous laugh came out. 'You're kidding me,' she said.

Sister Shaw interjected before Margaret could reply. 'Right, class, I hope you have all successfully completed your tests. I need you to mark your partners' answers out of the total of twenty, and pass the sheets to me,' she said, wandering around the room to collect the papers.

As Ruby wrote fifteen on Margaret's paper, the other girl gleefully marked a big number six on Ruby's. It was no surprise to Ruby that it was a low mark – she had struggled with a lot of the questions. But, she thought, it provided her with a starting point; she would just have to study harder was all.

'We'll have tests like these over the coming weeks to ensure you are retaining the information we learn in class, and also doing your own reading outside of the classroom. But as you know, you will be sitting exams at the end of your training,' Sister Shaw continued.

Margaret leaned in towards Ruby. 'Sitting,' she hissed, quietly enough that no one else could hear her. 'What do you do with that tail of yours when you sit down?'

Ruby's brow formed a deep furrow as she turned to Margaret. But the other girl was already up and strutting off to join Jean and Grace, leaving Ruby alone.

Minutes later, chairs screeched across the floor and bags clattered onto desks after Sister Shaw dismissed the class for the day.

'You ready, Ruby?' Connie enquired. 'How did you get on?'

'It was OK, I guess,' she replied. 'I only got six on the test.'

'Six? Oh Ruby, man, I got eighteen, and I'm thinking I need to do more work. You really have to knuckle down and study,' Connie urged her sister.

'Yes, I will do. But you know I struggle to take in all this information at once.' Ruby sighed. 'But then again, I don't know why

I should worry. Margaret did well but she's either crazy or stupid. You should have heard what she was saying to me! She thinks we have tails, Connie. Now what kind of nonsense is that? She makes out she's all intelligent and fancy, but then comes out with rubbish like that. And in an anatomy class, of all things!' Ruby laughed as the idiocy of Margaret's comments sank in, and now her latest encounter with the girl was over, this was the bit of fun she needed to help her to relax.

'Tails! What?' Connie was flabbergasted. 'She must have been making fun of you, Ruby. That's like the punchline to a joke.'

'I don't think she was,' Ruby chuckled. 'I think she was quite serious. Now I know we ain't learned about the coccyx yet, but I'm quite sure we don't have any tails coming off ours.' She paused for a moment and wiggled her bottom at her sister.

'You're crazy,' Connie giggled.

'No, sis, I'm not the crazy one around here, Margaret is,' and now Ruby laughed so hard that she was almost bent over double. 'What a thing!'

Chapter Nine

Connie

That Saturday, Connie and Ruby headed to Four Oaks train station. It was a crisp, bright March morning and they could hardly contain their excitement – they were going to meet Devon in London.

'I know you can't wait to see Devon, Connie, but is it bad that I'm most looking forward to seeing the sights?' Ruby winced a little. 'Devon is lovely, but I want to see *London*,' she said emphatically.

Connie rolled her eyes; a tiny part of her regretted inviting Ruby to tag along, but she also knew that there was no way she could have taken her first sightseeing trip to London without her. Not only did she know her sister would have been really disappointed if she had, but Connie also wanted to share these first experiences with her.

'No, it's fine, Ruby – I'm looking forward to both things. Well, maybe I'm a bit more excited about seeing Devon,' she grinned, and Ruby could see a flash of mischief in her sister's eyes.

'Well, if you two want to go off for some canoodling you can just leave me at Buckingham Palace, because I have a date for tea with the Queen, you know,' Ruby said, imitating a royal wave.

'Ruby, you are silly!' Connie groaned.

Boarding the train to London Liverpool Street, the sisters took their seats and soon the buildings and church steeple of Four Oaks had faded into the green of the countryside, this time with early spring blossoms dotting the landscape.

'It's prettier than I remember from our journey up here,' Connie said.

'It is, and it's nice to see some sunshine for a change – I was starting to wonder if they ever had any sun here in England,' Ruby replied. 'Then again, I'm surprised you remember much about that journey at all other than Mr Grant.'

'Hush, Ruby,' Connie said, her cheeks feeling hot.

Ruby stopped teasing her sister, and was thoughtful for a while. Then she said: 'Did you tell Billie we were going to London today? I'd have thought she would have loved to come along. She's been strange lately, though – I've hardly seen her other than in the classroom, and even there she seems different. I wonder why she's been so quiet.'

'Maybe she's getting into her studies. We have so much to learn I can't really blame her. I almost thought about rearranging this trip for a few weeks' time,' Connie said, downplaying things. She also failed to mention the conversation she'd had with Billie the previous night when the Jamaican girl had told her she was still sick with worry.

'Oh my goodness, no. We need breaks from all the study, you know, Connie.' Ruby's eyes grew wide. 'And we're going to *London*. You can't go about cancelling a *trip to London*.'

'But I didn't. I'm just saying that we have a lot of studying to do.' Connie's irritation piqued slightly.

'OK, you didn't and that's good,' Ruby smiled, ignoring Connie's reference to study, then she took a notebook from her bag. 'Devon said we should make a note of all the things we want to see, so tell me if you want to add any to this list I have: London Bridge, Buckingham Palace, St Paul's Cathedral, the Tower of London, Changing of the Guard, Tower Bridge, Hampton Court, Windsor

Castle, the Houses of Parliament, the River Thames – I know we saw that when we first got here, but I hear it's different in London – Madame Tussaud's, Oxford Street, Regent Street, Piccadilly Circus, Trafalgar Square, Leicester Square and Hyde Park.'

Connie wrinkled her nose beneath her warm brown eyes. 'Ruby, man, you don't think that list is a bit long? We only have a day, you know!'

'Yes, but I want to see as much as possible, and I was hoping Devon could take some photos of us that we could send back home to Mum and Dad,' Ruby replied.

'OK, love, yes – I believe Devon has a Kodak Brownie. We'll see how we get on, but girl, you're going to have us running all about the place!'

'It's OK, we're young, and besides, it's Sunday tomorrow – we can rest the whole day,' Ruby enthused. 'Though yes, we will study too,' she groaned, sensing Connie's sideways stare.

'Good, I'm glad to hear it!' Connie replied.

Minutes later the train pulled into Liverpool Street station, and they spotted Devon on the platform, looking smart in a steel grey flannel suit and trilby hat.

'Well, if it isn't my favourite sisters!' Devon's welcome warmed the cool spring day as he gathered Connie in his arms and pressed his lips to hers. Then he turned to Ruby and gave her a hearty hug, all the while Connie looked on smiling and half wishing she had him all to herself for the day.

'I hope you had a good journey. Now, did you come up with that list of places you'd like to see?' Devon asked the girls.

'Oh my goodness! Just wait for Ruby's list,' Connie smiled, noticing that she couldn't keep her eyes off her beau. Here with the three of them together, she could see just how much gentle care and attention Devon lavished upon those he cared about. It reminded her of their first date and how entranced he seemed to be by her, and she realized he was the first man that had ever made her feel as though she was the centre of his universe. And that, she thought, was a man to hold on to. Connie had thought she was in love with Martha's father, Cedric, but perhaps, she considered, she was only now finding out what love – and, importantly, what to be loved – really was.

Ruby directed a mock protest at Connie. 'It's my first time in the city proper, and I want to see *e-ve-ry-thing*. I didn't come all this way to England to sit in my room, you know!'

'Well then,' Devon said, giving a nod of his head and assuming a very serious expression, 'it sounds like we got our work cut out. Let's start at the beginning and work our way down the list in order of importance.'

Ruby's face lit up. 'Well, we better go straight to Buckingham Palace. I hear Her Majesty is in residence,' she said, putting on the most regal voice she could muster. 'And she likes to invite her subjects for tea.'

Devon and Connie chuckled as the three of them made their way to the underground platforms. 'Well, I don't know much about that, Ruby, but we can certainly call by and see if she lets us in.'

Half an hour later the trio walked the length of The Mall until they reached the black wrought-iron gates that encircled the imposing palace.

'Is this it?' Connie gasped.

'It can't be!' Ruby exclaimed. 'This whole place can't be for one family, even a royal one.'

'Oh, but it is. They don't live in one room like us,' Devon laughed ironically, but Ruby and Connie barely noticed. They were both pressing their faces through the iron railings to get a better look at the palace.

'My goodness!' Ruby said in awe. 'Connie, could you imagine living here? We could bring the whole of our street back home to live with us and we wouldn't see anyone for a week!'

Spotting the sentry box outside the gates with a guard in the red coat and bearskin hat of the Coldstream Guards within, Ruby turned to Devon. 'Lord h'mercy! Look at the guard – he's just like in the postcards we used to get from London at home. Did you bring your camera like you promised? Can we get a photo with the guard to send home?'

'Of course,' Devon replied. 'But Ruby, you mustn't touch him, you know. They have special rules about this, and I don't want them arresting you and throwing you in the Tower,' he joked.

'They wouldn't!' she said, shocked, making a mental note to be on her best behaviour.

As Connie and Ruby stood on either side of the Queen's guard, Ruby couldn't help but look up at him to see if his expressionless face would change. But catching no discernible shift in his countenance, she put one foot out to the left and slightly in front of her, then turned her head to look in the opposite direction.

'Come on, Connie – strike a pose. You need people to see how good you look now you're in England,' she urged.

Connie wrinkled her brow, baffled by her sister's sudden poise. But despite being amused by her affectation, she also didn't want her younger sister to outdo her; after all, this was going to be their first photo sent back to Barbados of them in England. So Connie positioned herself on the other side of the sentry box, in a pose mirroring Ruby's.

'Look at you, both here like fancy ladies,' Devon beamed, taking in Connie in particular.

'I don't know what you mean – we *are* fancy ladies, here to see Queen Elizabeth,' Ruby replied, her posturing now in full swing. 'I'm quite sure she'd like to meet some of her Barbadian subjects.'

With no Changing of the Guard that day, Ruby had to make do with her photo with the Coldstream Guard. Giving him a sweet smile and a 'thank you', she took Connie's hand and they skipped over to where Devon was standing. 'Where to next?' she enquired.

As Devon led the sisters towards Horse Guards Parade they paused as three glossy black horses clip-clopped by; the riders in their red and gold jackets had their own white manes tumbling from silver helmets.

'They look so smart,' Connie said, nudging Ruby to make sure she didn't miss them.

'Ah yes, they're from the Household Cavalry Mounted Regiment,' Devon explained. 'They're like the Queen's bodyguards.'

'Imagine, the Queen has all of these different troops protecting her – it's incredible!' Ruby said.

'Well, I suppose all of the British forces are there to protect the Queen and the Empire. It's what we were all defending during the war,' Devon said. 'Let's take this little pathway here.'

He took them down the side of Horse Guards Parade, and along a path out into one of the most famous streets in London.

'Wait! Is this . . . ? It can't be . . .' Ruby was agog. 'Oh my goodness, yes, this is Downing Street, and there's number 10, where the Prime Minister lives. Do you think Mr Churchill will be at home?'

'Well, I can see smoke coming from the chimney, so I expect someone is home,' Devon smiled. 'Or maybe he's baking bread,' he teased Ruby.

'I would love to knock on the door, tell him we've come all the way up here from Barbados to work in the National Health Service,' she continued.

'Well, I don't know that he would be so thrilled. The NHS came about under the Labour government and Conservatives like Churchill opposed it at first,' Devon explained.

'Can you imagine, a thing like free healthcare was not a popular idea when it started. People back home, boy they would love something like this.'

Next they walked along Whitehall to Trafalgar Square, where they stopped for more photos with the lions at the foot of Nelson's Column, and under the shadow of the crocheted dome of the National Gallery.

Their whistle-stop tour then took them to the Houses of Parliament, Westminster Abbey and Embankment, where they stopped for lunch, before hopping on a boat along the River Thames and getting off close to the left tower of Tower Bridge.

'But wait,' Connie said, looking up at the blue and white suspensions connecting the two towers to the drawbridge in the middle. 'I always thought this was London Bridge! Of course, I only ever saw it in books and I think on a postcard someone sent to Mum and Dad from London. But I could have sworn they said this was London Bridge.'

'Ah, you know, that's a common mistake people make,' Devon said, as the sisters' gaze then landed on the Tower of London.

'Connie, look, we're right next to the Tower,' Ruby said with the excitement of a child at Christmas.

'My goodness, it is! You know this is where they have the Crown Jewels,' Connie shrieked, her eyes as wide as saucers.

Devon beamed at the sisters. He was enjoying discovering London through their excited eyes just as much as he had enjoyed his first days in the city, perhaps more so – their glow and elation proving infectious. He was also falling more in love with Connie by the minute.

His hand found Connie's once more and she looked up at him with adoring eyes. 'Thank you, thank you so much for taking us around London today – it's . . .' And she paused, stopping to soak up the sights before her once more. 'It's magnificent.'

Before she could even fully finish the sentence, Devon planted a passionate kiss on her full lips. Connie's heart started beating faster, the excitement of the day mixing with the passion she felt for her beau, and she all but forgot where she was. The rush of the city faded from her consciousness fast, and it was just her and Devon locked in that moment.

That was until Ruby caught sight of them. 'Well!' she said, feigning shock. 'You two just can't keep your hands off one another, eh? I might have to find somewhere to take myself off to and leave you to it.'

Connie broke away from Devon and the pair looked sheepish. 'Sorry, sis,' she said, bowing her head.

'Yes, I'm sorry, Ruby. But sometimes, when you're in love with a beautiful woman like your sister, you just can't help yourself.'

Ruby's head spun round. 'What did you just say, Devon Grant?' And at the same time Connie turned to him open-mouthed, her palms feeling sweaty.

'Well, I didn't think it was a secret,' Devon smiled.

'I suppose not. I've seen how you look at each other. *All* the time,' Ruby replied knowingly, adding an eye-roll for extra emphasis. But Connie was far more shocked by Devon's revelation.

He loves me, and I . . . I think I love him too.

As this thought ran through her mind, Connie tried to push away any self-doubt and convince herself that what she had hoped to find for more than three years was right there in London, all beautifully packaged in this fine man.

'So, are we going in to see the Tower of London then, or what?' Ruby urged, linking Connie's arm to pull her along while also dragging her sister out of her thoughts.

Suddenly there was a loud boom, shattering the peace of the moment.

It was followed by another, and another. Birds burst from trees and flew in all directions, bringing chaos to the scene.

The girls whipped their heads around to look at each other, scared of what might be happening, just as another boom rang out. Then another, and another – forty-one in total, as smoke billowed from the ledge above them, and Connie felt Devon's hand pull away from hers as he flinched.

'It's all right, ladies. I guess they don't have many gun salutes where you're from, do they?' said a man in a tweed suit as the smoke cleared and he pointed up at the row of cannons. 'You almost get used to them round here, regular occurrence from the Tower, that is.' Then, 'Cor blimey,' he said, looking at Devon. 'You don't look like you're used to cannon fire either,' he chuckled as he carried on walking, his feet not missing a beat.

Connie looked at Devon and was surprised to see beads of sweat on his brow.

'Lord! These people really know how to create a ruckus, man!' he said, and then he smiled that Grant smile and Connie knew all was well in her world.

After a tour of the Tower of London, with the sisters taking plenty of time to marvel at the sparkle of the Crown Jewels, Devon had a suggestion. 'Let's head to the West End; I'm sure you girls would like to do a little shopping before you need to get your train.'

Within the hour, the girls and their gentlemanly escort walked from Oxford Street into Regent Street, the sisters buzzing with excitement at the enormous department stores shining with dazzling displays. This was especially true as they peered through the windows of Dickins & Jones.

'You want to go in and look round?' Devon asked, tickled once more by the sisters' awe.

'No, it's fine, we couldn't possibly afford anything,' Connie said earnestly.

'Ah, but Connie, that's not the point. Yes, I want to go in and look around please, Devon. I want to see what all the fancy London girls are wearing,' Ruby urged.

Inside, the shop was even more impressive than the girls had expected; its size and the incredible range of goods on sale left them astounded.

'This makes Cave Shepherd back home look like a cattle shed, and that's our biggest department store,' Ruby stated boldly.

'It's unbelievable,' Connie said, touching everything from the marble pillars that graced the building, to beautifully wrapped bars of 4711 soap, then landing eventually on a soft pink scarf with tiny blue flowers on it.

'It's quite the shop, isn't it?' Devon smiled. 'Do you like this scarf?'

'Yes, I was just thinking how beautiful it is. There are just so many beautiful things in this store,' Connie replied.

'Well, good, I'm glad you do,' he said, then turned to a shop assistant. 'I'd like one of these scarves please, and then, you see the hairpin you have here in the cabinet, I'd like one of those too, please.'

'Wait, what are you doing, Devon?' Connie said. 'You can't buy that for me. It must be so expensive.'

'Oh, but I can. I've a little money set aside, so why not treat a special lady? And her sister,' he said, handing a dinky paper bag to each of the girls. 'I can't have you both coming to London and not having a souvenir to take away.'

'Lord h'mercy!' Ruby cried, looking at the red silky rose that adorned the hairpin. 'Devon, it's beautiful, thank you! But you didn't have to do this, we've had such a lovely day already and you've shown us so much.'

'Thank you, Devon,' Connie locked eyes with him and gave him a kiss on the lips. 'I love it, and I love *you*,' she whispered to him, and the pair smiled at each other tenderly.

The sisters boarded the seven o'clock train from London as Devon waved them off from the platform. Exhausted but happy, they had a quiet journey back to Four Oaks. Then Connie saw Ruby staring at her, looking thoughtful.

'What's that look in aid of?' she quizzed.

'I was just thinking . . .' Ruby said wistfully. 'I was just thinking what colour I might wear as maid of honour at your wedding.'

'Oh hush, Ruby,' Connie said.

'Hush about what? You love him, don't you? He loves you. And he's very handsome and gentlemanly. What more do you need?' Ruby asked.

'Well, yes, and love is important, but a relationship takes much more than that, Ruby, man, come on.'

'Really? Like what?' Ruby pressed.

Connie looked out of the window, her eyes a little doleful as she was momentarily lost in her thoughts. 'It takes understanding, support and, well, acceptance.' She looked down at her feet now.

'Connie, I know what you're thinking about. But listen, Martha isn't here and Aunt Agatha is taking care of her. No one back home even knows that she's yours, so how would Devon find out?' Ruby pressed.

'But that's not the point, Ruby. I wouldn't want to keep something like that from him. I wouldn't want to keep anything from him. That wouldn't be fair, or right. And then I'm scared. What if he didn't want me any more after I told him? He's already said he doesn't like the fast girls in London – what if he decided I was just like them?'

Ruby looked her sister in the eye with a resolute steeliness. 'But Connie, you can't tell him. You can never tell him, no matter what he thinks about fast women. You're not a fast woman, mind you – you made a mistake and trusted a man that wasn't worthy of your trust; he wasn't worthy of you at all.

'But you tell Devon and word would get right back home. The whole neighbourhood would find out and Mum and Dad would never forgive you!' she said, panic written across her face. 'I'm only thinking of you, sis. Like Mum and Dad said, it's best that you forget about the mistakes you made in the past and focus on the future before you, and it looks like it's going to have Devon in it,' she beamed.

Connie nodded in agreement, but she wasn't at all comfortable with Ruby's advice. Not only did the idea of deceiving Devon not sit easily with her, but deep down, she wished to be a mother to Martha one day, and that would require her coming out of the shadows and being honest, first of all, with Devon and with her daughter.

Chapter Ten

Billie

In the next three weeks the girls became further immersed in their studies. Though Connie was the clear A-student, Billie, too, had been doing well and garnering praise from Sister Shaw for her knowledge of the digestive system when she answered questions in class. But when it came to putting her knowledge to the test, Billie faltered.

'Nurse Benjamin, I think you need to get back to basics. You seem to have forgotten all that we've covered in class. You're going to have to pull your socks up quite considerably if you are ever going to be a nurse at this hospital,' Sister Shaw said sternly one day as she handed back Billie's latest test paper with a score of ten out of twenty.

'Yes, Sister, I'll try to do better,' Billie said solemnly.

'Well, "try" will not be good enough, Nurse. *Trying* to treat a patient for the wrong condition or *trying* the wrong medication could very well kill them. We need all of you here equipped to give the correct treatment and to spot when something is wrong. That is what nurses do.

'If you do not have the wherewithal to pass your exams, we will have to say thank you very much and send you back home. The same applies to you, Nurse Haynes,' the training sister said as she handed Ruby her test paper. 'Another near failure. I expect you all to go away from here and study, study, study,' she concluded, rapping her hand on her desk to punctuate her words.

Billie shuddered. Going home was not an option for her. She still had family in Kingston, of course – her eighteen-year-old sister, Candice, was now living with a cousin. But the death of their mother had been a catalyst for the family's dissolution. Her mother had been its linchpin, and Billie and her brother and sister had looked to her for everything after their father, Francis, strayed from the family home.

Despite having six children to three different women across the island, Francis simply wasn't equipped to be a father. And Billie knew that there wasn't anything or anyone for her to fall back on in Jamaica. Moreover, a part of her hoped a day might come when Candice could join her in England, so she had to succeed as a nurse.

And Billie had been studying. Every night she made time to go over her notes from class and to read more from the textbook the hospital had provided. But she was still under a cloud of worry. And now, coupled with her poor test results, it was building into something Billie was rather unaccustomed to: self-doubt.

That night, after she had put away her books, she got out her clothes for the next morning. Closing the door to her wardrobe, she caught her reflection in the mirror and could swear she had begun to put on weight. She pulled her nightie tight behind her so the baby blue fabric hugged her figure. The very curves that drove men wild with lust now looked to have an extra layer, and she was convinced it wasn't only the stodgy food they served in the dining room that was adding to her weight.

Pulling up her nightie, she inspected her stomach in the mirror. There it was – a swelling in her lower abdomen.

How could I be so foolish? I always act like I'm invincible.

Ruby was right, I do behave as though I'm a man, but which woman can really do that? I should know better. I ain't lucky enough to get away with this, this time.

Society just don't allow women to live like this.

Her internal dialogue played over and over in her head as the next two days passed and she continued to struggle to concentrate on her training, let alone enjoy her time in England.

It was as though a light had dimmed inside her. Even on the Saturday afternoon, when an excited Ruby enquired what Billie's plans were for that evening, suggesting a night out at the Woodman's Arms, Billie was cool to the idea, saying she needed to stay in and study.

'Connie, I don't understand it,' she said later to her sister. 'When we started here, Billie was the first to be calling on us to go out and live it up. Now she's become all meek and studious.'

'Hmm . . . maybe she just feels she needs to commit herself to this course to get through, Ruby. You heard what Sister Shaw said the other day, and you'd be as well to listen to her yourself.'

'Oh I know, Connie, but it's the weekend, we all need a breather from study,' Ruby sighed.

Late that evening, Connie knocked on Billie's door. 'How are you doing?'

'Well, I've been better, Connie. I'm not sleeping very well, I'm not eating very well and yet I'm putting on weight. Just look at my stomach,' she said, lifting up a long and uncharacteristically loose-fitting jumper to show her friend.

'Oh Billie, you have been eating, at least a bit. And the food is different here, so that's bound to be why you're putting on weight – what about all that bread and dripping they serve up? That dripping is made from lard, isn't it? That can't be good for the figure,' she soothed.

'No, I suppose not, and it's pretty dreadful anyway. It isn't a dish worthy of ruining a girl's good figure,' Billie joked. 'But neither is . . . you know,' she said, instantly solemn once more.

'Billie, look, I think the time has come for you to see a doctor. Promise me you will go next week,' Connie urged.

'I've been thinking about it, but really, what would be the point? It's not as though they could tell me anything. There ain't any way for them to know until I really start showing, or until the baby starts moving around. If there is a baby . . . And I would be weeks off that yet,' Billie said.

'That's true, but at least he could suggest ways you could look after yourself. You know, just in case.'

'No, Connie, I can't do that. They would surely get word back to the hospital. It's a small town, and me, a young woman from the West Indies going in there – it wouldn't take any time at all for them to figure out I'm a trainee at St Mary's. And then they would expel me from here so fast.' Billie's angst was building again, so Connie backed down, careful not to upset her friend unnecessarily. Besides, she knew Billie was right. When Connie had had Martha, she had known something was wrong, or at least changed, inside her for weeks before her mother paid for her to see a doctor close to where Aunt Agatha lived, and he confirmed that she was pregnant.

'OK, Billie, fair enough. But at least get yourself to bed now and get some rest; it's nearly midnight,' Connie urged, then hugged her friend. 'I'm going to be praying for you, and I'll ask the Lord's forgiveness when I go to church tomorrow.'

'Thanks, Connie,' Billie said, trying her best to paint on a smile, but failing miserably. She was tired, weeks of study and worry now showing on her face. But as she lay in bed, sleep evading her for yet another night, she started counting sheep to avoid going over her fears once again.

The next morning, Billie woke to a hubbub of activity in the hallway. She could hear Connie and Ruby's voices as they headed off to church.

'See you later on, yes,' Ruby called to Jean.

'We could go to for a walk in the park if you like, the weather is set to be a bit warmer,' Jean replied. 'Though I bet it still won't be all that warm for you.'

'I'll be OK, I've got warm Caribbean blood. I'll give you a shout later,' Ruby said cheerfully.

Then Billie felt it – an all-too-familiar, and usually unwelcome, gnawing pain in her lower back, her abdomen swelling as the pain intensified and knotted her insides.

Could it be?

She got out of bed and made for the toilet. The small red spots on the toilet tissue were the most welcome sight. Billie had never been so happy to get her period – she would've danced back to her room had she not been in pain. But even then, she embraced the discomfort. Billie considered that she deserved these menstrual cramps, as though they amounted to a penance for her misde-meanours in the previous weeks – from Philip to John, and even Clive, although most of that had only been in her head.

Back in her bedroom she paused in front of her mirror. 'Yes, yes, yes!' Then she launched herself onto her bed, and burying her head in her pillow to muffle the sound, she let out a delighted scream.

Later, when she heard Connie and Ruby return from church, Billie was already up and dressed, she'd taken painkillers for her cramps, and now felt ready to take on the world. But first, she knocked on Connie's door.

'Connie,' she beamed. 'I don't know how many Hail Marys you must have said for me, but it's come!'

Connie's face was a picture of joy at seeing her friend smiling once more, but also confusion. 'What do you mean? What's come, Billie? Oh, wait . . . Really?'

'Yes, Connie! I'm not pregnant,' Billie hissed.

'Oh my goodness, and praise the Lord!' Connie exclaimed. 'I'm so relieved.'

'Me too, Connie. Me too!' Billie smiled, the burden she had carried in the past weeks dissipating and leaving her looking ten years younger – her face already back to the carefree beauty Connie had come to know in their first week in Four Oaks.

The same relief propelled Billie through her week, during which the training continued to look at the structures of the body. However, Sister Shaw also took time out to give the girls a lesson in observation.

'We have many tools at our disposal that enable us to diagnose and treat a patient. But besides the stethoscopes and all the technology like ophthalmoscopes and auriscopes, observation is an important tool. In fact I'd go so far as to say that observation is critical to the work of a nurse,' she stated.

'A nurse should be able not only to listen to what a patient is telling her, but she must also *observe* their condition – and, more importantly, note what they are *not* telling her. It may be in their tone of voice, their deportment, their facial expressions, or it may be down to other aspects of their body language.

'You can even learn about a person's condition from their family, so talk to their husband, wife or children to find out more about how that patient is faring. That being said, you must also be very aware that family relations may not always be good, and you can be receptive to that. But you must never, *absolutely never*, become involved in a patient's relationships, family conflicts or social concerns,' she stressed. 'That is most definitely not our place.'

After dinner that evening, Billie fortified herself against her period pain with a couple of aspirin, then joined the other girls in the sitting room for coffee.

'What you smiling about so much?' Ruby enquired. 'All day you been like this. Did you hear from one of your boyfriends? Are they going to pay you a visit?'

'No, not at all,' she replied.

'I had another kind of visitor,' she added quietly enough that only Connie, who was sitting next to her, could hear and the pair shared a knowing smile. Billie then tipped her head back to finish the last of her coffee, and left the room to make for one of the telephone booths in reception.

'Hello,' a deep Jamaican voice answered.

'Clive? It's Billie, we met on the Metropolitan train.'

'Ohh, hello, it's real good to hear from you. You've been running through my mind these past few weeks. I'm not sure if it was those eyes or that figure of yours, but you definitely taking up plenty space in my head.'

Billie smiled to herself. Clive was far from the first man to have charmed her, but she couldn't help but enjoy this game.

'I can only imagine – I have been known to make an impression before, you know,' she flirted back. 'I meant to call you before now, but it's been a real busy few weeks with all the training and thing. But I'm thinking about coming to London next weekend – you want to meet up?'

'That is perfect timing – some friends of mine are having a house party next Saturday. I was planning to go alone, but if you'd do me the honour of accompanying me,' he said, a ring of expectation to his voice. Billie was quiet momentarily, calculating that Clive wanted to have something pretty on his arm.

'Or if parties aren't your scene I could show you some of the sights and we could go for dinner,' Clive suggested, hurriedly.

'No, no. I always enjoy a good party, and maybe we can do some sightseeing too if you don't mind showing an island girl some of your new home town. Some of the girls here have seen a lot of the sights already and I feel like I've missed out.'

'Well, I would be delighted to escort you around this fine city.' Clive sounded pleased. 'I'll meet you at Liverpool Street station at twelve o'clock.'

'You have yourself a date, Mr Clive,' Billie said, laying on a sultry tone.

'I'm looking forward to it,' he replied.

Bouncing up the stairs, Billie went to see Connie.

'OK, what happened?' asked Connie. 'I'm getting to know this look you got about you.'

'Nothing. But you see, Ruby just reminded me of something. Well, *someone*,' she said with a glint in her eye. 'So I just called Clive and we have a date next weekend.'

'Oh, Billie!' Connie said, exasperated, but also unable to stop herself from slightly admiring her friend's confidence. 'You really don't waste any time, do you?'

'Life is too short for missed opportunities. For all I know, Clive could be the man for me.'

'Yes, I guess he could,' Connie said, unable to feign excitement. Instead she wondered just how Billie was able to turn on a sixpence like that. Just one day earlier she had been stricken with fear over her future, and here she was already back in the saddle, planning a date with yet another man. All Connie knew was, it wasn't how she herself would react.

'So Clive's invited me to a party next weekend, which I thought would be fun, and he also said he would take me to see some of the sights. I remembered you and Ruby saying how much you enjoyed your sightseeing a few weeks ago – I only wish I'd have had the energy to go with you at the time. But you know . . .

'Anyway, I was wondering, maybe you and Ruby could come to London for the party. Perhaps you could invite Devon too if you like?'

'Did you say a party?' Ruby gasped as she entered her sister's room. 'That would be great fun!'

'Ruby, wait, will you,' Connie said frustratedly. 'We don't even know that Clive would mind us going.'

'Of course, I'd check with him, make sure his friends won't

mind me inviting more people, but I've heard that folks from back home are having house parties where everyone's welcome. You've seen what it's like in Four Oaks – there ain't much action to be had. I'm sure it's quite different in London, of course, but I was chatting to my friend Esme, and she said they were starting up with parties more and more because we don't always get a warm welcome at the dance halls and thing,' Billie explained.

'Let me speak to Devon and see what he thinks. If he likes the sound of it, it could be a fun thing to do together. And I would get to introduce you to him too,' Connie replied.

'They're in love!' Ruby beamed.

'Is that so?' Billie enquired, taking Connie's quiet bashfulness as all the evidence she needed to back up Ruby's claim. 'Well, then I really had better meet him now. Need to size up if he's good enough for my friend,' Billie smiled at Connie.

'Oh, he is! Don't you worry – I've checked out all of his particulars already,' Ruby laughed.

Billie couldn't help but smile at the younger girl. 'You did?' she said, winking at Connie. 'I bet Connie has too. Or at least, that's what I would have done by now!' she teased.

'Yes, I'm sure *you* would have,' Connie replied dryly. 'And now I'm not so sure going to this party with you is such a good idea.'

'Come on, Connie, I'm only teasing. It'll be fun. Live a little,' Billie said.

'Yes, man, Billie's right, you got to loosen up them panties and live a little,' Ruby urged.

And by the end of another busy week of training, with Sister Shaw now moving the trainees on to exploring the immune and lymphatic systems, the girls were ready for a weekend off.

'I'm so excited about tomorrow night, Billie,' Ruby said. 'I'll be happy to forget about the differences between the left and right ventricles of the heart for a night and focus on matters of the heart. I might even meet a fella there and not be stuck playing gooseberry with you and Connie and your boyfriends,' she added, pressing the palms of her hands together as though in a silent prayer.

'Don't you worry, Ruby, I'll be on the lookout for a handsome man for you too,' Billie replied.

'Now I'm even more excited,' Ruby smiled, her dimples still making her look more adorable than womanly. 'Anyway, I hope you have fun tomorrow afternoon. I'd have loved to go sightseeing too, but Connie told me there will be plenty of time for that once we're through with exams.'

'Don't worry, it will all be worth it in the end,' Billie smiled. 'Now, what are you planning to wear?'

'I was thinking of my lilac jumper dress with a white blouse underneath it,' Ruby said, then wrinkled her nose as she saw Billie's expression and guessed that wouldn't be right for the occasion.

'No, no, no, you won't,' Billie said. 'If that's all you have, I'm going to have to lend you one of my sheath dresses. And do you have some heels?'

Ruby nodded.

'A sheath dress and heels will give that bottom of yours a little wiggle. It's what will turn you from a girl into a woman. I think this one would fit you,' Billie said, passing her a little black dress on a hanger, and Ruby couldn't wait to try it on.

It was just after midday the following day when Billie's train arrived into London. She didn't spot Clive at first because she couldn't quite remember what he looked like. But Billie, wearing a peacock-coloured sheath dress under her unbuttoned coat and black stiletto heels, was impossible for any man to miss.

'Welcome to London,' Clive said, taking her hand and kissing the back of it.

'Thank you. It's good to see the city, and especially you again,' she smiled.

'I don't know what you want to do before the party, but I was thinking of taking you to see one of my favourite places in London,' he said.

Billie loved the idea of Clive choosing where they would go for the afternoon, and linking her arm he led her to the underground. Unfortunately, when they arrived at St Paul's Cathedral, Billie was a tad underwhelmed.

Clive forged ahead though, taking her on a personal tour of the famous building's interior. 'It was just above here that they removed an unexploded bomb from the roof during the Blitz, but the cathedral largely escaped damage during the war,' he said, and Billie was struck by his apparent passion for architecture and history, when all she saw was an oversized church.

'Are you enjoying it?' Clive enquired.

'Man, you know what, I don't mean to offend you, but this isn't my thing at all,' Billie said. 'Is there somewhere else we could go for the next few hours? Or how about the pictures – I hear that *Hobson's Choice* is a fun film.'

'I thought this was the kind of thing you wanted to see. Girl, I had read up on the history and thing specially to impress you. Let's get out of here,' Clive said, looking relieved, and whisked her out of the cathedral.

Within the hour, the pair were seated at the Empire Cinema in Leicester Square, watching the film and sharing a small box of popcorn, the screen barely visible through a cloud of smoke from the groups of teenagers and young men that filled the other seats.

Billie was enjoying the film, but she also knew the cinema's shadows provided a perfect place for young couples to get to know each other more intimately. She leaned towards Clive and stroked his face, then, whispering seductively in his ear, she got the response she was hoping for. Clive turned towards her and kissed her deeply and passionately.

As they left the theatre, neither could recall much of the film, but they did feel as though they had discovered a little more about each other.

Later that evening, the pair took the Central Line to Notting Hill Gate underground station for the party. 'I'm glad your friends didn't mind me bringing some of mine along. I think you'll like them,' Billie enthused.

'I'm looking forward to meeting them,' Clive smiled. 'If they're anything like you, I expect they'll have my friends fighting over them.'

'Oh boy! Ruby is single, but Connie is bringing her sweetheart, Devon, who I haven't met yet, but I've heard only good things about him,' she replied.

Stepping off the wooden escalator and into the ticket office, they found Connie, Ruby and Devon waiting to greet them.

'This is Clive. He was trying to sophisticate me when I first got to London today, but I got him more to my level. I don't know why it is that all of you people are so into your churches!' she laughed.

'It wasn't just a church, it was *St Paul's Cathedral*,' Clive explained as Ruby and Connie looked impressed.

'Look, Clive, stop pretending it was your cup of tea. Anyway, I've always said you can't have much fun in church,' Billie joked, then turning her attention towards Devon she shook his hand and turned to Connie. 'Girl, you got yourself a real catch here, though!' She giggled in a girly fashion that Connie and Ruby hadn't seen from her before.

'It's real good to meet you,' Devon smiled back, then he shook Clive's hand too.

'Ruby, you're looking hot, girl!' Billie said next, focusing her attention on her fashion protégé.

'Thanks,' the younger girl said. 'I only wish I could walk properly in this dress. It's so tight!'

'Ruby, darling, that's the point of it; you got to take small steps, just like a Japanese geisha would. That's what will get your wiggle going,' Billie explained.

'But I don't know what one of them is. How do they walk?'

'I'll show you when we get to the party. Clive says it's not far from here,' Billie replied.

'No, no – it's real close, you won't have to walk far, Ruby. My friends have themselves in a little Caribbean corner of London,' Clive said.

A few minutes later Clive was introducing the group to his friends, Wilbur from Jamaica and Erwin from Guyana.

'Boy, you guys get here early, man!' Erwin said. 'You know things won't warm up much before eleven o'clock.'

'Eleven!' Connie said, shocked. 'But what about lock-up? Billie, you know we have to be back before midnight.'

'Well, I hadn't really thought about that, but you know our parties don't start early, Connie. You know how everything happens on BMT,' Billie said a little sheepishly.

'I don't care about your Black Man Time, Billie. We're West Indian girls in England, we got to play by their rules. The ones set out for us at the hospital,' Connie replied curtly.

'Ladies, ladies, it's not a problem. I can put you all up in London tonight, and you can get the first train back in the morning,' Clive suggested.

'Thank you, Clive. See, Connie, it will all be fine,' Billie said, smoothing over the cracks in her plan.

And Erwin was right, the party didn't get going until much later, but as the calypso songs blared out from a radiogram, rum flowed and food like curried goat was served up, the girls felt they'd found a warm slice of home amid the chill of spring in London.

Heading to the bathroom, Billie bumped into Wilbur, rum and stale cigarettes on his breath as he stumbled, then propped himself up against the wall, taking up so much space Billie would have to squeeze by him. 'Hey beautiful, what's up? You looking real nice and sexy in that dress, you know. Only thing is, I'm not sure old Clive would know what to do with a woman like you,' he sneered, then lunged for her bottom.

'Yes he does,' she snapped back, pushing his hand away. 'He treats me like a queen. You know, he's gentlemanly. Something you'd do well to learn from him.'

'Listen, darling,' he said, now blocking Billie's path. 'I know women just like you – big hair, big eyes, and your big breasts all push up in a man's face. You can't fool me that he's interested in you, or you in him. I know the likes of you need a real man,' he said, pressing himself against her till she could feel his crotch against her leg and his breath on her neck.

But Billie had met his kind before. After one swift knee to the groin he was doubled over, his glass shattered on the floor.

'Billie, are you all right?' It was Devon behind her.

'Yes, I am now,' she said, her voice slightly trembling. 'I need to go to the bathroom, but please could you hold on here until I'm out. And whatever you do, don't tell Clive about this one here,' she said, nodding her head in the direction of Wilbur's doubled-over frame.

'Of course. But you know, it would be better if you told him. Better he find out his friend ain't no friend from you now, than down the line,' Devon urged.

'No, it's very early days for us, and I don't want him to have to deal with knowing this worthless wretch betrayed him,' Billie stated.

By the time Billie returned, Devon told her that Wilbur had stumbled off. 'Will you be OK? I'd be happier if you told Clive,' he said. 'I know I'd want Connie to tell me if one of my friends had behaved so.'

'No, I'm fine, thank you, Devon. I've met his kind before, and I'd rather not make a scene. You know how lonely it can be here;

we need our friends, even if they're not all good ones,' she said philosophically.

It was around three o'clock in the morning when the group left the party, Billie arm in arm with Clive.

'Argh, my feet are hurting real bad in these shoes, you know. I don't know how you can wear heels a whole day and night, Billie!' Ruby moaned, staggering along the street.

'My place ain't too far from here, don't worry,' Clive told them.

'And I can soon get out of these shoes!' Ruby cried, hobbling along behind the two couples.

'Thank you so much, Clive, for putting us up for a few hours,' Billie said. 'We all really appreciate it.' Then she added, giggling, 'Especially Ruby's feet!'

Back at Clive's bedsit, he settled Ruby, Connie and Devon on two couches. Then, pulling a curtain across to conceal his bed, he offered it to Billie. 'Your first train will be at 6.15 a.m. and I guess you'll be going for that to slip back into the nurses' home unnoticed?' Billie nodded. 'I don't mind sleeping on the floor, but I can always keep you warm if you'd prefer.' His penetrating stare said even more than his suggestive words.

'No, come here,' she said, pulling Clive towards her, and they kissed passionately. Then she slipped off her dress and pulled at his shirt and trousers, until she could feel his muscular frame against hers and his heart beating fast in his chest.

It was all the invitation Clive needed, and he grappled with Billie's bra until her pert breasts filled his hands. As their passions fired, Clive's hands wandered up her thigh and pulled next at Billie's underwear, but she brushed his hand away and in the pale light from the street lamp outside, he could see her point at the curtain.

'We can't, they're just out there,' she whispered softly in his ear.

Clive sighed heavily, but reined in his passion.

Deep down, Billie was relieved to have her friends at close quarters. Despite the fact that she'd fallen straight into her old ways of flirtatious persuasion, given the past few weeks, she didn't feel quite ready to take another risk. Instead the pair lay kissing in the darkness. It was enough for Billie to sense Clive's desire for her, making her feel safe and cherished.

Chapter Eleven

Connie

The girls knew the nurses' home doors were unlocked at six o'clock each morning, so when they got back into the hospital grounds they only had to sneak in the side door to evade possible capture by Sister Shaw.

That didn't stop Connie's heart beating out of her chest with fear of being spotted, though.

'He he, we made it! We can breathe easy,' Billie said as the girls reached their rooms.

'Yes, we did, but I could do without the worry, man,' Connie replied, her fear mixing with tiredness now to leave her uncharacteristically stony-faced.

'Oh come on, Connie, it was an adventure!' Billie replied.

Ruby nodded approval. 'Yes, I can now say I've partied in London – imagine! And thank you so much for lending me your dress, Billie – I felt like a real glamour puss,' she whispered, but the joy on her face was all the thanks Billie needed.

'Right, I'm going to bed. We'll have to give church a miss today, Ruby,' Connie yawned.

It was early afternoon before any of the other trainees saw the girls. Connie knew she'd been overly fretful about having to stay over in London, but after a good sleep, she reflected on what a great night it had been. She felt as though they had discovered a little piece of home in west London. The music, the food and everyone dancing and telling jokes about common experiences had given her a boost, and she was surprised to find she felt more alive on that Sunday than she had done in weeks.

She also realized that the more she saw of Devon, the more she was falling in love with him. They had spent the previous night dancing and giggling together, and at times were so engrossed in each other that it felt like they were the only people in the room. Then back at Clive's flat, Connie woke to Devon tenderly kissing her forehead. For Connie, London was full of so much that was wonderful, and Devon was the best of all.

Monday morning came around all too quickly, and the girls were back in the classroom, Sister Shaw introducing them to the renal system.

Connie was, as ever, eager to learn, as Sister Shaw started describing how the kidneys clear waste and fluid from the body. Highlighting the process on a diagram, she said: 'The kidneys have about one million filtering units called nephrons. These include glomeruli, which filter the body's waste products, and tubules, which remove the waste before returning required substances to the blood.'

Connie could see her sister next to her slowly start to put down her pen.

'The *who* and the *what*?' Ruby hissed, her face contorted by confusion. 'Man, Connie, this thing is only getting harder and harder to understand.'

'I do hope you're paying attention, Nurse Haynes!' Sister Shaw bellowed. 'You are behind the rest of the class by a long chalk. This is *not* a time for you to be chatting!'

Connie couldn't help but feel sympathy for her sister. She was always so much more self-assured with academic study than Ruby, but, even as she looked at her with all that confusion and uncertainty denting her confidence, Connie knew Ruby cared deeply about people and that this would make her a fantastic nurse.

'Sorry, Sister, it was my fault, I asked Ruby something,' Connie butted in, in an effort to get Ruby into Sister Shaw's good graces. Then she scribbled on her exercise book: 'I'll help you later' and flashed it at Ruby, as the training sister glared at her. 'Well, I expected better from you, Nurse,' she said.

As class ended for the day, Billie wandered over to Ruby as she packed up her belongings. 'Are you OK, Ruby? Man, wasn't the class confusing today? The amount of things they're throwing at us is ridiculous.'

'Oh man, Billie, I ain't got a clue what Sister was talking about. Surely we don't need to know about all of these things. I would have expected that kind of thing would be for the doctors to learn, not us,' Ruby said, exasperated.

'I guess they want us to have a good grounding in everything, though,' Billie replied. 'Wait, where's Connie?'

'She went on ahead, said she wanted to check at reception to see if any post had arrived,' Ruby explained. 'She's looking forward to news from home.'

But when Ruby and Billie met up with Connie in reception, she looked a little deflated.

'Still nothing?' Ruby enquired, disappointed for her sister.

'Well, there's a letter from Mum, but still nothing from Aunt Agatha,' Connie sighed.

'Wait, Mum's written to us?!' Ruby cried, snatching the letter from her sister to race through its contents.

'Lord, she says she got my letter already and that she was happy to hear that we are settling in so quick. She says Dad is well, even though they keeping him so busy at work he's having to do extra shifts – he's a postman, and they sending him all about the island,' she said, turning to Billie. 'Harold is doing well at school and

Mum says he got a certificate at Sunday School the other day –
ah, I miss that boy so much. Wait! She says Miss Jacobs' daughter,
Doreen, is coming up to England in the next couple of months
too – she's our neighbour,' Ruby blathered, with a smile that
stretched the width of her face, the rounds of her cheeks disap-
pearing into her dimples. 'Oh man, it's just so good to hear from
home, isn't it, Connie?'

But her sister looked glum. 'It is, yes,' she said flatly. 'I guess I
was just hoping for something from Aunt Agatha by now.'

'Well, it's fairly early days, we haven't been here two months
yet,' Ruby soothed.

'I know, but that's long enough for her to write; she must know
I'm anxious to hear. Martha must have changed so much,' Connie
replied, and Ruby flinched, her eyes flicking towards Billie.

'It's OK, I told Billie already. We were having a heart-to-heart
one day.'

'You did? Billie, you're real honoured – Connie's been keeping
this whole thing under her hat for years. Though I suppose it's
not like you would tell anyone – you won't be going to Barbados
any time soon,' Ruby thought out loud. 'But wait! What about
Devon? She could tell Devon, you know, Connie. Did you think
about that?'

'I won't be telling anybody,' Billie said, looking a little offended.
'It's for Connie to tell Devon when she's good and ready. Though
you ought to tell him sooner rather than later. Rather that than
for him to find out for himself some time.'

'Billie, I can't do that,' Connie pleaded. 'Devon already told
me he doesn't like London girls because they're so fast. There's
no way I could tell him and risk what we have.' Tears were starting
to well in Connie's eyes now, her disappointment at not hearing
from Aunt Agatha combining with fear about having to tell Devon
she had a daughter.

'I'm sorry, Connie. I didn't mean to upset you,' Billie said, with a look of resignation. 'I just want you two to have strong foundations for this relationship.'

Ruby wrapped an arm around her sister's slim waist. 'I tell you what, why don't we have a hair and make-up party tonight to cheer you up? I can do your hair for you and maybe Billie can do our make-up and we can try out different looks. I saw some lovely styles in one of Billie's magazines the other day.'

Connie exhaled a long sigh. 'Ruby, we *must* study tonight – I told you we would work on what we covered in class today. You *have* to get to grips with it, there's only five more weeks left. That exam is coming fast.'

'Oh yes, sorry, I forgot. The whole thing is pickling my brain if I'm honest with you,' Ruby replied, with the same befuddled look as she'd had that afternoon.

'And it won't be any less pickled unless we go to your room and look at it now,' Connie said, all but frog-marching Ruby up the stairs in a spectacle that made Billie smother a giggle.

'I'll catch up with you girls later,' she smirked.

In Ruby's room that evening, Connie went over all the things the girls had learned that day, then the things they'd learned the previous week. Then Connie realized she needed to go back even further to the basics of anatomy and physiology they'd covered weeks previously.

'Oh Ruby, why didn't you tell me you were having so much trouble?' she pressed her sister.

'I thought I had a handle on things, Connie.' Ruby looked glum. 'But they expect us to learn so much and so fast.'

'They do, and it's not easy for me either. But we have to be ready because when we get on the wards we will have a lot of responsibility. Patients will need us to look after them properly,' Connie said.

'Yes, you're right, of course. And I want to be a good nurse, Connie, I really do,' Ruby sighed. 'And I don't want them to send me back home. I'm not really good at anything, Connie, you know that. If you find some of this hard, imagine how it is for me. But the last thing I want is to fail and have to go home shame-faced.' Frustrated tears now streaked Ruby's face. 'I came up here to make something of myself, to be part of something important.'

Connie was not used to seeing her normally ebullient sister under such pressure, but as Ruby put her fears into words, they were suddenly very palpable. And for the first time Connie realized just how important becoming a nurse was to her sister. Her horsing around when it came to study was merely to disguise her lack of confidence. Ruby looked vulnerable and Connie remembered how very young she was, and not just in years; Ruby was a nineteen-year-old who still had some growing to do.

'You will, Ruby,' Connie said finally. 'I'll make sure you qualify as a nurse and become part of this great National Health Service, because I'll be damned if you'll be going home without me, and I ain't going back to Barbados in a hurry. We won't be going home for years and years.' Connie did her best to encourage her sister.

'But . . .' Ruby said through sobs. 'But you said you wanted to go home as soon as you were qualified.'

'Did I?' Connie said with a glint in her eye. 'Well, as Billie would say, it's a lady's prerogative to change her mind. And someone may be making me reconsider life in England.'

'Devon!' Ruby grinned through her tears, but Connie merely offered up a knowing smile.

'Dry your tears, sis,' Connie said, handing Ruby her handkerchief.

The next day, not only was Ruby feeling much happier, but she even put her hand up to answer a question posed by Sister Shaw.

'That is correct, Nurse, yes. The kidneys excrete nitrogenous wastes including urea, catabolism, and uric acid in urine. Very good!' she said, looking equal parts surprised and impressed.

Looking at her sister, Ruby beamed. 'Well done,' Connie mouthed.

As lunchtime came, Connie and Ruby queued up in the dining room together with Billie and Jean.

'Cor, Ruby, you really know your stuff!' Jean said. 'I didn't have a clue what Sister was talking about today. How did you know about all that?'

'It was something Connie and I studied last night,' Ruby smiled, this rare praise boosting her confidence.

'Come on Jean, you know she's not as clever as you,' a voice came from behind them and all four girls spun around to see Margaret.

'Oh, I don't know about that,' Jean said sweetly, with a slight look of confusion. 'She knows all about the kidneys for a start.'

'Margaret, did anybody ask you anything?' Billie piped up. 'I don't remember anybody here talking to you.'

'I can say whatever I like, whenever I like,' Margaret spat.

'Hush up your mouth, girl,' Billie said, waving her hand at Margaret. 'Jesus Christ, we've heard too much from you already, and none of it's worth listening to,' she added, turning back to the other girls. 'And Connie, Ruby, don't tell me I shouldn't blaspheme. *Some* people deserve to hear much worse than that.'

'Thanks, Billie,' Ruby smiled, even though she'd felt a little crushed by Margaret's comment, and Connie echoed her thanks to their friend for stepping in.

Over lunch, the trainees sat together, but Margaret took herself to another table and demanded Grace sit with her. Being of a quiet nature, Grace did as she was asked.

'I wonder why Grace is sitting over there with that hateful cow,' Billie said.

'Yeah, I thought Grace was your friend, Ruby. I'm surprised she'd choose to sit with that nasty piece,' Connie agreed.

'Maybe Margaret's teaching her about the anatomy of people from the Caribbean. I'll have to set Grace right later,' Ruby guffawed.

'What do you mean?' Billie enquired, confused, and Ruby started explaining Margaret's tail comments to her during the anatomy test a couple of weeks previously.

'She said what? Ruby, man, that's outright offensive! The rude wretch!' Billie spat, while the other girls looked on, bewildered.

'I bet she was just being silly, she can't have meant such a thing,' Phyllis said innocently.

'Of course. She couldn't mean that,' said Jean.

But Lin, Mei and Kathleen's faces were a mixture of sullen and aghast. As fellow outsiders in this small town in Middle England, they could recognize Margaret's comments for what they were.

'Ruby, that's racist. It's as simple as that,' Billie stated. 'I don't know why, but there's this thinking among some of the English that we have tails. It must be something to do with them thinking we all hang about in trees like monkeys, or something just as damn ridiculous.

'Clive was telling me about this with a friend of his. He was renting a room in a shared house where some English people lived too. There wasn't a door to the bathroom, just a curtain, and every time he would have a bath he would see the curtain twitching. Till one day he overheard the other people living there talking about how they were convinced he had a tail and they were trying to spot it. So the next day he had a bath, and he made sure to take off all of his clothes and stand spreadeagle in the bathroom for them to see *everything* that he had and everything he *didn't*.'

As Billie finished telling the story, the group roared with laughter.

'You know what?' she continued. 'The curtain didn't twitch like that again!'

'Oh my goodness,' Connie said through fits of giggles.

'Ach, fair play to him,' Kathleen laughed riotously. 'I'm struggling to breathe, that's so funny.'

'It is, and I laughed real hard on Saturday when he told me. The stupidity of some people is astounding. But it's also offensive; I don't even know how people could think such things,' Billie said, now looking serious. 'It's like she's saying we ain't human.'

Connie nodded. 'I hadn't thought of it like that, but you're right,' she said. 'I really don't know where Margaret gets off with her high and mighty self, but we shouldn't put up with any nonsense from her.'

'But then, what should we do?' Ruby asked, wrinkling her brow.

'I'm not sure there is much we can do, Ruby. It would just seem like we're telling tales if we were to mention it to Sister Shaw or Matron Wilson,' Connie considered.

'I tell you what I'd like to do – I'd like to box her ears,' Billie stated, then, looking at the others' resigned faces, she added: 'But I guess we'll just have to ignore her for now. That said, if she comes up with any more of that kind of talk, Ruby, you tell me and I'll put that bitch right.'

Ruby nodded solemnly.

'Let's not dwell on any more of that kind of silliness now,' Phyllis said. 'I for one think you're all lovely.'

After lunch the nurses were back in the classroom, this time learning about the urinary system. Connie looked over at Ruby and was pleased to see her listening intently. She looked to be soaking the information up, and Connie was relieved to see how even in one day, Ruby's confidence seemed to be flourishing.

Later that afternoon, Connie went to reception for her now daily check on the post.

'Yes, what can I do for you?' Miss Bleakly asked. It wasn't usual for her to be manning the reception and her brusque attitude made Connie nervous.

'Oh, I expect you're here to check on the mail again, aren't you?' she tutted, then pursed her thin lips as if she had just taken a bite out of a lemon.

'Er . . . yes, I'm wai-waiting on a letter from home,' Connie stuttered.

'I thought I heard that one came for you and your sister yesterday. Unless this is some boyfriend of yours you're waiting on,' the older woman said, stony-faced. 'You know what will happen if you get into any kind of trouble,' she went on, searching through the day's letters. 'Here,' she said, thrusting an envelope towards Connie.

Connie's hands began to shake slightly as she looked at the envelope addressed solely to her, not to her and Ruby as the one from their mother had been the previous day. It had a Barbados stamp on it with Queen Elizabeth's head and a picture of the statue of Admiral Nelson that sat in the heart of Bridgetown. She also recognized Aunt Agatha's handwriting, and her heart leapt in her chest when she read the words 'Please Do Not Bend' on the envelope.

She's sent a photo!

'Thank you!' Connie yelled after her as she raced up the stairs to Ruby's room. Miss Bleakly merely cast her familiar look of disdain after her.

'Ruby, Ruby! It's come!' she panted. 'Aunt Agatha has written me a letter.'

And then, before she could even open the envelope, tears started to stain Connie's cheeks.

'Come on, silly. Read it first at least,' Ruby said, wiping the tears from her sister's face. 'Else you won't be able to read it at all!'

For a moment, Connie's fingers and thumbs fought with the

envelope, but then she finally managed to prise it open carefully. She popped the two photos contained within to one side, as though to save the best for last, and began to consume the news.

'She says thank you for my letter, that she was happy to hear we got up here safe. Mum and Dad had got word to her but she says it was nice to hear from me directly. Martha is doing really well, and has grown a lot, even in this short time. She has started learning her alphabet but she stalls at G, saying, "G-gee-gee G-gee-gee" before Aunt Agatha has to help her move along to H,' and then Connie found herself laughing and crying all at once.

'She has enrolled her at Sunday School and says that her favourite song is "Jesus Wants Me for a Sunbeam", but she sings "Shesus" instead of "Jesus". Oh, Ruby!'

'Oh Lord, she's so funny!' Ruby said as she hugged her sister. 'I just hope she's got a better voice than her mother,' she added teasingly, but Connie promptly dissolved into more tears.

'Ah, Connie, I'm sorry. Come, let me finish reading the letter . . . OK: "I have enclosed a couple of photos of Martha that were taken of her at church recently, as I think you only had the one photo before and I'm sure these will be a very welcome reminder of her for you. I'd better sign off now, Connie. But, please God, I will write again soon with more news. Now take good care of yourself and Ruby, and give her a hug from me. Oh, yes, I also have to tell you that when I told Martha I was writing to you, she said she wanted to give you a hug. So, a hug from Martha, and lots of love from me, Agatha." And she has signed it with three kisses,' Ruby smiled, as Connie now turned her attention to the photos.

Flipping them over, she saw a little girl with the same fine bone structure as her own, and a button nose that perhaps more resembled Ruby's, but she was unmistakably Connie's daughter. In the next photo she was a little blurry as she was tilting her head back and laughing, but Connie didn't mind this minor flaw – for her, everything about Martha was perfect.

'Isn't that lovely? I'm so glad you got the letter you were waiting for, Connie. And my, she's as cute as a button and growing so fast,' Ruby said, as she now looked at the two images.

'Yes, these are happy tears now,' Connie chuckled, and clutched the photos to her chest. 'I'm so glad to have these.'

That evening after dinner, Connie propped the photos of Martha up on her desk as she worked. The little face staring back at her from the images seemed to spur her on, and she tore through pages of her nursing textbook.

As she paused for a break she looked at the photos and smiled. *I'm going to make you so proud of me, and maybe one day, I'll be able to be your mummy and bring you to England.*

A knock at the door pulled her from her thoughts. 'There's a phone call for you, Connie,' came the voice.

As she rushed down to one of the booths and the call was put through from reception, she heard Devon's warm tones.

'Hello, my beautiful lady. How are you? I've missed you since the weekend,' he said.

'But it was only two days ago!' Connie protested.

'Wait, a man ain't allowed to miss his woman after two days? It's been two *whole* days, you know! In fact, longer than that because you left me at the station in London early o'clock Sunday morning,' he joked, but Connie was momentarily knocked off guard by the fact he'd called her *his woman*.

'I miss you too. I've been working real hard these past couple days though so I haven't had a lot of time, well, for anything else at all,' she said, feeling a glow spread through her that she only felt with Devon.

'Did you hear from home yet? I know you girls were waiting on letters,' he asked. Connie felt an urge to tell him the good news about the letter she'd received from Aunt Agatha. She so longed to share everything with Devon, but she knew it was much too soon. Perhaps there would never be a good time to tell him that she wasn't quite the pure girl he thought she was.

Just how do you tell someone that?

'Yes, we did. We got a letter from Mum just yesterday – it was so nice to hear all her news. Ruby was thrilled!'

'Oh that's good, that's good. This sort a thing means a lot when you're far from home. Family is important. Speaking of which, it's Easter next weekend – do you and Ruby have any plans? I was hoping I could come and see you,' Devon suggested.

'Ah yes, I almost forgot. With so much going on with the training, my head is constantly in my books. That would be wonderful. Ruby and I usually go to church in the morning, so we could meet in the afternoon?' Connie said.

'Then that's what we will do. I'll come up on the train and spend the afternoon with you, and don't eat lunch, I have a surprise for you,' Devon said cheerily.

Chapter Twelve

Ruby

The following weekend, Ruby was almost as excited as Connie for Devon's visit to Four Oaks.

'You would think I was going along with the two of you, this afternoon, I'm so looking forward to seeing him,' Ruby smiled at her sister as they walked back from All Saints Church, enjoying the feel of the warm sun on their faces after days of April showers.

'Ah, you know Devon wouldn't have you left home alone today, don't you? He said you must join us. It's Easter Sunday after all, he said – it's a time for families.'

'Family!' Ruby said, slightly aghast. 'He considers us family already? You two ain't got nothing to tell me, have you? There ain't wedding bells on the horizon, are there?'

'No, Ruby, man. He's just being nice – we're all up here away from our real families so you kind of have to make your family here,' Connie said, batting away her sister's question with a wave of her white church gloves.

'This may be the Motherland, but I haven't seen much sign of the kind of family we have back home yet. So I guess Devon is thinking we look out for him and he will look out for us. That's what family does.'

Ruby nodded. 'OK, that sounds good. And I've always wanted

a big brother. So *maybe* you two could hurry up and get married and then we could be family for true.'

'Ruby Haynes, cut out this nonsense talk, you hear me!' Connie protested. 'We've only been stepping out for a few short weeks.'

'I *know*. And *you* know I'm only teasing you,' Ruby giggled.

'Yes, but next thing you'll say this for him to hear and Lord only knows where we'll be. He'll probably run away and I'll never hear from him again,' Connie scowled playfully.

'No, this man is for keeps, you know, Connie,' Ruby gave a knowing smile, but Connie couldn't help but wonder what her inexperienced sister could possibly know about men and love.

The twelve o'clock train steamed into Four Oaks bringing Devon with it, and he gathered Connie into his arms in a big hug, planting a kiss on her lips.

'I'm glad the weather has turned out nice up here too because I've brought us a few things for a picnic,' he said. 'And then I thought, if it gets cooler later, we could perhaps go for a drink somewhere. I don't know if you've been to a pub here yet? Oh, where's Ruby?'

'Yes—' Connie began, but was interrupted by her sister.

'I'm here, I'm here,' Ruby cried, her cheeks bulging. 'I thought as it was Easter I would treat us to some chocolates, because the English are all eating their chocolate eggs, so I thought we better do as they do. We saw some great big eggs when we did a tour of the children's ward the other day. I wished we were working the wards already just so I could get a taste,' she chortled as she chewed.

'Look at that – Devon's brought us a picnic and you've got chocolate; we better go find somewhere to enjoy all these goodies before the rain comes again,' Connie said.

As they settled in a pleasant spot in Memorial Park, they were lucky enough to be graced with sunshine.

'Ohh, this is the stuff,' Ruby said, turning her head towards the warm sun. 'Doesn't everything seem so much better and brighter in the sunshine?'

'Ah yes. Winter here can be long and pretty bleak, so this is nice,' Devon said, taking three bottles of lemonade and some neatly wrapped corned beef sandwiches out of a bag.

'I'm glad that the weather has improved. Not that I'm planning on going anywhere fast. Not at all. I'm going to get this course under my belt, finish all my training on the job, and find a nice man to marry – maybe we could live in London. So it's good to see how nice the weather in England can be,' Ruby said, looking thoughtful, as though planning her future in considerable detail.

'Sounds like you have it all thought out, Ruby,' Devon laughed a little. 'My mind is set on saving for now. I'm hoping to save enough to build a house back home. You know, for me and my family.' He glanced at Connie, who gulped down a mouthful of lemonade.

'Well, you got big plans, Mr Grant! Though I hope they don't include taking my sister back with you already – we got things to do up here, you know,' Ruby replied. 'I'm still hoping one day we could get up to Scotland and maybe to Wales.'

'Well, they may do, so you better start travelling fast. That is, if she'll follow me back home,' Devon said, his gentle eyes seeking approval from Connie.

'Right now I can only think about the exam we have to sit in a few weeks' time, but in a few *years*, maybe,' Connie replied with a smile.

'Yes, you all have work to do up here yet. But that's OK, it will give me time to save up,' Devon said. Ruby eyed her sister thoughtfully. She couldn't help but notice Connie's shift in position from when they'd arrived a few weeks previously, when she had sounded in a hurry to get home. Perhaps she was starting to enjoy England, Ruby thought.

As the evening closed in and the sunlight faded, Connie

suggested they head to the Woodman's Arms. 'I invited Billie to join us there too, as I didn't want her to spend the whole of Easter Sunday on her own. She said she might bring Kathleen along with her. She's an Irish girl we're training with,' Connie told Devon.

Soon they were in the hubbub of the Woodman's Arms as it came alive with the early-evening drinkers. There were men mostly, but especially on this festive weekend, many were there with wives and girlfriends sipping port and lemon.

'Good evening, it's good to see you again. And it's nice to meet you,' Devon said as Billie and Kathleen arrived at the pub and found the trio.

'Hi Devon,' Billie replied. 'How are you getting along, handsome?'

'So you're the famous Devon! I've spent the whole day with me nose in the books for this infernal exam we have next month, so I'm jealous of you two girls spending the day in such grand company,' Kathleen continued.

'I'm a little worried that Ruby and I lost a whole day of study, but we can get back to the books tomorrow,' Connie said.

'Ach, all work and no play makes Jack a dull boy,' Kathleen retorted. 'There's time for that yet.'

'Yes,' Ruby replied, a part of her wondering why her sister seemed to find it so difficult to relax and enjoy life, especially after the lovely day they'd had. 'There's still plenty of time.'

The evening passed with Billie and Kathleen telling jokes about life back home, and Devon finding himself even more charmed by Connie. As the group went to leave the pub, Billie came face to face with John Whicker, the man she'd had a little dalliance with a few weeks earlier.

''Ello, darling, what you doing 'ere?' he asked, looking her up and down, his eyes focusing on her bust for a few seconds before he remembered her face.

'John! I came here looking for a good-looking English man, of course. How are you?' Billie said, fixing him with her big eyes.

'All the better for seeing you, gal, but it's been a good few weeks, eh?' he replied, looking around at the table. 'Fancy coming down here another night – just you and me like, you know?'

'Ah, this nursing course is keeping me real busy. I only came out today because these girls begged me. But I'll be spending the next month with my books now, so no can do I'm afraid,' she said sweetly, and John wandered away looking a little crestfallen.

'Wait, Billie, you passing up a date with him? I thought you said he was a looker?' Ruby said, surprised.

'Oh, he is. But girl, you must think I have time on my hands. I already have Clive in my life, and with all the study, I ain't got time for him too. Besides, I like Clive, I wouldn't want to be messing that up,' she said thoughtfully.

'Ach, you can't ride two horses in the same race and expect to win,' Kathleen agreed.

That night as she lay in bed Ruby thought about her sister and Devon and what a lovely day they'd spent together. Just like *family*, she thought, the word floating tantalizingly in her mind. Maybe one day Devon really would be family to her, and she would be delighted.

She also wished there was a boy interested in her. Since Sylvester had abandoned her for Sandra Blake she'd not so much as had a boy look in her direction. Sitting on the sidelines while the other girls were so romantically involved made her long for someone to show her attention. But this wasn't jealousy. Ruby had listened to enough church sermons to know that the green-eyed monster was the root of unhappiness, and as she fell asleep, she comforted herself with the idea that one day her time would come.

*

The next few weeks marched on, then finally, on a Friday afternoon, Sister Shaw brought the preliminary training school to a close.

'I have addressed all of you trainees as nurses from the outset. This isn't merely because you are here and set to work as nurses at this fine hospital. It is because I have had faith in each of you, that you will achieve just what is expected so that you do indeed become nurses here at St Mary's,' she said. While Ruby was listening intently to the training sister, she also couldn't help but catch sight of Margaret sitting at a table opposite, smirking at her, but she tried to quash the sense of unease that started swirling in the pit of her stomach.

'Your exam is next week, and you will be expected to pass that before you can continue with your training to become state enrolled or state registered nurses, and commence working on the wards where you will start looking after patients. We are, of course, desperately in need of qualified nurses here at St Mary's, and you will continue to learn on the job for the next two years. But the important word is *qualified*,' Sister Shaw stressed.

'So I expect you all to do your very, very best, and I hope to see you in your nurses' uniforms and heading to the wards as soon as you have passed your exams. Class dismissed!'

A sense of apprehension at the challenges to come and accomplishment for what they had already learned filled the air as the trainee nurses chatted while packing their bags.

'Goodness, how nerve-racking this all is. Do you think you're ready for the exam, Ruby?' Grace sighed.

'I'm as ready as I'll ever be,' Ruby said, surprising herself with her confidence. But she also knew that she had been working very hard the past few weeks. Connie wouldn't allow it any other way.

'I know my left ventricle from my right, and the function of each. And I also know all about the nervous system,' she said brightly, her confidence shining like the sun on that fine May day.

'Well, don't some people have a lot of chat,' Margaret sniggered. 'Bet that's about all you know though, isn't it?'

Connie overheard her comment and glared at her. 'Hush your mouth, Margaret. Nobody here asked you anything. You're always prancing about the place like you know everything. You leave my sister alone.' She kissed her teeth with uncharacteristic feistiness.

Billie stepped in too, putting herself between Margaret and the Haynes sisters. 'You see you, your mouth is always running, in't it?' she hissed from between gritted teeth, her beautiful features contorted with disgust. 'You think because you come from here, because you have your pale white skin and your blue eyes, that you're something special, don't you? But you're just a nasty piece of work. And when we get onto the wards you know you're going to be wiping up the same amount of muck that we will. So don't get all up in yourself, and let this girl alone,' Billie fired off.

'Tut. Come on, Grace.' Margaret's voice broke a little but she quickly buried any fluster and forced a grin onto her face. 'I think it's time for us to go. We don't have to put up with this.'

Grace, though visibly unsettled by the fallout and unclear as to how she had any possible role in it, knew better than to argue with Margaret, and followed her out of the room. 'I'll see you later,' she mouthed to Ruby, who stood looking dejected.

'I wish she would just leave me alone,' Ruby said, finally.

'She's a bully, Ruby, plain and simple. But maybe she'll back off now she sees that we're not standing for it,' Connie said.

'Yes, I hope so,' Ruby replied as she felt her sister place an arm on her shoulder and take her bag out of her hands, lightening her emotional load as well as the physical one.

'Come on, let's go into town and I'll treat you to an ice cream sundae at Minstrels,' Connie said. 'You want to come?' she asked Billie, Kathleen and the other girls still in the room, but they all recognized this was time the Haynes sisters needed on their own.

The trip to Minstrels proved a welcome break for Ruby. But later that evening the sisters sat in their rooms revising, and they did so for much of the weekend.

As Monday morning rolled around, Ruby woke feeling confident and ready for the exam that day.

Putting on her trainee's white coat for what she realized would be the last time, she stared at herself in the mirror. Gone was the girl that had arrived in England three months earlier, who hadn't known the first thing about the human body; gone too was the inexperienced teen who had only ever travelled as far as her aunt's home in the north of Barbados. Ruby knew she had grown considerably in the past few months, and she was loving the exciting new life she was forging in England, even though she missed home and the rest of her family. And surprisingly, even with something as academic as an exam before her, she was brimming with confidence.

This time next week, I'll be wearing the proper nurses' uniform, with the belt and everything.

An hour later, though, as the trainees waited to enter the exam room, nerves twisted inside Ruby, putting pressure on her bladder. 'I've got to go to the loo, Connie,' she muttered.

'OK, well you have ten minutes to get back here, so hurry along,' her sister urged.

Walking into the toilets, Ruby found the first cubicle occupied so made for the second one along. Before she'd finished, she heard the other toilet flush, and then, as she came out of her own cubicle, she found Margaret fluffing her fringe in the mirror.

'Oh, it's you,' said Margaret, her lips pursing into a pout. 'I thought there was a bad smell in here.'

'Any bad smell could only have come from you. You were here before me,' Ruby replied with more mettle than she realized she had. Though she thoroughly disliked confrontation, Billie and Connie leaping to her defence the previous week had given her some strength, and she was no longer prepared to be pushed around.

'Perhaps you lot from the colonies don't understand where you are in the pecking order. So you listen here – this is not your country, it's not your home and your type isn't welcome here,' Margaret spat, launching herself at Ruby and pointing her finger in her face, her own face flushing red with fury.

Ruby tried her best to remain calm, to not let Margaret see that she was upsetting her. She narrowed her eyes, a look of defiance taking hold, then through gritted teeth, she said: 'I belong here just as much as you do. I'm a British citizen and I've come here to help. Now get out of my way.'

Ruby brushed her aside and turned to wash her hands in the basin. Margaret watched her for a moment, incredulous that Ruby would ever talk to her in that way.

'You may be from the colonies, but you only just stepped off the boat, my girl, and I can see you heading right back home on one too. Think you're going to be a nurse? Pah, you've got another think coming – you're too stupid to be one. I don't know why you're even wasting everyone's time taking the exam,' Margaret taunted with a dark, exaggerated laugh, then she turned and flounced from the room.

Ruby looked at herself in the mirror and forced back the tears that burned behind her eyes.

Why was Margaret so hateful, she wondered. She looked at her skin in the mirror, now already beginning to her to look a little paler without the constant kiss of sunshine it was used to back home. And for the first time in her life, Ruby realized she was different. Not only that, Ruby realized she was black.

She wasn't unaware of the chocolate brown hue of her skin. But in Barbados, its colour was all but an irrelevance – almost everyone had skin similar to hers. They were the majority. And though there were white Barbadians, and Ruby had heard that they had certain privileges she didn't – like access to better jobs – Ruby hadn't had much personal experience of the dagger of racism. In this moment, though, it felt like the deepest cut.

Suddenly the door swung open. 'Ruby, what on earth are you still doing in here, man? Sister Shaw was hollering for you – the exam is about to start. Come!' Connie urged, not noticing her sister's sullen expression as she rushed her back to the exam room.

'Ahh, Nurse Haynes, so you have decided to sit this exam, have you? Hurry up and take your seat over there.' Sister Shaw pointed to an empty table where an exam paper lay face down.

As Ruby hurried into her seat she caught sight of Margaret, two tables away, who scowled at her as she went by.

'You have three hours to complete the paper, starting from now,' Sister Shaw instructed, then the trainees turned over their papers and began to study the questions before them.

Ruby sat quietly, her stomach a churning sea of confusion, nerves and anger. She couldn't understand why Margaret was so ghastly to her, how it could be that her skin – the very fabric of who she was – seemed to offend her. She was warm and friendly to everyone – why was this one girl so hateful towards her?

It was a question that tumbled over and over in her mind as the clock ticked down over the next three hours, and Ruby spent a long time watching the other girls furiously writing before focusing on her own paper. So when Sister Shaw brought the exam to a close, Ruby was still frantically scribbling her answers down.

'Nurse Haynes, that's all the time you have,' the training sister warned, and Ruby put down her pen feeling a little defeated.

'How do you think you got on?' Connie asked her sister as the girls filed out of the room.

'I don't know, Connie,' Ruby said, her brow furrowing and her voice sounding weak. 'I didn't get time to finish it all. I had a lot on my mind during the exam.'

'*Ruby*,' Connie prepared to chide her sister but then she saw her lip trembling and her face begin to crumple. 'Come, let's go to the toilets a minute.'

Billie also saw what was happening and followed the sisters into the same room in which Margaret had abused Ruby and undermined her confidence just hours earlier.

'Oh Connie,' she said, her anger now dissolving into hot tears that coursed down her cheeks as Connie and Billie looked at each other, bemused.

'Ruby! Whatever is the matter?' Connie asked, gathering her little sister into an embrace. Ruby tried to explain, but Connie found it hard to discern through her sobs.

'I want to go home,' Connie heard Ruby say. 'I think I made a mistake coming here.'

'Ruby, it's natural to feel homesick. I miss home too,' her sister soothed.

But Billie had caught more of what Ruby had said. 'Wait, Margaret said what? That nasty bitch,' she spat angrily. 'She's just hateful. She's a hateful, racist bitch. You hold your head high, Ruby Haynes, cos Margaret ain't worth the mess on your shoes!' and she took off out of the room.

'Ruby, you can't let her upset you. I think Billie's right, and you and me . . . we're just going to have to develop strong back-bones to deal with this kind of thing,' Connie said.

'She said I was stupid, Connie, that I would fail the exam and be sent right back to Barbados. And now I think she might be right. I didn't finish the paper,' Ruby said through sobs. 'I let her get to me, when I'd studied so hard these past few weeks.'

Just then, they heard Billie's voice in the corridor outside and the sisters knew she must be speaking to Margaret. 'You know what, you ain't no better than any one of we here. Actually, I think you do know. That's why you're such a bully – because you know your intellect and your abilities are limited,' she said, her voice a growl, so ignited was she by rage.

Connie opened the door just in time to see Margaret trying to shove Billie aside. 'Who do you think you're talking to? Get out of my way,' she stormed.

But Billie, the stronger and bigger girl of the two, stood firm in Margaret's path and there was a tussle. Margaret punched Billie's cheek. Then she broke free and ran off in the direction of the nurses' home.

Connie rushed to Billie's aid followed by Ruby, and the other trainees still in the vicinity ran over too.

'Oh my goodness!' shrieked Jean.

'Billie, are you all right?' Connie cried as her friend, looking a little dazed, clutched her face.

'Yes . . . I think so,' she said with frustrated resignation. 'But let me tell you all here and now, you best keep that nasty piece of work far away from me.'

'I expect she'll be staying away from all of us,' Phyllis said. 'She barely mixes with us now anyway, she's so very high and mighty. I hear she comes from a lot of money – her dad's some sort of aristocrat.'

'Well, I don't care where she comes from, she just better stay away from me and my girls here,' Billie replied, motioning towards Connie and Ruby, who had now stopped crying but was still feeling fretful.

Her worry was a sinking feeling that she couldn't shake. At the end of the week when the nurses went to the training room to collect their results, Ruby still had a deep sense of unease.

'Oh my goodness, we've all passed!' Grace cried as she quickly scanned the list of names.

'We have!?' Lei said, rushing up to find her name on the board.

'Move out of the way and let me see the board, will you,' Margaret said, shoving her way to the front, then she stepped away smiling. 'I knew I had it in the bag!' she gushed.

Connie was next in line and her face lit up as she came across her name. Billie's name was next on the list, then she looked for her sister's.

'Well done, Billie. We've made it!' She grinned at her friend.

'Thank heavens for that – I haven't been wasting my time these past three months after all,' Billie said.

Then Connie froze, and Ruby, who was standing a little behind her, immediately knew what was wrong. 'Ruby,' she said slowly, 'there must be a mistake . . . your name isn't on the list.'

'Ach no, tell me it didn't go arseways for yer,' Kathleen said, concerned.

'There must be a mistake,' Grace cooed.

'Yes, Grace is right, maybe they just forgot to put your name here,' Connie said, clutching for a buoy of hope in her sea of despair.

Ruby just stared at Connie, so numb she was unable to utter a reply.

'Come on, I'll go with you to find Sister Shaw,' Connie said as the trainee nurses parted to let them pass, their high spirits suddenly brought crashing down. As they wandered off Ruby could hear subdued chatter, but also squeals of delight from one girl – Margaret.

'You just wait till I call home. They're going to be so impressed by this. But then, I always told them – there's no holding me back,' she prattled on, but no one was listening.

Minutes later, Ruby was called into Sister Shaw's office, and Connie waited outside the room, tension turning in the pit of her stomach at the possible outcome of this meeting.

'I was very disappointed in your exam paper, Miss Haynes,' she said, and Ruby was struck by the way she called her 'miss'. *Sister Shaw always refers to us as 'Nurse'*, she thought as her brow furrowed and she became terrified of where the conversation was going.

'You have a mark of just 34 per cent, so I had to fail you,' Sister Shaw said bleakly. Ruby felt as though the walls of the room were caving in on her; her heart started beating faster and droplets of sweat formed on her forehead.

'But . . . but y-you can't send me home, I'll do better, I promise I can do this,' she pleaded. 'I so want to be a nurse.' Then she started sobbing.

'Please stop this now,' Sister Shaw said, then in an uncharacteristically tender and supportive tone she went on: 'Ruby, I know you can do this. I have seen just how you've grown in your knowledge and also in your confidence over the duration of the course. I *know* that you have more to offer than what you submitted in the exam.'

Ruby looked up at her, her face painted with a mixture of fear and astonishment.

'That is why, the *only* reason why, I am arranging for you to re-sit the examination. I have set it for this Friday.'

Ruby's jaw dropped as tears streamed down her face. 'I thought you were going to send me back home. I know I can do better. I won't let you down, Sister,' she said through her sobs.

'I'm quite sure you *can* and that you *won't*,' the sister said. 'I will see you back here at nine o'clock sharp on Friday.'

'Yes, Sister, I'll be here – and I'll be sure to do more revising before then too,' Ruby said, then dried her tears as she left the room.

Connie was anxiously waiting outside.

'I've got to come back and re-sit the exam,' Ruby said, then recounted her conversation as her sister cuddled her.

'Oh, you're so very lucky Sister Shaw saw the work you were putting in and has given you another chance to prove yourself,' Connie said.

'I know. I am. But Connie, I looked at the paper and I knew all the answers, it's just that I didn't have enough time to finish it all,' Ruby explained, feeling almost as flustered as she had done earlier when chatting to Sister Shaw, her worry at being sent back to Barbados still very present. 'The trouble was, I spent the first forty-five minutes or so trying to understand why Margaret hates me so much.'

'You listen to me, Ruby Haynes: you have worked your behind off to be a nurse at this hospital and there is no way we'll be letting that nasty wretch get in the way of your ambition. I will help you study over the coming days in readiness for Friday, and you're going to go in there and show everybody just how ready you are to be a nurse.'

Connie was as good as her word, and a few days later, Ruby sat with just Sister Shaw in the exam room. The exam questions were different to the previous one, and though this threw her at first, she planned things out, allowing herself enough time to consider all the answers and then write down everything she knew.

It was a nervous weekend for Ruby and Connie, and even though Devon had invited Connie to London to celebrate her results, she refused. There was no way she could enjoy it under the circumstances.

'Connie, you don't have to explain,' Devon said on the phone. 'Let's just hope Ruby passes this re-sit. Then we can have a celebration for you both.'

On Monday afternoon, as the rest of the trainees readied themselves for a tour of the wards on which they would be given their first three-month rotations, Ruby walked to Sister Shaw's office. She was quietly confident that she'd done a far better job, but she couldn't deny her nerves.

'Nurse Haynes,' Sister Shaw said as Ruby entered the room. 'Please take a seat – I think you might need to.'

Ruby really didn't need to be told twice, since by this point her legs could no longer carry her.

'I am delighted to say that not only did you pass the paper on this occasion, but you came in with flying colours – 87 per cent,' Sister Shaw smiled enthusiastically.

'It's the second from top mark in your group, and I'll let you into a secret,' she said conspiratorially. 'Only your sister, Connie, scored slightly higher.'

'Lord h'mercy, Sister, you really frightened me – I thought you were going to send me home. Thank you, thank you so much. I'm going to work so hard and be the best nurse St Mary's has ever seen,' Ruby said excitedly.

'You don't need to thank me, Nurse, you did all of this yourself,' Sister Shaw said. 'Your training is of course far from over, but this is where your nursing career begins. Now you may go – I'm sure you want to tell your sister.'

Ruby was out the door like a bullet from a gun, running, skipping and laughing all the way back to the nurses' home.

'Connie, Connie, I've passed. I'm a nurse just like you and the others!' Ruby cried, as her sister returned from her ward tour.

Chapter Thirteen

Connie

Connie could barely contain her joy at her sister's news. She could not have imagined being in England without Ruby, and had gone through the motions of her day exploring the wards and being measured for her uniform in perfunctory fashion. Her own achievement – passing her exam and stepping up a rung on the ladder towards being a fully qualified nurse – had felt hollow.

'Ruby! That's wonderful, I'm so relieved!' she squealed.

'I know, I thought I was a goner. But thank the Lord, I made it! And it's also thanks to you, sis. You helped me get here.' Ruby hugged her sister tightly.

'Wait! You got through?' Billie beamed hopefully at the door to Ruby's room – with Kathleen, Jean, Mei, Phyllis, Grace and Lin all behind her.

'Yes, I did. I did it – I got 87 per cent!' Ruby's excitement was palpable as the other girls cheered.

'Congratulations, dear. I knew you would do it,' Billie said. 'This is cause for celebration.'

'Well done,' said Jean.

'We're all nurses here now,' said Mei, and the girls continued to congratulate Ruby as Connie looked on, feeling deeply proud of her little sister.

'Right then, we need to party,' Billie stated. 'We're going to be heading onto the wards from Wednesday, so tomorrow's our only opportunity to let our hair down.'

'I was thinking we could go to the pictures in town,' Connie said, and Billie's glare told her immediately that this was not the kind of celebration she had in mind.

'Come on Connie, where's your sense of fun?' she groaned.

'I thought you said you'd had a good time at the pictures with Clive when you went last month?' Ruby said.

'Yes I did, but Ruby, that's different, man. We made our own fun there, you know,' Billie winked, leaving Ruby momentarily aghast. 'Ugh, OK, fine, why don't we go to the pictures tonight then. But tomorrow we're all going to the Woodman's – this needs a proper celebration.' Billie was insistent.

That evening at the ABC Cinema in town, all of the trainees bar Margaret, who grandly stated that she had no interest in stupid films, took their seats in a row to watch *Prince Valiant*.

'Lord, this is boring,' Billie hissed to Kathleen ten minutes into the film.

'Maybe, but that there Robert Wagner's a looker, so I'm prepared to put up with it,' Kathleen smirked.

'It's a good job I brought this along,' Billie said, pulling a small flask out of her bag.

'Billie, what is that you've got there?' Connie nudged her.

'It's just a little tipple to *liven* things up in here. It's what's left of my rum from home,' Billie explained, offering the flask to Connie.

'Goodness me! Is there any stopping you?' Connie replied. 'No thanks, I'm watching the film.'

'Ooh, did you say you had some rum there?' Ruby whispered across Connie. Then she took the flask, took a gulp and pulled a face as the liquid burned down her windpipe.

Connie flashed her a mildly disapproving glance.

'Come on, sis, she's right.' Ruby gasped momentarily, then

licked her lips as if to savour every drop of the rum. 'We really do have reason to celebrate. I certainly do.'

'Hmm,' was Connie's response, but she knew she couldn't deprive Ruby of enjoying her success, and she was enjoying her own as well.

The next morning, there was a telephone call for Connie in reception.

'Hello?' she answered.

'Hello there, is that Nurse Connie Haynes?' a familiar voice said.

'Devon!' she smiled. 'It certainly is.'

'I wondered just what a nurse does on a fine day like today?'

'Well, I was about to go into town – I was going to see if Ruby and any of the other girls . . . I mean *nurses*, wanted to join me,' she said.

'What would you say to me escorting you into town myself?' Devon enquired.

'What? Where are you?' Connie asked, intrigued.

'I not long stepped off the train from London, wanted to surprise you. I thought we ought to spend the day together before you start working all those funny hours on the wards.'

'Oh, what? You're here!' she cried.

Half an hour later, Connie was on her way into town to meet Devon, after arranging with Ruby and Billie for them all to meet later that day at Minstrels. She spotted him on the steps of All Saints, where daffodils and tulips now lined the pathway through the churchyard.

'Hello, Nurse Haynes. I can't tell you how proud I am of you – and of Ruby, too. I got you these,' Devon beamed, handing Connie a posy of flowers.

'Thank you,' she smiled. 'I'm so happy, Devon. I made it! Now it's just about learning the ropes on the job. I'm most happy for Ruby, though. I was so worried for her.' She began to tell him about the past week, Ruby's encounter with Margaret and the effect it had had on her performance in the exam.

'Boy, some people can be so nasty,' he said, shaking his head as the pair wandered through the centre of town.

It was market day, and the heart of Four Oaks was thronging with people. Headscarfed women filled wicker baskets with fresh fruit and vegetables from the stalls, while a group of small children kicked a runaway potato around the square.

They heard the cattle market before they came upon it. Traders yelled in double-time patter as cows mooed and metal gates clanged shut behind them as they were herded into pens ready for auction.

'This really is the country,' Devon laughed, taking Connie's hand, as they began window shopping around the town centre.

Then, a few hours later, they wandered into Minstrels to find Billie and Ruby already there, enjoying milkshakes.

The group had a meal together before Billie reminded them that they had big plans to celebrate that evening, and they made for the Woodman's Arms.

As they rounded the corner to the pub, a group of young men were gathered outside, chatting around a slew of motorbikes.

'This looks like a motorcycle club,' Devon observed as the men revved and spun wheelies on their bikes. As they grew closer Billie recognized one of the bikers as John, and as he waved at her, Connie caught her friend flash him her killer smile, and she could have sworn she saw her batting her eyelashes too.

Bang! Pop-pop! Bang!

The sound startled Connie as one of the motorbikes backfired and she jumped. But soon her mild fear was overrun by the sound of laughter, and her attention switched to the group of young men.

Most of them, John included, were pointing in their direction and roaring with laughter. Connie figured the other girls must have been as startled as she was and that they were laughing at her and her friends. All rather ungentlemanly, she thought.

'Look at him on the ground!' one of them guffawed, apparently pointing at her. It was then that she realized she'd lost hold of Devon's hand, and turning around to speak to him, her eyes eventually fell to the cold cement of the pavement beneath her feet. And there he was on the ground, fear tensing his face, his eyes fixed on the space right in front of them. Kneeling down, Connie took his face in her hands.

'Devon, you OK? What happened? Are you hurt?' she pressed.

But Devon didn't respond; he was frozen to the spot. All he could do was stare right ahead, not even at Connie. The expression in his eyes was pained.

'I'm . . . O . . . K,' he said slowly. 'I'm . . . OK,' he repeated, but it sounded as though he was trying to reassure himself more than Connie.

'Let's help get you up, eh,' one of the lads said, moving away from the laughing group to kneel beside Devon. Then, as Connie continued to fuss, the man looked Devon straight in the eyes. 'I was there too, I know,' he said quietly enough that Connie missed the exchange.

'Come along, mate,' he continued, helping Connie to get Devon to his feet, then he used his hands to dust the remains of grit from the pavement off his grey flannel suit.

'Fred Rosby,' he said, shaking Connie's hand and smiling from beneath piercing blue eyes. 'I think your friend here could use a stiff drink – good job you're at the Woodman's already.'

Then, turning to Devon, who Connie could feel trembling in her arms, he said in a low voice: 'It's over. You'll be right as rain soon, don't you worry.'

As they settled at a corner table inside the pub, Devon pushed his chair back against the wall, his eyes frantically searching the room. Connie removed his suit jacket and placed it on a hook, and eventually the tension on his face started to evaporate, as though he was slowly coming back into the world he shared with Connie and the others.

'Devon, you are real funny, you know,' Ruby grinned.

'And I'm sure he doesn't need you pointing that out,' Connie huffed, but her little sister didn't register her annoyance.

'Will someone get that man a drink?' Kathleen said. 'A whisky will do it, that's usually a good answer to any ills.'

'I'll get them,' Devon offered, but Billie was already on her feet, heading to the bar.

'No, no mister, you sit yourself down there. You've had a funny turn – relax, man.'

'I don't know what happened,' Devon said. 'I must've blacked out for a moment. But I'm all fine now.' He smiled at Connie to reassure her. 'Maybe I just hadn't eaten enough. Billie, would you get some peanuts for me please?'

Connie looked at him quizzically. She couldn't figure out what had happened, and despite his slight smile, she didn't feel the comfort she usually got from his gaze. Instead, there was a growing unease in the pit of her stomach.

As the evening turned to night, though, her worries eased a little as the girls celebrated their achievements.

'Imagine, tomorrow we're going to be on the wards,' Ruby sighed.

'I just hope we don't have to do too many night shifts or weekends,' Billie said, rolling her eyes. 'I didn't come to England to spend Saturday nights emptying bed pans.'

The next morning, Connie woke early. She'd been tossing and turning in her sleep with something niggling at her that pushed itself ever further forward into her consciousness until she could sleep no more.

What happened to Devon yesterday?

He'd been back to his usual attentive and loving self when he'd walked them all back to the nurses' home the previous night, before he headed off to London. But Connie sensed there was something he was hiding from her and, in the pale light of the early morning, she couldn't shake her upset. She wanted Devon to be able to share everything with her, to feel able to trust her.

Then she felt a pang of disgust. How could she be so upset with Devon for keeping something from her when she hadn't even told him about Martha?

But surely that was different, she thought. Martha was a secret forced upon Connie herself, one she knew would break her family if word got back home. And how would Devon react if he were to find out she was not who he thought she was? She *had* to keep Martha secret . . . at least until she knew there was going to be a future with him. But even as she thought that, she doubted herself. Wasn't there a future with Devon? He was already making plans for the years ahead that included her. And she knew that this kind, thoughtful, handsome man was the one for her.

Connie continued to have a backwards–forwards debate with herself until her alarm rang two hours later.

Forty-five minutes after that, she pushed the dilemma to the back of her mind, knowing she had an important day ahead. Getting dressed, she put on the lilac pinstripe nurses' uniform of a first-year trainee and adjusted the elasticated belt – whose pattern matched the dress – around her middle. The belt buckle snapped together solidly, the latest piece in the puzzle of her new life in England falling into place, then she looked at herself in the mirror and smiled.

'Connie, you ready for breakfast?' Ruby's voice accompanied a knock on the door.

'Ruby – look at you! You looking so smart, man. I'm so proud of you.' Connie smiled at her sister.

Ruby beamed back. 'And I'm proud of you. We both made it!

The only bad thing is that they're separating us now. I wish I was going to be with you on the women's ward. But I checked the Change List and they've gone and assigned me to the men's general ward for my first rotation.'

'I'm sure it'll be very interesting, though, Ruby, and we'll get to work on lots of wards in the hospital in time. Sister Shaw said we need to become proficient in every area of general medicine.'

'Yes I know, but it's so much better when we're able to do things together,' Ruby replied. 'But I guess I'll be all right.'

Connie gazed at her younger sister, happy to see her confidence growing. Since passing her exam there seemed to be a spring to her step.

Later that morning, as she arrived on Lavender Ward, Connie, Mei and Phyllis lined up with other, more experienced nurses as they were greeted by the ward sister.

'We have twenty-two women on the ward currently, each with different levels of needs. Some can get around and get to the toilet themselves, but others are post-operative and will require assistance to walk, or more often, a bed pan.

'Some are here with broken bones, others following surgery for things like appendicitis, and then some have a range of women's problems and are under our consultant gynaecologists,' Sister Lambert explained, her brown eyes earnest and her wavy dark hair peeking from beneath a heavily starched cap that fell down her head to finish in a point behind her.

'I've already taken the handover from the night staff who did their last vital signs check an hour ago; we will need to do that again in an hour's time for our acute surgical cases. However, we now need to get our patients breakfast, then get them washed and up out of bed for those that can. There are also bed pans that need cleaning. We've a busy day ahead, so let's get going, nurses.'

As they all set about their day, it soon became clear that the less glamorous job of cleaning was falling to the newly arrived trainees.

'Ugh,' Phyllis said as she joined Connie and Mei among a clutter of bed pans, kidney dishes, duck-billed metal specula and glass syringes in the dressing room. 'This is not how I thought we'd spend our first morning!'

'Yes, it's . . . erm . . . well, let's just say I'm glad I only had a very light breakfast,' Connie replied. 'But I'm sure you must get used to this,' she said, pouring the contents of a bed pan down a gurgling drain.

'I hope it happens soon, but in the meantime I'll be holding my breath and looking the other way,' said Mei, wrinkling her button nose. Then the girls removed syringes from a sterilizing machine and the room filled with steam.

By lunchtime, they thought they'd cleaned up well and left the whole area spick and span, expecting that on their return they would be helping patients. But as they came back from the dining room, yet more dirty instruments were there for cleaning, and Sister Lambert instructed the young trainees that that was their job for the afternoon.

'Goodness,' Connie sighed. 'I really didn't think we'd be doing this all day.'

'I guess us trainees get all the worst jobs to start,' Mei sighed, watching as qualified nurses and more experienced trainees, whose full year of training was symbolized by their white belts, darted around the ward, busily tending to patients.

'Please, nurse,' a greying woman called to Connie as she rushed by the ward, her arms loaded with cleaned kidney dishes. And for a moment, Connie turned to find a nurse, before realization dawned that the woman was talking to her.

'Mrs Peters,' she said, hurriedly looking at the woman's name on a board attached to the metal bedstead. 'How can I help?'

'Nurse, I need the toilet, but they say I'm supposed to ask one of you to take me,' the woman said as she struggled from the bed and got unsteadily to her feet.

'Hold on, wait right there,' Connie replied, rushing to put down the trays and support the woman, then slowly she led her to the bathroom.

No sooner had she got Mrs Peters back to bed, and picked up the kidney dishes, than she heard Sister Lambert calling for her.

'Nurse Haynes, is it? Come along, we need those clean dishes *before* they're dirty again. There's no time for dilly-dalliers here, you know,' the ward sister said curtly.

Connie went to reply, to tell the sister that she had been helping a patient, but immediately thought better of it. She knew it was not the place of trainees to answer back.

'Coming, Sister,' she said, grabbing the clean dishes.

Once she'd delivered the dishes, a staff nurse beckoned to her. 'It looks like Mrs Roberts in there has been sick – this happens quite a lot with the drugs some of our patients are taking. Could you go and clean up the area around her bed and help her change, please? Get Mei to help you make her up a fresh bed, as I think the sheets are soiled.'

'How was your day?' Billie asked as she met her friend on the stairs of the nurses' home later that afternoon.

'Ugh. Honestly, I don't think I've ever seen so much mess in my entire life. I've been elbow deep cleaning up blood, urine, faeces, vomit, you name it,' Connie said exasperatedly. 'I didn't think this was what nursing would be about at all.'

'Goodness,' Billie replied, aghast. 'That's some nastiness you were having to deal with there. But it could be worse. They have me on the paediatric ward with a whole heap of sick children. Me! Looking after pickneys. Can you imagine?' She rolled her large brown eyes, and Connie noted that despite a day of labouring on the wards, her friend's beauty still shone.

'I saw that you got the paediatric ward first. I would have loved that – all those children to look after. Although I'd have been feeling so sorry for them, too – it surely can't be nice seeing your child sick. I-I mean it can't be nice if you see *a* child sick,' she stammered.

'You know you told me already,' Billie smiled gently. 'And even if you hadn't, and I was only just finding out now, I wouldn't judge you.'

'Oh I know, it slipped my mind for a moment and well . . . It's just . . . Oh, Billie, I guess it's worrying me that I haven't been open with Devon.'

'I can only imagine. The thing is, he's a grown man, and a good man at that. I can't see him treating you badly because of that,' Billie comforted.

'Hmm,' Connie sighed, furrowing her brow. 'I hope not.'

'Well, look at you two, how you still looking so good? I'm exhausted,' Ruby said minutes later. 'They had me running around cleaning everything until it was shining. I barely even saw any patients.'

'Sounds just like my day,' Connie said, rolling her eyes. 'Other than that, how was the men's ward?'

'Well, the little I saw of it outside of the dressing room it was fine. Grace got to do some rounds and assist with the meals and giving out the drugs. They said we would swap around and I'd get to do that tomorrow. But I'm still loving it!' Ruby smiled, if a little wearily. 'I'm just glad to still be here.'

Chapter Fourteen

Billie

If there was one thing Billie felt she'd learned in her first month after starting work on the wards, it was that there was little glamour to nursing. And although she had never been under any illusions that the job required a strong stomach for some of the sights she would witness, she realized working in paediatrics meant caring for little people, many of whom couldn't take care of their most basic needs. At first, with three months of this ahead, it seemed a trial.

But as the long days of summer stretched out before the new nurses, Billie was making little friends on the ward and finding joy in her work.

'Sally, your parents are here, it's time for you to go home,' she said, and the seven-year-old beamed back at her as though reflecting the bright afternoon sunshine that filled the room.

'Fanks, Nurse Billie,' she said with a gummy grin. 'I'll see you when I come back to see the doctor one day.'

'Oh no, you'll see him in the clinic, darling,' she said, then looking down at the little girl, she saw her face begin to crumple.

'Don't get upset now. It's a good thing that you won't see me any more. It means that your leg is all mended. Well, very nearly – don't get out your skipping rope right away, but I expect very soon you'll be running and dancing and everything. Just don't be climbing any more trees,' she said softly, gathering the little girl up in a cuddle to comfort her.

Soon Sally was discharged, and then it was a little boy called Peter's turn; then, three days later, it was time for Billie to say goodbye to five-year-old Bobby, who'd had his tonsils out.

'Now you be a good boy, won't you, Bobby. And next time I see you I expect you'll be singing to me,' she said, patting the youngster's head as he wandered off, his arms stretched out to his parents on either side of him.

'Thank you for everything, nurse,' his father smiled back, and Billie felt the warmth in her heart that she did every time one of the tiny patients went home. She delighted in seeing the colour come back into their cheeks, the light back into their eyes and even their sense of mischief return. But most of all, she was just thrilled to know that they were healthy again, and that she had contributed to their recovery.

'It's always nice to see, isn't it?' a voice said behind her, and Billie turned to see one of the general medicine doctors looking on at Bobby and his parents.

'It's joyous,' Billie said. 'I didn't expect to enjoy spending so much time with these little ones, but it's even more delightful to see them going home with their parents. That's how it should be.'

'Yes, it is. We're seeing so much positive change in the health of young children since the NHS started,' he said, then he exhaled slowly. 'Sadly, for every few that we can get back to full health and send home quickly, there is one child that will be here much, much longer. Or possibly will never be themselves again.' Billie followed the doctor's solemn gaze as he looked towards a bed with a tiny figure in it – Pear Tree Ward's longest-stay patient, Mandy Ford, who was in a coma.

'We know it will be a miracle if she recovers,' he said of the ten-year-old girl who had come into the hospital eight months earlier, limp in her father's arms. 'The aseptic meningitis has ravaged her, and left her with considerable brain damage. I'm not sure she will ever be able to lead a normal life again.'

'Yes, Doctor, so I heard. It's so very sad,' Billie said, her eyes locking on Dr Ezra Becker's concerned face and for the first time, noticing his dark blue eyes. It wasn't the first time she'd seen Dr Becker – he checked in on many patients on Pear Tree Ward and Billie had been present when he'd briefed the ward sister, Sister Brown, on drug and treatment regimens for the children. But this was the first time he had spoken to her directly, and the deep pools of his eyes stood out more to her in that moment, perhaps because they were just a little glassy as he stared thoughtfully at the small girl in the bed. A raw moment of silence passed between them.

'If only there was more we could do,' Billie said finally.

'Dr Becker,' a deep voice bellowed, pulling them both from their thoughts. 'We must continue our rounds.'

'Yes, of course, Mr Stone,' he replied to the consultant physician, and they wandered off in the direction of the next ward, leaving Billie to wonder what hope there was for the young girl before her.

She checked that the fluids were still flowing well through Mandy's drip, stroked her blonde curls away from her face, and went back to the desk by the doors into the ward.

'Nurse Benjamin, I've just been informing the other nurses. From Monday, the hospital will be allowing parents to visit their children for a few hours every day,' Sister Brown explained. 'It's part of a new national drive. Some recent research has suggested children do better from more regular visits, and suffer less separation anxiety.'

'That makes a lot of sense,' Billie nodded. 'They're so little and a month between visits is a very long time for them.'

'Yes, I've seen some of the children who are here a long while become quite withdrawn, so I do think it will help. Though I hope the parents know that we will be busy, and that they won't get in the way. That would never do,' the sister bristled.

'Yes, Sister,' Billie agreed.

Soon it was time for the last drugs round of the day and Billie assisted more experienced nurses in taking temperatures and the children's blood pressure as they handed out the medicines.

'Come on, Barbara, one more gulp – it'll put hairs on yer chest!' said Kathleen. 'Good girl.'

The little girl scrunched up her face in disgust as she swallowed the medicine, then looked up at Kathleen from a bed far too big for her to fill it. 'But I don't want a hairy chest. I'm a girl!' she said, her face now a mixture of confusion and dismay.

'Don't you worry yourself, Barbara,' Billie said, smiling. 'It's just Nurse O'Hare and her silly sayings. You won't be getting a hairy chest, but you will get better.' Then she fluffed up her pillows and tucked in her sheets.

Kathleen looked over at Billie as though seeing her friend in a new light. Though they were only a month into their time on the wards, she was definitely seeing a warm and caring side to Billie that she hadn't seen before – and that she was sure her friend would deny.

Soon the weekend arrived and Billie found out she would have to fill in for another nurse on her first weekend shift, starting work at seven thirty each morning. She had lamented the fact two days earlier when chatting to Ruby and Connie. 'But you get two days off in the week in lieu of that time,' Ruby encouraged.

'Yes, but who goes out anywhere on a Monday or a Tuesday? Besides, Clive will be at work by then and I was hoping to get to see him this weekend,' she said, frustratedly.

'Billie, man, people are sick all the time. This isn't a Monday to Friday kind of a job,' Connie said, mildly exasperated.

'Yes, yes, I know. I guess I'll just have to be happy enough that I at least get to see my little ones at the weekend,' Billie replied.

'You do surprise me, Billie,' Connie said. 'I would never have had you down as a lover of children.'

'Well, it just goes to show that you don't know me well enough yet,' Billie replied with an air of grandiosity. 'That said, I would never have expected to care so much about any pickney that wasn't my own, or wasn't at least family to me.'

Connie's eyes met Ruby's as their thoughts clearly aligned – *who is this Billie?* – and the sisters couldn't help but laugh.

'What's so funny, you two? Didn't you think I had a heart till now?' Billie shot them an accusatory stare.

'No, it's not that,' Ruby said through giggles. 'It's just . . . well, you aren't exactly the motherly type.' And with that, the sisters shot from the room, just in time to miss Billie's scorn and cushions being flung in their wake.

'That's right, the two of you better run! What a slur on my gentle character,' Billie cried in mock annoyance.

Then Lin popped her head into the sitting room. 'There's a call for you, Billie.'

'Hello, beautiful, how has your week been?' Clive's voice came down the receiver. 'I'm calling to confirm our weekend plans. And I was thinking, there won't be anybody on the other side of the curtain this time,' he said suggestively, recollecting the last time Billie had stayed at his bedsit with the other girls and Devon.

'Oh, Clive, I'm afraid you're going to have to wait a bit longer!' she told him. 'Unfortunately one of the other girls is sick and I have to cover her shifts this weekend. I can't even come to London tomorrow night after my shift, because I have to be up and out of here first thing on Sunday morning,' Billie explained, only wishing she could change things to be able to see him. It had been two weeks and she missed his embrace.

'You do? Girl, you don't know I've been thinking about you

every day and missing that beautiful body of yours,' he said, sullen. 'And I was just about to tell you that the boys are going to watch the cricket at Lord's tomorrow and they have tickets spare. I was going to see if you fancied it.'

'Oh man! Of course I would have loved to go – you know we all love *cricket lovely cricket*,' she cooed, reciting the lyrics to the famous calypso song. 'I don't believe I'm missing this opportunity to see the West Indies up here! Wait – who do you mean by the boys? Erwin and Wilbur?'

'Yes, they both going, along with Wilbur's brother and a next friend of his,' Clive explained and Billie felt her skin turn pimply, a sickening chill taking hold as she thought back to her last encounter with Wilbur at the party.

'Well, I'm sure you'll have a good time. Give the team a cheer for me, I'm so vexed I'm going to miss it and that I won't get to see you, honey,' Billie said, and she meant it, even though she was relieved not to have to face Wilbur again.

'I will do – you know all the West Indians will be in the stand cheering loud for the boys from home,' Clive enthused before hanging up the phone.

Early the following morning, Billie pulled on American tan tights – a colour about five shades lighter than her own skin, but they proved the closest match she could find. Next she zipped up her uniform and tied up her very sensible black work shoes with a stacked heel that took her a mere inch and a half off the floor. Then she smoothed back her wavy hair, fixed it into a bun, applied some Vaseline to her lips and then the merest hint of eyeliner. Looking at herself in the mirror, she realized she was a picture of everything she would have railed against just a few months earlier.

She still thought the uniform made her look square, and she disliked her all-but-make-up-free face, but having a sense of what lay before her that day, she also felt her appearance was of little importance. Nothing really mattered except helping the children of Pear Tree Ward become fit and well. Finally, Billie felt as though she had found her calling.

It was a busy day on the ward, which started with Billie and Kathleen sterilizing needles, then they joined the other nurses in getting the patients their breakfast, and washing and changing them.

When it came to Mandy, they gave her a gentle bed bath, washing the comatose girl with a damp flannel, then they adjusted her pillows and turned her little body in the bed. Noting that her drip was coming to an end, Billie reported it to one of the senior nurses, who refreshed it.

In the afternoon, once the workload had eased, Billie went to a toy box on the ward, pulled out a jigsaw and gathered three of the children to do the puzzle together.

'This one fits into the beach,' she said, grabbing a puzzle piece.

'How do you know that?' a little boy named Freddie asked, astonished.

'It's because the sand is golden. Just like it is where I come from in Jamaica,' Billie smiled, fitting the piece into the rest of the puzzle.

'I've never seen the beach before,' Freddie said, wide-eyed. 'Does it have lots of sand and everything?'

'Yes, darling, and there's the sweet sound of the ocean, and the breeze carries the heavy, salty smell of the sea as waves roll in. Then as the water soaks away from the shore it makes a very low hissing sound like air seeping out of a balloon, as it trickles into the sand. And then in Jamaica the sun shines bright, bright, bright in the bluest sky. Now you have me thinking about home and all the things I miss,' she said longingly, a half-smile gracing her lips.

The hubbub of the ward seemed to fade away as Billie cast her mind back to home, but around her the usual activity continued.

Kathleen and Lin helped a more senior nurse change a child's dressings, and Dr Becker was busily writing up a patient's notes nearby. Hearing Billie reminiscing, he couldn't help but pause and turn to look at her, quickly becoming as enthralled as the children were by her charming descriptions.

'It sounds like something out of a dream,' he said softly.

Billie smiled. 'Oh, it is. I dream of home quite a bit these days. But I wouldn't change a thing. I'm happy here, there's still so much I want to see and do.'

'I'm sure. I just can't imagine that you'd find much of it in Four Oaks,' Dr Becker replied.

'You know this is true! And I had thought with us being so close to London, I'd be able to visit every weekend and see all the lights and the action of the big city. But the hours here are long and I haven't been there as often as I'd like. I'm even missing a chance to see the West Indies playing cricket today,' she explained.

'Oh, you are? I have a radio set in my office, I can bring it to the nurses' station if Sister agrees, then you could listen. Though to be honest I'd probably like to tune in myself too,' he said with a mischievous glint in his eye. 'Give me a moment to talk to her.'

Twenty minutes later Billie packed up the puzzle and got the children into bed for an afternoon nap. Once they were settled, she hurried to the nurses' station, where Sister Brown, Dr Becker and the other staff were gathered around the radio.

Through the crackle they heard: 'And he hits it . . . it's in the air, the fielder's underneath it, but it's still going . . . and going . . . for six!'

'Yeah, man! West Indies are whopping them!' Billie squealed gleefully, then remembered where she was. 'Um . . . sorry, Sister.'

But the group gathered at the station just laughed at Billie's enthusiasm.

'It's quite all right, Nurse Benjamin. I understand – sport can be rather exhilarating. Just keep your voice down so you don't wake the patients.'

'Yes, of course, Sister,' she said.

Billie's shift ended before the cricket match did, but she stayed on the ward, listening to the radio so as not to miss a wicket.

That evening after dinner, she telephoned Clive, but getting no answer, she instead went to the sitting room to mingle with the other girls.

'Is Clive not home?' Connie enquired.

'No, he must still be on his way home after the match today. It's a shame, really, because I'm missing him something bad this weekend, and I'm soon going to have to call it a night. These early mornings are the work of the devil himself,' she yawned.

'Well, I didn't think I'd ever see the day,' Ruby gasped in mock shock. 'First you're missing that nice gentleman of yours and not thinking about hopping like a rampant bunny onto the next one, and next thing you telling us you're off to bed early. And on a Saturday night!'

'Ruby, don't tease her so,' Connie scolded. But Ruby was too gleeful to care.

'They work us hard in the day, you know, so you can kid all you want to, Miss Ruby, but this girl has got to get her beauty sleep,' Billie said indignantly, then left the room and made for bed.

As the sun broke through her curtains to herald a bright June morning, Billie woke with thoughts of Clive. She decided she would call him that evening, see if they could spend Monday evening together.

Pear Tree Ward was oddly quiet that morning and Billie had time to shadow another more experienced Jamaican nurse, Ruth Campbell, to pick up on different aspects of the job.

'Sister told me you'd show me how to clean a drip line,' she said. 'It's good to meet you – there ain't many of us up here, especially not someone with years' more experience on the job.'

'That's true, though I'm seeing plenty, plenty more people from home coming up here now. But I think it's fair to say that I was a pioneer. I came up here on HMS *Empire Windrush*, you know,' Ruth replied, a certain pride shining through her last sentence, as though wearing her pioneering immigrant status like a badge of honour.

'Really? You've been here years!' Billie said, clearly impressed by the other woman's experience.

'Yes, since June 1948. And you know what? It's exactly six years to the day today!' Ruth nodded.

'My, what an adventure!' Billie replied, her big eyes urging Ruth to tell her more.

'Yes, and we didn't even know if we would be welcomed at the time. There was word circulating on board that the authorities might not let the ship dock. But one of my friends was a former wireless operator in the RAF and somebody asked him if he would go and play dominoes outside the ship's radio room to eavesdrop on incoming signals.

'They heard Arthur Creech Jones on the BBC. He was Secretary of State for the Colonies, and he said: "These people have British passports and they must be allowed to land." He also reckoned that we wouldn't even last one winter up here anyway – I think he said that to comfort the English that there was nothing to worry about,' Ruth laughed. 'And now look at me – six winters have passed and I'm still here!'

'Oh my goodness, you've done well, dear,' Billie said, awed by Ruth's adventurous spirit. 'And what was it like when you came to land? I came in February and it was *cold*. Girl, I could never have imagined it. I was so glad to see my friend Esme come to greet me at the docks and she brought me some warm clothes.'

Ruth laughed again, flashing a row of perfectly white teeth

beneath her spectacled eyes and flat nose. 'You would have thought that the weather would have been nice when we got to Tilbury, seeing as it was June. But there was this mist! I couldn't believe how terrible the weather was. And then there was the greyness – the whole place was so glum-looking. You have to remember this was just three years after the end of the war, and so a lot of places – whole communities, you know – they were just shells.'

'Oh goodness!' Billie exclaimed. 'I thought it was pretty bleak when I came, but I can't imagine. I heard that a lot of places were bombed pretty bad in the war.'

'Sister Brown, SISTER BROWN!' a voice urged, interrupting the nurses' chatter. It was quickly followed by Sister Brown and three other nurses racing down the corridor towards it. 'Call Dr Becker and Mr Stone!' the sister shouted behind her to Lin.

'What's happening?' Billie asked, as Ruth looked alarmed.

'Oh, Lord! That will be Mandy!' the other nurse replied anxiously, and they raced to the end of the ward.

'She's turned blue, Sister,' Billie heard one of the staff nurses say as she pulled a curtain around the little girl's bed, the huddle of nurses causing the curtains to swell in volume.

'Right, let's start chest compressions,' Sister instructed, and began pumping her hands on the little girl's chest in time to Ruth's count.

Two minutes later and the girl's skin still had a pale blue hue. The blonde curls that fell around her face bounced with every compression the sister made. But that was the only movement from her.

'Is there anything we can do?' Billie said, feeling as helpless as many of the other nurses gathered there.

'Not exactly, Nurse – just watch and learn how we deal with emergencies,' Sister Brown said. 'Right, she's still not breathing. I'm going to try mouth-to-mouth resuscitation.' She locked her mouth over the child's mouth and nose to breathe life into her body.

Another frantic few minutes passed as Sister Brown and the experienced nurses carried on working to save their tiny patient. Then as the sister paused between breaths, the nurses all stared, willing the girl to breathe for herself.

Once or twice, Billie thought she saw it – a sign of life. Was that a flicker of her eyelashes? A quiver of her lips as air was sucked through them?

But there was nothing.

Slowly, silently, Sister Brown stepped away from the girl, her ruffled curls crowning her head in a way that would have looked adorable, had the whole scene not been so heartbreaking.

'Time of death: 2.32 p.m.,' the sister said quietly. 'Keep the curtains closed and we will leave the body here to rest for an hour, by which time Dr Becker should have arrived to register the death.'

As the sister went to step outside the curtains, the nurses stood silently, and Billie felt frozen in place. She'd never seen someone die before.

How could such a tiny little girl be so suddenly ripped from this earth and sent to the Lord, she wondered.

The nurses slowly left the curtained area and Billie could hear Lin gently sobbing. But Billie didn't cry. The emotion was far from lost on her, but she felt shocked. It was as though a darkness had descended over the ward in those few minutes since she'd been talking to Ruth, and Billie didn't know what to do. So she prayed silently for the first time in years.

Dear Father in Heaven, please look after this little angel, she did not have long here on this earth. Please have St Peter welcome her and may she join in your heavenly choir.

'Come along, nurses, chop-chop now. I know losing a patient is terribly sad, especially when it's one of Pear Tree's little darlings. But unfortunately this is all part of the job,' Sister Brown said stoically.

Slowly, the nurses filed out of the area surrounding Mandy's bed, leaving the little girl's lifeless, tiny frame all alone. Billie looked back at her as the last nurse closed the gap in the curtain and she felt a sadness she hadn't felt since her mother died.

Soon Dr Becker arrived on the ward and completed the death certification, then later Ruth and another nurse prepared Mandy's body, and sometime after that, hospital porter Fred Jones arrived to wheel her to the mortuary. A silence fell across the ward as a gurney, now with a white sheet covering Mandy's body, slowly squeaked out through the ward's double doors.

Billie felt her shift couldn't end soon enough. She had spent the afternoon unable to shake the pervasive sense of loss that seeped through the ward.

Getting back to the nurses' home that evening, Billie went to her room and even avoided Connie, Ruby and the other girls. She just didn't want to have to tell them about it and relive that sadness so soon. She didn't answer when the other girls called for her at dinner time, then sat in silence in her room munching on a few cream crackers.

Before she knew the girls would be back, Billie wandered downstairs to phone Clive. She was longing to hear his voice. To her it was like a reassuring, long-distance hug.

'Hello, darling, it's Billie. How was your day?' she enquired as Clive picked up the phone.

'Oh, hello. Yes, it wasn't too bad,' he mumbled.

'I've been thinking about you. How was the cricket?'

'Yes, it was all good. We enjoyed seeing the boys from home get some good runs, and then seeing some wickets tumble,' Clive said.

'That's great. I listened on the radio when I was on the ward yesterday. But . . . goodness . . . that feels a lifetime ago already – I've had a terrible day today. Anyway, I was just calling to tell you that I miss you,' Billie said sadly. She wasn't looking for sympathy, but she was surprised that Clive didn't ask what had happened that day. Instead there was silence on the other end of the line.

'Clive? I said I really miss you, I was wondering what you were doing tomorrow. Maybe I could come to London for when you finish work and I could stay over,' she suggested.

'Er . . . I don't know. I mean . . . I don't think so, Billie. We need to talk,' Clive said flatly, and Billie's heart sank to the floor. 'Wilbur was telling me about the party, and how you were flirting with him.'

'No, Clive, I didn't do anything of the kind. He tried to force himself on me,' Billie protested, but Clive wasn't listening to her.

'I've come across girls like you before. All of you are just up for a good time. You've come to England, but you've come to escape the shackles of home, and to carry on however you like,' he said, anger blunting the edges of his voice. 'I knew it all along, I could see the kind of girl that you were. But I thought no, don't listen to the warning voice in your head. This one could be different. And I guess I must've had my head turned by that pretty face and that curvy body of yours, too. I must've been crazy! I should never have trusted a woman like you.'

Billie tried to protest a little more, but then she fell quiet. She had experienced a situation similar to this before, and she knew it was hopeless trying to argue. If someone can turn a person's mind against you, especially if you're someone that person cared about, you have lost them forever, she thought.

Tears were rolling down her face now. She felt frustrated by the injustice of it all, saddened that Clive had so little trust in her, and so little respect. By avoiding Wilbur's advances, she had fallen foul of the code that allowed men to get away with things women simply couldn't.

How could he let this so-called friend of his bad-mouth her like that and lie to split them up?

But quickly Billie realized that the tears that rolled so freely down her cheeks were nothing to do with the end of this love affair. She was crying for the little girl who had died in front of her that afternoon.

'You know what, Clive? I'm sad to find after all this time that you think so little of me that you'd let a low-down snake like Wilbur deceive you like this, and convince you of his lies. But at least it's made me realize something now before I was in too deep: I was looking for a man, and that ain't you. I'm glad you enjoyed your cricket yesterday, because that's the most balls you'll ever find between you and your friends.' Billie slammed the phone down and stomped up the stairs to her room.

Back in her sanctuary, she stared at herself in the mirror, thinking back to what she had witnessed that day. Then, wiping tears away with a tissue, she told herself that there were more important things in life than men.

Chapter Fifteen

Ruby

'Wait, did anybody see Billie? I ain't seen that girl for the whole day, you'd think we'd done something to her,' said Ruby, leading the charge as the girls returned from the dining room.

'Now, Ruby Haynes, why would you say such a thing?' Billie replied, forcing a smile.

'There you are! Why didn't you come to dinner?' Ruby asked.

'I didn't feel like it at all. I had a horrible day. A little girl died on the ward,' Billie explained.

'Oh, Billie, no!' Ruby exclaimed as Connie and all the other trainees looked horrified.

'Yes, it was that ten-year-old I've mentioned before, Mandy. She was so sick, but it was still a shock. Seems as though the brain damage was so severe that her heart packed in,' Billie said sadly, as Ruby hugged her.

'That's terrible,' Ruby said. 'I guess I could expect it – I have a few geriatrics on the men's general where I am. But you just don't imagine that little children will die like that.'

'Maybe not, but I think we'll have to get used to this – people die at any age,' Connie said dolefully.

The incident cast a shadow over the evening, but it also made the girls even more committed to their work. It was as though their role suddenly had greater significance. They couldn't help everyone, and some people would die, even little girls. But they could get some people fit and well again. It was this fervour that Ruby took onto Oak Ward at eight o'clock the next evening.

'Good evening, Sister Davenport,' she said.

'Good evening, Nurse,' the night sister replied. 'I understand this is your first night shift. We have breaks at midnight and at four o'clock in the morning. It is a longer shift, but it should be fairly quiet, of course, as we try to ensure the patients have a full night's sleep, even with vital signs checks and any drugs that need to be administered. The doctor will complete his ward round shortly, then it will be over to all of you nurses here for the night. I am on call, and I'll come by again before morning handover.'

'Oh OK, thank you, Sister,' Ruby replied, then retreated to help a staff nurse with the drugs round.

She'd been enjoying her time on the ward, despite the fact that Margaret had been allotted Oak Ward for her first rotation too. Their paths had crossed a little in the preceding weeks, but Grace and Jean were also on the ward and did their best to keep the two girls as far apart as possible. And now that Ruby would be working nights for the next few weeks, she was able to avoid her as Margaret was still on days.

'Good evening, Mr Bailey, you ready for your medication?' Ruby smiled.

'Hello, love, you're back here already, are you? I was just saying to old Bert over there how hard you girls all work. You can't get much time to yourselves,' said Fred Bailey, who was in hospital to have kidney stones removed.

'I'm happy to be here. I love working here and I want to make sure you're doing well,' Ruby replied.

'You're a good nurse,' he said, and Ruby's pride swelled. 'I think the best thing that ever happened was your lot coming over here and staffing our hospitals. It must be making a massive difference to the NHS.'

'Thank you, I'm glad you think so. All I ever wanted to do was come here and help, so I'm happy to hear that we're doing just that.'

'Oh, absolutely. I remember what it used to be like – working men like me couldn't afford to go into hospital. Not only would you lose your wage from your job, but then you had to pay to be treated and the like too. Gawd knows what I would've done if I'd had this problem back then,' he said.

Two hours later, the ward was quiet, the lights dimmed to allow patients to settle down and sleep.

'Nurse, nurse,' a man called as Ruby walked by.

'Yes, Mr Bentley, what's the matter?'

'I've got something I wanted to show you,' he said.

'Oh, OK, what is it?' She moved over to the foot of his bed.

'It's here, nurse. You'll have to come closer,' he pressed, his voice soft.

In the low light of the ward, Ruby walked slowly to the side of the bed, minding her step so she didn't walk into the chair next to it, or clatter into the metal bedstead and wake the other patients.

As she got to the bedside, her eyes took a few moments to adjust and focus in the dark corner. As they did, she realized the man had pulled back his bedcovers and lowered his pyjama bottoms to reveal a swelling in his nether regions.

'What is it? What's the problem?' she asked, but her innocence seemed only to encourage him.

'Well? Do you like it? I don't know if it's what you're used to,' he said keenly.

'Mr Bentley!' Ruby said a little too loudly, then remembered she was in a ward of sleeping patients. 'That sort of thing is for your wife to see, not me. Would you want someone to do that to your daughter? I'm here to help you, now cover yourself!' she hissed, pulling up his pyjamas and the bedding in one swoop.

Back at the front desk, she told Sybil Russell, the senior staff nurse on duty, what had happened.

'Goodness! Unfortunately some of our patients seem to forget what is and isn't appropriate behaviour in hospital. I will speak to him right away – that's completely unacceptable. And you a young girl at that,' she said.

'I don't want him in any trouble, I just don't want him thinking I'm a certain kind of girl,' Ruby said.

'Don't you worry about that, Ruby, he's the one in the wrong here,' Sybil said. 'It can happen – thankfully not very often.'

'Thank you,' Ruby said, and gave Mr Bentley a wide berth for the rest of her shift.

The next afternoon, she woke tired after finally getting to sleep around eleven o'clock that morning. The little alarm on her bedside table ticked to just before four o'clock and she realized that she had only enough time to get washed and dressed, eat dinner and perhaps have a quick catch-up with her sister before heading back on shift.

'How was your first night shift, sis?' Connie enquired as they headed to dinner with Billie later.

'It was OK. But I don't know about some of these men, you know. They can be really disgusting.' Ruby wrinkled her nose.

'What a funny thing to say, Ruby. Whatever did they do?' Connie asked.

As they sat down to eat, Ruby proceeded to tell them about her experience the previous night.

'He did what?! Oh my! And what did you do, Ruby?' Billie exclaimed.

'The dirty beast,' Connie said, outraged.

'I covered him up and reported it to the senior nurse on duty,' she said.

Billie roared laughing. 'You covered him up! Were you worried he might get cold? Only you would make sure he was comfortable again, Ruby – you even care for the dirty old men.'

'Well, it wasn't quite like that. I just didn't want to look at it or for anyone else to have to,' she said as Billie continued to chuckle.

'It's not funny, Billie, man,' Connie scolded her.

'No, it's not that. It really isn't funny at all. It's just the idea that Ruby covered him up first that made me laugh. Seriously now, Ruby, it's terrible,' Billie said, trying to show she was being earnest. 'I'm glad you reported it to the ward sister.'

'Hello ladies, you seem very jolly over here,' a voice said behind them.

'Oh, Dr Becker, hello,' Billie replied. All three girls now stopped and looked, astonished to see the doctor breaking the unwritten code that segregated the nurses from senior nursing staff and doctors in the dining room.

'Erm . . . how are you?' Billie enquired.

'I'm very well, thank you, I just couldn't resist talking to you when I saw such frivolity and laughter. The conversations in here are usually as dry as the food,' he chortled, amused by his own witticism.

'It wasn't exactly funny, just an experience my friend Ruby here had yesterday on Oak Ward.'

'Really, what happened? Oak is on my rounds this month,' he said.

Ruby looked panicked and urged Billie to keep quiet with a swift kick under the table.

'Oh nothing, just girly nonsense,' Connie jumped in, while Billie let out a low yelp and flashed Ruby a glare that said she knew better than to say a word.

'OK, well, I hope you enjoy your dinner, ladies. See you later, Nurse Benjamin,' he said, and Ruby noticed his eyes linger on Billie's face.

'And perhaps I'll see you later too, er . . . Nurse . . . ?'

'Haynes, I'm Nurse Haynes,' Ruby piped up. 'Yes, I'll be on shift later.'

Dr Becker walked towards his table but Ruby saw him looking back in Billie's direction.

'Goodness, Billie! Whatever next!' she said.

'What? I didn't say anything, *did I*?' Billie said pointedly.

'No, I don't mean that. I saw the way you two looked at each other,' Ruby said.

'What? Ruby, you must be crazy!' Billie chuckled. 'I mean to say . . . he has lovely, gentle eyes, but he's not my type at all. He's so . . . I don't know. He's a *doctor*, Ruby! And he's so straight-laced, you only need take one look at him.'

'Mm-hmm, well now look at that – you ain't saying you wouldn't be interested in him because of Clive or nothing. You're so fast!' Ruby chastised. 'That poor man of yours!'

'Well, as it happens, he is not that man of mine at all. Clive ended it with me the other day,' she said flatly.

'What? Why ever . . . ?' Connie sounded disappointed for her friend, while Ruby sat open-mouthed.

'She's got to be making sport with us. Come on now, Billie,' Ruby said.

'No. I wouldn't joke about something like this,' Billie said sadly. 'It was that damn friend of his, Wilbur. He tried it on with me at the party a few months ago. He said Clive wasn't man enough for me – implying that *he* was, the nasty piece. He tried forcing himself on me, and he only stopped when I kneed him in the groin. Sweet Devon saw what happened,' Billie explained.

'What? How did I not know about this?' Connie shook her head.

'Because I made him promise not to say anything. And like I always say, he's a gentleman, Connie. It's a shame there aren't more men like him. Wilbur went and told Clive I'd been flirting with him – he *wished*. And then Clive ended everything.'

Billie looked sad for a few seconds, then took a deep breath.

'But you know what? I couldn't care,' she said. There was a quiver in her voice, but she buried it with as much bravado as she could muster, because she knew that if a man was prepared to take his dumb friend's word over that of his woman, then he wasn't worthy of her.

'Oh Billie, I'm so sorry,' Connie said.

'Me too. I didn't know. And I didn't mean to say you were, well . . . anything like what Wilbur was suggesting,' Ruby added, wishing she'd had an ounce more tact and timing.

'It's fine, girls. There's more to life than men,' Billie stated.

Ruby looked at her agog. 'Wait. Who are you? That's not the Billie I know.'

'It's true. I don't know, I guess Clive and me just weren't meant to be. Besides, there's plenty more fish in the sea and I'll soon get my fishing rod out again,' she winked.

'Now *that* is the Billie I know and love!' Ruby said, and the three girls laughed heartily.

All too soon it was time for Ruby to start her shift, and as she got to the ward, she hung her cape in the nurses' rest room, then busily set about the tasks set by Sister Davenport before the night sister went on rounds to other wards.

She spent the first few hours working with a staff nurse on the drugs round and vital signs checks, and she spoke to each of her patients – the senior nurse had been sure not to put Mr Bentley in her care – and made sure they were all as happy and comfortable as possible. She even allayed any fears they had about their pending surgery or how their recovery was progressing. She was determined to be the best nurse she could be and to her, that meant covering all bases.

'Well done, Nurse, you've been working so hard and we're all impressed with the energy and enthusiasm you're bringing to the job,' said Sister Davenport, as she completed her ward round the next morning and heard comments from staff and patients alike about Ruby's fine work.

It was how she continued on Oak Ward as the weeks of her three-month rotation rolled by.

'Nurse, can I ask you something?' said a patient with acute appendicitis one day.

'Yes, Mr Porter,' Ruby responded a little cautiously. 'What is it?'

'You seem to work all the hours and you're so attentive to everyone here. But why are you here and not out with a nice young man this evening?'

'Me?' Ruby's shock was clear. 'Oh no, I don't have a boyfriend.'

'Well, that surprises me – you're a very sweet and caring girl. I imagine you'd be a great homemaker; I've seen how busy you are and all the energy you put in around here. Yet you take time for everyone. I'm sure you'd make someone a lovely wife.'

It was all Ruby could do not to guffaw at the suggestion. Since her first love, Sylvester, had abandoned her, crushing her hopes of marriage, she had considered that perhaps she wasn't good enough for anyone to want to marry her. But her mother had always told her to accept compliments graciously. So she smiled sweetly and said thank you.

As she headed to the cleaning area she emptied bed pans and bottles and made sure she left the area spotlessly clean in preparation for when the day staff would take over some hours later. All the while, she couldn't stop thinking about Mr Porter's comments.

Why can't I find a boyfriend? she mused. She had to admit to something she would only ever admit to herself: that as much as she loved them both, she couldn't help feeling a little envious about what Connie had with Devon. She knew jealousy was a one-way street to misery, but she couldn't understand why it seemed no one was interested in her.

I'm not ugly . . . I don't think so anyway. Yet here I am, still sitting on the shelf.

The thoughts rolled over and over in her mind until her meal break came around.

'Ruby, it's quiet round here and I know you've been working really hard all night. Do you want to have a sleep for a while? I can call you if anything happens, or if Sister Davenport comes back up,' said Sybil, who had just come back from an extended break of her own.

'Well, if you think that would be all right. I don't want to get into any trouble for it – I know Matron would be appalled. But some sleep would be wonderful right now. I just can't seem to get enough rest in the daytime.' Ruby yawned. She was starting to feel the strain of weeks of night shifts.

'Of course. I'll call you in a couple of hours,' Sybil reassured her.

Heading into the nurses' rest room, she took her cape from the hook, pulled two armchairs together to form a bed, then tossed the cape over her for comfort and its woollen warmth. It took no time at all before Ruby was gently snoring in a deep sleep.

It only seemed like a short while had passed when she felt someone nudging her.

'Ruby, Rubyyyy, wake up,' a voiced hissed, and eventually she opened one eye, feeling a little confused as to where she was.

'Quick, Ruby,' Sybil urged. 'Something has happened. It's Mr Partridge in bed five. Sister Davenport is on her way now, you need to look busy.'

'What? What's happened?' Ruby enquired sleepily. But Sybil had already rushed back onto the ward. She checked the time on her nurse's watch, pinned to the front of her uniform.

Six forty-five! Oh my goodness, how did they let me sleep for so long?

Ruby flipped her cape back, jumped up, smoothed the creases

in her crumpled uniform, then hurriedly tied the laces on her shoes and popped her white cap on her head. She was still wiping the sleep from her eyes when she left the room to race back onto the ward, knowing that her morning duties should be well underway in preparation for handover in the next hour.

Looking down the length of the ward, she saw Sybil and another nurse rushing around but couldn't figure out what the fuss was about.

Then Sister Davenport arrived on the ward, accompanied by the on-call doctor, and as they went to the desk to speak to the nurses, Ruby tried to stay out of sight so they wouldn't realize she was coming back from the rest area.

Instead she tiptoed into the top end of the ward, creeping quietly through the rows of beds, hoping not to draw any attention to herself from patients who might be awake.

She got part way down when Sister Davenport and the doctor rounded the corner into the ward, startling her. Jumping into action, she shoved a half-closed curtain to one side to take the pulse of the nearest sleeping patient, in a bid to show that she was hard at work.

'Good morning, Sister,' Ruby said, hiding her nerves with a hearty smile. 'I'm just doing some extra vitals checks,' she added.

Sister Davenport looked confused. 'Er, Nurse, I don't think you need to do them on this patient.'

'Well, yes, erm . . . actually, Sister, I was thinking that this man's pulse is hard to find. I wonder if you can help me, it's dreadfully confusing, maybe I'm doing it all wrong though,' she babbled, entirely missing Sybil who was by now standing behind Sister Davenport and the doctor, animatedly mouthing the word 'No' and drawing a line across her throat as if to say stop.

'Nurse,' Sister Davenport's voice was a mix of confusion and concern. 'You know this man has died, don't you? So therefore he would no longer have a pulse. Dr Frances and I are just here to complete the death registration.'

Ruby's cheeks suddenly felt hot and her mouth became dry.

'Oh . . . this is Mr Partridge, of course – yes, he was *very* sick. I thought this was Mr Peters. I'm sorry, Sister, it's been a long shift and I got terribly confused. I'll, erm, just leave you to it here.' Ruby gently placed the man's right hand back on top of his abdomen, patted it and walked off.

'Why didn't you tell me?' she whispered to Sybil as they went back to the front desk.

'I tried, but there was no time. I thought my hand gestures were enough to tell you that he was dead, though. Poor old Bill, he went off peacefully in his sleep.

'But, oh Ruby,' she howled. 'Sister Davenport must have thought you'd taken leave of your senses. And your face! It was an absolute picture when she told you he'd died!'

'Man, I'm so embarrassed! Sister must think I'm a terrible nurse,' Ruby said. 'And I haven't even seen a dead person before. I thought he looked a little pale,' she added, and by now Sybil was doubled over with laughter.

'Oh, my. Oh my goodness – it's terrible, I feel bad for old Bill, but Ruby, you've exorcised any sadness from this situation,' she giggled, and by now Ruby couldn't help but chuckle too. She was concerned Sister Davenport might think her slightly daft, but relieved that at least she didn't know she had been sleeping on the job.

The rest of the week passed uneventfully, with Ruby learning as she went and throwing herself into all kinds of jobs on the ward. As she arrived back at the nurses' home on the last day of her run of night shifts, she all but bumped into Matron Wilson.

'It's Nurse Haynes, isn't it? Now which sister are you? Ruby?' Matron pressed.

'Yes, that's right, Matron,' Ruby said.

She was exhausted after a busy week of nights, but now she was also rather worried, especially as she could see Miss Bleakly at the reception desk, scowling in her general direction as she shuffled papers.

'I've been hearing lots about you, Ruby,' the matron said, deepening Ruby's fears – especially after Sister Davenport had found her taking a dead man's pulse.

'All good things. Let's just say your thorough and hard work has been noticed by the senior nursing staff,' Matron Wilson explained.

'Oh . . . thank you, Matron. I've been trying, and I'm loving every minute!' Ruby enthused.

'That's marvellous! Keep up the good work,' the matron said, continuing on to the wards.

'Yes, I will,' Ruby gushed, the commendation making her feel really proud. She realized she wasn't just going to be a nurse, she was going to be a good one.

'Morning, Grace!' Ruby said as she arrived back on Oak Ward feeling rested and refreshed after three days off.

'Good morning,' Grace said, an uneasy smile on her meek face.

'Come on, Grace, we're working together today. You don't need to be hanging around here,' a familiar voice said, and Ruby turned to see Margaret, throwing her a look of disgust as though she'd just been assaulted by a bad smell.

Ruby rolled her eyes. She was happy to be back on days, but less so about her shifts coinciding with Grace and Margaret's.

She liked Grace – she was one of the first friends she had made at the hospital – but Ruby had been disappointed by her not standing up to Margaret's bigotry, and realized that not only was her friend too shy, but Margaret had a controlling influence on her.

Ruby made sure to steer clear of them that day, and for the

rest of the week, as she continued to care for her patients the best way she knew how.

On Friday Ruby joined her sister, Billie, Kathleen and Jean at breakfast. She was working a half-day, and was thrilled to learn that they would all be off duty for a few days. And not only that, but it was the August bank holiday weekend.

'We should have some fun,' Jean said.

'Oh, I'll be seeing Devon on Sunday as it's his only day off this week,' Connie explained.

'And I'm planning to go visit my friend Esme in London,' Billie said. 'But I'll be back by Sunday.'

'OK, well how about Monday, then? They say the weather will be blazing hot – we could go to the seaside!' Jean said excitedly.

'Well, I've never been to the seaside here in England before. What a great idea,' Ruby gasped.

'Ooh yes,' agreed Connie as Billie grinned and nodded approval.

'We could go to Southend-on-Sea, I hear it's just lovely there, and easy to get to from here,' Jean said.

'That sounds wonderful – we haven't been on a day trip in a long while. I haven't even been to London because I've been working so hard. And I don't usually have much money left from my wages each month to do anything very exciting. This will be fun!' Ruby was clearly thrilled.

'You're very cheery,' said Mr Porter as he saw Ruby towards the end of her shift that day.

'Yes, I'm pretty excited about the weekend. We're going to go to the seaside, a place called Southend, I think it is,' she said.

'Ah yes, that's a great town. You must be sure to get some rock while you're there, and maybe fish and chips at the end of the pier,' said her patient.

'That sounds real good,' Ruby said. 'And I can't wait to see the sea – I used to be at the beach often at home but I haven't seen the water since I got here.'

'Mr Porter?' said a voice, and Ruby turned to see Dr Becker, who was the doctor on call for the day.

'Hello, doctor – don't suppose you've got good news for me, have you?' asked Mr Porter.

'Well, I'm pleased to say that your surgery went well, but I'm afraid you won't be going home any time soon. We will be taking you off this dextrose–saline drip, though,' Dr Becker explained.

'All right, doctor, that will be good,' Mr Porter nodded, trying to sound as though he'd considered the doctor's course of action and it was the best option, but knowing he had no clue what he'd been told and merely accepted the doctor's analysis.

Ruby watched as Dr Becker's dark brown hair flopped onto his forehead as he scribbled the new treatment plan in the patient's notes, and she thought again about how he had spoken to Billie a few weeks ago at dinner. He didn't seem like the other doctors, she decided; he was friendly and very approachable. That said, she still wouldn't have dared to speak to him as Billie had, but, she thought, Billie was always very confident.

'Right, Nurse, I'm going to be off now for a week, but please remove Mr Porter's drip. And then be sure to enjoy your trip to the seaside. You take care of yourself, Mr Porter,' Dr Becker said.

'I will, doctor,' the man replied.

'Um, thank you Doctor,' Ruby said shyly, then immediately busied herself with turning off the drip, before going to get a dressing pack to remove Mr Porter's cannula and stopping to check with a senior nurse that what she had done was correct.

But on returning to her patient's bedside, she found he was again attached to the drip.

'Wait, Mr Porter, why are you back on a drip?' she asked, confused, quickly double-checking his notes to confirm everything. 'Yes, Dr Becker ordered that it be removed.'

'Oh I know, but another nurse came along and put it back up,' he replied, as Ruby started to turn it off once more.

'You! Get off that!' Margaret spat, shoving Ruby to one side.

'Margaret, Dr Becker changed his treatment, we need to remove this drip now. And look at it, it seems to be running real fast,' Ruby reasoned with the older girl.

'Do you think I'm going to listen to a dummy like you? Like the doctor would trust you with something important like this! Get out of my way. Besides, hasn't your shift finished?'

'It has now, yes. I was just dealing with this before I left,' Ruby said defensively.

'Well it's best you get yourself off home then, isn't it? Sister won't be impressed at you coming in here meddling when these patients have been assigned to me,' Margaret snapped.

With as much calm as she could muster, Ruby lifted Mr Porter's notes from his bed and handed them to Margaret. 'You'll see Dr Becker's instructions here.'

'That's what the doc said,' Mr Porter agreed. But as Ruby moved towards the bed to remove the drip, Margaret blocked her path.

'If that's the case, *I'll* take the drip out. I'm sure the patients would prefer not to have someone like you messing with things like this anyway. If it was down to me, I'd keep you on bed-pan duty where you belong.'

Ruby felt her last ounce of control dissolve as she saw Mr Porter looking on weakly at the spectacle before him, clearly lacking both the physical strength and the confidence to question Margaret's antics. Vulnerability and embarrassment fused into a tight tangle of emotion in Ruby's chest, and she turned and ran from the ward before hot tears could run down her face.

It had been quite some time since she had been confronted by Margaret's antics, but Ruby was distressed to find that the hateful girl still had the capacity to make her feel small. She loathed Margaret having so much power over her emotions. And despite everything that was going so right for her at St Mary's, and in

England, Margaret's vicious racism made her feel belittled, unwelcome, and as though she wanted to run and hide. Given the choice there and then, Ruby would have bought a ticket for the SS *Sorrento* and sailed right back home.

Home.

Ruby thought back to her first night in England, how she had come to the Motherland with a heart full of expectations. She had hoped for fun and adventure like many of the girls who travelled there from foreign shores. But Ruby had also anticipated finding acceptance – in fact, it had never crossed her mind that she wouldn't be accepted. Why wouldn't she? At school she'd learned that Barbados was an extension of England via the chains of Empire. She had assumed that England was equally an extension of Barbados with an indelible connection between the two islands, and that people like her could just travel to Britain and be . . . at home. She hadn't anticipated lines being drawn in the sand, differences manifesting from little more than intolerance, and hatred poisoning her experience.

She felt as though Caribbean girls like her had been brought to England on a promise, and it was about more than just employment. It was an offer of a new life alongside a wider family. But faced with such hatred, Ruby decided, that promise hadn't only been broken, it was a fallacy in the first place.

The links that bound Britain to its empire now seemed to her to be based on what Britain wanted and needed, not on familial kinship.

But walking back into the nurses' home, Ruby didn't want Connie or Billie to see her tears; they had been through enough with her problems with Margaret already. So that evening and for the entire weekend, Ruby kept what had happened to herself, and all of her emotions locked within.

It helped that the nurses had a fun weekend planned. On Saturday Ruby went shopping in town with Connie, then to the matinée at the cinema; on Sunday she went to church, and then spent the day relaxing and reading magazines, ahead of the girls' big day out.

As the train pulled into Southend-on-Sea, they were all thrilled to be exploring somewhere new and exciting.

'Shall we start with a walk along the pier? It's the longest in Britain – it goes for one and a third miles!' Jean said incredulously.

'That sounds like quite the walk to me; I'm not sure I can go the distance in these heels!' Billie said.

'I said you'd want something more comfortable on your feet,' Connie said, pointing at her own sensibly flat shoes.

'Yes, but then I would look like a dwarf,' Billie shot back, rolling her eyes.

'There's another option,' said Kathleen. 'We could get on that there train – it looks to go to the end.'

Minutes later, the girls were hopping on the pier railway. 'Hello love, are you going all the way?' A cheeky conductor winked at Billie.

'I never was one to know when to stop,' she flirted, throwing a seductive look his way.

At the end of the pier, the girls got ice creams, Ruby following it up with a large ball of candy floss almost the size of her head.

'This is some real funny stuff,' she said, finally coming up for air. 'It's this big thing, but then melts away to nothing at all.'

'It's just like a lot of men. Most of them are empty suits!' Billie joked, and the other girls roared.

'I wouldn't know. I'd just like to find one in the first place,' Ruby lamented.

'Oh you will dear, you will. That God of yours has a good one lined up for you,' Billie promised.

'Well, he better send him to me soon. I'm getting bored waiting and waiting for a nice fella to come my way. The only men in my life right now are on Oak Ward, and most of them are over fifty-five!'

And with that, the group started laughing again, setting the tone for a day of fun in the August sunshine.

At the end of the pier they had a lunch of fish and chips, eating them straight from the newspaper it was wrapped in, while looking out to sea. 'Do you think if it was a very, very clear day, we might be able to see Barbados from here?' Ruby had a look of yearning on her face.

'Lord, Ruby, you can be real daft sometimes, you know. Look how long it took us to sail from Barbados to here. You'd need some mighty strong binoculars!' Connie poked her sister in the ribs.

'I'm just missing home, I guess,' Ruby sighed as Connie put her arm around her shoulders.

'Even if we were blessed with super-long-range vision, yer cannae see yer home from here,' Kathleen informed them. 'We're right over on the east coast – if anything we'd be looking towards continental Europe.'

From the pier they headed to the Kursaal amusement park, where they hopped on a number of rides including the water chute and the Cyclone rollercoaster, which left them dizzy with glee.

'What a thing!' Connie said, slightly shaken after her experience on the rickety wooden ride.

'OK, I can't take any more thrills because I might just spill my lunch soon,' Billie said. 'Let's head to the beach – I haven't enjoyed a bathe in the sea in so long.'

Laying out their towels, though, the girls were bemused by the shingle. 'Man, they ain't got no sand here?' said Ruby.

'Looks not. It reminds me a lot of home, though – Killiney Beach, near Dublin, is like this,' Kathleen said.

'I ain't too sure of bathing in the sea neither. I guess it's all right, a lot of people are out there swimming, but it's a little murky looking to me. I think I'll wait till I can visit Jamaica,' Billie said.

By the time the girls were heading for home, though, they'd had a perfectly wonderful day out, and had many stories to share with the other trainees.

Tuesday came around all too soon for Ruby. She was partly dreading having to work with Margaret again, but happy at the prospect of seeing her patients, and was wondering how they were getting on.

As she arrived on the ward, though, Matron Wilson was at the front desk.

'Nurse Haynes, just the person I need to speak to next. Would you follow me to my office, please?'

'Er, yes, Matron. Shall I put my cape and bag away first?' Ruby enquired.

'No, no, best you bring all of your belongings and come with me,' the matron replied.

In her office, Matron Wilson sat at her large wooden desk and Ruby wondered what on earth she could want to speak to her about. She worried that maybe it was something Margaret had said, but surely Matron wouldn't concern herself with her divisive behaviour.

'Nurse, we have had an incident on Oak Ward and I want you to think very carefully and be very honest in your answers to my questions,' the matron said, and Ruby nodded slowly.

'Mr Porter ended up in a critical condition. It would seem his treatment was not changed as per the instructions that Dr Becker wrote up before going on leave this week, and worse – the dextrose–saline ran in too quickly and overloaded his circulation, making him breathless.

'Now as I understand it, you were the nurse on duty at the

time and responsible for Mr Porter's care. I have spoken to other nurses on duty last Thursday, and I'm receiving mixed information. Staff Nurse Russell tells me you enquired about changes you were making to Mr Porter's drip and that it all sounded correct. But then Nurse Allen tells me that when she started duty, Mr Porter's drip had not been changed.'

Ruby felt her pulse rate increase and beads of sweat start to form on her forehead; her lip began to tremble.

'What? No, oh my goodness, Matron, is Mr Porter going to be OK?' Ruby's voice quivered.

Chapter Sixteen

Connie

It was just after four o'clock when Connie began the last vital signs round with Phyllis before their shift ended. She was loving her time on Lavender Ward, but she had just received an envelope with her next placement and was thrilled to learn she would be going to the hospital's maternity ward for the next three months.

'Oh my God, you never got that!' Phyllis said. 'That's the one I've been hoping for.'

'I can't believe it – this is the best day. You wait till I tell Ruby. Though I think even Billie will be impressed by this. She's changed so much since she started on Pear Tree Ward. I think the children have melted her heart,' she chuckled.

'I know. I didn't think I'd ever see the day that Billie was so, I don't know . . . so motherly, I suppose. She seems to care about the patients there as if they were her own,' Phyllis said, her comment chiming with Connie's.

Would the maternity ward change her, she wondered. Would every birth remind her of those first precious moments when Martha was born?

Either way, she was already committed to the rotation, and she was excited.

'Ruby,' Connie called a little later, knocking on her sister's bedroom door. With no response, she made for Billie's room to tell her the news.

'What? You're going to love that! I almost wish I was going there with you, dear. They've got me lined up for Oak Ward from Monday. I have to chat to Ruby and see if she has any tips for me,' Billie said. 'I'll be sad to leave all my little ones behind.'

'I can imagine. You've really been enjoying it up there,' Connie said.

'Yes, well a lot of those little children remind me of my siblings, especially my baby sister, Candice. Man, that girl used to get herself into so many scrapes. So when I see children there with broken bones from climbing trees and things like that, my mind goes back to her.'

'Oh really? It must be hard being so far from her,' Connie said.

Billie nodded. 'Yeah, I miss her. Maybe once I'm fully qualified and get some money saved I can send for her to come here. Who knows, maybe she'll want to be a nurse too.'

'Wouldn't that be something? You could guide her in everything she could expect – although I'm not sure the men of Britain could handle another Benjamin woman,' Connie teased. 'Speaking of sisters, I wonder where mine has got to. It's nearly dinner time and it's not like Ruby to miss a meal.'

'Here she comes up the path now,' Billie said, peering out of the window. 'Oh wait, Connie. I think there might be something wrong. She looks like she's shaking. I think she's crying.'

The girls raced from the room.

'Ruby, where have you been? What's happened?' Connie's voice shook with worry.

Ruby tried to speak. She tried to explain what had happened that day, that past week, but she could barely get the words out between her sobs.

'Come, dear. Sit down. Now take your time and tell us what happened,' Billie's voice soothed.

In the echo of the lofty lobby, Ruby told the girls everything.

'I told Matron that Margaret said she'd take the drip out but it's my word against hers and no one saw Mr Porter without the drip . . . And now Matron has said they will have to put me on basic duties until they investigate everything. But she warned me. She said if the inquiry concludes that I was at fault, then that would be "very serious indeed". She said I would be suspended, pending dismissal,' she finished, barely daring to look at Connie and Billie, both of whom were trying but failing to hide their horror from each other.

'I'm scared. I'm so scared,' Ruby said.

'Oh sis, I can only imagine. Being a nurse has been all you've wanted for so long, how dare Margaret try to take that away from you,' Connie said, feeling as though her heart might break for Ruby. All she could think was how much Ruby had grown, not only since they'd been in England but since training had ended and she'd started working on the wards. She had become a picture of confidence and was maturing as a young woman as well as becoming an excellent, caring nurse. Looking at her sister's crumpled face, and her shattered self-belief, Connie couldn't help but think how unjust her situation was. It felt so visceral.

'But it's not about me, Connie. I'm scared for Mr Porter . . . he . . . he's so sick. They had to call the doctor to get fluid off his lungs by giving him an intravenous diuretic. They're waiting on the results of a chest X-ray to see if he has pulmonary oedema,' Ruby said, then started sobbing loudly into a handkerchief. 'What if he was to die? And . . . and . . . it would be all my fault.'

'No, no it would not, Ruby,' Billie said. 'It is not your fault and you must not take the blame for this, not now or in the future. You removed the drip, just like Dr Becker ordered; it was Margaret who reinstated it. And then she can't have taken it out even though she insisted you leave it to her. Don't you blame yourself for what she did,' Billie all but ordered her friend.

'No, but Billie, don't you see? I saw Margaret had reinstated the drip and she'd left it running so fast. I told her she shouldn't have but she didn't listen to me. She said such hurtful things that I just ran. I ran away and left my patient when he needed me, Billie. It *is* my fault. I should have stayed to make sure it was taken out or told the sister what she'd done. But I let Margaret intimidate me. And now . . . Mr Porter's so sick. And . . . it . . . it's at . . . my hands,' Ruby's reply came in fits and starts as she hyperventilated through her tears.

Connie wrapped her arms around her sister and gently rocked her. 'Shh . . . No, sis, you mustn't think like that. You mustn't, you hear me? And don't you worry. We will get through this, and we'll get through it together. Just like we always do.'

'Come, Connie, Ruby, let's go upstairs. I kept a little of my Appleton's rum back for emergencies, and I think this definitely counts. I think we could all use a drink to calm down,' Billie said.

The rest of the week passed relatively peacefully for Connie as she finished her rotation on Lavender Ward. By coincidence, Ruby had been assigned to Lavender Ward on the Change List, starting the following week, and under normal circumstances Connie would have been excitedly telling her about the other staff there and the patients that were currently on the ward; but she knew that though Ruby would be making the switch, she wouldn't be dealing with any patients.

For the rest of that week, Connie felt no joy in her job as she constantly pushed fears for Ruby to the back of her mind.

Though Matron Wilson had already interviewed Margaret over the incident, none of the girls saw her that week. After working over the weekend, she was off duty. But rumour had it that she too had landed the maternity ward for her next rotation, and Connie was already mentally preparing to give her a piece of her mind.

As the weekend came, Connie vowed to spend time with Ruby, and the sisters went to the cinema in town with Billie and Kathleen, then for milkshakes at Minstrels.

On their way into town, they were stopped by people they recognized who had been patients on the wards.

'Hello, Nurse Haynes?' a woman shopper said, stopping Connie in her tracks. 'I thought it was you, but my husband Bert here, he said how could I be sure, and I said, "Well, you don't see many of their sort around here." And I was right. It is you,' she smiled. 'You helped me recover from . . . well, you know, my *women's problems* a couple of months ago,' she said, lowering her voice in a conspiratorial fashion. 'Mrs Peacock.'

'Yes, of course, it's so good to see you, and you're looking so well,' Connie replied.

'Yes, well that's all thanks to you and the other nurses up there. I know the doctors did my surgery and all, but you girls do all of the heavy lifting afterwards.'

'Oh, thank you! Well, it's wonderful to see you again,' Connie smiled and the woman walked on.

'My, I didn't expect that. How nice! I can't believe how well she looks, and it was lovely to hear how much difference we made for her. It really makes it all worthwhile.' Connie smiled, but Ruby's head stayed down, a dark cloud seeming to follow her.

A few hours later, on their way home, a man waved frantically from the other side of the road. 'Hello!' Neither Connie, Billie or Kathleen recognized him, and Ruby was too consumed with her thoughts to notice, so the other girls smiled but continued walking.

'Nurse, nurse! You're from St Mary's, aren't you?' He started crossing the road and speaking directly to Ruby.

'Oh, Mr Rogers, I'm so sorry, I didn't see it was you,' she replied.

'Not to worry. I know you're a good-hearted soul, so I didn't think you were ignoring me,' he smiled. 'I keep meaning to come back up to the hospital, and thank you all for what you did to get me back on my feet, you know. I'm ever so grateful and you were one of the best up there.'

With all the stresses and strains of that week, it was the boost that Ruby needed. Connie looked over at her sister to see her smiling for the first time in days, and she too was bursting with pride to know that they were helping people, and to hear how much they appreciated it.

'See, Ruby, I told you. You're a wonderful nurse, don't let anyone tell you any different,' Connie said, and Ruby smiled back at her.

'Well, let's just hope Matron sees that, and I'm not stuck on basic duties forever. This week has been terrible. I'm not allowed anywhere near patients and I'm stuck cleaning. Even the other day when Mr Philips was calling out to me for help, I was told I couldn't get involved. I was so embarrassed.'

'She will, sis. She has to,' Connie said encouragingly.

'Ruby, have you seen Dr Becker around? Surely he could back you up – he knows you made the changes he instructed, doesn't he?' Billie asked.

'No, he's been on leave. So he doesn't even have any idea of what's happened to Mr Porter.'

'Look at that!' Connie interjected, pointing at a house on the corner of the street with a 'Rooms To Let' sign in the window. 'I sometimes wonder what it would be like to live out in the community, you know. I guess we can't live in the nurses' home forever.'

'I suppose in time you'll be setting up house with that good-looking man of yours,' Kathleen nudged her.

'Not before we're married!'

'Ach, get away, it won't be long before the wedding bells are ringing, of that I'm sure,' Kathleen replied, and Connie looked bashful.

'In the meantime, I wonder how much a room here might go for. Maybe we could scrape the money together and share, Ruby,' she said.

'Ugh, no . . . Get away. The horrible sods!' Kathleen spat, glaring at the sign. 'Right below "Rooms To Let" it says "No IRISH, No BLACKS, No DOGS". I've heard about this, but this is the first time I've seen it,' Kathleen explained.

'What?! How can people be so disgusting? So we rank only slightly higher than dogs to some of these people? I bet they wouldn't be thinking that if they needed to come to St Mary's for treatment. They would be glad of us then.' Billie was shocked and Connie was too.

'I told you. Some of these people *hate* us,' said Ruby sadly, and she continued walking.

Connie thought her sister cut a terribly dejected figure. But even though she understood her pain, even though she felt it deeply herself, she refused to let Ruby wallow in her anguish.

The next morning, as the girls walked home from church, Connie tried to cheer her sister. 'Devon's coming up this afternoon and he says he's taking us both out on the river. He's going to hire a little rowing boat. How about that?'

'It's OK, Connie, you go – I need some time alone anyway,' Ruby said. 'I'll be all right, and I don't want you wasting valuable time you could be spending with Devon with me hanging about the place all miserable.'

'Ruby, you know he wouldn't mind at all – you're family to Devon, and he's as upset as I am by what's happening to you. At least come for a little walk in the park with us later on.'

'No, honestly, sis, I'll be all right. Billie's around this afternoon if I need someone to talk to, though I won't. Go and see that man of yours and give him a big hug from me.' As if to reassure her, Ruby forced a smile and stroked her sister's arm.

'I just don't know what to do with Ruby,' Connie said to Devon later as he rowed them out onto the river. 'This is so deeply unfair. She's a diligent nurse and she didn't mess up the treatment, she was just intimidated by Margaret – who, incidentally, has been off work ever since this happened. I do hope Matron has spoken to her, because Ruby shouldn't be shouldering the blame for this at all.'

'The thing is, unfortunately this is how it goes up here. Ruby is a good nurse, but it's not enough to just be good. People like us, from the Caribbean? Man, we have to be exceptional to be recognized. We have to have covered all the bases to be considered beyond reproach should anything go wrong,' Devon said, cutting the oars through the water gently, barely making a splash.

'I guess you're right. I just never thought living here could possibly be so difficult – we've come with such pure hearts and a willingness to learn and fit in.'

Her sadness tugged at Devon's heart. 'Everything will be all right, Connie, you just have to learn the ropes is all. Once you all have it figured out, you'll know how you need to behave to get by.'

It turned out to be an idyllic early autumn afternoon, and as the buildings of Four Oaks melted away and they found themselves surrounded by verdant countryside, Connie started to relax a little, as though her troubles had been left behind in the town.

As Devon moored the boat, they stopped for a while and lay back in each other's arms, watching puffs of white clouds float on the breeze above.

'This is wonderful,' Connie said. A part of her still wished Ruby had taken her advice and come along, but she was also enjoying the escape and being in the arms of her sweetheart. As Devon caressed her face, they talked about their hopes and dreams for the not-too-distant future.

'You see, Connie, you're just starting to understand things up here now, and maybe this experience with Ruby . . . it's tough and very unfair, but maybe it will show you why I'm keen to get from up here and back home soon enough,' he said. 'England for sure has its benefits. Just look around us now – this is beautiful. And there are opportunities here, that can't be denied. But it isn't everything people back home have it cracked up to be.'

'I know. I just, well, it feels like I've only just arrived here and am getting settled. We've fallen in love,' she said, as Devon's arms squeezed her closer. 'And you want to go home already, when I still feel like I have things to do up here.'

'Oh no, wait, I ain't going anywhere yet, young lady. I need to earn my way back home and have enough to build a house when I get there. And besides, I won't be going until you're good and ready to come with me. Of course not.' His words went straight to Connie's heart and were as warm as his embrace.

'And then, when we're ready, whether it's up here or back home, we'll start to raise a family too. I want at least a girl and a boy, how about you?' He smiled.

'Oh, the same,' Connie said quietly, wondering to herself how on earth she would ever find the right time to tell Devon that she already had a daughter.

Suddenly Connie felt overwhelmed. It was as though she was back on the rollercoaster in Southend and it was running out of control at top speed. She wanted the future Devon was painting. She loved it. But she was also terrified of it, because the more involved they became, the more she knew she would have to reveal about herself.

'Devon, I can't stand this any longer. It's just not right or fair to you,' Connie said, sitting up to look him in the eye, and he was at first struck by the pained expression on her face.

'I have a daughter.' The words flew from Connie's mouth at such speed that even she was shocked. And then they hung there between them, like a blot on the landscape of their idyllic day and their perfect relationship.

'Wha—? Connie!' he said, shock and confusion fusing in his voice, followed by an expression she had never seen before. Was it anger? Disappointment? Disgust?

If she could have swept up her words and thrown them away, preventing Devon from hearing them, she would have done. But they were out there, and Connie realized there was no telling what those four words would do. She feared, however, that they would immediately change everything between them.

'I wanted to tell you, but Devon, they made me keep it quiet, they . . . Oh Lord, if they knew I'd told you now . . .' Despair tinged Connie's words and though she knew they didn't make sense to Devon, who was hearing her story in a jumble of broken pieces, it was all she could manage as fear over his reaction crystallized within her.

'She's called Martha, she's two, and she lives with my aunt in St Lucy. I didn't know what I was doing, Devon,' she said, shaking her head. 'I was so young. But goodness, she's the sweetest little girl.' Her angst was palpable now as she searched Devon's face for clues to what he was thinking.

His eyes were wide, staring intently at Connie as she spoke. He listened and then, when her rush of words came to an uneasy stop, he took hold of her hands and looked into her eyes.

'Connie, I don't know what to say. I'm shocked.' He shook his head slowly in disbelief. 'Not only am I taken by surprise, because I thought I knew who you were. But I'd have thought you would have told me before. I thought you knew you could trust me with your heart. Honestly, I don't quite know what to think. But right now I'm more disappointed than anything, that you didn't think you could trust me with this.'

'I'm sorry, Devon, it's just . . . I hadn't told *anyone* from home. My parents, they just wouldn't allow it. Martha . . . well, I've never really been allowed to be her mother – that would've brought too much shame on the family,' she rushed to explain.

'*Shame?* The shame of it is all this secrecy,' Devon replied. And Connie couldn't help but think of how this secret had caused her so much pain – not only in her past, but now it could very well impact her future happiness too.

Their afternoon idyll shattered, Devon rowed them back into town, saw Connie back to the hospital grounds and left to get his train home to London.

'I'm so sorry, please forgive me,' she said.

'I'll call you, Connie,' he replied; his shock and disappointment in her seemed to be ebbing away. 'I just need some time.'

'OK, I'll wait for you to call,' she said sadly as he kissed her on the forehead before he turned and walked away.

'Connie, how was your afternoon? And how is *Devv-uhn*?' Ruby all but sang Devon's name later that evening, seeming much brighter than earlier that day.

'He's OK, yes,' her sister said quietly, but Ruby immediately sensed that something was not quite right.

'What happened?' she fired off. 'This isn't like you. You're usually full of smiles after seeing him.'

'Ruby, oh man. I don't really know where to begin,' Connie said, her face taut with anxiety.

'Come, let's get some tea. I hear them all talking about it on the ward as though it cures any ill.' Ruby laughed slightly, but sensing Connie's tension, she soon stifled it.

As the kettle started to boil on the hob over a blue gas flame, Connie sat at a table in the kitchen and proceeded to tell Ruby how Devon's plans to start a family with her had left her terrified.

'I so want what he wants, Ruby. I want that future with him, and children of our own – a boy and girl too – just like he said. But I couldn't let him carry on like that. He needed to know the truth.'

Sarah Lee

Ruby handed her a steaming cup of tea, sat opposite and glared at her. 'Oh, Connie, man. What did you say?'

'I was so upset, I felt like I'd been deceiving him. I just had to tell him. I told him everything, Ruby.' Connie's voice was dull.

'You never did!' her sister exclaimed. 'Oh my goodness, oh my goodness! Connie, what did he say? How did he take it?'

'Pretty well, I suppose. I thought he would raise his voice – shout and scream at me, that he'd feel completely betrayed. But you know Devon, he barely ever gets into a rage about anything. But it was worse than that. Instead of him getting angry, he was upset. I think he was disappointed in me. Oh, Ruby, he thought he could trust me and I've kept things from him. I've trampled all over his faith in me.' Connie was sobbing now.

'Connie, you did nothing of the kind. You were protecting yourself. In fact, it wasn't only yourself you were protecting. You were protecting your whole family. I'm sure he could understand that,' Ruby soothed.

'I don't think so. Oh, I don't know . . . maybe,' Connie replied. 'He left saying he needed time to think; he said he felt like he didn't know me any more. That he knows having a child isn't a bad thing necessarily – quite a few women come up here and leave their children back at home in the Caribbean, but that's for practical reasons, not because they're hidden away from sight. I guess I'm not the girl he thought I was – I'm a mother, a woman with experience.

'Oh, Ruby! I'm so scared it will frighten him off. Whatever was I thinking, telling him? But I just couldn't stand it any longer – all the secrecy, all the separation, all the sacrifices that we have to make as young women, as young mothers. It's all so unfair,' and then Connie sobbed, burying her face in a handkerchief.

'Surely everything will be fine when you see each other again; it certainly doesn't sound as though he doesn't want anything to do with you. When will you see him next?' Ruby asked.

'I don't know, we don't have anything planned, and that's another thing – he usually sets up our next meeting each time we part. But this time all he would say is that he'd call me,' Connie explained.

'Gosh, Connie, you have got into a mess. But you know what? I think this is really hopeful. I know Devon loves you more than anything and I'm quite sure he will come to understand what's happened. You were so young when you had Martha, and I know you had expected to settle down with Cedric. Anyway, that damn fool man would have made a terrible father for Martha, so it's as well that he cleared off,' Ruby decided.

'Ruby!' Connie exclaimed. Even now, about three years later, she was not prepared for Cedric's name to be mentioned in a negative light, no matter how much he deserved it.

'I'm sorry, sis, but you know what I mean. Devon is ten times the man that Cedric was,' she said. 'Anyway, don't you worry. I think everything will be just fine – I expect he'll be in touch sooner than you know. Perhaps even tonight.' And Ruby put her arms around her sister's shoulders and hugged her tightly.

It was as though she had transferred a large helping of hope and inner strength to Connie, and her older sister smiled. She knew Ruby needed her in England. But Connie needed Ruby too, and in that moment she realized just how much.

The following day, Connie made sure she was early for her first shift on the maternity ward. She wanted time not just to meet all the staff, but to be able to spend a little extra time looking around the ward, too.

She was instantly drawn to a young mother who was sitting up in bed, nursing her newborn. 'Hello Mrs Simms,' Connie said, looking at her name board. 'How are you getting on this morning?'

'Hello nurse, yes, I'm OK. I'm finding breastfeeding pretty

tricky, but now that he's latched on, it seems to be going all right this time,' the woman said, looking down at her tiny son.

'Yes, I know, it can be challenging. I mean, that's what I hear,' Connie caught herself. 'But let me or one of the other nurses know if you still need help with it.'

'Thank you, nurse, I will,' Mrs Simms replied, looking back down at her suckling baby, and Connie's heart immediately began to swell.

She remembered how she had breastfed Martha for a couple of weeks before she had to return home and leave her daughter with her Aunt Agatha. They were the moments she remembered most fondly, especially when she got to grips with feeding and it was just the two of them in the peace of her aunt's home. Mother and baby building an infrangible bond. It made no difference what challenges life threw at her, or how far Connie was from Martha, she thought. That bond, created in those very first moments of her child's life, was the one true constant they had.

'Good morning, Nurse Haynes, Nurse Roberts, Nurse Chang. I'm Sister Harding, and I'm pleased to welcome you here to maternity. It's good to have you joining us for your next rotation and I expect you'll learn an awful lot during your time here,' the ward sister said.

'Good morning, Sister,' the girls chorused.

'I believe there's another of you scheduled to be here with us, a Nurse Allen? Has anyone seen her?'

'Morning, Sister, I'm so sorry I'm late. Matron Wilson wanted to speak with me,' Margaret said as she raced into the ward.

Connie cut her eye at Margaret, feeling utter contempt for her. But the other girl didn't seem to notice, never mind care. As they went about the duties Sister Harding set them, Connie seized her opportunity to give Margaret a piece of her mind.

'I need to speak with you,' she said.

'Oh yes, what about? Not that witless sister of yours? I'm

hoping Matron sends her packing for what she did to that poor man,' Margaret snarled.

'You know what you did, Margaret, and you better own up to it,' Connie seethed, her uncharacteristic anger startling the Hampshire girl. 'How could you jeopardize someone else's health like that? And Ruby's prospects?'

Margaret maintained her surly air. 'I didn't do anything, and I'm not admitting to anything either. Your sister can go back to where she belongs for all I care, and you with her!'

Connie realized she was wasting her time. People like Margaret only lived to cause others pain; she would never do anything to help Ruby.

She went about her work and was largely able to stay away from Margaret for the rest of the morning.

By lunchtime, Connie was already feeling pretty tired after a busy morning, but she had co-ordinated her lunch break to co-incide with Ruby's and after a good first morning, she met her sister in the dining room. She was bursting with updates from the first few hours on the ward, but seeing Ruby's downcast face, she didn't dare share her glee.

'How was your morning?' she asked, even though she feared the answer.

'Well, they really do have me doing all the rubbish,' Ruby said sadly. 'Sister Lambert seems nice, and she was sympathetic, but she said all she could let me do was cleaning jobs. So I've been emptying bed pans and washing up kidney dishes the whole morning.'

'Oh, but Ruby, that's what they had me do when I was first on Lavender too,' Connie said, trying to be encouraging, but her words fell flat.

'Yes, but that was right after we qualified; we're now over three months in, and Kathleen and Jean were caring for patients and learning all sorts of new things today. I'm not even allowed to speak to anyone up there. I've got to go back soon, but I need some fresh air. I'm going for a walk.'

'I'll come with you,' Connie said, getting up.

'No, thank you sis, but I need some time alone,' she said, and Connie barely knew what to do. All she did know was that this was not her gregarious sister.

'Penny for your thoughts,' Billie said, as she took the chair Ruby had just vacated.

'You wouldn't want to know – but I'll tell you this much, they ain't Christian. That wretch Margaret! She's wrecking Ruby's chances here and my sister just ain't herself right now,' Connie said, infuriated by the situation.

'Oh I know. I can barely believe what's happening to her. But I don't intend to let Margaret get away with this. Leave it with me, Connie, I have an ace up my sleeve,' Billie said mysteriously.

Chapter Seventeen

Billie

Injustice was something that weighed heavily on Billie, especially when, as in Ruby's case, it had come about as a result of someone's hatefulness.

As she got onto Oak Ward after lunch, she checked on Mr Porter, and rage built within her.

It wasn't only for Ruby. If Margaret hadn't reinstated his drip with her usual arrogance and rudeness, she thought, Mr Porter wouldn't be so sick, and Ruby wouldn't be facing possible dismissal. Billie felt Margaret shouldn't be working in the hospital, least of all on the maternity ward. What if her next incident of spitefulness and poor nursing put a baby at risk?

Billie couldn't let that happen. Matron needed to know the truth about the incident with Mr Porter, and Billie only had to wait two hours before she could set the wheels in motion.

'Dr Becker . . . hello.' A touch of shyness threw Billie off guard as she saw the doctor later that afternoon.

'Nurse Benjamin!' he said, turning around, his smile catching Billie rather by surprise. It wasn't only politeness, nor the patriarchal way in which a man in a senior position in the hospital might look upon a young trainee. Something between his gentle eyes and his warm smile conveyed that he was genuinely pleased to see her.

'It's good to see you. I take it your next rotation is here on Oak?' he enquired.

'Yes, Doctor, I started just today,' she replied.

'Oh well, you won't find it too different to what you're used to. I'd wager a lot of the men up here are no more mature than the little ones you left on Pear Tree.' He laughed heartily at his own joke.

Billie looked at him, unsure how to respond, but then she realized she should laugh too, so gave an affected giggle. 'I can only imagine,' she said. But she quickly changed the subject, to broach the topic concerning her most. She *had* to do something. 'Doctor, I wanted to speak to you about Mr Porter over there.'

'Ah yes, he's in a poorly state, unfortunately. Terrible business that went on. I just couldn't for the life of me understand what happened after I went off duty. I'm sure I saw the nurse that was here remove his drip, just like I'd asked,' he said.

'You *saw* her do it?' Billie asked. 'The nurse, I mean.'

'Yes, yes, no sooner had I written it down than I'd told the nurse what to do and she had made the change,' Dr Becker said.

'Doctor,' Billie pressed. 'Could I ask you something? It would be a wonderful favour to me. You see, that nurse is my friend, and now she's in trouble. Matron Wilson has removed her from normal duties while she investigates and she says that if Mr Porter's condition has been caused by Ruby's, er, I mean Nurse Haynes' negligence, she could be dismissed. But it's not her fault – she did take out the drip, and you saw that. The trouble is she was later bullied by another nurse, Margaret Allen. She's real nasty, and she has been bullying Ruby for months now. She hates us all because . . . well, I suppose because we're from the Caribbean. She seems to think she's better than us. So Nurse Allen overrode what Nurse Haynes had done, and reattached Mr Porter's drip. Nurse Haynes tried to talk to her, she showed her your notes and Nurse Allen said she'd see to it but she was so abusive to Nurse Haynes that she didn't know what to do, she was terribly upset and fled the ward. But, Doctor, she's devastated about Mr Porter; she blames herself for him being so ill.'

Dr Becker listened to Billie's every word. And as she spoke, his expression turned from friendly and relaxed to one of horror and outrage.

'Nurse, this is utterly horrendous. Mistakes sadly happen. But this – this is different. Personal issues should never come in the way of providing care, and putting a patient at risk in this way is absolutely intolerable. I am due to see Matron Wilson about this incident, she left me a note, but I've only just returned to duty today. Still, I had no idea this was going on in the background.' Dr Becker's normally calm countenance was now jagged at the edges, his anger building.

'I'm not entirely surprised, racism can be insidious. It can hide, stealthily, in plain sight. And before you know it, a whole nation, a continent even, can be corrupted by vile, seeping intolerance. I saw it happen before my very eyes as the Nazis started marching across Europe. Nurse, I shall speak to Matron Wilson right away. Thank you for informing me of this. I will update you once I have spoken to her.

'We can't do much more than we are already doing to help Mr Porter, but let's hope we can at least help your friend, and remove this other woman and her vile poison from the heart of our hospital.'

'Thank you, Doctor. I really appreciate your help,' Billie said.

Ruby's sadness continued to cast a shadow over the rest of the week for some of the trainee nurses, and Billie didn't mention her conversation with Dr Becker to her for fear of raising her hopes before she had heard anything further herself. But as the week passed, Billie wondered if Matron would do anything at all.

She had only fleetingly seen Dr Becker, and with busy ward rounds she didn't have a chance to speak to him again.

By Friday, Billie was wondering how she could join with Connie in cheering Ruby up for the weekend.

'Where's Ruby?' she asked her at tea time.

'You know, I'm not too sure. These days she could be almost anywhere,' Connie said, shaking her head. 'I just don't know what to do.'

Minutes later the two girls were walking along the path from the dining room when someone flew towards them like a whirlwind.

'YOU! Where's that nasty little sister of yours, where is she?' Margaret roared, pushing Connie in the chest with both hands.

Billie was taken aback as she saw Connie grapple with Margaret to handle the other girl's unfettered rage.

'Where is the little bitch? I don't know who in the hell she thinks she's playing with. Her and her lies! She's had me fired!' she ranted as angry, bitter tears stained her incandescent face.

'Get your hands off her. Anything that's happened to you, you've brought on yourself!' Billie shouted back at her.

Margaret took off, running from the hospital grounds, but hurling a promise in her wake: 'You just wait – when I find her, I'll see to her. Nobody does this to me!'

Connie and Billie looked at each other, then turned on their heels and ran to the nurses' home, hoping they'd find Ruby before Margaret did. As they raced through the lobby, Miss Bleakly scowled. 'Such unladylike behaviour!' she shouted after them.

'Ruby, you here?' Connie called along the corridor lined with the nurses' rooms, then banged on her little sister's bedroom door. But there was no reply.

Running downstairs, they came under Miss Bleakly's glare once more, and just as they were about to run out of the door, they came to a sudden halt.

Ruby had emerged from the corridor that led to Matron Wilson's office.

'Ruby!' Connie said in a fluster.

The younger girl looked confused to see her sister and friend, angst lining their faces as each girl caught her breath.

'I'm OK,' Ruby said, even though she didn't quite know what they were concerned about. 'Matron Wilson. She's said the investigation has been concluded and they know it wasn't my fault. Not exactly anyway. She ticked me off for not reporting Margaret for reinstating Mr Porter's drip, and said I should have stayed to make sure it was removed again. She said I needed to have the courage of my convictions.

'I wanted to tell her that it wasn't that I didn't believe in myself, but that Margaret's comments had upset me so much. And,' she said, turning slightly towards Billie, 'it seems as though I have that nice doctor to thank for this. Matron said Dr Becker had come forward, he told her he had seen me implement his instructions, and that he understands that the real culprit was another nurse on the ward. She said they had already spoken to Margaret and she has been disciplined.'

'Disciplined? Not just that, Margaret's been dismissed,' Connie said. Ruby exhaled a long, deep breath, and Billie saw a look of relief wash over her friend. 'Oh Lord, I'm so happy. Not about Margaret being sacked – I take no joy in that.'

'Why ever not?' Billie said. 'That nasty bitch. She deserves just what she got, worse probably.'

'It's just not Christian, Billie,' Connie said. 'Leave her to the Lord, because remember, Romans 12:19 says: "Vengeance is mine, I will repay". We shouldn't carry on with vengeance in our hearts; the Lord will always take care of things, you only need to pray for his guidance.'

'I don't know if it was the Lord exactly but regardless, I'm relieved for you, Ruby. And I'm so glad Dr Becker was as good as his word.'

'You spoke to him?' Ruby asked, aghast. 'I don't believe it! Billie, you're so bold.'

'I guess so,' Billie replied.

'Well, I'm real glad you are, but I don't know how you do it,' Ruby said.

'I just couldn't let you take the blame for poor Mr Porter's unfortunate position, dear, and Dr Becker is a nice man, I was sure he would help. At least, I hoped he would,' Billie replied.

'Thank you. I'm so grateful to you, and to Dr Becker too. Matron said she will speak to Sister Lambert for me and get me back on regular duties. She said, "Nursing requires confidence and you have to be prepared to advocate for your patients," but she said she was really happy to reinstate me because aside from this incident, she had heard such good reports about my first rotation. Can you believe it?' Ruby beamed.

'Well, yes I can, Ruby – you're a far better nurse than I am,' Connie replied as the three girls walked upstairs and into the sitting room, their panic easing now the day's drama was over and Margaret would no longer prove problematic.

Opening the door, though, they found Grace in the sitting room, her eyes red and her face blotchy with tears.

'Wait, what's happened, Grace?' Ruby enquired.

'You! It's all your fault,' she cried.

'What?' Ruby was flabbergasted.

'It's Margaret,' Lin said. 'She's been dismissed.'

'Yes, we know – she tried to blame Ruby when she was the one who completely disregarded a doctor's instructions, because she always seems to know better.' Connie's annoyance manifested itself in sarcasm and Billie couldn't help but be impressed by her steeliness. She figured it was most unlike her friend, but then recognized Connie was jumping to her sister's defence, and would walk over hot coals to do so.

'Matron Wilson has found out the truth and that is why Margaret's rightly been sent packing. Just because you're from here, and you're from a rich family, doesn't mean you can treat people how you like, or put patients at risk like that,' Connie continued.

'But you don't understand,' Grace protested bitterly. 'You might not like her but she was my friend and she was never the person she made herself out to be. It was all just talk. She isn't from a rich family – well, they're not any more. They used to live in a big house, but her dad has been made bankrupt. So she needed this job, just like the rest of us here.'

'But she always made out like she was from some kind of nobility,' Ruby said slowly, her face a picture of confusion.

'I know, I know,' Grace said. 'I used to think she was daft for doing it, but she seemed to think it made people listen to her more.'

'You know what? She just sounds like your typical bully if you ask me,' Billie interjected. 'She knew she was nothing special. Instead of facing up to her own inadequacies she tried to make herself feel bigger and more important by making someone else feel small. I don't know how anyone could feel sorry for someone like that, not at all.'

'Connie, there's a call for you, I think it's that fella of yours,' Kathleen said, popping her head around the door, and was then taken by surprise when she saw Grace.

'Thank you,' Connie said, looking flustered, then she raced downstairs.

As Billie and Ruby recounted the events of the past hour, Kathleen couldn't help but echo their sense of relief that Margaret had been let go.

'She's a bad penny, that one. I'll wager she'll be all right though, people like her always land on their feet in the end,' Kathleen said ruefully.

'Ruby, I'm so sorry,' Grace said to her. 'I didn't realize all of this had gone on, or quite how spiteful Margaret was towards you. I knew she didn't like you, but I didn't really know why, and I felt like I had to be her friend as no one else here seemed to like her.'

Billie looked at Grace, her face red and blotchy with tears, and then at Ruby, to see a glimmer of forgiveness in her eyes. 'It's all right, Grace. I understand. We're all here just trying to get along in life,' Ruby told the timid girl.

An hour later, Billie and Ruby were still in the sitting room when Connie returned.

'Girl, I thought you would never get off that phone! I guess you had to tell Devon the news about Ruby too,' Billie said.

'Partly. I was relieved he called, so I didn't want to hang up until I felt all was well.' Connie exhaled deeply, then proceeded to explain to Billie how she'd told Devon about Martha.

'Wait, what? How did he take it? He's OK, right? I'm sure he is,' Billie quizzed.

'He needed time to let the news sink in, I guess. I don't know, he seemed to be OK just now, thankfully. He wants to see me at the weekend,' Connie explained.

'Well then, Connie, that sounds fine. He's a big man and he always strikes me as open-minded. I'm sure all will be fine. It sounds like he's accepted it already.' Billie did her best to sound encouraging.

'Yes, sis, I agree,' Ruby added and a relieved smile crept across Connie's face.

On the ward the next day, Billie keenly awaited Dr Becker's rounds so she could let him know the good news about Ruby.

'Doctor?' she said, as he finished his assessment of Mr Porter. 'I wanted to thank you. Whatever you said to Matron Wilson, it made a whole lot of difference. It saved my friend Ruby's job. She's a wonderful nurse and she cares so much, I'm so happy to see her going back to work as normal. The other nurse was dismissed.

'I don't know how I'll ever be able to thank you. But if there is some way in which I could repay your kindness, well, just let me know.' As she said this, Billie felt the kind of awkwardness that was quite alien to her; it was as though Connie and Ruby's deference for the doctor had rubbed off on her.

'Oh nurse, that's marvellous news. I could not have lived with myself if I had allowed such an injustice to stand,' said Dr Becker, tucking a pen into the inside pocket of his blue-grey flannel suit.

'I take no pleasure in seeing nurses dismissed – the National Health Service needs all the able hands it can find to increase healthcare provision for the people of Four Oaks, as well as towns up and down Britain. But I would venture this is best for all involved. It is certainly best in the name of all that is decent – I've seen how racism can spread like a cancer. But, most importantly, it is the best outcome for our patients. They must never be afflicted by high-handed and negligent behaviour from the people that are meant to care for them. As for thanking me – there really is no need for you to repay me in any way.' Dr Becker shook his head. 'That is, unless . . . Well, I wonder if you might . . . I . . . well, I was thinking . . . do you ever go out? With, erm, gentlemen, I mean,' he stammered.

Billie was confused, until she saw the intent with which Dr Becker had locked her with his gaze.

'Wait – Dr Becker, are you asking me on a date?' Billie replied quietly, a little surprised, but with an unexpected fizzle of excitement in her tummy. 'Of course I do, I mean I have done. No, I would love to,' she said, absent-mindedly tucking a few wavy strands of hair behind her right ear and fixing him with her cat-like eyes as she took in his kindly face and slightly dishevelled brown hair.

'I don't want you to think that this was in any way a condition of my assisting you, Nurse Benjamin. It's just, well, by way of explanation, I have seen how you relate to people here. You have a good, honest heart, and I'd be honoured if you would come to dinner sometime.' His face softened. 'At my house, I mean, so do let me know if there's anything you don't eat. I've got used to rustling up a few dishes in the past few years. And of course with rationing ending a couple of months back – well, I can double up and use four ounces of butter now!' he joked. 'I'm working this weekend but I'm on early shifts, so how about Sunday for dinner? I could pick you up at seven o'clock.

'Oh, and I hope you don't fear I think of you as a certain kind of girl – you can, of course, bring a chaperone with you,' he added.

Billie smiled, charmed not only by the doctor's joviality but also his honourable, if old-fashioned, nature. She was quite sure she didn't need to take a chaperone with her – she wouldn't want anyone cramping her style. But the mere fact that he had suggested this made her feel as though he considered her a lady.

'That sounds wonderful. I would love to,' she said.

'Well, I am truly looking forward to it, Nurse Benjamin,' he said, then caught himself, the formality of the statement too much even for this relatively formal man.

'Billie. I think you should probably call me Billie,' she said.

'Ezra.' He smiled gently with a look of relief on his face as her comment dissolved the awkwardness between them. 'It's very good to meet you, Billie,' he added.

'You too.' She smiled back, her eyes sweeping up to lock with his. 'It's probably best that I meet you in town on Sunday – how about outside the church?' Billie said. 'I don't think Matron Wilson would be too impressed were she to find out that we were . . . well, you know. And I can just imagine how the other girls would talk, too.'

'Yes, that sounds a very wise suggestion. That is what we shall do,' he said, and as he left the ward, Billie was sure she noted a certain spring in his step. She certainly felt her own afternoon had livened up.

I've got to call Esme – she won't believe a doctor has asked me on a date!

For the rest of the day Billie tried to carry on with her duties as normal – serving up lunch, doing drugs rounds, checking on drips, preparing patients for discharge and beds for admissions – but she couldn't stop thinking about the conversation she'd had earlier.

'What's got you looking so jolly?' Phyllis enquired later, Billie clearly revealing more than she realized of the excitement she was feeling.

'Oh, it's nothing, I'm just happy in my work,' she said brightly, keeping close counsel. It was all Billie could do, though, not to mention her news to Connie or Ruby later. They were her closest friends there. But something about this dinner date, and whatever might come from it, felt risky, and as though it should be kept under wraps, at least for now. Besides, she thought, why tell everyone about something that may never develop. Dinner was one thing, but would he really be keen on her, a nurse, in the longer term?

It was rare that Billie suffered from a crisis of confidence, especially where men were concerned. But *this* man was so different to any she had ever known. First of all, he seemed to have seen more to her than just her body – although, she mused, that was no great surprise as the nurses' uniform did little for anyone's figure. But he had said he saw her heart, that it was 'a good, honest heart', and this appeared to appeal to him. It was something she had never been told by a man before, even though she cared deeply about others.

As the weekend arrived, she thought she might need an excuse as to why she would be busy on Sunday, but Ruby was working a late shift, and Connie was in London seeing Devon.

Looking at her reflection in the waist-length mirror in her room, she thought that although Ezra might not have been as taken by her curves as he was by her heart, dressed as she was, he surely couldn't miss them either.

Smoothing out the lines of her dark red pencil dress, she slicked on Revlon's Certainly Red lipstick, which was a close match in colour, used a pencil to line her eyes into a feline flick and feathered block mascara onto her lashes.

As she got to the church, at just after seven o'clock, the doctor was there waiting for her in a pale blue Morris Minor.

'Hello, nurs— er, Billie. It's so good to see you. How are you?' He smiled broadly.

'I'm well, thank you. I've been really looking forward to this evening,' she said, placing her right hand gently on his thigh as she turned to him and fixed him with a look that said far more than the doctor was anticipating.

Clearing his throat, he turned the key to start the car's engine.

'You didn't care to bring anyone with you?' he asked.

'No, I'm sure I can trust you to behave yourself. Now you just have me to worry about,' Billie giggled, as Ezra laughed a little nervously and kept his eyes on the road, leaving Billie unsure how to take his reaction to her slightly suggestive joke.

Twenty minutes later, they were at his home, a neat end-of-terrace house with a light grey painted fence running around a patchwork front garden.

'This is all yours?' she asked, stepping into the narrow hallway.

'Yes. It's nothing grand, but it's quiet. I've lived in the city before, you see, and I've realized I'm much more suited to suburban life on the edge of a market town.' Ezra took Billie's jacket and showed her into the living room, where he invited her to sit on a green sofa before sitting down next to her.

'Did you live in London?' she said excitedly.

'For a little while, I did, yes, I lived in the East End when I first came to England. It was just the sort of community I needed back then. There are quite a lot of other Jews there. People would go to synagogue on Saturdays, there were Jewish theatres and even street signs were in Yiddish. It was a friendly and welcoming community, despite everything. But I arrived here in 1943, and much of the area had been badly bombed, so I didn't stay in London for long at all,' he sighed.

'Oh, you're Jewish. I don't think I've met anyone Jewish before. Though yes, I heard it was terrible during the war,' she said.

'Let me get you a drink – would you like some lemonade? Tea? Or I have a new drink, called Babycham – it seems to be pretty popular. Now it does have a little alcohol in it,' he warned, leaving for the kitchen across the hall.

'I'd like to try that,' Billie said.

Moments later, he returned with a glass of golden bubbles for Billie, and a glass of beer for him, which they clinked in a toast. 'Cheers!'

'Ooh, this is tasty,' she said. 'So where did you come from before you lived in London?'

'I grew up in Groningen in the Netherlands. It's a city in the north of the country, about 200 miles from the border with Germany,' he said.

Billie looked deep into Ezra's steely blue eyes as he talked, and she observed him in a way she hadn't done before. She noted a sadness to him, and the delicate crow's feet that had started forming at the corners of those deep blue pools, giving one of a few signs that he was perhaps older than she had realized.

'How old are you?' she quizzed.

'Oh dear, I may have given all my secrets away too soon,' he smiled, and Billie saw a few more lines deepen around his eyes. 'I would guess I am considerably older than you, so I would quite understand if you felt it inappropriate and asked me to drive you home now. Although I have prepared a lovely supper for us so you really should stop and try it first.'

Billie laughed. 'Come on, how old are you?' she pressed.

'I'm thirty-six years old. Well, not old. I like to think of it as experienced,' he chuckled and Billie joined him.

'I wasn't expecting that!' she said. 'You're twelve years older than me – whatever would your neighbours say? And Matron. I'm sure Matron Wilson would have an awful lot to say about that!' she added dramatically, and Ezra found himself becoming ever more enchanted by her.

'The good news is, if I've learned one thing in my very many years on this earth, it's how to cook. I got hold of a rather popular cookbook actually, *French Country Cooking*. So we're having potato and watercress soup, then roast beef with dauphinois for dinner.'

'Oh, you're very international,' Billie said.

The meal did not disappoint, from the soup to Billie's last spoonful of dessert, and sitting together at a small table in his kitchen also gave them time to talk and exchange stories about their lives. She discovered that Ezra had left Groningen to escape the Nazi invasion of the city, and the deportation of Jews. As an immigrant, arriving on British shores with a suitcase loaded with not only her clothes, but her hopes and dreams, Billie could barely imagine the heart-rending circumstances that had brought Ezra to Britain as a refugee.

'My goodness. That must have been dreadful!' she said, sensing that she had started to unravel just a little of the sadness she'd caught in Ezra's eyes earlier.

'Europe's dark history. It was a terrible period, and something I hope none of us will ever, *ever* have to endure again. I lost my wife, Hannah, and Elijah, my baby son during the war,' he said bleakly, his gaze falling to the table as he momentarily bit his lip, as though to ward off the pain that still burned within.

'It's part of the reason I went to see Matron Wilson the other day. When you told me about how vile that nurse had been towards your friend. I just couldn't abide it – the hatred she exhibited, I mean. It reminded me of the hate that ignited in our community in the 1940s. Before that, Groningen was wonderful – in fact racial tolerance seemed rather redundant a concept. Everyone just lived side by side . . .' Billie nodded, her face tensing and her mood darkening momentarily.

'I'm sorry about your family. That must have been heartbreaking for you,' she said, but Ezra waved his hand as though to bat away his memories.

'It's not something I like to talk about. I only felt you should know that much at least. But Billie, we must remain positive,' he said, his tone already changed, more upbeat, and Billie considered that his keeping the conversation in perpetual motion relieved him from dwelling on his difficult past. 'The Nazis – they didn't win the war. And that nurse – Nurse Allen?' he said, searching Billie's face for confirmation. 'She didn't win either. If we hadn't remained hopeful during the war, we would have long perished. Also, the world has changed so much since then, and that gives me faith for the future,' he concluded, leaving Billie touched by the sentiment of his words and the hope in his heart.

'I agree. You always have to have faith,' she said, optimism filling the space between them as she caught Ezra smiling back at her.

She realized there was much more depth to Ezra than she had found in any man she had met before. Not only that, but over the course of the evening he was challenging her to think more deeply about the new world she was inhabiting and perhaps even to better understand her place in it.

'Thank you for a lovely evening,' she said many hours later, as Ezra helped her into her jacket in the hallway. Then she turned towards him and waited. If Billie knew anything about men, she knew this was the time – at least a goodnight kiss was inevitable. She took a step towards him, looked at his lips, then her eyes flicked up towards his and she waited.

'Can I drop you back at the nurses' home? I can stop right around the corner so no one sees us, but I really don't like the idea of you walking all the way back from town on your own,' he said, fumbling in his pocket for car keys and then reaching past her to the front door.

Billie was taken aback. She'd never met a man who hadn't raced to become intimate with her; at the very least to kiss her.

It then occurred to her that perhaps Ezra didn't like her, not in that way at least. But she found it confusing; he seemed so keen and comfortable in her company otherwise.

She spent much of the drive back contemplating what could be going on, while Ezra continued chatting until he realized he was doing most of the talking.

'I would love to see you again,' he said, as they arrived in the dark lane beside the nurses' home and he turned off the car's headlights.

'You would? I mean, I would too. Like to see you again, that is,' Billie said. She had really enjoyed the evening and getting to know Ezra. His gentle nature and his background, his story, were fascinating to her. She felt as though there was something so wonderfully different about him. He was an intelligent man with a really charming manner.

'Well, it looks like that is what we shall do then,' he smiled, then took her hand and kissed the back of it.

Chapter Eighteen

Ruby

Ever since her close shave with dismissal Ruby had been keen to show just what a committed nurse she was set to be, and routinely arrived half an hour early for her shift.

'Morning, Staff Nurse,' she said as Ruth arrived on the ward later that week.

'Look at you, all very formal,' Ruth said.

'Yes, I'm trying to be all present and correct,' Ruby replied. 'I don't want anyone here to say I'm not putting my best foot forward.'

'Far from it – I've been hearing all kinds of good things about you, since everything got sorted out with that dreadful girl. What was her name again?' Ruth pulled a face.

'Margaret.' Ruby shuddered, her facial expression mirroring Ruth's. 'Yes, that whole thing was terrible. Praise the Lord, the patient was OK in the end. I hear he went home a couple of days ago.'

'Ah that's a relief! I can't imagine what it would have been like to have that hanging over you,' Ruth said.

'I was very worried about what would happen to him. But he's better and things are much better around here now. I've been enjoying it on this ward too,' Ruby said.

'You have? That's good, I'm usually on Pear Tree Ward, but

they asked me to come here to help out for a few days as they said it's very busy,' Ruth explained.

And it wasn't long before Ruby could see why. After a few new admissions, every bed on the ward was full, plus there were a number of emergency cases that the staff dealt with that day.

But Ruby took it all in her stride.

'Mrs Robertson, you must stay in bed. The doctor has ordered bed rest for you, and bed rest is what you're going to get. I know you're used to running around after five children but not for the foreseeable future,' she said, tucking the patient into bed.

'Oh, nurse, I can't keep on in here, it ain't right. I know that my Johnny will be at a loss as to what to do with the kids. It's a good job my neighbour, Mrs Lyons, is looking in on them. I know she can at least get them an evening meal. But I can't be staying in here for much longer,' the woman pleaded.

'We plan to send you home when you're well again. So the sooner you stop worrying about everyone else and set your mind to getting better, the sooner you'll be back taking care of the family,' Ruby said.

'Oh all right, nurse,' Mrs Robertson exhaled in resignation. 'I'm so worried about them, but you know best, and I know you have my welfare at heart.'

Ruby smiled, not only pleased to see her patient relaxing, but also at what she had said. She was finally back to doing what she loved, and her patients knew she cared for them too.

Next, she went over to assist Mrs Bowes with her meal, as she had broken her wrist.

'There you go, I hear the soup is good today,' she said, holding up a spoonful so Mrs Bowes could sip it. She paused to look at the bloat of swollen skin on the woman's face and black-purple bruising around her right eye that had come up since she'd been admitted the previous day.

'We'll get you all mended again, Mrs Bowes, you wait and see.

And then I don't want to hear of you having fallen down the stairs again, you hear?' Ruby encouraged.

Her bruised eye swollen shut, the woman looked at her out of the other eye, and Ruby saw an unfathomable sadness within.

Later, Ruth took Ruby to one side. 'That woman. I think I've seen her before. The one you were feeding the soup.'

'Mrs Bowes?' Ruby asked.

'Yes, I think she was black and blue the last time I saw her too. One of her sons was admitted to Pear Tree with a broken collarbone. I'm sure neither of them got their injuries accidentally.' Ruth gave Ruby a knowing look.

'What? Really? I wonder why would they say that, then.' Ruby was bemused.

'Well, you haven't seen Mr Bowes yet, have you?' Ruth said flatly. 'He's a big brute of a man and girl, I tell you, if he should ever put his hand on you, you would know.'

'You're kidding me!' Ruby's shock was obvious. 'You think he did that to them? But why?'

'You haven't seen this kind of thing before? Sadly, it can be quite common – some men like to assert themselves over their women. Over the whole family. I don't know, but perhaps it makes them feel bigger, more of a man or something, and this is the end result. I've seen it happen at home too, but I don't know, it might be even more commonplace here,' Ruth explained. 'It's a terrible thing.'

'It is,' Ruby said thoughtfully. She wasn't just surprised, but saddened that a family could experience such turmoil. And it was a feeling that stuck with her not only for the rest of the day, but for the whole weekend.

It was Monday morning before Ruby was able to catch up with her sister at breakfast time, and soon Billie joined them at the table too.

225

'But wait a minute, where have you sprung from suddenly, Billie?' Ruby said. 'I ain't seen you in . . . what? It must be three or four days. Not even at dinner.'

'Well, you were working all weekend, weren't you, while I've been relaxing,' Billie said grandly, but her smile was enigmatic. 'I've been around, I've just been busy is all.'

'Busy? What, too busy to eat? You must be eating somewhere, and busy with *someone*,' Ruby said, raising a laugh from Connie.

'So you saw Devon? How is that lovely man?' Billie asked, neatly moving the conversation on.

'He was OK, I think. He said he had just needed some time to let my news settle in,' Connie explained.

'Not only that. He said he didn't think any less of you and he still loved you,' Ruby butted in.

'Yes, he did say that too.' Connie tried to sound upbeat, but her tone was flat.

'I would try not to fret, Connie. His response must be pretty normal – it would have been a shock for him to hear. I expect he just needed time to come to terms with everything,' Billie said.

'Yes, sis, it will be all right,' Ruby agreed. 'Right, I need to get off to the ward.' And all three girls made their way in different directions along paths around the hospital grounds.

'Hello, darling, are you one of them from up on Lavender?' a dishevelled-looking porter called to Ruby as she started up the stairs to the ward. She turned and took in his unshaven face and scruffy, ash-blond hair.

'Yes, I'm going up there now,' Ruby replied. 'Do you need something?'

'Well, since yer offering, like. The name's Archie Bannister. Want to have some fun?' He winked, looking her up and down.

'Fun? In Four Oaks? Well, I'd be interested in that. My friend Billie is always saying that this town is lacking any real fun,' Ruby began innocently, before realizing Archie's interest wasn't in the surrounding town.

'I meant fun with me . . . like a date. I've seen you around here a bit and I keep thinking I'd like to take you out and show you a good time. How about we meet up on Thursday – I hear there's a new film coming at the cinema if you fancy it?' Archie grinned and Ruby noticed his gaze focus on her bust.

'Oh,' Ruby said. She wasn't exactly enamoured by Archie's chat-up lines, nor his approach, but she also felt a tingle of excitement that a young man was asking her on a date. 'I didn't realize you were asking me out. Well, if you promise to behave yourself, I guess I might be interested in going out with you,' she said, feeling pleased with herself that she was open, yet keeping him in his place. 'I'm not a free-and-easy type you know.'

'I'm sure you're not. You're beautiful, though, and I'd love to take you out on the town, you know.'

The pair set a date, and Ruby showed Archie onto the ward and to the patient he was due to take to theatre.

'I'll see you, then,' he said, his eyes following her bottom as she walked away.

Ruby was in a dizzy state as she went around the ward. Excitement sparked inside and she daydreamed much of the afternoon away thinking about Archie and what he had said to her.

An English boy – interested in me. Imagine!

It was all she could do to focus on her patients. But Ruby was a committed nurse, and she wouldn't let her private passions get in the way of her work entirely.

As visiting time began, Ruby ushered families in to see patients. She was struck by a burly man in a navy donkey jacket who appeared at the front desk, his dark hair flopping over a jagged scar on his forehead.

'I'm here to see Tilly Bowes.' His countenance was stiff and his voice gruff, not leaving an ounce of room for congeniality.

'Are you Mr Bowes?' Ruby enquired.

'Who'd you think? Unless she's got some fancy man,' he bristled. Then muttered: 'But who'd have her?'

'Oh . . . OK, I'll show you to her bed,' Ruby stammered, unaccustomed to dealing with such an abrasive character.

As soon as Mrs Bowes saw her husband appear, she melted. But it was not desire Ruby could see on her face; instead, she saw dread and fear. It was as though a dark cloud had descended over the woman's bed and she became a quivering mess before Ruby's eyes, her skin turning pale aside from her bruising.

'Are you OK, Mrs Bowes?' she enquired.

'Er . . . yes. Yes, I'm fine. It's OK, love.' She forced a smile.

'You can leave now,' Mr Bowes ordered and Ruby stepped away, but she tried to look busy with other patients and stay close enough to hear what was going on.

'When you getting out of this place? I need you home, woman,' Mr Bowes told his wife.

'I don't know, they say I'm not quite well enough yet,' Mrs Bowes whimpered.

'Don't give me that, this is about your husband and your children. You do remember you have nippers to care for, don't ya?' he said, then leaned over her bed and Ruby could just about see him grabbing the woman's jaw, forcing her head towards him.

'Look at me – you get yourself sorted and back home sharpish, else there'll be hell to pay, do you hear?' And with that he stormed out of the ward, and Ruby could almost see the dark cloud follow him.

'Are you OK?' Ruby asked, rushing over to the woman's bedside. She observed red marks on her jaw, a perfect imprint of Mr Bowes' large hand.

'I'm fine, nurse,' the woman said, as boldly as she could muster, despite her voice being reed thin. 'But I do need to get home now, I'm dreadfully worried about my children and my husband was just saying how he misses me. He really needs me at home. Can you arrange for me to be discharged, please?'

'But Mrs Bowes,' Ruby interjected. 'You're still not well enough, and you shouldn't be going home just because of what he said. You shouldn't let him bully you like that.'

'No, I'm not, not at all,' she laughed weakly. 'I need to leave and that's that. You can't stop me, you know. You're here to help people, not hold them against their will.'

Ruby thought for a moment, struck by the fear that she could plainly see on Mrs Bowes' face. She knew it was all because of her husband – he had threatened her, just as Ruby was sure he did often. Ruby wanted to do something, to talk the woman out of leaving the hospital. But she stopped herself, remembering Sister Shaw's warnings during class that it wasn't their place to get involved in anything more than a patient's medical care, and Ruby was not about to get into trouble again.

'I do wish you'd reconsider, Mrs Bowes, but as you seem to have made up your mind, I'll speak to Sister and check if you need any further medication to take with you,' she said sadly.

By the end of Ruby's shift, Mrs Bowes had already headed for home.

'I so wish there was more I could have done. I wish I'd stopped her from leaving, Ruth,' she said as they walked through the hospital grounds.

'That's the trouble, you couldn't have done any more. There's no love left in these marriages. It's as though these women shack up with the first man to show them interest, then get lumbered with a string of children and they see that as their lot in life. Some are lucky, and their husband treats them good, but unfortunately some are not.' Ruth's comments weighed heavily on Ruby's usually joyful state of mind.

Unease and a sense of injustice nagged at her throughout the evening and when she was alone in her room, a tsunami of thoughts rumbled through her mind. So much had happened that day and she turned the events over and over. She had been touched by Archie's proposal, but then Ruth's comments rang in her ears.

What if Archie was one of those sorts of men? He was more than a bit rough around the edges, she thought. Maybe *she* was about to hook up with the first man to show her interest. And there and then, Ruby decided she wouldn't go out with Archie; she recognized that she deserved better and promised herself she would wait for the right man to come along.

Chapter Nineteen

Connie

With Ruby back to work and her future secured once more, Connie had time to focus on her own work and her relationship with Devon. One Sunday, she headed to London to spend the day with him, and as she lay in bed that night back in the nurses' home, she thought about how protected she'd felt in his arms when he kissed her in Hyde Park that afternoon, as the late September sun melted into a fiery orange sunset.

She'd also returned with some treats picked up from a West Indian bakery Devon had taken her to in Notting Hill. And she had shared black cake and sweetbread – each a sweet taste of home – with Ruby.

'Morning, Billie. I didn't see you last night, but I brought some of this home for you from London,' Connie told her friend, and watched as Billie's eyes grew wide over her cup of tea as they sat in the kitchen.

'Where on earth did you find these?' she asked.

'They're from a West Indian bakery. Somehow they got hold of more rum than you have, Billie – the cake is full of it,' Connie joked.

'I heard that Jewish people here have set up their own businesses and thing, but I had *no* idea that we were branching out and not just working in hospitals and on the railways,' Billie replied, taking a big bite out of her slice of cake, despite the fact that she hadn't yet had breakfast. 'Mmm . . . man, it tastes good!' she enthused.

'Yes, you're right, I was telling Connie she brought home the goods!' Ruby said emphatically. 'Morning!'

'Morning, Ruby, how was your day yesterday? Things getting back to normal now?' Billie enquired.

'It was great. There are some lovely ladies on Lavender – it's so nice to be back, working with the patients. And a relief to be off bed-pan duty,' she laughed.

'Too right, sis,' Connie smiled.

'Oh, and Grace told me that Margaret has packed up and left Four Oaks, apparently she's gone home to Hampshire. Grace said she had to because she couldn't afford to pay her rent down here and it would be difficult for her to find a job now she has a dismissal on her record,' Ruby explained.

Connie took little pleasure in Margaret's misery. But she was happy that Ruby was looking herself once more, her dimples gracing her face again as her smile filled the room.

'I heard about Margaret,' Kathleen said, joining them in the kitchen. 'And speaking about people getting their come-uppance, do you remember that house in town with the rooms to let that we saw a few weeks back?' The other girls nodded. 'Well, I just couldn't get the shocking prejudice of that sign out of my head. So over the weekend, I went looking for a room.'

'You did what?' Billie said, a picture of open-mouthed surprise combined with eagerness to hear more.

'I'd been chatting to some of the other nurses from the Caribbean that have been here a while, and they were telling me that they would call up for a room, get an appointment to view it, only to turn up and the people would lie to their faces, saying the room had already been rented.

'Now I figured if there's one thing I have in my favour for this situation, it's this,' she said, stroking the milky white skin of her arm. 'So I phoned and asked to view that room down the road. I went there on Saturday, met a lovely couple called the Browns. And then,' Kathleen continued, sounding more like Queen Elizabeth II than a girl from Dublin, 'I put on my very best English accent. And guess what? They offered me a room!'

'You didn't!? But you're not going to go and live there, are you?' Ruby was confused.

'God, no! They wouldn't have me, Ruby, and I couldn't keep up with this ridiculous accent forever. I wanted to teach them a lesson. So when they offered me the room, I smiled sweetly, said, "Thank you so very much," in my very best English accent. And then I let them have it.'

And now she resorted to her normal Dublin accent, though the usual softness of her tone had been replaced by a more aggressive one. 'I said: "I wouldn't let my *dog* stay here with you rotten bastards, let alone my friends from the Caribbean!"'

'Ohh!' Ruby squealed, clapping her hands.

'You didn't!' Connie was bent double laughing.

'I damn well did! The mean bastards. But you should've seen their faces – they couldn't wait to shove me out the door.' Kathleen was indignant, but she also had a self-satisfied look about her as she laughed heartily.

'Oh my goodness! Kathleen, you're my hero. This is the funniest thing I've heard in a while!' Billie howled with laughter.

It was a glorious start to the day for Connie, and somehow it also gave her hope. Hope because there were good people in the world, prepared to put themselves out in the defence of others, or where they saw unjust situations.

'Right, girls, I've got to get off to work. Lin said it was a busy weekend on maternity,' Connie said.

It wasn't long before she was on the ward and had a tiny

newborn in her arms. 'Oh my! Sister Harding, I'll be happy to look after all the babies today,' she grinned.

'I can understand that,' the sister smiled back, mentally noting how well Connie was supporting the baby's head. 'I always think this is the best ward in the hospital. But we're due to have a couple more ladies admitted who are having complications with the latter stages of their pregnancies, so make the most of the time we have to fuss our littlest patients now.'

'Yes, Sister,' Connie replied, looking down at the little boy in her arms, whose tiny mouth gaped open in a satisfied yawn, as though tasting the air for the first time.

The morning passed with Connie admitting patients and helping a new mother to give her baby her first bath.

'How are you getting on with breastfeeding now, Mrs Williams?' she asked a patient due for discharge that afternoon.

'Ivy's latching on much easier now. Thank you for checking on me, nurse. You've all been so wonderful. My mum says she wishes the National Health Service had been around when she was having us. She had seven of us kids and said she could've done with all sorts of help but couldn't afford to have a baby in hospital,' Mrs Williams explained.

'Well, that's great to hear – I'm glad we've been able to get a good start in life for little Ivy,' Connie replied, smiling down at Mrs Williams' baby. And she wasn't just smiling out of adoration for the little girl. Connie felt an immense pride about the difference the NHS was making to people in the town, and the part she played in that too. She remembered something Ruby had said to her when they'd first arrived at the hospital: 'Nursing is very noble work and this is a chance for us to contribute.' In this moment, Connie couldn't have felt that sentiment more deeply.

That evening she reminded Ruby of this conversation on their first day at the hospital.

'Ah yes, I remember! Goodness, that seems so long ago,' Ruby smiled. 'It's true, though. I doubt there is a nobler job than this. And I'm so happy to be back helping patients and learning on the job.'

It was a similar sense of pride and responsibility that propelled Connie through the next few weeks.

One evening she felt the first sting of a crisp autumnal breeze and saw amber leaves slowly floating down from the trees that lined the pathway, as she headed home from the maternity ward through the hospital grounds.

October had arrived and the ward had been full of happy but tired new mothers, soon-to-be mothers, their bumps rising like molehills in their beds, and newborn babies, a couple of whom were wailing as though they had just learned a new trick and were enjoying the attention it garnered. But even though she was loving her time on the ward, Connie had been working non-stop in the previous few weeks and was looking forward to a few days off, and especially to catching up with Devon.

He had been busy with work too so it had been some weeks since they'd seen each other, but Connie had become used to speaking to Devon at around eight o'clock most evenings. Though those conversations had taken a more serious tone in the weeks since she had confessed to him about Martha, she still relished them.

'You know in two and a half years, when you qualify as a state registered nurse, you'll be able to work anywhere in the country. I was wondering if you might have better prospects to get work down here in London,' he said. 'You got to think beyond where you are now and start planning for the future.'

Connie loved him for the care and interest he took in her; his voice alone was a soft woollen blanket of comfort to her. Devon had also started asking more about Martha, but since she had not had a letter from Aunt Agatha in a number of weeks, Connie could only share old news with him and anecdotes of their brief time together.

This she considered the hardest part of the separation from her daughter. However, the lack of regular updates hadn't only happened since Connie left Barbados. In fact, it was easier for her to receive news of Martha now she was living independently and didn't have to keep contact with her daughter a secret from her parents.

One thing she hadn't kept a secret, though, was that she and Devon were stepping out, and her parents had responded positively. 'I always thought he was a nice young man and your dad says he's pleased you have someone looking out for you over there,' her mother had written some weeks earlier. So Connie knew she was doing the right thing. She did, however, add a warning: 'But I beg you, be sure you don't go doing anything stupid and mess up this opportunity you got. We've already had to sort out one mess you brought upon us . . .'

'Did you say you were seeing Devon on Saturday? I'm thinking about doing some early shopping for Christmas, and I need you out of my way,' Ruby smiled as she walked into Connie's room one day, proud that she had saved enough money to buy her sister a small gift.

'You're real cheeky you know, Ruby Haynes. Though don't you go spending too much money now – neither of us have it to give away. But yes, I am planning to go to London. Devon said he'd take me to the West End. So who knows? I might even get a little something for someone I know too.' Connie had a glint in her eye.

'I knew it!' Ruby said. 'Well, I won't make any hints. But if you happen to see any of that Yardley perfume . . .' She trailed off with a mischievous smile.

'Yes, yes.' Connie rolled her eyes.

Later that evening she called Devon to make arrangements for the weekend.

'My train gets in at eleven o'clock,' she said, thumbing a paper timetable. 'Do you think that will be enough time for everything we plan to do?'

'Oh wait, it's this weekend?' Devon said. Then, as though searching for information, 'I have something I need to do in the morning, I have to go south of the river. I'll try my best to get back for you in time, but if I don't make it at the station for eleven maybe you could meet me at the pub across the road? Dirty Dicks, it's just along Bishopsgate.'

'Devon, I can't go into a public house on my own, you've got to be crazy!' Connie laughed nervously.

'But you also can't stand around in this cold weather, Connie. I'll be there just as soon as I can,' he said.

Unease swelled inside Connie. It was one thing going into the pub escorted by a man, or even on the few occasions when she had gone to the Woodman's Arms with Ruby, Billie and Kathleen. Though she wouldn't have told her parents or the vicar at church that she'd done so. But to go in on her own? Surely only certain types of girls did that.

'I'm out with the fellas after work tomorrow night, so I won't get the chance to speak to you, but I'll see you on Saturday. It will all work out fine,' Devon said, in a determinedly positive voice.

As Saturday came, on the train to London, Connie's exterior was calm but her tummy was a bundle of excitement and anxious anticipation at seeing Devon – it had been a while, and it was only the third time since she'd told him about Martha – plus nerves at him possibly not being there to meet her off the train.

An hour later, the train spewed its last plume of black smoke then pulled up before the imposing Victorian archways of the Great Eastern Hotel.

Connie searched the throng of bright headscarves and dark hats for Devon. Then she waited a few minutes for the crowds to dissolve in the hope she would see his warm eyes scanning for her too. But he wasn't there, and her eyes fell to the pavement as she weighed her options.

A frigid wind whistled through the station, swirling litter and leaves around her feet, and for a moment, Connie felt very alone.

Devon said to go to the pub, he'll be right along soon, she coaxed herself.

Crossing Bishopsgate, Connie took a deep breath, and with her head held as high as she could muster, she wandered into the pub. It was early in the day so it was thankfully pretty empty, but even then, Connie sensed a number of men shuffling in their seats, turning their heads to look at her.

'Erm, hello, er, would it be possible to have a lemonade please?' she said, sure she could see astonishment on the barman's face. 'I'm waiting for someone,' she added hurriedly, hoping he didn't think her *that* kind of girl.

'There ya go, love. You can take a seat in the snug, you won't get no bother there.'

And there she sat, sipping her lemonade and wondering how Devon could have surmised this to be a good idea; he was usually so much more considerate, she thought.

When an hour passed, Connie became anxious, wondering when on earth Devon would arrive. Half an hour later she ordered another lemonade and was sure the barman gave her a pitying look.

He thinks I've been stood up. But Devon will be here soon . . . he has to be, else we'll never get to the shops.

Another hour later, and Connie could feel hot anger burning her cheeks and stinging her eyes. She blinked away furious tears, unable to fathom why Devon would treat her in such a way. He knew where she was, and how uncomfortable it had made her to go there. She'd have thought he would have made a point of getting there quickly.

Questions went round and round in her head as to where he could be, until she landed on something. What if he didn't care that he'd made her wait – and in a pub of all places – because his opinion of her had changed? Perhaps he now considered that she was a certain kind of girl.

That must be it – he thinks less of me because of Martha.

Connie could no longer control her emotions and dissolved into tears.

'You all right over there?' the barman said. 'Don't let him upset you, love. I see it a lot round here. Some of these lads, they have two or three girls on the go – come in here with a different one each time. At least you know what he is now.'

'No, it's not that,' Connie started to counter, angry at the barman's presumptuousness – he didn't know who she was waiting for, he didn't know Devon, how dare he assume he did? But then she lost all will and ran from the pub in tears, out into the icy city air, self-doubt mixing with her misery.

The sun had faded to a pale straw colour, behind the slate grey billows of London's infamous smog, and Connie felt the city suffocating her as much as the questions that tumbled through her mind were.

How could he do this to me? He must have done it on purpose. But why?

Oh my goodness, what if he's trying to teach me a lesson for having deceived him?

Don't be silly, Connie. He wouldn't do such a thing.

So what could have happened?

If he didn't leave me here on purpose then something must have happened. Lord, what if he's sick or something?

In an instant, Connie darted across the road and found a red telephone box. But finding she didn't have the correct change, she ran to a woman walking by. 'Excuse me, you wouldn't have change for the phone box, would you?'

'Of course, dear. Ah, you've got a tanner there,' the woman said, taking Connie's coin and counting out six pennies in exchange into her hand.

Dialling Devon's number, Connie's hand hovered on the 'A' button to connect the call. But with no reply after a couple of minutes, she pressed 'B' to have her coins returned.

Feeling helpless, she headed back into Liverpool Street station. Perhaps Devon would turn up on the next train. Or maybe he'd forgotten their plan to meet at the pub and he was scouring the station looking for her.

But once more, with no sign of him, Connie was left confused, and forced to formulate her own answers to this puzzle.

The next train to Four Oaks wasn't leaving until three o'clock, so Connie went to the ladies' waiting room and sat in its relative warmth for the next forty-five minutes – hoping against hope that Devon would turn up.

Why on earth didn't he suggest I wait for him in here? Surely this would have been more suitable.

Later, as the train departed the city, it escaped the gloom of London's smog but immediately descended into the darkness of an autumn evening, only adding to Connie's glum mood.

Soon after she got back to the nurses' home, Ruby arrived from town.

'Wait, what are you doing here? You trying to sneak up and see the gift I got you? I didn't think you would be home until much later tonight, or tomorrow even. I know lovely Devon doesn't like to let you go once he has you in his arms,' she teased.

'He didn't show up. I waited for hours in a horrible old pub, like some kind of a loose woman, and he didn't even come.' Connie saw Ruby's countenance change to one of shock. 'I thought maybe when I got back there would be a message from him, but nothing.'

'That's very strange, Connie. You sure something hasn't happened to him?' Ruby replied, concern wrinkling her brow.

'I wouldn't know if it had. I called his lodgings, but nobody answered. But Ruby, he would *never* have done this to me before. Not before I told him about Martha, that is.' Connie's eyes were doleful.

Ruby put down her bags and went to comfort her. 'Connie, that's silly. I'm sure there will be a simple explanation for what happened today. You wait, he'll call tonight, or first thing in the morning at the latest. I can tell you've been crying, so let's turn that frown upside down, eh?' she said, and Connie couldn't help but let out a little laugh.

'What? Where on earth did you hear that?' she asked.

'Oh, it's one of my patients on Lavender, she says it's something she tells her children a lot. I thought it sounded nice, and just the kind of thing we all need sometimes.'

'I guess you're right. I'll just have to wait to hear from him. There must be a good explanation,' Connie sighed.

And wait she did, for the evening, that night, the following morning before church, and more. By Sunday afternoon, Connie was very anxious once again.

'Still no word?' Ruby asked as Connie moped in the sitting room.

'No. I'm going to have to phone his lodgings again. I'm really getting worried now, this isn't like Devon at all.'

Picking up the telephone, she dialled Devon's number, her hand trembling over the last digit as if dreading what would come next.

What if something's happened to him? But what if nothing's happened, but it's that he doesn't want to speak to me?

'Kentish Town 6874. Hello? Hello?'

'Mrs Silver, it's Connie – you know, Devon's friend,' she said. 'I wondered if he was there?'

'I haven't seen him, no dear,' she said.

'Oh. Do you have any idea where he could be?'

'No dear, but he's a busy man, and I don't like to pry. He's paid up on his rent for a month so I'm not too worried,' she explained.

Connie thanked her, but Devon's landlady had been no help at all, and she felt utterly desperate. How could she be so deeply involved, so in love with someone, and yet now have no way of contacting them or knowing where they were?

As she mused over this, Billie and Kathleen entered the reception area.

'Connie? What's the matter, dear?' Billie asked, immediately sensing her friend's distress.

Through heavy sighs, Connie explained that it was now over twenty-four hours since she was supposed to have met Devon in London, and approaching forty-eight hours since she had last spoken to him.

'Goodness, that's not at all like him, now,' Kathleen said. 'Come let's get a brew and you can tell us all about it. We'll figure something out, of that I'm sure.'

Connie felt so sad, so worried, so tired of all the guilt and deceit that had knotted her insides for months, that she told Kathleen everything – all about Martha and how she'd told Devon.

'He seemed to take it OK, we saw each other in the weeks after I spoke to him and I thought he was fine, but now . . .' Her despondency seemed to stifle the air in the room. 'I think I misread the whole situation. It looks like he's decided he wants nothing to do with me. And I can't even blame him. Who would want me? I'm a witless girl who got herself lumbered with a baby when I wasn't very much more than a child myself.

'But it's so much worse than that. Then I deceived him. For months. All the time he was planning our future together, I didn't dare tell him about my past for fear that he wouldn't want me any more. And now it's becoming clear that he really doesn't.'

'Connie, you have to stop this. Devon seems to have disappeared, and you're right to be worried about him, but you can't go thinking you're to blame. He could have been busy with something, or perhaps he's been taken ill. I know – didn't he have a friend in Peterborough? Maybe he had to go to see him at the last minute,' Billie said, searching for answers where there were clearly none.

The mystery of Devon's disappearance would hang over them for the rest of the night; in fact, for the rest of the week.

By Friday, a full seven days after Connie had last spoken to Devon, she had tried calling his lodgings on two further occasions, but having got no further information from his landlady she became convinced that he had told Mrs Silver not to disclose anything to her regarding his whereabouts. For all she knew, he could even have gone home to Barbados.

Chapter Twenty

Billie

Two weeks later, Billie hurried through the darkness of a cool December night.

She knew she hadn't been herself for the past few weeks, and that this was now clear to her friends too, but they still hadn't figured out what had changed about her. Though it wasn't as though anything was wrong – in fact, everything was *right*.

Arriving at their usual meeting place, outside the church, she found Ezra waiting in his car.

'Good evening, Dr Becker,' she said with a glint in her eye.

'Oh, it's Dr Becker now, is it?' He laughed.

'I've always called you Dr Becker, haven't I? It's only appropriate for a nurse, and a trainee at that. I know my place in the pecking order, you know,' Billie teased, then put her hand on Ezra's knee and planted a peck on his cheek.

He placed his hand over hers; the awkwardness that had been a feature of their first few dates had dissipated.

'You know, I was thinking, we're going to have to consider how we can be more open about this. About us, I mean. That is, if you don't mind people knowing. And I don't want you to get into any kind of trouble or anything,' Billie said. 'It's just that my friends, they've realized I've been missing quite a bit over the past few weeks, and they're asking questions.'

'So our clandestine liaisons haven't been as clandestine as we might have liked, eh?' Ezra smiled. 'I don't mind you telling them, if you aren't concerned about what people may think? I *am* a lot older than you, and a doctor. I'm sure you don't want anyone thinking you're somehow trying to win favour during your training or something.'

'That thought hadn't crossed my mind,' Billie said, bewildered. 'I would have thought more that *you* might be worried about people finding out, as, you know, I'm only a nurse. Maybe people would think I'm not good enough for someone like you. Or perhaps you'd worry people would think it inappropriate that we're having *liaisons*,' she said, gently mocking Ezra's earlier description.

'Why – because I'm Jewish and you're a beautiful Christian? Or a beautiful black woman?' He smiled again.

'Well, we're not exactly average here,' Billie said, taking in Four Oaks' suburban landscape. A woman with a navy blue coat and matching felt hat pushed a pram along the pavement, and under the streetlight Billie could see her white face had been turned a bright pink by the frosty air.

As he pulled up outside his house, Ezra turned the key towards him to cut the car's ignition.

'You, my dear, are more than good enough for me. You are everything to me. And don't you ever let anyone at all tell you you're not their equal,' he said, and Billie felt something she'd never felt before, an inner glow radiating from her heart right to her face.

'You're very special to me too,' she smiled broadly. 'I've never known something like this, someone like *you* before.'

And she meant it. Despite having had many previous boyfriends, and countless other dalliances, even Billie couldn't kid herself that there had been anything special in her many flirtations, the discreet and the indiscreet kisses and more. But for weeks now, she had known that there was something different about what she had with Ezra.

He was different.

It wasn't just that he was gentlemanly – opening doors and pulling out chairs for her. Billie had enjoyed being treated like a lady, but she realized, as much as she'd previously longed to meet a gentleman, many of those small things were just that, small things.

It wasn't his appearance, because as much as Billie had grown to love his deep blue eyes and the strong arms that gathered her close to his lean but muscular chest, Ezra wasn't a traditionally good-looking man, and nor did that matter to her. What she had come to appreciate about him was much more than skin deep; she knew he cared for her, and that he was interested in her.

Instead of a merely physical preoccupation, Billie and Ezra would have conversations on any number of topics and she realized that he was intrigued by her, that he valued her thoughts and opinions. He had not only entrusted her with his heart, but he had taken her into his world and also wanted to discover hers.

For Billie, it was a deeper connection than she had ever experienced with a man before and, for perhaps the first time, she was falling in love.

As much as she had previously been quite free with her body, Billie was rarely free with her heart. But with Ezra, once again she found that things were different.

As Ezra chopped carrots for dinner, they talked.

'You know, I admire you. I can't imagine the courage it must have taken to leave a tiny island in the Caribbean, journey three weeks from home and come all the way to not just another country, but another continent to start a new life,' he said.

'Yes, and I still haven't earned enough money to pay the government back for my ticket here, never mind enough to get myself back home yet. So you're stuck with me, mister.' She paused to take a sip of beer from his glass, staring over the rim at him.

'I just hope St Mary's continues to pay a pittance so you're stuck with me forever,' he said, leaning forward to kiss her forehead.

'Oh don't you worry, I don't think that will be changing fast,' she laughed, and Ezra chuckled too.

'But you must also use this time as an opportunity. You can travel,' he said, then noting Billie's expression, which suggested that anything beyond a trip to London would be out of her financial reach, he corrected himself. 'We can travel. I would love to go to Scotland, Wales, and even further – who knows, maybe even to France. And I want you there for all of that. I'd also love to take you to the Netherlands one day, and show you where I grew up.'

Billie smiled, excited at his plans, and by the fact that he was including her in his future.

'And then – now, I don't want you to worry that I'm trying to rush you into things – but one day, I want to have a house in the countryside and have children; as many as you would like,' he said, then caught himself at the same time that Billie started weighing his comment, recognizing that this was a whole new plane for them. 'Oh Billie, I do hope I'm not moving too fast or scaring you. But I am twelve years your senior,' he sighed, and his tone became solemn. 'It feels as though I'm onto my second life now, you know, since the war – that terrible time and losing my family, it made me realize, life is fragile. Everything we know to be normal, everything we think we have . . . it can turn to dust, and in no time at all. I never want to be there. Not again,' he said quietly and there was a moment of stillness between them, as they both reflected on what his words meant for their future.

'But I don't wish to be maudlin. We have to move forward positively, and in a peaceful, free country *we* can make our lives what we wish them to be,' he said, taking a deep breath. And Billie sensed hope in his words and in his eyes.

'Yes, we can, my darling,' she said, stepping towards him to stroke his arm. 'Yes, we can. Ezra, I know you have scars from the war. I understand you don't like to talk about everything that happened and how you ended up here in Britain.'

'Let's just say that while you came here by invitation, I arrived on these shores through adversity.' His doleful gaze dropped to the floor and Billie sensed an impenetrable wall of pain surrounding him. She caressed his face and, lifting it up to meet hers, she said: 'I want you to know, though, that I'm here for you whenever you're ready to talk about it. And no matter what, I'm ready to be with you forever.'

'I will. I do want to talk to you about it all one day; I don't want there to be secrets between us. Only . . . it's now eleven years since I escaped the horror of war in Europe, and I still find it difficult to speak of. But I love you, Billie, I open up to you more than you know. We talk more than I have with anyone since, well . . . since Hannah . . .'

Placing his hand over hers, Ezra tenderly kissed Billie's lips.

There was a hiss-hiss-splutter as the saucepan of carrots boiled over, and he turned his attention to the cooker.

'Damn and blast, now I'll have to clean down this cooker. Is a man's work ever done?' he said with a smile, stamping his foot and tossing his arms into the air in frustration, and Billie couldn't help but giggle a little at what she considered one of the quirky, endearing traits of the man she was falling in love with.

After dinner, though, Ezra decided to temporarily forgo the cleaning to spend more time chatting to Billie. They talked about topics she had never discussed with any man before, perhaps anyone at all – from politics to world peace. Billie found spending time with Ezra to be a joy, and part of that joy was the fact that he discussed such matters with her. No subject was ever avoided or her opinions cast aside because she was a woman. On the contrary, Ezra seemed to relish her opinions because they were sometimes at odds with his own, and it was clear that he was as mesmerized by her brains as by her beauty.

As the small clock on his mantelpiece struck eleven, Ezra knew he'd shortly have to drive Billie back before the nurses' home doors were locked. But as they sat on the small green sofa in his living room and by the pale glow of a table lamp, Ezra turned to Billie, tenderly took her face in his hands and placed a kiss delicately on her full lips.

He would normally have stopped there, and ever since their first date, when Ezra had been cautious, as he put it, 'not to take advantage of her', Billie had been uncharacteristically anxious not to push things too far too soon with him.

But she was falling deeply for him and it was clear he was for her too. She moved her hands behind his head to caress his brown hair, and pressed her lips to his once more, and then again. This time, the longing of his kiss pushed her back on the sofa, until the pair were falling into each other's arms, their passion unleashed.

As Ezra nuzzled her neck, and then caressed her breasts through her fitted blouse, her hands drifted to his trousers.

But Ezra pulled away. 'Billie, I love you and I respect you. Let's do this right,' he said.

Billie was, once more, a little surprised. Men she had known previously had always been ready to take things to the next stage. But there it was again: Ezra was different, he was proper, and Billie adored that about him.

'Of course,' she said. And instead they lay entwined in each other's arms, making the most of every second together, before it was time for Ezra to take Billie home, with the promise that they would see each other again later that week.

*

The chill of winter was biting the next morning as Billie opened her eyes, the hot pipe that ran through each of the nurses' rooms having little impact on the below-zero temperatures. But Billie woke with a smile on her face and an inner warmth that seemed to radiate from inside out.

'Lord h'mercy, is it ever icy this morning!' Connie shivered as she came across her friend in the corridor. 'It was cold, cold, cold when we first came here, but I don't remember it being as bad as this.'

'I know. We all gonna need a good man to keep us warm. Could you imagine if they allowed us to bring in men friends? For medicinal purposes, you know,' Billie laughed then caught herself, her unusual lack of tact pricking her conscience.

'I'm sorry, Connie. I forgot,' she said, her brows furrowing with concern. But Connie just shrugged. 'Thank you, but you can't tiptoe around my feelings all the time. And besides, girl, you're such a joker! *Medicinal purposes*, indeed,' Connie said, seeing the funny side, but it wasn't enough to force a smile to her lips.

Seeing this as her opportunity, Billie said: 'So, I have something to tell you. But I can't speak too loudly. Don't they say, "the walls have ears"?'

'Ruby's coming soon and we can get off to breakfast, we can walk and talk. You know, out in the open air, where there aren't any walls to listen in,' Connie said, a mild sarcasm to her voice.

'I'm coming,' Ruby yelled from her room, after hearing the other girls in the corridor.

Though all three were wrapped up in their woollen capes, these proved no match for the biting wind and frost that cloaked every blade of grass and each leaf on the trees in white, as though freezing the scene in time. Propelled by their desire to get back into the warm, the girls hurried along the pathway to the dining room, steamy trails of breath floating behind their heads.

'But wait, girls, I had something I wanted to talk to you about

– quick, come with me to the toilet,' Billie said as they entered the dining-room block.

'Man, Billie, I'm hungry, you can't wait till we're sat down at a table to talk?' Ruby implored.

'No, definitely not. Come with me,' Billie said, opening the door to the toilet and checking that all the cubicles were empty.

'What is all this secrecy?' Connie asked, bemused.

'Funny you should say that, he's been calling it our clandestine relationship,' Billie said.

'What? Who did? Billie! Have you been dating somebody?' Ruby shrieked.

'Shh, Ruby!' Billie urged.

'But what's all the secrecy about? I already know who it is,' Ruby said confidently. 'It has to be that fella from the summer at the Woodman's. What was his name again? John?'

'Ah yes, him! I nearly forgot about him,' Connie said.

'No. It's not,' Billie said.

Ruby looked thoughtful for a while. 'Oh, I know!' she cried. 'What's that young porter called again? Not Archie, the other one. He's always turning his head to look at you when he walks past. Though that's not unusual, of course. Every hot-blooded man in this place is always eyeing you, like you need any more attention,' Ruby said, lacking a little grace.

'No, I don't think it's anyone here in the hospital. She's been out and about so much, he can't have anything to do with St Mary's,' Connie mused.

'Girls, will you stop running your minds all over the place and listen? I'm about to tell you everything,' Billie implored them.

'His name's Ezra,' she said, and the sisters looked perplexed. 'Ezra Becker,' Billie smiled, loving just saying his name out loud.

A few long seconds passed and then Ruby's mouth fell open as wide as a tunnel. 'No!' she said, aghast. '*Dr* Becker? The one who saved my job? I don't believe it!'

'Oh my goodness, Billie!' Connie said and Billie saw a degree of joy on her face, and noted that it was the first time in days that she'd seen her look in any way happy. 'But *how*? When did this all come about? What is he like? And why on earth did you not say anything?'

'I'm telling you now, aren't I? You girls are like my sisters here, so I had to tell you first – I will probably tell the other girls later on. But man, it's been killing me that I couldn't tell you how happy I am, because I've been walking on air,' Billie said, a contented glow beaming from her face as she spoke about Ezra. 'He just makes me feel . . . well, so important and appreciated. He makes me blissfully happy. And I'm sorry I didn't tell you earlier. But I just didn't know . . . *we* didn't know what this was, or where it was going. Quite truthfully, I didn't think it was going anywhere, because he's so unlike anyone I've ever met, and well, because he's a doctor, and I'm not even a proper nurse yet. But last night, he started talking about us – where we might go, what we might do, you know – our future life.'

'Oh my *goodness*! Billie, man, is this for real? This is just like one of those romantic movies,' Ruby said. 'I can barely believe it.'

'I know. It took me by surprise too. But it is real,' she assured her friend. 'And I think he has been keeping me focused – on why I'm here in England, and the things I want to achieve from being up here. The real things that matter.'

'Billie, I'm delighted for you,' Connie said, then she let out a long sigh. 'I always felt as though having Devon here really helped me. It was as though he grounded me.' Connie's eyes were glassy now, but though emotion welled within her she pushed herself to continue. As sad as she was, she felt this was Billie's time, and she felt honoured that she wanted to share her happiness. She didn't want to put a dampener on things or spoil her moment. 'I think you might find something similar with your doctor. He's always seemed a very nice and respectable man,' Connie said.

'He truly is. He makes all those other boys I've been messing about with all these years seem . . .' Billie paused as if trying to calculate a difficult sum, then threw her hands in the air. 'Well, there's just no comparison. So I wanted to tell you, because like I say, you girls are my family up here. And this family is branching out in all directions.'

The girls looked at her curiously.

'Ah yes, I didn't tell you he comes from the Netherlands originally. But he's been here many years now because he came as a refugee during the war.'

'Did he fight in the war too, similar to Devon?' Ruby asked, her naivety showing.

'No, it's quite different to Devon. Ezra's Jewish and he came here to escape the Nazis, else they would have rounded him up and then God only knows what would have happened. It was a horrific time for him. He lost his wife and son in the war, but he can't even talk about it properly yet, it's so painful. Though hopefully he will do one day,' Billie explained. 'He's been here since 1943 working as a doctor, first in London at a hospital treating people during the war, and then he moved out here to Four Oaks.'

'So what's it like dating a white man, Billie? Though I don't know anybody that's Jewish,' Ruby said, clearly thinking out loud.

'Oh, I know – he's white and I'm black, he's a doctor, I'm a nurse. He's in his thirties and I'm still in my twenties. Goodness, there are countless differences between us. He's completely different to anyone I've ever known.' Billie paused now, thinking about Ezra, and a smile slowly spread across her face. 'And you know what? We're all foreigners here, Ruby.' Given her experiences in the last few months, Ruby couldn't disagree.

'Well, I don't think any of that matters. The important thing is that God delivered him here to safety in England. And now, he's delivered him to you.' Connie managed a smile and touched her friend's arm, while Billie couldn't shake her joyful expression for the rest of the day.

Chapter Twenty-One

Ruby

As the days had turned into weeks with still no news about Devon, Ruby noticed her sister's sadness had turned to anger – an emotion she rarely saw in loving Connie.

'Come on, Connie, let's go into town. The place is covered in Christmas lights. It's really nice, and you could do with a day away from all this upset,' Ruby implored her sister.

'I don't know, Ruby, I really ain't feeling like going anywhere. And I'm not upset. I'm livid. That mean wretch, how could he do this to me? How dare he just disappear without a word, without any kind of consideration at all. Not only for me, Ruby, but for what we had. It's as though all that time, all those special moments we had together counted for nothing.'

'Yes, I suppose it's one thing for him to be angry if he felt deceived, but was it even deception? It wasn't as though he found out about Martha himself, or if he ever asked you directly if you had children. You simply kept the information to yourself until the time was right and you felt you could trust him,' Ruby pointed out.

'And it turns out I couldn't trust him at all. Especially not with my heart,' Connie bristled. 'Oh, Ruby, he knows me. He's the only person that knows me anything like as much as you. And yet now, it's as though he thinks I'm a terrible person. I remember how he talked about girls in London and how free they can be with their morals. And now all I can think is, he started to see me as one of those girls. He's come to the conclusion that I'm not as innocent and pure as he wants,' she ranted to her sister. And though Ruby didn't agree with everything Connie said, her heart was quickly turning to stone against Devon.

She had absorbed so much of Connie's upset that a sense of foreboding had followed her around for the past few weeks. She kept coming back to the same question – how could he behave in such a way and walk out of Connie's life without a word? It was so unbecoming of the man Ruby had thought he was.

But she was not about to let Connie suffer. Their first Christmas in England was fast approaching and Ruby was determined they were going to enjoy the festivities.

'Come, Connie, let's go into town – aside from anything, you really could do with the fresh air,' she encouraged.

And an hour later, they were wandering the marketplace and the high street in Four Oaks watching as a pale blue hour became dotted with white lights strung in rows across the street, then snowflakes attached to lampposts gently flickered on and off as though dancing in the twilight.

'Lord, it's so pretty. Don't you think, Connie?' Ruby said.

For the first time that week, she thought she saw some light in her sister too.

'It is,' Connie said, and then Ruby noticed that she was weeping.

'Connie, come here.' Ruby hugged her sister.

'I'm sorry, Ruby. It really is lovely,' Connie stuttered, misery choking her words.

'You can't let him upset you like this,' Ruby said.

'It's not really that.' Connie fought to get her words out through her emotion. 'It's just— Devon. He said . . . he said he would show me the lights in London. That he wanted me to see them with him. And . . . And now he won't even speak to me,' she stammered. Connie's tears fell onto the apples of Ruby's cheeks and her coat. 'We had so many things planned, Ruby.'

'I know, I know,' Ruby soothed, stroking Connie's face to wipe away her tears.

'I just . . . my heart is breaking into pieces. I regret it so much. I shouldn't have said anything,' Connie said. 'If I'd known this would happen, I would never have told him.'

'But Connie, I think you did the right thing. You couldn't keep it from him forever. I know I suggested you should, but it was silly of me,' Ruby admitted. 'Martha will not stay little forever, and you want to be a real mum to her one day. You had to discuss all of that with him.

'Still, it's better for you to know about him now. Even if the truth of the matter is that Devon is not worthy of your tears, least of all your love. I'm sorry, Connie, but it's something I've been thinking for a few days now. He didn't deserve someone like you. You may have made a mistake, but does that mean you should pay for it for the rest of your days? No, you shouldn't,' Ruby said emphatically. 'You were young and we all make mistakes. Connie, I want you to know something,' she said now, taking her sister's gloved hands and lifting her head to look her right in the eyes. 'You have the biggest heart of anyone I've ever known. You're beautiful inside and out, and if this damn fool man couldn't see that, then he's the one who's losing, because one day, I'm sure in the not-too-distant future, you will find someone who loves you. And I mean everything about you,' Ruby said, clenching her sister's hands tightly as if for emphasis.

'I really thought he was that person, though. That he was the one,' Connie whimpered.

'No, darling, he was just the first. The one is still out there waiting to meet you.' Ruby smiled confidently. She hoped this confidence and her strength was rubbing off, that she could somehow fortify Connie.

As they stood in the deepening darkness of the town's square, tiny crystals of snow started to fall, and before they knew it, penny-sized flakes were tumbling from the sky.

'Oh my! This would be so beautiful if I wasn't so very sad,' Connie said.

'No, Connie, man, this isn't beautiful. It's wondrous!' Ruby said, turning circles in the snowstorm and laughing uncontrollably with glee. Soon Connie couldn't help but share her joy, and she joined Ruby in spinning and running around the square, leaving grumpy-faced passers-by in no doubt that this was the first time the sisters had seen snow and they found it magical.

The spirit of Christmas that gripped Ruby that night flourished in the next few days as St Mary's was full of festivities. Each ward had a Christmas tree, which the nurses decorated with glass baubles, while garlands of silver tinsel were strung liberally – running the length of windows, draping the front desk and even some patient's beds – and sprigs of holly were brought in from the cold to add a splash of colour to the nurses' home reception. There was even a sprig of mistletoe hung in a corner of the room, although under Miss Bleakly's cold, watchful eye, not one of the nurses would have dared smuggle in a boyfriend to use it for anything as nefarious as snatching a kiss.

Instead, cards were exchanged, new traditions were cemented and Ruby had previously unknown foods to try, such as mince pies.

'These taste delicious – Ruth told me they sometimes put a little brandy in with the mincemeat, though I don't know why they call it that when it's all made of fruit,' she said, licking her lips during a tea break.

'I don't care much about that, but I wouldn't mind finding the ones with a bit of booze. I wonder if they have any made with rum – now that would be *something*,' Billie suggested.

'You're always on the lookout for your rum. Don't you know

drink is the work of the devil,' Connie said thoughtfully. 'They had a sermon about that, and a few other sinful things we take for granted just the other day at church.' Then she stomped out of the sitting room.

'That's as may be but I thought this was a hospital, not a convent,' Billie protested after her.

'Oh, ignore her, man,' Ruby said. 'I know that sounded judgemental, but you know her, Billie – Connie's not like that. She's shrunk away these past few weeks. And the church thing, well, it's as though she's looking for answers to what's happened with Devon, and deciding it has to be down to how she lives her life. That somehow she has a life of shame.'

'Ain't that Connie all over – to blame herself, I mean,' Billie said exasperatedly. 'That church girl needs to wise up to all that she has, because she is such a good soul. Just because some worthless man couldn't see that, and didn't have the decency to even tell her it was all off because of *his* ideas about her, well, it doesn't mean she's a bad person. Having a child out of wedlock doesn't make you a bad person, it makes you a *mother*, and we all know that mothers are wonderful beings,' Billie ranted, clearly angered by the injustice of Connie carrying the burden of Devon's actions.

'I . . . I guess you're right,' Ruby replied, unsure quite what to make of Billie's comments, which flew in the face of her own Catholic upbringing. Billie's views could be so modern that they could challenge her friends, and this was one of those times. 'From what I understand of what you're saying, at least. Our mother is wonderful. I know Connie sometimes feels as though she made things difficult for her, but Mum has always looked out for us. Although, I think if Connie is allowed the chance to be a mother to Martha – a real mother, you know – she would be wonderful too.' Ruby smiled wistfully.

'Of course she would, dear. This is what I'm saying. Connie cares, her heart is as big as the ocean, and for me, that's what you need to be a mother. The rest you can learn. So anybody that can't see that . . . they ain't worthy of her love.' Billie shook her head.

'Yes, I think you're right. It's such a shame. I loved Devon like he was my own brother. But now . . .' Ruby pulled a face, and for the first time Billie could see the bitterness she felt over the demise of her sister's relationship.

'But I don't know what to do with her, Billie. It's been three weeks now and she doesn't seem to be coming to terms with it even a little bit. And I think with Christmas coming it's even harder for her . . .' Ruby's voice trailed off as Connie returned to the room.

'You OK, sis?' she said meekly.

'Please, stop asking me, Ruby.' Connie rolled her eyes. 'I keep telling you, I'm fine. Or at least I'm as good as I can be, for a woman who has been abandoned by the man who said he wanted to spend the rest of his life with her. And worse still, for a mistake I made years ago. Imagine being punished twice for this,' Connie said, her head bowed so the other girls couldn't see the tears welling in her eyes.

But they didn't need to witness her tears to appreciate her emotional state. Connie's sadness had been undeniable – a creeping misery that seemed to stifle the air in the room when she entered. Somehow she had managed to paint a smile on her face while at work because she genuinely loved helping her patients, and working on the maternity ward especially. But beyond that, the heartache she was suffering was clear to all her fellow trainees.

'Oh my, Martha's birthday!' Ruby exclaimed suddenly, covering her mouth with both hands. 'I completely forgot. She was three last week, wasn't she?'

'Yes, she was,' Connie replied, then her despair unfurled completely and she wept.

'Right, we can't carry on like this. Connie, Ruby, it's Christmas

Eve on Friday. I'm supposed to be spending the day with Ezra as he's on call on Christmas Day, so how about we go to the Woodman's on Thursday evening – neither of you are working, are you?' The sisters shook their heads.

'Let's see if we can't get some Christmas cheer going around here? I'll see if Kathleen and the other girls want to come as well,' Billie suggested.

'I don't think I'll be up for that at all,' Connie said through tears.

But Billie's index finger was pressed to her plump, heart-shaped lips, shushing Connie before she could protest further.

'You need this. I think we all need this. And besides, it's Christmas, and it can't just be a time of goodwill to all men – let's have some cheer and goodwill for all us women here too.' Billie gave a positive nod of the head.

As Friday evening came, though, and Ruby had finished getting ready for the night out, she found Connie listening to the radio, and as Dean Martin's 'The Christmas Blues' started up, her sister began to cry.

'Connie! I'm sorry, sis, but you have to stop this,' she implored. 'He isn't worthy of your tears. He didn't even have the decency to see you, or the backbone to tell you to your face how he was feeling.'

'No, Ruby. It's not really that, it's . . . it's this song,' Connie sobbed. 'I thought I'd be excited about my first Christmas in England. But the lyrics are just so sad and they're just how I feel. The bit about how usually Christmas is a time of joy, but when you're lonely it's only for little girls and boys. It's so true,' Connie said miserably.

'You're right about one thing: if anyone has the Christmas blues, it's you,' Ruby stated flatly. 'It's so unfair that he's done this to you. You deserve to be having fun with the rest of us this Christmastime.'

'Well, I'm coming out tonight. I'm not excited about it, but I'm going. Billie all but bullied me into it,' Connie said.

'And that's because she cares about you. We all do, and we want to help shake you out of this misery,' Ruby explained.

'Only Devon can do that, Ruby. Only he can fix this – fix me and make me whole again.'

'Oh no, I don't want to hear any of that,' Billie said, quickly sensing the despair tingeing the air as she walked into the room. 'You don't need a man to make you whole, Connie. They only accentuate the woman that you are, but it's what you have in here that matters.' She tapped her chest. 'It's your courage, your strength and your heart that make you who you are. Men, they're just accessories, pretty ones – you know, like how a lovely hat finishes off an outfit. But no man can make you whole, you have to do that for yourself. And I know you can, you just have to get beyond this . . .' She paused, searching for the word. 'This . . . *grief* that you're going through.'

Connie looked at her friend, clearly startled, and for the first time it was as though someone had got through to her and made her see that she couldn't continue mourning Devon's loss.

She sat there looking thoughtful for a few long seconds.

'I suppose his actions have said it all,' Connie said slowly. There was a moment of quiet between them, each girl inwardly reflecting on the situation.

'I guess we'd better get ready to go out this evening.'

Ruby and Billie caught each other's eye and beamed.

As it was Christmas, all of the trainee nurses got dressed up for the night out. As the evening at the Woodman's progressed there were games and songs, then things became more raucous.

'Cor, get a load of that.' A man eyed Ruby's rounded bottom as she walked by.

She whipped her head around to glare at him, now growing tired of the comments and advances of lascivious men.

'Why can't I just find one nice man? Just one,' Ruby grumbled.

'Give it time, dear. Do you think I found mine just like that?' Billie replied. 'No girl, I had to kiss a whole lot of frogs first.'

'I must be getting all the frogs since you stopped kissing them. I'm so tired of the way men carry on. When they're not making rude comments they're exposing themselves,' she whined.

'What? What do you mean, Ruby?' Phyllis said, eyes wide with surprise.

'A patient called me over just to show me his privates when I was on Oak Ward. I don't know what he took me for,' Ruby said.

'Ach, the dirty bugger!' Kathleen retorted. 'Don't you worry about it though, Ruby, the right man could be just around the corner. That said, I don't know about you girls but the way they have us working double shifts and all, I've barely enough time to bless myself, let alone worry about finding a fella.'

Mei, Lin and Jean nodded.

'You're right, we are pulling some long shifts. Are any of you working on Christmas Day?' Grace asked.

'Yes, I am – a night shift,' Connie replied.

'Connie!' Ruby was surprised. 'You didn't tell me. We won't get to spend time together now. Phyllis was going to bring a record player over on Christmas evening for us.'

'Well, they put me down for it, and I didn't think to ask Sister if I could swap with anyone because . . . I don't see much to celebrate right now, to be honest,' Connie replied matter-of-factly.

'Oh . . .' Ruby sat back in her seat, looking deflated. It was their first Christmas in England and once more, she found the situation with Devon to be a barrier to Connie's happiness, and even her own. 'I guess someone needs to look after the patients. We can't all be off enjoying ourselves,' she said after some thought.

'Hello, ladies. I hope you don't mind, but Billie invited me along to join the festivities. Also, I figured you could perhaps do with a male chaperone; I've heard things can get rather rowdy in here.' The nurses turned to see Ezra smiling awkwardly.

'I'm so happy you made it!' Billie said, hopping out of her seat to place a kiss on his cheek.

'I guess you know everyone, but just in case, this is Connie, Kathleen, Mei, Lin, Grace, Jean, Phyllis,' she said, pointing to each girl in turn. 'And oh yes, I know you know Ruby.'

'Hello, Doctor,' the girls chorused.

'Oh . . . yes, erm . . . please, call me Ezra. At least while we're out and in our civvies. I guess it'll be different when we're back on the wards. Matron doesn't tend to approve of mingling across the different tiers of staff at St Mary's.' He sounded apologetic.

'So how is it you two are *mingling*, and carrying on like you are, then?' Ruby had a puzzled expression on her face.

'Ruby, you're something else!' Billie exclaimed, rolling her big eyes heavenwards. 'For your information, we ain't "carrying on", and we haven't been placed on the same ward since we met on Pear Tree, but if we do I'm sure we can keep things strictly professional.'

'Yes, yes, of course we would,' Ezra said, taking Billie's hand with his right and using his left hand to stroke the back of it.

'But what Matron doesn't know – or anyone else not here at this table . . . what any of them don't know won't hurt them.' Billie smiled a knowing smile.

Soon the party joined the other revellers in singing and dancing, and by the time they left the pub, the girls were all very merry. Ruby noticed how even Connie was smiling for the first time in weeks.

'Girls, I'll be back a little later, I'm going to see Ezra home,' Billie said with a mischievous look in her eye.

'You're going to see him home? But Billie, he's a grown man, why—' Ruby said, before the penny dropped. 'Oh, all right, guess we'll see you later.'

And though Ruby didn't see Billie, because she was fast asleep when the Jamaican girl climbed through an open window to sneak back into the nurses' home, Billie didn't stay out all night as she once would have.

'Ruby, Ruby!' An intense knocking on her bedroom door woke her the next morning. It was Connie, her voice a mixture of excitement and worry. Sleepily, Ruby let her in.

'I just had a phone call. It was Joseph Grant – do you remember him?' Connie urged. 'Devon's brother?' she prompted. But Ruby was still confused.

'What? He called from Barbados?' she said, perplexed.

'No, he's here. He's looking for Devon. He said he arrived in England three weeks ago, and he already had a job lined up in Manchester so he went straight there. But he was due to meet up with Devon in London just as soon as he got the chance. That was this weekend just gone.

'But Devon didn't turn up, Ruby. Joseph doesn't know where he is. Luckily he had taken his address with him, so he went to Devon's flat in Kentish Town and asked for him. But Mrs Silver told him how she hadn't seen Devon in weeks and even I'd stopped calling for him. She allowed Joseph to go and look in his room, to see if he could find any clues to his whereabouts. He found my number and telephoned me. Ruby, Devon's not been ignoring me all these weeks. He's missing!'

'What? Lord, no!' Ruby crossed herself, horrified.

'I know. I don't know whether to jump for joy or feel absolutely terrified,' Connie said, and Ruby saw anxiety winning the battle on her sister's face.

'I don't believe it!' Ruby said. 'Has Joseph reported it to the police already?'

'He has and he's waiting to hear from them. They said they'd be making enquiries. But Joseph said he wants to get the train up to see me today to see if we can piece together where Devon might be,' Connie said.

'I'll come with you to meet him,' Ruby said emphatically, springing up from her bed to get ready.

Joseph Grant reminded Ruby of a younger, slighter version of his brother when he strode off the train from London that afternoon.

She remembered him from back home. She had gone to school at Our Lady's Convent, while he went to St Michael's School for Boys, which was right across the road, and their families were friendly. But with Joseph three years her senior, she didn't feel she knew him well.

She did note his resolve, though. There was something about a person's first few weeks in England, she considered, the experience of travelling 4,000 miles from home, that seemed either to make them bolder – and in the case of men, appear more debonair – or make them subdued and almost meek as they strove to get to grips with their new surroundings. Joseph appeared to be the former.

'Hello, Connie. Ruby! I'm so pleased to see you,' he announced, a broad grin stretching from ear to ear as he hugged them both.

'Is there any further information?' Connie urged as the trio sat together at a nearby tea room.

'No, nothing at all.' Joseph shook his head and sighed, his deep concern for his brother evident. 'It's some kind of madness – my brother has just disappeared into thin air. And the police . . . I wouldn't like to say that they didn't consider this an emergency, but they were a little casual.'

'They said they'd investigate, though, didn't they?' Connie's voice pleaded.

'Yes, yes, they did. But I wanted to see if there was anything else we could figure out,' Joseph explained, and Ruby noted longing in his gentle brown eyes.

Studying his face further, as he spoke to her sister and Connie recounted her last conversation with Devon, Ruby saw yet more that intrigued her. Joseph's face was slimmer than Devon's, but his skin was no less fine and unblemished. It was as though God had carved the brothers out of the finest, shimmering chocolate, pulling their flawless skin taut across their frame.

Then she noticed his mouth and how his bottom lip was thicker than his top one, as though matching his strong jawline, where a light covering of stubble stretched from his cheeks to his chin.

Ruby was all but consumed with Joseph's appearance, wondering how she'd never noticed how attractive he was before. So much so that she wasn't listening as he and her sister tried to piece together Devon's last known activities.

'Do you remember, Ruby, did Devon tell me where he was going with his friends on the phone that night?' Connie asked.

'Er, oh, n-no,' Ruby stuttered as she was pulled back to the tea room's reality. 'I don't think you mentioned anything like that.'

'I just can't imagine where he might have gone,' Connie said next. 'But I'm glad of one thing at least: he didn't just abandon me. You know he was supposed to meet me in a pub near Liverpool Street station.'

Ruby watched as Joseph's brow furrowed. 'Well, that's strange. And he never showed?' Joseph enquired.

Connie slowly shook her head.

'But Connie, I hope you don't think he was trying to let you down easy. Devon is crazy about you,' Joseph smiled, and Ruby noticed it was the same smile that Devon had, his eyes lighting up his face like one of the Christmas displays in the shop windows in town. 'He wrote a lot about you in letters home.'

'He did?' Connie asked, her joy momentarily overtaking her worry.

'Of course!' Joseph nodded. 'It was clear that you were special to him. We just need to find him now. Aside from anything else,

I got plenty jokes to share with him from back home.' He smiled, and soon the trio found themselves reminiscing about life in Barbados.

'And do you remember when Archibald was in front of Mr Thomas's yard and humbugging him?' Joseph was laughing so much he struggled to get the words out. 'He said, "Boy, if I catch you 'bout here again I'll set this billy goat on you." And that would have been ridiculous if it were any other goat. But everybody knew that goat would chase anyone and anything that went past the house, horns down, constantly ready to butt you!' He roared, and soon Connie found herself giggling away. The memory of simple times back home brought them all some much-needed light relief, their worry dissipating for a moment. Ruby realized it was the first time she had seen Joseph laugh that day, and it was much longer since Connie had laughed so heartily.

A few hours later, as Connie excused herself to go to the bathroom, Joseph caught Ruby's eye as she looked at him over the rim of her third cup of tea.

'You like that, don't you?' he observed.

'It's more that I've become accustomed to it. I know we would drink tea at home, but not like here. Back home it's for breakfast alone,' she wittered.

As she put down her cup, Joseph leaned over and took one of her hands in his.

'Ruby, I hope you don't think this forward of me, or in any way . . . I don't know . . . inappropriate, perhaps – because of everything with Devon. But I wondered if you would like to meet up some time? You see,' and his eyes dropped to his cup, as though trying to read his tea leaves to cover his bashfulness, 'well, I always liked you, but you were so involved with Sylvester Adams. When Devon wrote to me and said that he was stepping out with Connie, boy, I have to admit, I was really jealous.' He shook his head with disbelief that he could have felt so negative over something he knew deep down was beautiful. 'Don't get me wrong, I was happy for Devon. Your sister is a fine woman. But, well, I had always hoped that *I* would be the one romancing one of the Haynes girls. By that I mean *you*, of course. It's always been you for me, Ruby,' he mumbled uncomfortably, as though afraid that sharing those words and the feelings associated with them would leave his heart wide open to injury.

'But . . .' Ruby was agog, her heart bouncing in her chest. 'Wait, you say you've felt this way for a long time? Why? Why didn't you tell me before?'

'Ruby Haynes, you are perhaps the most beautiful girl I know. But sometimes – and this is no criticism, mind you – sometimes you seem oblivious to everything around you. All that time you were with that waste of space Sylvester last year, I was secretly yearning for you,' he confessed.

'What? You're kidding!' Ruby said, staggered.

As Connie returned to the table she didn't seem to notice the slightly uncomfortable atmosphere between the pair.

'Joseph, your train is leaving soon. I guess we better get you to the station,' she said.

'Yes. Yes, of course. I'll wait to hear from the police, Connie, and let's hope they have some answers.'

'They must have. Please tell them this is wholly unlike Devon and we're desperately worried about him,' she replied. 'But also, Joseph, be sure to look after yourself, and if you need anything at all, you know where Ruby and I are.'

Connie was so consumed with her fears over Devon that she didn't notice the furtive glances Ruby shared with Joseph over the table, nor the strange silence between them as they all wandered to the station.

But she did notice when the whistle hooted, the engine of Joseph's train reverberated into action and Ruby slipped her arm out of Connie's to race along the platform. Joseph was looking out of the window and a smile filled his face as Ruby came through a plume of smoke to appear level with where he was sat.

'Yes. I will meet up with you. I'm off the Wednesday after Christmas. Call me!' she yelled through the thunderous sound of the engine, and Joseph beamed.

Chapter Twenty-Two

Connie

It was a strange sense that consumed Connie in the days that followed. It was as though, during the previous few weeks, she had expended all the emotion she had within her on Devon, and now, although she was deeply concerned for his wellbeing, she felt numb.

All of her anger, anguish, sadness and torment seemed to disappear and Connie was left with her practical head, while something deep within her – perhaps her faith – told her he was alive, she only had to find him.

On Christmas Day the sisters went to church in the morning, just as they always had back home.

'Merry Christmas!' Kathleen and Billie said to the sisters later when they pulled crackers at Christmas lunch in the dining room.

'Billie, are you not going to wear your paper hat?' Ruby enquired.

'What, and mess with my Christmas hair? No, dear, not today. Besides, I'll be seeing you-know-who later and I want to look my best.' She stroked her bouffant and puffed it up slightly, away from the nape of her neck.

'Ohh, it's all about *him* these days, eh?' Ruby replied.

'Ruby Haynes, I don't know how you could sound so innocent! Tell them about your date on Wednesday,' Connie said.

'A date! What? You seeing a boy?' Billie replied.

'Good on yer!' Kathleen said, noticing the shy but pleased-as-Punch look on Ruby's face.

'Yes. It's a first date, so we'll have to see how it goes. But he is sweet. It's Devon's brother, Joseph. Connie told you about us meeting up with him.' Ruby felt an intense heat rising within, setting her skin aglow.

'Now that is exciting,' Billie decided. 'Let's raise a toast to that,' she continued, holding her glass of water in the air. 'And we'll do it properly later on, too – my friend Esme gave me some more rum from home; someone brought it over for her, but she's not much of a drinker. Said it should go to a better home,' she chuckled.

'Ooh, nice. I'm looking forward to our get-together tonight – it's a shame you won't be there, Connie,' Ruby said.

Connie looked a little glum, but deep down she didn't mind working as it was keeping her thoughts in check. When she was busy on the ward, she didn't have time to worry about Devon or focus on her fears.

That evening, and for the rest of her shift, the maternity ward was quiet. Only three new mothers had been kept in during the holiday weekend, and, with their babies happily tucked up in their cots between feeds, Connie was able to join her patients around a television that had been shipped in specially for them to watch *Television's Christmas Party* on the BBC.

Though her mind drifted during the show, a string of comedy acts and the all-round festive cheer had everyone laughing happily.

Two days later, Connie managed to find a modicum of happiness too, when Joseph called to speak about Devon. He didn't really have much news to share, however.

'The Christmas break seems to have put the police's enquiries on hold. They said they couldn't get hold of anyone at Devon's work as they're closed for a couple of weeks for the holidays,' he told her on the phone.

The next day, however, Joseph came up to Four Oaks again to take Ruby on their planned date. They were going to the cinema, and Connie suggested they also go to Minstrels, but when she saw how Ruby was dressed she thought she may as well have suggested the Ritz.

'Man, Ruby, you really are dressed to the nines! Who did your hair like that?' she asked as she came home from work.

'Do you like it? Billie used her hot comb and then curled it under and poofed it up, just like Eartha Kitt wears hers. You know, I've heard her singing "Santa Baby" everywhere I go this year,' Ruby replied.

'Just don't be getting any ideas about Joseph buying you sables and yachts like in the song,' Connie teased, but she was immensely excited for her sister's date that evening. 'Tell Joseph I said hello, and I expect him to get you back home at a respectable hour,' she warned.

'Yes, Mum,' Ruby giggled cheekily, as Connie threw a cushion at her.

'Get going!' she shouted after her. 'And have a lovely time!'

And Ruby did. Three and a half hours later she was back home, and found all the girls in the sitting room to regale them with tales of her night out on the town with her new beau.

'And he said, "Ruby" . . .' And here she paused for dramatic effect. '"Would it be inappropriate of me to kiss you?" I said, "I don't think so," and then he did it – he leaned over and kissed me.'

'No! He didn't!' Jean shrieked, hanging on Ruby's every word.

'Oh my goodness. Girl, you've wasted no time at all,' Connie sighed.

'Ach yeah, she's a fast cat, so she is,' Kathleen joked.

'I don't even know you. Where's innocent-as-a-lamb Ruby Haynes disappeared to?' Billie said in jest, though with a little genuine surprise at how Ruby was changing. But they were all thrilled that she had found a man who seemed as keen on her as she was on him.

For Connie, however, ever since Devon had gone missing, it was her work that was driving her – it had become a safety net, and she felt at home with the women she met on the maternity ward. Most of them were young, just like her, and mothers, just like her. That kinship made her appreciate her time on maternity all the more.

So as the first working day of 1955 arrived, and the girls were given their new assignments on the Change List, Connie was devastated.

'Oh no! Billie, look at this. How could they put me *there*?'

'What's up, dear?' Billie said, taking the piece of paper from her friend. Her next placement was to be on the maternity ward but, seeing Connie's upset, she quickly folded her notice and put it into her pocket.

'Not only do I have to leave my beloved maternity, but they want me to go and work in the psychiatric unit!' Connie cried.

'And I'll be with the children on Pear Tree!' Ruby grinned. 'You loved it there, didn't you, Billie? What have you got?'

'Yes, I did. And I'm sure you will too. I'm sorry, Connie. They've given me maternity,' Billie said flatly.

'Oh no, no! This is so unfair, how am I going to cope with all those . . . those *crazy* people? I don't know anything about that kind of work.'

'Yes, but isn't that why they give us different wards to work on?' Phyllis asked innocently.

'Tell me something, Phyllis, where will your rotation take you?' Connie demanded.

'I'm going to accident and emergency,' the other girl said.

'Right. And have any of you had to go to the psychiatric unit yet?' Connie said, emotion welling within.

'No, I haven't, but neither's Jean,' Phyllis replied.

'Exactly, and I bet she won't, but you'll probably find that Ruby or Billie are up there next. This is something I've heard about before – Caribbean nurses are given all the worst jobs, and the toughest placements,' Connie said. 'That Jamaican staff nurse Ruth Campbell once told me she got stuck on psychiatry for a double rotation – six solid months. She thought she'd never get away from there.'

'I'm sure it's not that, Connie. I'm sure we will all have our turn there,' Phyllis tried to reassure her. 'After all, we don't get a choice where we're sent.' But Connie was livid, her deepening concerns for Devon fusing with her frustration over her placement and tipping her over the edge into a fiery pit of rage.

'I'll be back later,' she said, storming out of the nurses' home as she went for a long walk. It was a blustery, icy winter's morning that seemed unlikely to warm up enough to melt the hard frost that shrouded the hospital grounds in a white cloak.

But for once, Connie found the frigid air restorative, tempering the burning anger within her, while the wind helped to blow out the cobwebs that had gathered in the recesses of her mind since Devon's disappearance. And yet, her brain whirred with questions.

What if he's sick? Will the police have phoned all the hospitals? When will they have information? What if they never find him? What if I get stuck on psych forever more? However will I cope with that?

What am I going to do?

It was rare that practical Connie felt quite so helpless.

Later that week, she said her goodbyes to the patients and nursing staff on the maternity ward. And as Monday morning came around, Connie woke with her alarm.

It was still dark, and with the sound of rain pounding the roof and pavement outside, and the howling wind, she didn't want to get out of bed, let alone suffer the misery of the psychiatric unit.

'Come on, Connie.' She spoke to herself as though in an effort to propel her body from her bed. 'These people deserve your care as much as anyone else.'

An hour later she leapt over puddles that were too big to side-step, on her way to the unit. The weather was so dull that even when the gloom of the early morning lifted, it still seemed more like five o'clock in the evening than half past eight in the morning. Dense, dark, lead-grey clouds filled the sky. Despite the winds that swirled around the hospital grounds, the clouds appeared unmoving, as though they were fixed in place for the day.

'Good morning, you must be Nurse Haynes,' said the ward sister, who was waiting by the door as Connie entered the ward.

'Oh I'm sorry, I'm not late, am I? I set off in good time, but this weather! I couldn't even walk along the path properly what with the huge puddles,' Connie explained.

'No, no, you're right on time. I'm Sister Jeffries,' the woman said, looking at her over silver-rimmed cat-eye glasses. 'You're our only trainee, currently. And we're very pleased you're here, as there's always a lot of heavy lifting to do. But before we get started I must give you an orientation. This is of course the hospital's psychiatric unit, but more than that, it is one of the leading centres for psychiatric care in the country. So we don't only treat patients from Four Oaks, but they're referred to us from all over the south-east and as far away as the Midlands.

'Now most of our patients are just fine. They may be having a few problems at home and are a little depressed, is all. Then there are some that can get very distressed and want to hurt themselves or someone else, because, you see, we treat all kinds of conditions here, from depression through to various forms of psychosis. And so we have rules that must be followed for every-one's safety, but you'll pick everything up as you go along,' Sister Jeffries said. 'I have Staff Nurse Robinson set to work alongside you while you're here, and we've co-ordinated your shift patterns so you have someone with you showing you the ropes at all times. Any questions?'

A sinking feeling came over Connie – what if they wanted her to stay here forever?

'Sister, how long have most people stayed up here? Nurses, I mean?' she said.

'Most will just do the usual three-month rotation, but some have stayed a little longer. But you'll likely find that it isn't as dreadful here as you might expect,' she said curtly.

'Yes, Sister,' Connie replied with the broadest smile she could manage, as she sensed a little of the other woman's ire. Perhaps she hadn't been the first trainee nurse to want to run for the hills rather than work here, she thought.

Try as she might to paint a smile on her face, though, Connie felt like the weather – dull, unsettled and rather miserable at the prospect of three whole months working in psychiatry.

She spent her first day shadowing the staff nurse, Mary Robinson, on the east wing of the unit, where they were caring for thirty-five female patients.

'Oh my goodness, Mary, is the unit always full like this? I've not seen a ward so busy in the hospital yet,' Connie puffed as she raced to keep up with the more senior nurse.

'Yes, it's like this quite a lot. It's because people come here from all over the place,' Mary explained.

Though it was only mid-morning, with the gloomy weather turning the day to near night, the room was drenched in stark fluorescent light that caught the patients' blank, disassociated faces. Looking around, Connie found most of the women were staring off into space, a couple mumbling incoherently to themselves, while two others were tied to their beds with straps.

'Wh-why are they tied like that?' she asked cautiously. 'Surely that's not right.'

'Oh, those are a couple of our long stays – that's Mavis and

Betty, they like to go wandering, and right off the ward if we don't keep an eye on them. And as you can see it's far too busy for us to keep watch on everyone all the time, so we have to nail them down, so to speak,' Mary said with what Connie considered jarring joviality.

The afternoon was punctuated by behaviour Connie was unaccustomed to, such as a woman repeatedly shouting: 'I'm in love with the Lord.' But despite that, and the empty, at times haunting stares of some of the patients, she found the unit to be much like any other ward at St Mary's: there were sick people there who needed her care to get well. The only thing Connie did hope for was that her time there would be short because, she thought, no matter how anyone tried to window-dress it, it was one of the least desirable appointments in the hospital.

'So, how was it?' Ruby asked as she got in from her shift.

'I guess it is an opportunity to learn, which you know I always relish, but it sure as hell ain't somewhere I'd like to be working long term. There's something so dismal about it,' she replied.

'It probably wasn't helped by the miserable weather today. It made me miss home more than ever,' Ruby said longingly.

'Wait, you miss home? Ruby Haynes, I never would have expected it. You're always so upbeat about living in England,' Connie said.

'Oh, I love it here! But it doesn't stop me missing Mum, Dad and Harold, they're my heart. But sometimes I miss other things, too – like I might remember Miss Jacobs and how she all but lived at our house, and I start to miss her. Or I'll think about different people from the neighbourhood and before I know it, I miss them.' She sighed. 'But you know, that's another reason I feel so comfortable with Joseph. It's as though he's brought a little bit of home with him here.'

And then she caught herself. Ruby brought her hands up to cover her mouth. 'I'm so sorry, Connie, I can be so insensitive sometimes. How could I say such things when you're desperate for news of Devon?'

'No, Ruby, you don't need to apologize. Life can't come to a halt because Devon isn't here and I couldn't be happier for you. Joseph is lovely. I guess that was something I loved about Devon, too – he reminded me so much of home. It was little things really, like the way he spoke or just his mannerisms. Man! It was as though I'd found a piece of home up here.' A half-smile graced Connie's face as she thought back to all the ways in which Devon enriched her life. 'I just hope there's news on him soon, you know.'

'I know, sis. I'm with you – if only he knew how anxious we all were about him, he'd be real vex at us getting so worked up.' Ruby smiled at the thought.

'Anyway, back to you and Joseph,' Connie said, taking her younger sister's hand. 'Now remember how you used to mess about and tell Devon you needed to check him out in Mum and Dad's absence? I want you to know that I'm keeping my eye on you too, young lady. Joseph's all right, in fact I think he's a fine young man, and I have high hopes for you and him. But I don't want you getting all carried away now. I know you've been writing to one another and you've known each other since we were all kids back home, but you've only been on one date with him. Take things easy and steady, my sweet sister. I don't want you to jump in with both feet and come unstuck. The most loving relationships are built on solid foundations, and that requires time to get to know someone and develop a mutual love and trust,' she cautioned.

'Connie,' Ruby smiled, hugging her sister. 'Man, when did you get so wise! Love you, sis, and thank you. I promise to slow down and try not to run before I can walk with this one. Though we do have plans to see each other this weekend,' she said with a sparkle in her eyes.

At that moment Mei appeared in the doorway. 'Connie, there's a call for you. Someone called Joseph?'

'Speak of the devil,' Connie replied.

'Indeed,' Ruby said, and also wondered fleetingly why he was calling to speak to Connie and not her. 'Do you think he might have news on Devon?' she added seconds later.

'Oh,' was all Connie could utter. Her heart started pounding hard in her chest and her palms became sweaty as she raced from the room.

'Hello, Joseph?' she said, tension strangling her words. She swallowed hard to contain her emotion.

'Connie, hello. I have news. It's not good news, but it's not bad news. It's just—'

'Man, Joseph, spit it out,' Connie said, her anxiety quickly morphing into mild irritation at Joseph's inexperienced delivery.

'A Sergeant Smythe of Camden Town police called. He said they've finally been in touch with the foreman at the freight yard where Devon was working, now that they're back after the Christmas break. They say that on the Friday before he was due to meet you last month, Devon was involved in an accident in the yard.'

'What? My goodness! Is he OK? Joseph, tell me he's OK,' Connie cried.

'They said there was a collision between two of the wagons on a siding. Devon was nearly caught in between them and he could have been crushed. But one of the other fellas he works with pulled him out of the way at the last minute. They both tumbled down a bank, and he ended up with some broken bones. He was in the Royal London Hospital for a few days. He had some sort of fracture. Um . . . let me see . . . I wrote it down here . . .

'That's right, he fractured the femur and the tibia of his right leg, so he had to stay in hospital for a few weeks while he recovered,' Joseph explained.

'So that's where he is, at the Royal London? Why didn't he

get them to call you or me? Oh my goodness. I'll come down tomorrow, Joseph. I can come and meet you right after my shift ends if you're free.'

'No, Connie. Wait. You see, that's the trouble. He *was* there, but they say he's not at the Royal London any more. The policeman told me they were waiting to speak to the consultant that was in charge of his care tomorrow, then he'll call me back with more information.' Joseph's words were a sharp pin in the balloon of Connie's hope.

'Oh,' she said, deflated. 'I guess it's something. At least we know he was treated, that he's alive . . . or at least, he . . . *was*,' she mumbled, her last words all but inaudible.

'I wanted you to know just as soon as I did. I know it's not exactly the news we hoped for, but it's something. At least we now have some information. I'll call you again when I hear back from Sergeant Smythe,' he assured her.

'Thank you, Joseph. It's such a relief to hear this news at least,' Connie said, and for the first time in a month, she didn't feel the suffocating unease she had felt about Devon. She realized he hadn't purposely stood her up that day. He probably hadn't had any intention of abandoning her.

It wasn't my fault.

Connie passed the phone to Ruby for her to speak to Joseph. A few minutes later, as she hung up, she was all smiles.

'My goodness, it's such a relief to finally get news about Devon. It is strange though – he's no longer in hospital, and he hasn't been in touch with either of you. Why ever not?' Ruby's brow furrowed as she bit her lip.

'Yes, I don't quite know how to take this news, because we still haven't found him, but at least we know he was being looked after in hospital. I can't even bear to think about that accident and what might have happened to him. It makes my blood run cold. But one other thing I'm happy about, Ruby, is that it seems he didn't abandon me, or stand me up at the pub that day. It looks as though this isn't about Martha at all,' Connie said.

'The police will find him, Connie. I'm sure of it!' Ruby hugged her sister.

The chink of hope provided by the police's information had brought some light to what had been a pretty dark day, what with the storm and the sad, empty eyes of the patients on the psychiatric unit. But Connie had a restless night's sleep.

So as she headed to work the next day, she was tired and for the first time since she'd arrived in Four Oaks, she was wishing she could be anywhere but there.

'Morning, Nurse. You'll be working with Staff Nurse Robinson on the west wing today. The doctor's just finished his rounds,' Sister Jeffries said, breezing to the front desk and then marching quickly off again.

'Staff Nurse Jackson, follow me please, we need to look in on Mrs Saunders,' she bustled, as another nurse hurriedly fell into step beside her.

Connie looked around, but not seeing Mary she headed to the west wing to find her. As she wandered the corridor populated by men, she could hear shouting from patients who seemed to be rowing with themselves, while others sat on their beds mumbling incoherently. Then she found Mary.

'Morning,' she said. 'I'm just finishing the drugs round, then we can organize breakfasts.'

'OK, sounds good, are there many more to give out?' Connie enquired, busying herself by handing Mary small cups with the drugs inside.

'Just the two at the end by the window; the patient in bed three on the right needs this one. Then when you're done with that you can take this to the man in bed four on the left,' Mary said, and Connie took the first cup of drugs down to the bed at the end. It was curtained off, like many of the others, as Sister had informed her that it tended to help calm the patients.

'Hello, Mr Bailey,' she said, looking at his name above the bed. 'I've got these for you.' She made sure the tired-looking man had swallowed the pills before she left him to rest, and moved on to take the medication to the next patient.

As she pulled back the curtain, she recoiled in horror, almost dropping the cup.

For a few seconds, Connie thought her eyes were deceiving her, or that perhaps somehow she was seeing things.

There, lying in the bed, was Devon, his eyes barely open.

She rushed to his bedside, almost crashing into the counter-weights of the traction that connected to his leg. Then, putting her face close to his, she took in each line, every hair on his head in an effort for her brain to corroborate what her eyes were seeing.

'De—' Her voice caught in her throat, as though she feared uttering his name could wake her from a dream.

'Devon,' she whispered, then a little louder: 'Devon. Can it really be you?'

He stirred, and as he turned his head, she could see all of his face. Then, looking the length of the bed, she saw the white of his plastered right leg as it hung in mid-air supported by the traction, a sharp contrast to the heavy charcoal grey woollen blanket that covered the bed.

'Devon, it is you, it's really you,' she said, gently stroking his face. Her own was hot, sweat beading on her forehead, as she fought to hold in her tears. Though they would have been tears of joy, she didn't want anyone to see her crying over a patient.

But how is he a patient here?

Connie's thoughts drifted until she was pulled back into the room by Devon's voice.

'*Connie?* Wh . . . what? Where am I?' his sleepy voice croaked and she saw confusion line his face.

'Devon, darling, it's you. It's OK,' her voice soothed, as she saw him physically tense. 'You're safe. You're safe here. I've been so worried, so upset. I looked all over for you, and Joseph too. He's been looking for you everywhere.' Words tumbled from Connie, as she held Devon's face and gently kissed his forehead. It felt almost inappropriate – she had kissed a patient – but Connie, still shielded from view by the curtain and finally having Devon in her arms again, didn't care.

'You're in Four Oaks, you're in St Mary's. I don't know how you ended up *here*, though,' she said, taking up his chart to review his notes as Devon's eyelids drooped heavily and he drifted in and out of sleep.

Connie's mind was fired up as she frantically scoured the notes for the answers it was clear Devon was unable to provide. Then suddenly, she found it, scrawled in the hand of a consultant psychiatrist at the Royal London: 'It would appear as though the accident at the patient's place of employment has triggered symptoms which can only relate to combat stress reaction, following the patient's time in the forces during the war. We are therefore transferring Mr Grant from here to the specialist psychiatric unit at St Mary's Hospital in Hertfordshire for further treatment,' it read.

A chill ran along Connie's spine and prickled at her skin, raising goosebumps in its wake.

'Good Lord, Devon,' she exhaled mournfully, looking at the man she had fallen in love with through sad eyes.

The heavy blanket that cloaked his frame in the bed made him look so small, Connie could barely believe this was the same man whose strong arms had made her feel so loved and secure only weeks before.

Where was his light? Where was that devilish smile and twinkle in his eyes? He looked thinner, shrunken, and when she looked into his sleep-heavy eyes, this time she also saw fear.

'Devon, darling, I'm so sorry. I didn't know. I could have helped you, if I'd only seen the signs,' she said, cradling his head in her arms.

'No . . . It's not your fault,' he whispered, and for the first time in weeks, Connie felt able to breathe.

'I'm going to help you. I'm a nurse, and I'm going to help you get better. Starting from now – take these,' she said, and placed the cup of pills along with a glass of water into his quivering hands. Though neither of them had realized it, they both now had tears rolling down their cheeks.

'I thought I'd lost you forever,' she said.

'Never,' he said quietly. He looked bewildered and more exhausted than she'd ever seen him and Connie realized those few words were about as much as he could muster.

'I'm going to go now. You need your rest. But as soon as I can this evening, I'll call Joseph and let him know I've found you. He's been so, so worried,' she said, and placed a kiss lightly on his cheek.

'You all right? You look like you've seen a ghost or something,' Mary said as Connie walked towards her.

'Yes, yes, I'm fine. In fact, I think I'm better than I have been in a long time. But I must speak to Sister,' she said and hurried to find Sister Jeffries.

Within the hour, Connie had told the sister how she knew Devon and had even spoken to the consultant he was under, Mr Battersby.

'Did you ever notice any of the following conditions in him?' he asked. 'Depression, sleep problems, headache, irritability, anxiety, shaking, poor concentration or avoidance of social contact? Did he ever complain of having nightmares? They're among the most typical symptoms we see in the ex-servicemen we treat for combat stress reaction. They used to call it shell-shock years ago, but we're starting to better understand it now – that there's a little more to it than just shock.'

'Oh my,' Connie said, her eyes widening. 'Devon was in the army during the war. He seemed so calm and together most of the time so I would say no to the depression.'

But slowly, a look of recognition began to grow on Connie's face.

'Now you mention it, I do remember one very strange episode. It must have been his anxiety peaking,' and she told him all about the incident outside the Woodman's Arms.

'Yes, that sounds about right. It seems as though unexpected loud noises can spark dreadful memories for him and he's right back there, on the field of battle – facing all the fear and horrors of war time and time again. He said that all he remembers from his work accident was a hell of a commotion as the train wagons collided, and then he blacked out,' Mr Battersby explained.

'When we checked on his service record with the War Office to find out more about the problems he was having, there were details of an incident. It would seem he was clearing a house in France during the D-Day operation and the area came under some heavy shelling. The building collapsed around him and he was stuck under rubble for two whole days before a search team was able to rescue him.'

Connie looked shocked, but then remembered that Devon had once told her about being sent on a mission to France near the end of his time in the forces, and she thought of how he otherwise never spoke at length of his time in the military.

'It seems that his physical scars healed, and his leg will heal just fine too in a few more weeks. But the mental scars, they can take much longer, I'm afraid,' the consultant continued. 'The future is very much unknown for someone with his condition. But for now, we're giving him sedation so he can at least get some rest. He had weeks of sleeplessness at the Royal London. I dare say, though, with a little love and support he will rally.'

'Thank you so much, Doctor,' Connie said, finally understanding far more about what had brought Devon to the hospital and more too about the strange incident a few months earlier.

Before leaving the ward at the end of her shift, she went first to see Devon and found him sleeping soundly.

'I'm off now,' she whispered to him. 'But I'll be back, every day, and I will help you recover. We will beat this together, my darling.'

In another part of the hospital, Billie threw her woollen cape over her shoulders at the end of her shift and rushed across the hospital grounds. She had a new dress hanging in her wardrobe and she wanted plenty of time to get ready and get out to meet Ezra that evening.

As she hurried along the path, she met Connie racing from the opposite direction.

'Billie! I found him, he's OK!' The relief on Connie's face was evident.

'What? Devon? Did Joseph call? They found him in London?' Billie asked.

'No, he's *here*. Gosh, there's so much to explain,' Connie said, slowing her thoughts and her speech to detail everything to Billie as the pair sped through the hospital grounds.

'I don't believe it! Poor Devon. What he must have gone through with the war and everything. It's dreadful!' Billie said with a look of dismay.

'I know – my heart nearly broke in two when I saw him there in the bed, Billie. He looked so different – thinner, tired, I don't know. But he didn't look himself at all. I was so shocked. But the good news is that we've found him. I need to call Joseph,' she said breathlessly as they arrived home.

'Ruby, Ruby!' she called to her sister.

'What's up?' Ruby said, poking her head out of her door. 'Oh my! You look like you've seen a ghost, Connie.'

'Not a ghost, but Devon, I've found Devon.'

She then proceeded to tell her sister the whole story. When she had finally finished, she said, 'So I must call Joseph – do you know when he finishes work?'

'This is so wonderful! He should be home in about an hour. He's been so, so worried, Connie – he'll be thrilled,' Ruby exclaimed, and she was right.

When Connie was able to get him on the phone, Joseph was overjoyed. 'I'll take a couple of days off work, come straight down tomorrow morning – my employer knows I've been searching for Devon so he said I could take time off as needed. Lord Jesus, it's such a relief to find him! But what saddens me is that he has been going through all of this and he was keeping it to himself for so long. I remember a few incidents when Devon came back to Barbados right after the war. He had nightmares, and he could be very quiet and a bit withdrawn. He was still my brother, but the Devon that had left us a couple of years before was not the one that returned. So when he left to come up here, well, we felt it was something he *had* to do in some respects. As though he needed to come back up to Europe to exorcise some of these evils.

'But Connie, thank you. Thank you for loving my brother. I'm sure he'll be feeling better already having seen you and knowing that you're by his side.'

Joseph's words ignited a warmth in Connie's heart and she felt flush with respair. After weeks of disappointment, anger, worry and upset, she now had fresh hope for her future with Devon.

'You don't need to thank me, I couldn't not love him,' she smiled. 'Also, I know you're coming to see Devon, but Ruby will be so excited to see you too.'

'Yes, it's been a few weeks since I've seen her now. Her letters have been wonderful, but somehow that just isn't enough,' he said.

Chapter Twenty-Three

Billie

'Look at you!' Billie soothed with a half-smile as she came downstairs on her way out. She felt immensely happy for Connie. 'I know Devon's diagnosis is unexpected, but like you said, I'm sure having you here will help him tremendously. If anyone can help him pull through, it's going to be you, Connie. Not only are you a caring nurse, but you love that man. I'm so happy that you found him again and he's safe, at least.'

'Me too. And yes, I will, Billie; I will do whatever it takes to help him,' Connie said. 'Enjoy your evening with that lovely doctor of yours.'

'Thank you. We're lucky girls really, Connie. They're both lovely men. And now there's Ruby dating that sweet Joseph. Who knows, maybe one day, we'll all be married ladies, and we'll give up looking after others to look after our husbands,' she said.

'Wait a minute! You? Never. I could see you married, yes. He's *bound* to ask you soon. But giving up work to look after your husband? Most women would, but most women are not Billie Benjamin,' Connie said.

'Well, ain't that the truth,' Billie couldn't help but laugh.

Minutes later she hopped into Ezra's car, and their lips met in a passionate kiss, Billie's relief for her friend making her hold her man tighter and for a few seconds longer.

'Oh Ezra, we've had such good news – well, it's hopeful at least,' she piped cheerily as he started up the engine. 'Connie has found her boyfriend, Devon.'

During the drive Billie told Ezra all the news.

'Ah, combat-related stress. Yes, I've heard it spoken of but haven't witnessed it myself,' Ezra explained. 'My, what terrible ills we have wrought upon ourselves through war.'

'Yes, it's dreadful,' she agreed, picking lint off Ezra's navy blue suit jacket.

'We'd planned a dinner tonight, but I wondered if you'd like to go to the cinema first? There's that new Mickey Spillane film on,' he said.

'Yes, let's. As long as I'm with you, I'm happy wherever we go,' she smiled.

As they watched the film, Ezra placed his arm around Billie and she rested her head on his shoulder, and when he kissed her head, she felt as contented as she'd ever been.

'Do you ever think about getting married again?' she asked him later, as he fixed them a late supper.

'I, erm . . . not really,' and Billie saw him use his flop of hair to cover his bashfulness. There was an uneasy quiet between them for a couple of minutes, then he said: 'If I was to marry anyone, though, it would be you.'

'What took you so long to answer, mister?' Billie said with mild indignation. 'I thought you were trying to suggest I wasn't the one.'

He laughed. 'You are definitely the one, and I most certainly am committed to you. It's just, well, marriage . . .' He tailed off, a sadness momentarily dimming the light in his eyes. 'But yes, we will *have* to marry one day, because I want our commitment to each other to be known publicly and I want to get to know and love every part of you.'

'Exactly. I've been waiting a long time to get to know you too,'

Billie flashed him a suggestive stare. 'So don't keep me waiting too long now.' And, placing her arms around his neck, she pulled him towards her and they kissed deeply, Ezra's hands running from her small waist up her back and down again to gently caress the generous curve of her bottom.

As Billie's lips moved to kiss Ezra's neck, he moaned lightly, and taking that as encouragement, she undid the buttons of his shirt and ventured a little lower, her lips stroking his chest as she felt his heart beating faster and faster.

'My darling, you win. We will marry one day, and soon,' Ezra breathed. 'The truth is, I can't wait for you much longer.' Then, lifting her face to plant a passionate kiss on her lips, he did up the buttons on his shirt.

'Well you'd better propose soon enough, spoilsport!' she giggled. But deep down, as much as her lust for Ezra was in danger of boiling over, she appreciated him taking things slowly. Not only did it show her how much he cared about her, but she was enjoying getting to know him, including what she saw as his eccentricities.

The next day and the next few weeks made Billie realize how much she enjoyed working with people and nursing too. For her, it went beyond prepping mothers for birth and seeing newborns on the ward – Billie realized she was keen to see that the mothers were well enough to go home, as well as ensure that they were suitably equipped to look after their babies when they left hospital.

'Yes, Mrs Williams, that's right, be sure to support baby's head now too. That will give you both the best experience while feeding him,' she advised.

Later, Sister Harding took her to one side. 'You know, you show great promise in the way you relate to patients and I know you're passionate about their care beyond the walls of St Mary's. You may want to look into community nursing when you've finished your training. There's a lot of great work done by community midwives and health visitors,' she said.

'Oh, that's not something I've thought about before,' Billie replied.

'Yes, well you see the National Health Service is providing services to people who need many levels of care, and as such it's opened up more areas of work to young women,' the ward sister explained. 'It's just something to think about.'

And think about it Billie did, then she resolved to speak to Ezra about it later and get his thoughts.

That afternoon, she was called to assist with her first delivery. The baby was breech and there were concerns for the mother, who seemed to be in some distress. Billie watched, trying not to let worry show on her face as the midwife calmed her patient and then handled the bottom-first delivery with aplomb. The mother pushed and pushed until the baby's scrunched-up face appeared, then, blinking, he took his first look at the world around him, and at Billie, as he was passed to her for washing. As she did so, she felt joy filling her heart at the new life that had entered the world. And, later, when the boy's father arrived to see his wife and son back on the ward, Billie looked on gleefully as she witnessed the birth of a new family.

'Connie,' she said later that evening, recounting the highlights of her day, 'you didn't tell me maternity was such a delight! I loved seeing the three of them there together, now not just husband and wife, but a family. You know I lost my mother at a young age, and I only wish my father had been around more, so seeing them together . . . it just made me realize how beautiful family can be,' she gushed.

'Oh I know,' Connie smiled. 'It's one of the many wonders of the maternity ward. I think it's possibly the best place to work here.'

'And now tell me, how's things going with Devon? Are you seeing any improvements at all yet?' Billie asked her friend.

Connie sighed. 'Well, his leg is mending,' she said, as though searching for positives. 'But his mind . . . oh Billie. I think it's shattered into pieces. Everyone up there is so kind, and I try not to spend too much time with Devon during my shifts, but instead I stay on afterwards to talk to him and make sure he's comfortable and at ease, but he's still terribly anxious. Dr Battersby and Sister Jeffries have been wonderful, though, and they've taken time to explain a lot of his symptoms. I even bumped into Matron Wilson today and she'd heard all about Devon too. She told me how she'd lost her husband and son in the war. Her husband was an air-raid warden and he died when Four Oaks was bombed. And then her son was just twenty-two when he died while serving in Bomber Command in the Air Force. She said it was devastating that we're nearly ten years on from the end of the war, yet our menfolk are still suffering the effects of it. She said, "Why can't nations come together to work for a better future for all?"'

'Goodness, I can understand her sentiment. I didn't realize she'd suffered so much loss,' Billie said, feeling unexpected empathy for the matron. 'But yes, it seems as though the war had terrible effects on everyone up here; I only need to speak to Ezra to appreciate that.'

It wasn't until three weeks later, however, that the legacy of war would again reveal its destructive hold on the hopes and happiness of the people of St Mary's.

It was a freezing February evening as Billie shared a beer and a chat with her trainee friends in the sitting room. It was now one year since they'd all met and they were celebrating their achievements, the establishment of firm friendships, and reminiscing over the highs and lows of their first full year of training.

'Billie, there's a call for you downstairs,' Ruby said, entering the room. 'I think it might be your fancy man. I'd just finished speaking to Joseph when he called.'

'Girl, you're so cheeky! And how is that boy of yours?' she shouted as the door started closing behind her.

'Oh, he's good – I'm excited as I'm looking forward to seeing him at the weekend,' Ruby grinned as Billie smiled back then raced downstairs.

'Hello,' she cooed into the phone.

'Hello, Billie,' Ezra said, urgency and apprehension coating his tone but at first Billie didn't notice.

'Hello, handsome. I guess you're calling to tell me how in love with me you are and to propose, because you can't bear to be separated from me for a moment longer,' she said, sultriness dripping from her voice.

'Billie, I have to see you. Are you free? Can I pick you up now?' he replied flatly.

'Oh, it's like that, is it? Well, of course, I'm always at your beck and call,' she flirted.

'Good, I'll be there in twenty minutes,' he said.

Billie flung herself up the stairs, smoothing her hair as she went, then rushed to her bedroom to change from her comfortable cigarette pants into a slim-fitting light grey woollen pencil skirt and a white turtleneck jumper. Then she secured a black and white scarf around her neck, being sure to pop the ties to one side. Deep down, she knew that Ezra didn't care what she wore. She knew his interest in her went way beyond her appearance, but Billie didn't feel like Billie until she had changed and topped off the look with a slick of red lipstick.

'Where are you off to?' Connie enquired.

'I'm going out,' Billie replied. 'Ezra said he wanted to see me urgently and you know, it's not good to keep a good man waiting,' she winked.

Minutes later she hopped into Ezra's car and leaned over for a kiss, but her lips landed on his cheek as he started up the engine.

'Hello, I desperately needed to speak to you,' he said. But as Billie did most of the talking during the drive, by the time they had arrived at Ezra's house, she felt a little confused.

'So, mister, what gives? And why haven't I got a kiss yet?' She stepped towards him as the door closed behind them.

'Please,' he said quietly, taking her by the hand. 'Let's sit down.'

He turned on a table lamp, which instead of lighting the room, seemed to emphasize dark shadows that gathered in the corners.

'Ezra? What's up?' Billie said, now sensing his brooding disquiet.

'I barely know where to begin, Billie.' He shook his head. 'I— You know I love you.'

'Yes, I do. But you're scaring me, Ezra. I've never seen you like this before, your face is ashen. What on earth has happened? You can tell me anything, my darling, I would never judge you.'

'I had a letter this morning,' Ezra said slowly, reaching into his pocket. 'It came from Israel. I don't know anyone in Israel, or at least . . . I didn't think I did.'

Billie struggled to place the look on his face, it was somewhere between apprehension, nervousness, sorrow and guilt. Whatever the contents of the letter, it was obviously utterly unexpected and seemed to have thrown him into disarray.

'Billie, I told you about how I came to be in England, about how the Nazis invaded my city and rounded up people like me, but I escaped with the help of the Resistance. Honestly, I try not to talk about it – the memories are so painful. But I think now I have to tell you the whole story,' he said quietly, thumbing the envelope that he had taken from his pocket, on which Billie could see his name and address written in a neat hand.

'Ezra, it's OK. Take your time and talk to me,' she soothed.

'There is one day in my life that I find it impossible to forgive myself for, and it is one of my final days in the Netherlands. I told you how I was married before,' he said slowly, as though talking about his life was a burden he could barely carry. 'My wife, Hannah, she was a beautiful and stoic woman. We were twenty-four when we were married, and the following year, Hannah gave birth to our son, Elijah.'

Billie looked at him intently, her eyes widening in surprise as she went to speak.

'No, please don't say anything just yet. Please, my sweet girl, hear me out. Ugh,' he sighed as though struggling to tell his story, to find the beginning. 'I need to tell you what it was like back then. I need you to understand.

'When the Nazis invaded the Netherlands they seemed to see the Dutch as Germanic brothers and tried to convert them to Nazism. Some people were all for it, but there were also strong voices against the Nazi occupation and their attacks on Jewish liberty. For a while, Jewish supporters won, they pushed the German authorities back and they weren't able to restrict our movement and freedoms or put us into ghettos like they had in other parts of Europe. But by the summer of 1942 . . . everything changed. The German police were running things, and city by city they were rounding us up, all of us Jews, and deporting us. We'd heard rumours of what happened to those that were being shipped out of the country, of work camps and so on, but information was scant and no one really knew what the camps were like. Not until the end of the war.

'But we were scared of what might become of us under Nazi rule, so Hannah and I, we had long been working to help the Resistance. It was little things at first – Hannah used to ferry messages for them. But then she became pregnant, and we were worried for her safety. Meanwhile I was a trainee doctor at the main hospital in the city at the start of the war, but because I had been stopped from working by the regime since 1941, I helped the Resistance if someone was ever injured or if a family in hiding needed medical help. We were lucky, though; for some reason they didn't look to deport us until 1943. One night, I had a message from Lina, one of my contacts in the Resistance, that a man called Pieter had been injured. He had been shot by a German soldier and was losing a lot of blood, so I went to see him. There were rumours circulating all around the city that the Nazis were going to be raiding our homes that night, or the next day. But Hannah promised me she would be OK – she fed Elijah and then gave him a little jenever so he would sleep.' Ezra shook his head slightly.

'So I left them alone in the house. I went to the safe house where Pieter was, and it was a good job I did – he had lost a lot of blood. I removed the bullet and stitched him up as best I could, then stayed a few hours to make sure he was OK. But when I came to leave, Lina said I couldn't go home. The Nazis had blockaded roads and they were all over the city, rounding up Jews. It wasn't until just before daybreak the next day that she was able to help me get back to my house.

'My neighbours – they were a terrific Dutch couple, they saw me before I got into my house. They wanted to cut me off at the pass so I didn't have to see for myself how the soldiers had ransacked my home. And they told me Hannah and Elijah had been found by the soldiers, and they'd taken them.'

Billie had seen sadness in Ezra's blue-grey eyes before, but now there was pain and grief too; it was as though she could see and feel all that he had lost.

'I'm so sorry, Ezra,' she said, reaching out to touch his hands that still held on to the envelope. He didn't look up; instead his eyes remained transfixed on a spot on the floor. It was as though to look at her would have broken him, and he would dissolve into a pool of despair.

'All the people that were in the city that night were taken to Westerbork, a transit camp, about 40 kilometres from Groningen.

Sarah Lee

My neighbours told me the Nazis were looking for me too; they knew I was a trainee doctor and they were searching for me – they wanted to rid the city of every last Jew, especially professional ones.

'Lina insisted I left. She told me there were secret routes out of the country, and so I travelled for eight days via a series of safe houses until I was smuggled onto a ship bound for Southampton, before ending up in London.

'I didn't want to leave the Netherlands, I desperately wanted to find Hannah and Elijah, but Lina made me see sense. There was little hope, we all knew what happened after Westerbork. From there, the Germans transported our people to work camps across Europe,' he said dolefully.

'Oh, Ezra,' said Billie, her lip starting to tremble and her eyes filling with emotion. 'I can't imagine.'

'But I'd hoped to find them again, and in the years that followed I searched, Billie. I wrote letters, scoured lists, reports and archives. I tried for years to find word of Hannah and my boy, but there was just so much confusion after the war, so many people displaced, millions of souls lost. It was six years before I got word. I had a letter from an organization called the International Tracing Service to say they had been sent to Auschwitz and both had perished there. All I could think was, it was my fault. If I hadn't left them that night, if I had been there, I could have saved them. I had such intense guilt for a very long time. In truth, I don't think it's ever left me.'

Billie stood up now and with tears rolling down her face, she embraced Ezra, cradling his head against her abdomen. 'I'm so sorry. I'm so deeply sorry that you had to endure all of this and carry such a terrible burden for all this time. But it wasn't your fault, Ezra – surely if you had been there that night, you'd only have ended up in one of the camps too.'

'I know.' He shook his head. 'But that news cut so deeply into my heart that I truly wished I had perished alongside them, and it was the longest time before I could feel happy again, before I could feel anything again except guilt and devastation.

'And then I met you, Billie, and you have this warmth, this inner glow that made me feel filled with joy just being with you. Your heart is so open and so true. I fell in love with you and I felt as though I could live again, that I could shine in the light you were emitting and, finally, I could allow myself some happiness once more. And I'm grateful to you for that. I love you for that,' he qualified. 'You have been the greatest joy in my life in eleven years. But Billie, this letter arrived,' he said, and looking down, Billie realized he was still holding the neatly addressed envelope.

'It . . . it's from Hannah. She's alive. Elijah is alive, and they're living in Jerusalem, in Israel. They were among those few fortunate souls liberated by the Russians in January 1945.'

A numbness fell over Billie as he told her the contents of the letter.

She took a step back and looked down at the man she loved. His sad eyes, those deep, steely blue eyes, were now red with tears. His hands still held on to the envelope, but they were trembling.

'She changed their names when the Russians arrived. Hannah . . . she says she didn't know what would happen to them next, but she had seen so many people sent to the gas chambers, and there were so many rumours going around. They didn't know if they could trust the Russians, if they'd get out of Poland alive, if they had a home to go back to. She says they were shoved from refugee camp to refugee camp for some time – just two more people displaced by the war. She tried to find me for many years, but by then Lina and Pieter . . . someone had reported them and they were captured and executed by the Gestapo. So she could find no information on me, until now. I wrote an article for a medical journal last year, it's been very well received and has gone all over the world. Seeing my name, she traced me to St Mary's.'

Billie sat back down in stunned silence, staring at the envelope Ezra held between tense fingers. It was just one letter, she thought, one letter that had suddenly changed everything.

'What will you do?' she mumbled, despondency dulling her voice.

'My son. He's eleven now.' Ezra shook his head, his face a picture of anguish. 'All those years . . . we lost all those years.'

'I love you, Billie. I love you more than I've loved in a long, long time. More than I thought it was possible to love again. I don't know if I can ever be happy without you . . . but I'm not free to be with you. I don't know what I will find. But I have to go to them,' he said. 'I have to go to Israel.'

And with that, he went to sit beside her and they cried in each other's arms until the pale evening light turned to the darkness of a moonless night, neither of them wishing to release the other from their embrace.

The following Saturday, and with Ezra confirming a sabbatical from St Mary's, he placed his suitcase in a taxi.

'I'm going to the train station, but I need to stop at the hospital first, please,' he instructed the driver.

As the car arrived at the guard house he showed the guard his credentials, then asked the taxi driver to wait for him outside the nurses' home. He rang the bell, and Billie came down to meet him.

'You still wearing that grey overcoat? I told you to leave that old thing here,' she gently chided him. 'You want to be looking your best, or what?'

'Ah, but I didn't know if perhaps it might be a bit chilly when I got there,' Ezra replied.

'Boy, you know you're going to Israel, right? It ain't the

Caribbean, but cold it is not. Give me that thing,' and she took the sad-looking overcoat off his arm before slinging it onto a chair in the lobby.

'There, now you look like someone I'd like to meet after twelve years,' she said, noticing how much lighter, fresher faced and more rested Ezra looked.

'I wanted to give you this – it was my mother's,' he said, taking a jewellery box from his green suit jacket. He opened the box to reveal a gold pendant encrusted with diamonds. 'I used to carry it everywhere as it's a chai – a Jewish symbol that means alive, and it would make me feel more alive and closer to her, even when she'd died. The thing is, so much of me died during the war. But like I said, Billie, you've made me feel more alive these past few months than I have in years. So I want you to keep this.'

Billie looked at the pendant; overwhelmed, her shoulders and head slumped. 'No, Ezra, I can't take this,' she said, shaking her bowed head.

'You can, and you must,' he said. 'I want you to have something to remember me by, to remember *us* by. Please,' he urged.

'Thank you,' she breathed heavily. 'I will remember us always. I will miss you, mister, and I'll always reserve a special place for you in my heart. Travel safe, and promise me you will live your life with every fibre of your being,' she said, fighting hard to raise a smile.

'Billie Benjamin, you are the most incredible woman I have ever met. I promise I will do my very best to live the life you wish for me. Stay strong and make me proud – I want to hear of all your achievements once you qualify,' he said, taking hold of her hands and moving in to kiss her, his lips brushing the side of her mouth before landing delicately on her cheek. Then he walked to the waiting taxi. Looking up at Billie from the back seat, he waved, then looked away again as his eyes filled with emotion and the car drove off.

Watching her future happiness disappear into the distance, the enormity of the moment and all that she was losing tore at Billie's heart as tears fell relentlessly down her pretty face.

Ruby and Connie had stayed out of sight, but seeing their friend's anguish, they now appeared behind her, placing a supportive hand on each of her shoulders.

She looked at them, desperation weighing heavily in the air between them as she sobbed, 'I've lost a loving, caring, decent man because he's a loving, caring, decent man.'

And for the first time since the death of her mother, Billie felt the raw, unforgiving, piercing pain of total loss.

Chapter Twenty-Four

Ruby

It was two more weeks before Ruby was able to see Joseph again and Billie's sorrow had hovered in her mind like a cloud. *What if Joseph has someone else back home, or even in Manchester?*

But as he arrived at Four Oaks station with a whole four days ahead of him, Ruby knew Joseph was devoted to her from the moment she saw him.

'My beautiful Ruby! I couldn't be happier to see your pretty smile. Man! Those dimples get me every time,' he said, his broad grin setting Ruby's heart aglow.

'Hello, stranger! It really has been too long. I was starting to wonder if I'd ever see you again,' she said. 'I know you'll be wanting to see Devon while you're here, and I believe Connie has arranged things so you can go and spend time with him on the ward each day. You might even be able to take him out some-time – Connie can arrange that. She said he's doing so much better, and some fresh air and a change of scenery would no doubt do him a world of good too.

'But I'm so excited that you'll be here for a few days and we get to spend time together,' she smiled.

'Me too, my sweet, me too,' he said, and the couple wandered hand in hand through the streets of Four Oaks, until they arrived at the boarding house where Joseph would be staying.

'Come on in – I've told them we're married!' He winked and Ruby, though aghast, followed along, keeping quiet as a no-nonsense woman gave Joseph a room key.

Once he had unpacked, Joseph lay back on his bed, looking tired after his long journey. 'Come here,' he said, 'and lie next to me a while.'

'Joseph Grant! What do you take me for?' Ruby said, feigning a little more shock than she actually felt. But despite her inexperience, she had heard enough from her sister and her friends to know that she needed to be wary of men trying to take advantage of her.

'Ruby, man, what *you* take *me* for?' he said. 'I just want to cuddle with you is all.'

And he was true to his word.

As the pair lay on his single bed, they talked and talked about what they had been doing, what they had missed about each other, and even about the future.

'You know, I wasn't sure how long I'd stay here,' he said, turning to look Ruby in the eye. 'I had heard mixed reports about England from Devon, but I knew it was a place where I could make some money and I could send some home, you know, and save up. And I thought to myself who knows, you may even meet the woman of your dreams, then we could go back home to get married and build a dream house that we could fill with children.'

'We? You know you said "*we*",' Ruby said, losing herself in his dark brown eyes.

Joseph was quiet as a moment of bashfulness took hold. 'I know,' he smiled. Then he placed his hands on either side of her face and pulled her towards him. His rounded lips pressed against hers, and she felt an urgency in his kiss. But it was also gentle, loving.

'Oh, Ruby,' he murmured.

And for a moment, Ruby lost herself in the passion that burned between them. It was unlike anything she had ever felt before. But then, before they allowed things to cross the boundary of what she knew to be acceptable, Joseph pulled away to stare deep into her eyes.

'You know you're special to me, don't you?' he said, and then a broad smile spread across his face.

'Man, if I could go back now, say maybe a year or two, and tell myself that one day, I'd be here, with Ruby Haynes in my arms. Well! I just wouldn't have believed it – not even if I was talking to myself,' and he laughed heartily, while Ruby appeared lost for words.

'But . . . I didn't even know! How could you be harbouring these feelings for me all that time and say nothing!?' she demanded, and Joseph could sense her mild irritation, which made him chuckle.

'No, no, no, hold up. Girl, you didn't even look in my direction. Not once!' he said.

'But I didn't know you so well then! And anyway, we're together now, aren't we?' she protested, and Joseph chuckled to see the way her nose wrinkled with frustration.

'We are, my sweet, and I'm hoping we'll be together for a long, long time,' and his smiling eyes stared hopefully into Ruby's.

'Oh, we will,' she said, with great self-assurance. 'I don't plan to let you go, not ever!' And they held on to each other for another two hours before visiting time started at the hospital.

Joseph looked a little nervous as they arrived at the ward, and Ruby observed how he had been the same way the last time they were there, as though seeing his older brother in the psychiatric unit was a heavy burden. Having an older sibling who she too looked upon as her closest friend and confidante – someone she could turn to for guidance, counsel, strength and support – Ruby could understand how Joseph felt.

At times the unit was a maelstrom of chaos with voices raised in a wild range from joyous songs through to angry threats. And seeing Devon, a strong, robust man with a delightful disposition, so overwhelmed by the demons lurking in the recesses of his mind was a challenge for everyone that loved him. Ruby barely knew how Connie was able to handle it so well. But in the past two months she had seen her sister grow too, learning more about psychiatric care and bearing the weight of Devon's recovery across her broad shoulders, and Ruby decided Connie's dedication must stem from a combination of her love for her work and that for her beloved.

'Devon, you're looking good, man!' Ruby said, touching him on the shoulder.

'Well, perhaps I'm looking better than I'm feeling,' he grimaced. 'This leg is still hurting and I'm not getting a lot of sleep in here.'

But to Ruby, he looked better than he had done in some weeks.

Still, she knew better than to push things or to judge him in any way. Connie had told her about how the combat stress was affecting him, from anxiety to rage, guilt to sleeplessness. And when he did manage to sleep, he was cornered in the shadows of his subconscious by all-too-convincing nightmares. But Connie had also mentioned how he had become irritable at times and started snapping at her as she tried to help him. It was as though his pride, too, had been weakened by his struggles.

Joseph chatted to Devon, updating him on things at home and at his work; then as the conversation drifted onto cricket, Ruby sat quietly and scanned the room. Connie had told her this section of the unit was the quietest, and Ruby felt she could see why – there were so many empty faces, so many men sedated to the point where all their energy and character, their very lifeblood, had been repressed. She was so glad that Connie was there to watch over Devon and help bring him back to his old self.

'Yeah, man, I tell you, England held Australia to a draw in Sydney the other day. So now we gonna have to wait and see what happens when they play against the West Indies in a couple of weeks – West Indies vs Australia, it's the big one!' Joseph enthused, and Devon managed a slight smile.

'Lord h'mercy, Joseph Grant, don't you go getting him all excitable now, I beg you,' Connie said as she walked towards Devon's bed.

She was still on duty, so she made a point of not staying too long at Devon's bedside, but she did give Joseph a big hug. 'It's so good to see you,' she said.

'You too. I finally got myself a few days off in a row, so I said I had to come down to see my girl. And I figured I'd better come visit this old boy too,' Joseph teased, prodding his brother.

Connie saw Ruby's face light up. *He called me his girl*, Ruby thought. She had never been someone's girl before, and she thought it sounded wonderful.

'I'm pleased you made it down to see us all. But you better mind yourself with my sister these next few days, you hear?' Connie replied with mock admonishment.

'I will, don't you worry about that. Devon's already told me that you can be fiery when you want to be, and I don't want to get on your bad side,' he joked.

As they left the hospital, Joseph turned to Ruby, and for the first time since he'd arrived he looked at her seriously.

'Ruby, how do you think Devon's doing? I mean really. Do you think he'll ever get back to being his old self again?' he asked her.

'Oh, Joseph, I don't really know. Connie tells me that there's been a marked improvement in him, and I can see that too, but it's hard to know and the consultant up there says it can take months or even years for people to recover from combat stress reaction.'

'Ugh, my brother, man. This is so upsetting.' Joseph shook his head.

'I know, darling. But you know what? He's in the best place, getting the best care in the country. I know they're still learning about how to treat people with combat stress reaction, but they have some of the finest psychiatrists here at St Mary's, and I'm confident he will get better,' Ruby said, employing the same encouragement she offered her patients and their families, while feeling proud of the NHS, the hospital where she worked, and how they were rebuilding lives shattered by the war.

'I hope so, Ruby,' he said, slipping his hand into hers, and she squeezed it gently, knowing that Joseph needed support through this time as much as Connie did.

And support Joseph she did over the next few days, but they also found time to enjoy each other's company. Joseph took Ruby shopping, to the pictures, to Minstrels and on walks in the countryside surrounding Four Oaks, something that she had never thought to do before – but then she realized that there was much that was different when you had a boyfriend, and she loved every bit of it.

The pair were inseparable for Joseph's entire stay, except for on his last night, when he told Ruby he needed to spend a little time alone with Devon during visiting hours that day. Ruby didn't mind at all; she knew how important her times were with Connie, when it was just the two of them sharing their thoughts as siblings.

'It's OK,' she said. 'I have to do some washing anyway, so I'll meet you later this evening.'

Almost as soon as she'd left, Joseph made a phone call. 'Hello, Connie?' he said when she finally picked up the receiver. 'I was wondering if I could see you – but could you come and meet me at my lodgings? And please, don't tell Ruby anything about this,' he said.

At first Connie was uncomfortable with his cloak-and-dagger approach, but then, thinking she had an idea of what he might wish to speak to her about, she agreed to go and see him.

An hour later, the pair walked back through town and up to St Mary's to see Devon, Connie ensuring they took a back route to avoid Ruby spotting them from the nurses' home.

'I'm so excited, Joseph, and you know, I think despite everything, Devon will be too,' she said. And she was right: on hearing Joseph's news, Devon's face lit up, and it was the first time Connie had seen that Grant smile since she'd found him again.

'Connie, Connie! You won't believe it!' Ruby called to her the next day as she raced into her sister's room, Joseph following right behind her, smiling.

'Joseph's asked me to marry him. And I said yes!'

Connie's eyes widened to see Joseph in the nurses' home, Ruby dispensing with convention in her excitement.

'How did . . .' she started to ask, wondering how the pair had escaped Miss Bleakly's glare, but her surprise was quickly overwhelmed by the joy emanating from Ruby. Connie was thrilled, but it was impossible to match her little sister's delight.

'Oh my, Ruby! But I knew he was going to – Joseph had already let me in on his plans,' she said.

'What? Why, you two! You were conspiring!' Ruby shrieked.

'Not exactly, Ruby,' Joseph said. 'It's more that in the absence of your dad or mum being up here, I thought I should ask Connie for permission to ask you.'

'And of course, I said yes. I know you'll make each other so very happy, and Mum and Dad will be real happy when they hear too,' Connie smiled, her heart exploding with glee.

'Wait a minute, did I just hear right?' Billie said, arriving at the joyous scene. 'Joseph, you dark horse you, and little Ruby Haynes – well, you ain't so little no more! You're about to be a married lady. What lovely news!'

And there were hugs all round.

'OK girls, I'm going to walk Joseph back to the station now, but when I get back here, we need to talk. I have a wedding to plan, and I need my two best girls on the case!' Ruby said, and Connie was taken not only by her sister's ebullience but by how much she had grown in the past few months. Not only in experience and maturity, but now it seemed to be affecting her physically too, as though her relationship with Joseph was adding to her stature.

'Right, go on, you two, or Joseph will miss his train. Brother-in-law-to-be, I hope to see you again soon, long before the wedding no doubt,' she said, hugging him warmly. 'Hold on – did you two fix a date yet?'

'Ah, yes, we did talk about it – we were thinking about late May, when the weather is a little warmer,' Joseph said.

'Wait, you say what?' Connie shrieked. 'That's only two months away! Ruby, man, we gonna have a ton of things to do before then.'

'Yes, I know, but . . . well, we didn't want to wait. You know, until we could say we were husband and wife,' Ruby grinned, looking back at her beau.

'Lord h'mercy! Right, OK. Well, you best get going.'

'Don't you worry, we'll take care of things. I'll help you girls. To be honest, it will be so nice to share in two people's happiness. It's been in low supply for me for a while.' Billie smiled ruefully. Ruby touched her arm, and thanked her and her sister, then the young engaged couple headed out.

'Thanks, Billie,' Connie said. 'I know the past few weeks have been so difficult for you. I don't know exactly what you're going through. I still have Devon – well, sort of. We're trying to bring him back to a place of stability but he's been so distant lately that it sometimes feels as if I've lost him to the war too.

'Honestly, I would never have thought all those years ago, when we were growing up with war raging far away in foreign countries, that it would have such an impact on me. No one ever expected the war to last the six years it did, let alone for us to still be being touched by its cold hand all this time later,' she said.

'Tell me about it,' Billie lamented, her joy having left the room with Ruby and Joseph. 'I just hate everything about that goddamn war right now. But I guess we just have to move forward, Connie, because what else can we do? It happened, it's passed, and now we have to face whatever may come and do our best to get through it. And you will get through it. Devon's a strong man, and I have so much faith in you as a nurse, and in what you two have,' she encouraged her friend. 'Come, Ruby will be back soon. Let's go and see what we can conjure up here this evening, and have a little get-together for her.'

Connie smiled. 'That's a great idea, she'll like that.'

The two girls set about tracking down the other trainees, making sure they'd be home later, then Billie popped out to the shops for snacks and drinks as Connie made decorations for the sitting room.

Then that evening, just as the nurses would usually be thinking about heading down for dinner, Connie instead escorted her sister to the sitting room.

'Congratulations!' cried a crowd of voices as Connie opened the door, and Ruby found her fellow trainees in the room, as well as some of the other nurses from around the hospital like Ruth, Sybil and Mary. Then later, even Sister Davenport and Sister Harding looked in to offer their well wishes to a smiling Ruby.

'Ach, God love them,' Kathleen said as she heard of Ruby and Joseph's plans for a May wedding. 'Now are you sure you're not . . . you know.' She winked.

'What?' Ruby asked innocently.

'Well, Ruby, there's usually only one reason why a young girl will marry a fella quite so fast,' she explained as Ruby's eyes grew wide with shock.

'Do you mean am I pregnant? No!' She shuddered with horror, and the other girls laughed until they were bent double.

'What a thing to say, Kathleen!' Jean tittered.

'I guess she has a point,' Phyllis piped up.

'Well I never,' Ruby said with mock indignation. 'If you must know, it's because we love each other too much to be separated.'

There was a chorus of 'ahhhs' as Ruby looked thoughtful.

'And, we can't wait to get our hands on each other,' she added, and the girls fell about with bawdy delight.

Riotous laughter was soon overtaken by excited planning as each of the girls started to share details of their dream wedding.

'Oh my goodness, all this time I thought it was just me that used to think this way,' Ruby said. 'You see, Connie, I'm not alone, we all have our dreams for the future.'

Connie smiled and shook her head. She couldn't have been happier for her sister and she had grown so much, but, she thought, Ruby was still a dreamer.

Chapter Twenty-Five

Connie, Billie, Ruby

Connie

The following morning, Connie woke to the echoes of the previous night's excited wedding chatter, and something else – a persistent, wretched fear. What if Devon never recovered? What if he was lost somehow to this terrible illness? Mental health seemed to her so much more fragile and more challenging to heal than a broken bone or other injury.

Connie wanted to be with Devon so badly; she too wanted the dream wedding and the future the girls had spoken of. She had only ever seen Devon in her future since first setting eyes on him at Tilbury Docks. But, she feared, what if his condition had changed him and he no longer saw her as anything more than his nurse? More importantly – could he ever be her Devon again?

Her deepening concerns were only exacerbated that day when Dr Battersby took Connie to one side.

'Nurse, you're as good as next of kin to Mr Grant. Although I understand that he has a brother here now too, is that right?'

Connie nodded.

'I guess he should be notified too, but we are reaching the end of the road with what we can do to assist Mr Grant here on the unit,' he said, and noticing Connie's shoulders slump, he quickly continued, 'No, you see that's a good thing. He is improving, all the time, little by little. But as a result, he's moving out of the bounds of the acute care we provide here, and instead he could do with more ongoing support and occupational therapy.

'I'd like to refer him to an organization called the Ex-Servicemen's Welfare Society. It's a charity that has been doing simply marvellous work, helping rehabilitate veterans and get them back into some sort of gainful activity. Truthfully, there is still much we don't know about combat stress reaction and the NHS's resources are simply too limited for the powers-that-be to invest in something like this. I actually think sometimes that the government would prefer to sweep the suffering of these men under the carpet rather than help them. But this charity, well, it seems to be really making a difference to men, and their loved ones too – all too often the effects of the men's trauma on their families is overlooked.

'So with the permission of Mr Grant, I'd like to discharge him from our care and refer him there,' he concluded.

Listening to the doctor's reasoning, Connie could see it made sense, and she so longed to see Devon leave the psychiatric unit.

'OK,' she said, 'but Doctor, would you give me just a week or so to organize some lodgings for him? I'd like to have him close, where I can keep an eye on him,' Connie said.

'Ah, don't worry about that, the Ex-Servicemen's Welfare Society has taken over Walton Manor, the estate on the edge of town. They've turned it into a sort of convalescent home. There are psychiatrists there and nurses too for those men that need help, but they also give the men jobs in workshops on the grounds – it gets them back to work, and gives them a sense of pride and some purpose. They would provide him with a room there. We'll also get him a wheelchair – it'll be a little while yet till he can put all his weight on that leg, but we've taken X-rays and it is mending well,' he said.

'Oh Dr Battersby, that would be wonderful. Of course, talk to Devon and make sure that he's comfortable with everything, but if he is, I'd be more than happy to see him living in the community, and I can still help him too,' Connie said.

Later that day, with each of the trainees receiving new assignments on the Change List, and with Connie set to move to orthopaedics in a few weeks, she was relieved because she realized she would no longer have been able to keep an eye on Devon during working hours.

The following week, Connie rang the bell at Walton Manor, noticing the logo of the charity over the door – a purple cross and the words: *For Those Who Suffer in Mind*.

Soon Devon was showing her around, as other ex-servicemen, smartly dressed in collars and ties, headed into the workshops. 'It's not bad, is it?' he said, as they found a bench in the extensive gardens, and for once Connie thought she saw a tiny glimmer of hope in his eyes.

'I've seen the consultant psychiatrist and he seems happy with the progress I'm making. So I'll be starting in the workshop tomorrow making parts for electric blankets.' He went on to explain how the charity's work was supported by the Queen Mother and its company, Thermega, was based in Surrey, but sold the blankets all over the Empire.

Connie smiled, pleased to see a little light in Devon once more. 'So your work is helping to warm people up all over the world? Bet they won't sell many of those blankets in Barbados,' she chuckled. 'Man, I still miss that Bajan sun!'

As the next month passed, day by day, little by little, Connie saw improvements in Devon – and not only in his physical health, as it became clear that his mental health was strengthening too. And once more, instead of only focusing on the horrors lurking in his past, Devon was talking about the future.

'Would you like us to bring Martha here to live with us sometime in the future?' he asked her thoughtfully, one day in late April as they watched white blossoms float down from a wild cherry tree in the manor grounds.

'I would love to, but I . . . Well . . . it's just not practical, Devon, is it? I mean, she doesn't know me and my mum and dad, they'd be so upset, they don't want anyone to know that I had her out of wedlock. And, as much as I'd thought about it before, it's simply impossible,' she sighed, her expression gloomy.

Devon stroked her face and lifted her chin up to look at him. 'My darling, all I'm hearing from you is barriers, but it seems as though you're the only one putting them in your way. Connie, I've lived too long with negativity. The misery of the past, man, it nearly destroyed me, damn it. And I don't want the sadness we each have in our pasts to limit our future happiness. But most of all, I want us to go forward in life together. As a family.'

Connie looked up at him, her eyes wide with shock. 'Devon Grant!' she cried. 'You're not saying what I think you are, are you?'

And with that, Devon reached into his pocket. 'I'm only sad that I can't get down onto one knee. But Connie, you are everything to me and I want to be everything to you,' he said, opening a little red box to reveal a delicate, rose and white gold ring with a tiny diamond at its centre.

'Oh Devon! You have a ring?' Connie said.

'Yes, I was saving up all my money. And you remember that morning back in December, when I was due to meet you in London?' he asked.

'Yes, but you got into that terrible accident and so I spent the day in that grotty pub thinking you'd broken up with me!' she accused playfully.

'Well, the jeweller where I got this was a friend of a friend and that's why I was going south of the river that morning – to pick the ring up,' he explained.

'What? You were planning this all this time? Oh my!'

'Yes, I was meaning to take you somewhere romantic and ask you to marry me that Saturday. Then I was in the accident, and next thing I know Joseph started dating Ruby, and the two of them became engaged before any of us could catch our breath. What a whirlwind romance! But I can't blame Joseph for falling hard for one of you Haynes girls – I have too.

'Still, I couldn't have my younger brother coming up here and upstaging me,' he laughed gently. 'I told him where the jeweller was and got him to pick the ring up for me a few weeks ago. He brought it to me at the hospital when he was here last.'

'And there I was for weeks before I found you, thinking you didn't want to see me again. I thought you had come to the conclusion you couldn't cope with me having a child, that you thought I was too fast, and that's why you didn't show up,' Connie said, emotion rising in her voice.

He shook his head. 'We all make mistakes, Connie. But yours wasn't Martha, far from it. Your only mistake was in trusting the wrong man with your heart all those years ago. Now,' he said, delicately removing the ring from the box and going to place it on her finger, 'I'm hoping that you'll entrust it to someone who will love you forever,' he concluded, an inflection of hope in his voice, his eyes not daring to move from her lips until he saw them say, 'Yes.'

'Yes, I do trust you, and I will love you forever also,' she said, and as he placed the ring on her finger, they both cried happy tears.

Sarah Lee

Billie

Just a few hours later, Connie was regaling the other girls with her news.

'Oh my goodness. Oh. My. *Goodness!*' Ruby cried. 'I don't believe it – we could have a double wedding, Connie.'

'As much as I would love to, Ruby, we won't be ready for all that. For starters, we can't keep up with you two, but really, I think Devon needs time still. He's coming along, but he's only just got settled at Walton Manor and started occupational therapy. He can seem so fragile still, I don't want to do anything to risk his recovery.'

'But he *loves* you, Connie, where could be the risk in that?' Ruby said, and Connie couldn't help but sigh inwardly at her sister's naivety.

'If only it were that simple,' she replied.

'Simple? Nothing in love is simple,' Billie said, entering the room. Jean, Mei, Lin, Phyllis, Kathleen and Grace seemed to her to shift awkwardly in their chairs. But she knew Connie wouldn't take offence at her comments. Connie had already told her how resilient she thought she was, despite the sadness that tinged her heart since losing Ezra to his past life.

'Billie, did you hear the news? Devon asked Connie to marry him!' Ruby announced excitedly.

'What? Another Haynes–Grant wedding? You girls! I'm so happy for you.' Billie's broad smile quickly smothered the sadness that tinged her heart.

'Don't tell me – you two are going to get married on the exact same day?' She grinned then waited expectantly for their reply.

'No, no, I think we will wait a while,' Connie said. 'But thank you, Billie, thank you for being thrilled for us. You know . . . at a time like this.'

'Why wouldn't I be?' Billie replied, and then let out a long sigh. 'I lost a decent man, because he is a decent man. I can't hate Ezra for that. I can only admire him, and hope and pray that he finds what he's looking for. As for you two, you're like sisters to me – how could I be anything but ecstatic right now?

'Besides, I had some other news today, and I don't know if it will work out, but if it did, it would be the most terrific thing to have happened in a long, long time.'

'What? What is it? Don't tell me you got another boyfriend,' Ruby said.

'No, Ruby. It's much too soon for me and that,' said Billie, despondency furrowing her brow.

'Don't keep us in suspense, Billie, man!' Ruby urged.

Billie grinned at her, took a breath and paused for dramatic effect. 'You remember I told you about my sister back in Jamaica, Candice?' she said and the Haynes sisters nodded.

'She wrote me a letter. Girls, she's applied to come up here to England and train as a nurse! She's asking me all about what it's like and she's saying she's going to see about coming here to St Mary's as well, so we can be here together if they accept her.'

'I don't believe it!' Connie exclaimed excitedly.

'Ohh, you'll be just like us up here,' Ruby cooed. 'And it will be so perfect because you can help her adjust to life in Britain, and get to grips with the preliminary training. I couldn't imagine doing this without Connie being here. She's helped me a lot,' she said, slipping her arm around her sister's shoulders. 'I think you'll love having Candice here.'

'Now look at that – St Mary's is going to have two of the best nurses to come out of Jamaica,' Kathleen said.

'Well, maybe Candice will be a great nurse – that girl has always had a naturally caring nature. But me? No dear, I'm just here trying to make my way in life,' Billie replied.

'Ach, don't they say we're not a good judge of our own work?

Mark my words, you're already one of the best nurses here,' Kathleen told her.

It wasn't until a few weeks later that Kathleen's comments came to Billie's mind. She loved working on the maternity ward and found no greater joy than seeing new life come into being, but she also discovered that things weren't always so simple. Earlier that week, Billie had to quash the tangle of emotion that twisted her heart as she consoled a twenty-three-year-old woman who had miscarried at twenty-two weeks, only to then find herself, two days later, speaking to Valerie Harper, an unmarried woman of the same age whose wealthy parents had organized for her baby to be adopted.

'Nurse!' she yelled at Billie from the other side of the room, thumping her copy of *Harper's Bazaar* frustratedly onto her bed, the magazine's pages still seeming to flutter seconds later in the wake of her fury. 'It's still crying. Will you shut that baby up! I can't wait to get rid of it and get the hell out of here,' she screeched.

'Miss Harper, I'd ask you to keep your voice down,' Billie hushed. 'There are other patients here in the ward.'

'Trust me, I'm not making as much racket as that thing,' the girl seethed.

And Billie was seething too, but not at the baby, even though his screams revealed a loud voice for one so small.

She went to his cot and, wrapping a blanket around him, she picked him up, making sure that his little white cap was still firmly in place on his head to keep him warm, despite him writhing, red-faced from his frustrated tears.

'Good, get him out of here. I can't wait until I can hand him over to his parents – my mum says they'll be coming for him any day now,' Valerie spat.

'Yes, but Valerie, you also need to recover from the birth. Don't forget, it wasn't plain sailing for either of you. So please, settle down – we need to watch your blood pressure.

'There, there, little one,' Billie soothed as she carried the baby out of the ward and away from his mother's squall. She felt heartbroken for the little boy, an inconvenience, an unwanted package about to be shipped out to another family. But as disgusted as she was, she felt it was not her place to judge his mother; perhaps she wouldn't appreciate the gravity of her decision until much, much later, she told herself.

As she walked the baby up and down the hallway, Sister Harding, who had caught the exchange, stopped her.

'That was very well handled, Nurse. I've noticed the way you relate to patients over some weeks now, and I have to say, I am very impressed at the care and compassion you exhibit. You know, it's one thing to have an understanding of medicine and nursing, and you have that in spades. But compassion is something that cannot be taught.

'And look at that – I think you've found your calling, Nurse Benjamin!' she said, looking at the tiny boy, whose angry red face was now cooling to a pink blush, his tears drying and cries quietening as two blue eyes looked up at her contentedly.

'Keep up the good work,' Sister Harding concluded as she walked away.

But as Billie felt the warmth from the little boy spread to her heart, she thought to herself, there was one thing the sister had got wrong: this really wasn't work at all.

Sarah Lee

Ruby
25 May 1955

'Oh my! You look so beautiful!' Kathleen said, as she arrived at All Saints Church.

'Are you sure my eyeshadow is OK? I think I smudged it at the corner of my eye,' Ruby asked.

'Ach, you're OK! It's nothing that a man on a galloping horse would ever see,' she replied, leaving Ruby with a befuddled expression.

'It's just fine,' Connie translated, reassuring her. 'You look ever so lovely.'

'Ruby, you ready?' Billie beamed. 'We got to get in there before I start bawling and ruin *my* make-up and that will just never do.'

And with that, she motioned to the church organist, who began the Bridal Chorus as Connie and Billie followed Ruby up the aisle of the church.

From the pews, parishioners who the sisters had gotten to know, and their fellow trainees, beamed with delight at the occasion.

'My goodness, look at her!' Jean whispered wistfully to Phyllis next to her.

'I know – she looks beautiful, doesn't she?' Phyllis replied. 'And to think Connie's engaged to Joseph's older brother. Imagine, two sisters finding two brothers just right for them! It can be hard enough to find one lovely man and hold on to him. Just look at Billie and her sorry tale.'

But as she walked in step with Connie, Billie's eyes sparkled as much as the chai pendant she wore on a chain around her neck, as she found happiness in her friend's joy.

As the Wedding March played and church bells pealed from the tall spire above them, Ruby and Joseph emerged from the church as Mr and Mrs Grant.

'Ruby, I'm so proud of you. I only wish Mum and Dad were

here to see you now!' Connie exclaimed, a broad smile reaching right to her eyes.

'Can you imagine, Connie!' Ruby said, waving her hand at her sister, one finger now graced with a small gold wedding band, her other hand still holding tightly on to Joseph's.

'Congratulations, brother,' Devon said as he and Joseph embraced.

'I'm looking forward to when I can say the same to you,' Joseph smiled.

'Ah yes, that day is coming soon,' Devon replied.

'One day at a time, brother, one day at a time,' Joseph said, his pride at Devon's progress equalled only by that in his new wife.

It wasn't long before the couple were boarding a train, off for a few days' honeymoon in Southend.

But as Monday came around again, all the trainees were there to meet Ruby for breakfast in the dining room before they each started their shifts.

'You must have wanted to run for the hills and just be with your Joseph forever,' Jean said wistfully.

'Yes, we really enjoyed Southend,' Ruby said. 'But marriage is for a lifetime, so we have all the time in the world to spend together, and as Joseph has been able to get work in Four Oaks, we're looking for our own place in town. So I'm not sad to be back.

'Also, I expect there's been a whole lot of patients come in to Pear Tree Ward today. And I'm going to have to get to know more about looking after children, since Joseph and I want to have some of our own soon.'

There were gasps from all the girls at the table, but Ruby just smiled, feeling every inch the woman she had become.

As they got up, Connie linked her arm through her sister's. 'Well, you better get up there and ready yourself – children change everything,' she smiled.

Ruby thought for a moment, about Connie, Devon and Martha; about Billie, Ezra and his son; how Martha was thousands of miles away, Ezra's son lost over many miles and more than a decade, each seemingly set adrift, an ocean apart from their parents. But it was clear to her that people were tethered to their children as though through an invisible umbilical cord, and that no matter where their future took them, their lives, and their hearts, would be eternally entwined.

Author's Note

We hear a lot about immigration today. Stories of 'illegal immigrants' are often in the news, and we hear of people seeking asylum and more. But we rarely talk about migration in terms of the net gains that people bring to our communities or economy, nor how they benefit our society.

This seemed to me a missing link in the story of immigration. When I started researching *An Ocean Apart*, I became fascinated by people's motivations for leaving their homes to seek a new experience or whole new life thousands of miles from all they have ever known. They would have given up so much to do so.

I became fascinated by the idea of what people left behind when leaving the warmth of the Caribbean to live and work in Britain. Not every migrant leaves a life devastated by war, or one of abject poverty. Some people, especially those of the Windrush Generation, left home due to other motivators. In fact it could be argued that they didn't really leave home at all. With Caribbean nations colonized by Britain from the seventeenth century, Britain was the motherland, its Caribbean citizens British.

Britain's monarch was head of state, British – not Caribbean – history was taught in schools, and all aspects of life from laws to entertainment were the provision of the British. So coming here, though involving a journey of four thousand miles and three weeks by ship for those earliest pioneers, was merely an extension of their own home – at least until the realities of life in Britain set in.

Sarah Lee

Immigration does offer opportunity though, and I'm sure every one of those people who set out from the Caribbean for Britain between 1948 and 1972 had many aspirations of how the move would transform their lives.

My mother, Margery, was one of those people. She left Barbados by plane just after Christmas in 1960, aged twenty. I can't imagine what it must have been like to leave your parents, family, friends and all that you'd grown up with to travel thousands of miles away, not knowing when you'd be able to go home again. My mum and many more of her generation came here not only on a one-way ticket, but also not knowing when they'd be able to save the money to go home again. My mother didn't return to Barbados for the first visit until 1971, shortly before my grandfather died.

But when I asked her about the decision that led her to Britain, she said for her it was a great adventure. It made me think back to when I was twenty years old, possessed with a similar fearlessness of youth. I went on a three-month Erasmus exchange to Romania – this was only a few years after the fall of communism and Ceaușescu, and Romania wasn't somewhere anyone in Britain was visiting. But I embraced it with the same sense of adventure, so I could draw some parallels. Yet even then, I knew that I could go home, and that after a finite time I would go home. It was very different for my mother and her contemporaries.

For many, adjusting to life in Britain was a struggle. And during my research for this book I discovered some fascinating resources, such as *Going to Britain?*, a pamphlet penned by Caribbean men living in London, including renowned Trinidadian author Samuel Selvon (*The Lonely Londoners*), and published by the BBC Caribbean Service in 1959. It had advice on all manner of topics on making the move to Britain, such as how to make the decision to migrate, the challenges of finding work when you arrive, how to handle landladies, and even things more innocuous such as the English customs of queuing and tea-drinking. It also warned newcomers to the country of prejudice they may be faced with. So although *An Ocean Apart* is a fictional tale, the challenges Connie, Ruby and Billie faced in fitting in to a new country where they were not always made welcome were very much founded on real experiences.

The book also explores themes around the ghosts of the Second World War, because I believe something that changed the world so dramatically didn't end as soon as the last shots were fired in 1945. The war had a legacy, even down to the fact that rationing continued until 1954, and the Windrush Generation are a strong part of that legacy. Not only did many Caribbean men, like Devon, fight for Queen and country, but a war-ravaged Britain needed the able hands of its Caribbean citizens to aid its recovery and to build a better future, part of which was the National Health Service.

Devon's story revealed what was in the 1950s a little understood aspect of time in active service. Post-Traumatic Stress Disorder, or Combat Stress Reaction as it was known, is a complex psychological issue. Though it manifests from traumatic experiences, the impact it had on our servicemen was often swept under the carpet by the Forces and successive governments unwilling to acknowledge the impact of war, or rise to the challenge of supporting veterans. The charity Combat Stress, known as Ex-Servicemen's Welfare Society in the mid-1950s, has helped change this, offering support, counselling and occupational therapy to veterans and their families for more than one hundred years. If you or anyone you know is a veteran struggling with PTSD, depression, anxiety, anger or substance abuse, they are well placed to assist, and you can find out more on their website (combatstress.org.uk) or by calling their 24-hour helpline on 0800 138 1619.

In recent years, some of those who journeyed here to give their working lives to Britain, and some of their early descendants too, have been mired in a hostile immigration policy that saw many either deported to the Caribbean, or illegally held in deportation centres. The Windrush Scandal, as it became known, devastated families and the lives of people who came to the country as legal citizens. It is an important, if distressing, chapter in our recent history that brings the story of Caribbean immigration to Britain right up to the present day. The story was broken by Amelia Gentleman of *The Guardian*, and to get to grips with it I'd recommend further reading of her writing on the newspaper's website, or her book *The Windrush Betrayal: Exposing the Hostile Environment*. You could also look out for the wonderfully insightful documentary *Hostile*, by Galeforce Films, which I caught at an independent cinema earlier this year and which covers this issue (hostiledocumentary.com).

Despite the many challenges that the Windrush Generation has faced, the human spirit adapts and moves forward, and the central characters of *An Ocean Apart* embody and reflect the decency and cheerful optimism that I believe the vast majority of immigrants share.

My editor once described *An Ocean Apart* as a love letter to the NHS. I'm not sure that is something I set out to write. However, I would guess this came about because I am grateful for our NHS, and feel that as a nation are very lucky to have such provision at our disposal. At no time was this felt more deeply nationwide than during the Covid-19 pandemic. In the past year my loved ones have also received stellar treatment and follow-up care, and I have had cause to express gratitude for the service. I too am deeply proud of my mother and the people of her generation who contributed to the development of such a vital organization. Even today, immigrant workers – not just from the Caribbean, but all over the world – are the backbone of the NHS, and to each of them I say, thank you.